CHEYENNE CAPTIVE

GEORGINA GENTRY

ZEBRA BOOKS
KENSINGTON PUBLISHING CORP.

ZEBRA BOOKS

are published by

Kensington Publishing Corp.
475 Park Avenue South
New York, NY 10016

Second printing: July, 1992

Printed in the United States of America

To "Murph"
My Irish-Indian "once-in-a-lifetime" love

Prologue

In September, 1858, the Butterfield Overland Stage began its first cross-country routes, finally linking Eastern civilization with the roaring gold camps of California. Already, the Oregon trail and the Santa Fe trail carried a seemingly endless train of covered wagons into and across once uncharted wilderness.

Our young nation trembled on the brink of the coming Civil War. "Bloody Kansas" struggled toward statehood, enmeshed in the conflict of the Jayhawkers and John Brown's antislavery zealots, and there were rumors of gold in the "Shining Mountains," the Rockies.

The Fitzpatrick Treaty of 1851 had kept an uneasy peace among the Plains Indians, broken occasionally by minor scrimmages against each other or the hated "Bluecoats." Beset on all sides by broken promises, worthless treaties, and the beginnings of the wholesale slaughter of the buffalo, the Plains tribes struggled valiantly to survive and hold on to their way of life.

Less than two decades hence, the savage Cheyennes would join up with the Sioux to annihilate Colonel Custer at the Little Big Horn. In three decades, the final chapter would be written at bloody Wounded Knee Creek. But for now, the tribes struggled against the immediate problems of white encroach-

7

ment, whiskey, smallpox, and cholera.

Always, the white tide of immigrants swept forward, taking more land, more water, more timber. Hotheaded young braves talked war, but wise chiefs tried to hold them back, knowing the government hoped for an excuse to destroy the Indians, herd them like cattle to reservations. The discovery of gold at Cherry Creek in the Rockies marked the beginning of the end of the bloody tragedy. Now, the whites clamored even for that formerly worthless land, those last few acres promised to the mighty Cheyenne, the Arapaho, the Shoshoni, and the Sioux.

This then is a love story of two warring cultures, and a forbidden passion played against the gigantic panorama of the early West. Forever branded on the pages of history is the tale of beautiful Summer Van Schuyler, stolen in a stagecoach raid by the savage half-breed, Iron Knife, in that brief moment before the Civil War turned lives and land into fire and ashes. . . .

Chapter One

September, 1858

Summer Priscilla Van Schuyler had never given a thought to the possibility of being raped and murdered by a band of renegade Indians. With all her other problems, Indians were the last thing on her mind as she fled down the dark street to board the 3:30 A.M. stage out of Fort Smith.

The bearded driver eyed her with suspicion as he took her small bag. "You all alone, miss?"

"Well, yes." She avoided his dark eyes with her pale blue ones. "I have a job to get to in San Francisco," she lied lamely. That city seemed like a safe destination because of its distance. All she'd managed to grab was one small bag, forgetting even her corset in her headlong flight from the hotel.

The driver said nothing more as he loaded her bag and helped her into the coach, but she felt his eyes taking in the cheap red dress that clung revealingly to her tiny waist and full bosom. Her face flamed as she settled herself. She was glad now she had traded clothes with the dance-hall girl. Her own blue silk, Parisian-made gown would have brought her too much notice and too many questions. Wealthy girls of good family did not travel alone.

Overhead, she heard the driver climb up beside the guard and crack his whip. Summer heaved a sigh of relief as the Butterfield Overland lurched away. With any luck, she would be miles away before her maid awakened back at the hotel.

There was only one other passenger, a fat man snoring loudly, his doughy hands clasped across his plaid vest. He reeked of cheap, barbershop hair tonic. Finally, Summer dozed off, too, as the stage swayed rhythmically and the hours passed as they headed southwest across the corner of the Indian Territory.

She was startled awake by the sudden speed of the coach and the driver's shout, "Indians! Indians!"

The guard leaned down to shout in the window, his gray hair blowing in the wind. "We're being attacked! Cheyennes!"

Summer crashed to the floor as the coach raced forward, the driver cracking his whip to urge the snorting horses on. Choking on the swirling dust, she leaned out the window to peer behind the stage. The east gave an agonizingly slow and bloody birth to dawn, barely outlining a half dozen whooping Indians on paint ponies a few hundred yards behind.

The fat little man stared out his window. "It's Cheyennes, by God! And they're gainin' on us!"

She clamped her soft hands over her mouth for a moment, willing herself not to panic. Torn between excitement and terror, she watched sweat bead on the man's upper lip, his hands tremble as he dug in his valise.

"Lucky I still got my old Colt dragoon from my army days!" He cocked the big pistol and commenced firing out the window.

Summer vowed she would not give way to hysteria as she gripped the seat with white knuckles. The roar of the pistol and the guns above her set her ears ringing, and the interior reeked with the smell of gunpowder and the fat man's sweat.

The coach bounced wildly, and she felt her hairpins loosen in the chignon of long blond locks that now cascaded down her slender neck.

A scream of agony, and the guard fell from the top of the stage, falling past her window and into the dust of the road

10

behind them.

Summer never knew what happened next—maybe they hit a rock in the road, or maybe an arrow brought down one of the team horses, but the coach lurched abruptly. Everything was topsy-turvy, turning over and over in a swirl of cheap red satin and white crinoline petticoats. She lay where she fell a long moment, uncomprehending, the horsehair cushion harsh against her creamy cheek.

Dazed, she crawled across the plaid vest of the hapless fat man. His dead eyes stared in a last, surprised look at the doorpost, which had given him a fatal blow across the forehead. Blood ran scarlet down the pasty skin.

The coach wheels still whirled and creaked as she crawled out of the wreckage into the September chill. The stage horses, broken free, stood trembling and lathered under a nearby blackjack oak. Shouts and hoofbeats warned her the savages were almost upon her.

Looking around for the stage driver, she found him, three arrows sticking at odd angles from his back.

She promised herself that she wouldn't cry and she wouldn't faint as tears threatened to overflow her big eyes. With teeth clenched to stop her lips from trembling, she crawled back into the overturned stage, wrenching the pistol from the dead man's fingers. Fear tasted like bitter metal to her mouth, and she gagged on the sweetish smell of blood. Oh, how she wished now that proper young society ladies were taught to shoot instead of waltzing and speaking French.

Hiding behind the wrecked door, she watched the Cheyennes joking and laughing as they fanned out and crawled toward the stage to finish off any survivors. If she could only hold them off for a little while, the stage would be overdue at the next stop, and a search party might be sent out. And back at Fort Smith, Mrs. O'Malley had surely recovered from the sherry and would send help for her missing charge. But the maid didn't know she was on this stage, wouldn't know where to look, Summer remembered with a sinking heart. Anyway, she couldn't hold the savages off ten minutes, she realized, checking the Colt's chambers. She only had one shot left.

Frantically, she dug into the dead man's valise, hoping to find more ammunition. There was none. Should she use the last bullet on herself? She recalled the story in the *Boston Journal*, hinting at the terrible things Indians did to white women.

No, she decided, lifting her chin in that stubborn way of hers, she was going to get one more of those murdering savages and the devil take the hindmost!

Overhead, the sky clouded and a drop of rain plunked on the coach. Encouraged by the lack of movement from the wreckage, the Indians stood and moved toward her. *Why, they're drunk!* she realized, trying to cock the pistol at the nearest swaying figure.

She steadied the barrel against the window edge to stop her own trembling and pulled the trigger. The recoil threw her across the floor, and her ears rang. But over the roar, she heard the unmistakable howl of a wounded man, and peeked to see a dirty, pock-marked savage clutching his arm and dodging behind a boulder.

Darn! She had only creased him. Why was it acceptable for a proper Boston girl to learn to ride but not to shoot? Regretfully, she reached up to touch the tiny miniature of her mother hanging from a fine gold neck chain. She had been too sentimental last night to part with it when she had sold her other jewelry to pay her passage. Well, she'd see those bloodthirsty savages didn't get it! Summer jerked at it, breaking the delicate chain as she did so, tucking it carefully under one of the seat cushions.

Then, resolutely, she gripped the big Colt by its barrel, wondering just how much damage she could do with a gun butt before it was twisted from her hands and her skull cleaved by a tomahawk. She intended to go down fighting. Not for her the weepy hysterics and the begging for mercy! Some of the bluest blood in Massachusetts might flow in her veins, but somewhere in her past was a tempestuous vixen, coming through now, ready to claw and fight.

She could hear the braves rustling in the weeds just a few feet away. She held her breath, waiting, not wanting to give away her position, but knowing they must hear her heart hammering.

Any minute now, they would realize that her gun was empty when no more shots were forthcoming. Summer wondered for a split second if it would hurt as she died, and almost regretted that she had not obeyed her father.

The pock-marked one she had creased with her last bullet was at the end of the coach now. He was close enough for her to see the red paint smeared on his dirty face. She waited, gripping the pistol barrel with clammy fingers.

And then he exploded up out of the grass, jerked open the door and grappled with Summer.

"How dare you!" she screamed in fury. "How dare you attack a Van Schuyler! I'm not afraid! Do you hear? Not afraid!"

He seemed momentarily stunned both by her furious anger and her attack as she beat him about the face with the gun butt. Then she screamed in pain as his knife flashed, slashing her arm, and she dropped the gun.

Dizzy, she staggered as she fought him and smelled the rancid stink of him. His hands were like iron bands on her small wrists as she struggled, and then his arms went around her narrow waist, lifting her clear of the wreckage and carrying her out on the open prairie.

"You pay, white whore!" he said in broken English. "You pay now for everything!"

"Let go of me!" she shrieked, struggling. "Let go of me!"

But his brute strength overpowered her, and he dragged her out on the grass. The others ran out of the brush, dancing about, laughing and pointing at her. It must be high humor, she thought, to have been held at bay by a mere slip of a girl with an empty gun.

"You pay now, white woman!" her captor said again. "You pay for making Angry Wolf look the fool to his men! Tonight your mane of gold hair hangs from my lodge pole!"

Weakly, Summer struggled as he pulled her closer to him. The others yelped and danced about, helping themselves to trinkets, money from the strongbox, the coach horses. Out of the corner of her eye, she saw a knife flash over the fallen driver and willed herself not to faint as the culprit waved the scalp for the approval of the others. Then, satisfied with their loot, the pack gathered around Angry Wolf and his captive. They chortled and poked at her as they swayed drunkenly, seemingly excited over what was about to happen. Now they fell silent, like hungry wolves waiting to tear apart one small rabbit.

Angry Wolf jerked Summer hard against him. Her breasts ached from the hard pressure of his chest and she could feel the heat of his hands through the back of her flimsy crimson dress. His eyes gleamed moist with eagerness, and now his hot mouth was on hers, forcing her lips open, cutting off her screams. Summer gagged on the whiskey taste of his mouth and closed her eyes against the lust in the circling faces. The Indian twisted his hands in her blond curls, trying to force her to the ground.

Struggling, she attempted to run. But as she broke away from him, his fingers caught the low-cut bodice of the red dress, jerking her around. The fabric gave way, ripping almost to the waist, exposing her full, perfect breasts.

The pack set off a howl of approval, stamping their feet, eager now for their turn at the captive. She pulled her tattered bodice together, backing away slowly. It was impossible not to see the hunger in the drunken eyes as they devoured the image of the rose-tipped mounds. Angry Wolf's chest heaved, and he licked his thin lips. His eyes never left her breasts and his manhood was very apparent under the skimpy loincloth.

"Now, white bitch," he breathed heavily, "we will teach you what you were born for and use you like a dog pack does a bitch

14

in heat, again and again!"

He fingered the knife in his beaded belt and moved toward her stealthily. "And when we have had enough of your body, we will enjoy you in other ways, taking a very long time to finish you, making you beg for death!"

The others shouted approval at his words. "Tell her, Angry Wolf, tell her what we will do to her pale body with fire and blade! But let us get on with the sharing of her!"

Desperately, Summer backed away, but the pock-marked one grabbed her, lifting her completely off the ground as he buried his face greedily in her breasts. He swore angry Cheyenne curses as her nails raked his face and tore at his beaded shirt. He wrapped one leg around her long, slender ones and tripped her, falling heavily on her as they went to the grass. His mouth cut into hers brutally, and he struggled to jerk her dress up, forcing himself between her thighs.

Abruptly, she was aware of three riders charging into the confusion and her attacker being jerked away from her, thrown to his feet, and he stumbled backward. She raised weakly on one elbow, modestly pulling at her torn clothing and watching as her big Indian rescuer engaged in a hot argument with the one called Angry Wolf.

The three new Indians were obviously sober and wore no paint. Perhaps they had been hunting in the area, because two rabbits hung from the leader's Appaloosa stallion. She wondered if this were a prearranged meeting place or if the three had been drawn to the scene by shots or Summer's screams. The two men shouted at each other angrily, and there was much pushing and gesturing.

She studied her rescuer, thrilling in spite of herself at the knowledge that these two stallions clashed because of her.

The new Indian was much larger than the others, and not as dark. It dawned on her that he had white blood, for although he dressed like the others in beaded buckskin, his skin was lighter bronze.

His ebony hair pulled to a braid over his left ear, the right shone with an earring, a large gold coin. Scars showed in the neck of his open shirt and powerful muscles rippled as he gestured. Around his neck, he wore a small white object on a thong and a big knife with a bone handle hung from his belt.

He spoke with authority, gesturing in fury toward the overturned stage, and the others hung their heads and backed away. His two friends sat their horses like stone sentinels, seemingly awaiting his orders. Only Angry Wolf seemed defiant now. The others sobered and ducked their heads like small boys caught in mischief by three older brothers.

The tall one was handsome in a savage way, Summer thought, although his face was weathered and his nose broken. She had no idea how old he might be, but he was certainly much more than Summer's eighteen years.

Thunder echoed in the distance, and a drop of cool rain fell on her bruised lips—then, another.

Angry Wolf spoke in English this time, leering wickedly at her, and she knew he wanted her to hear. "This white squaw is worth nothing, my brother Dog Soldier, only a small plaything for men to enjoy!"

"You, Iron Knife," he gestured to the big man, "you and your cousins forget the Treaty and this worthless peace and share along with us! We will give you some of the loot we have taken from the stage and you, too, may lie on this woman's silken belly. When at last we grow tired of her, we will cut her throat with a tiny slash, and watch her writhe as her life bubbles out into the dust! Then we will leave arrows and other things from our hated enemies, the Crow and the Pawnee so the soldiers will chase them!" He fingered the hilt of his knife. "It will be a good joke!"

His fellows nodded approval, but Iron Knife shook his head and barked orders in Cheyenne. The others fell back, but not Angry Wolf. His enraged face showed he had no intention of giving up this tasty morsel before he had tasted it. He exclaimed angrily and pushed the half-breed with his open hand. The other pushed back. Summer clutched the shreds of her dress against the rain as she slowly stood up and watched the shoving turn into a full fight.

They wrestled, grunting from the exertion as they went to the ground, and the others urged them on. Even the two sentinels came off their ponies to watch the fight. The struggle was as old as time and Summer tingled with excitement in spite of herself, knowing as females always do that this battle was for possession of her body.

Whoever won would do as he wished with her, and she would have no say in the matter. There was something primitive unfolding before her, something that frightened her civilized soul, yet made her blood race.

Furtively, she glanced around. The men were all intently watching the fight, ignoring her completely. The ponies strayed across the prairie, munching grass while their rawhide bridles dragged behind them. A red and white pinto caught her eye a few hundred feet to one side. If she could reach that pony, there was a forest on the other side of the rise that she might lose herself in.

She took a slow step sideways, then another. As she moved, she waited for the braves to notice, but they were too intent on the struggle. The time was now!

She whirled, jerked up her crinoline petticoats and fled in a dead run across the buffalo grass. She was going to make it! Her heart pounded in her dry throat as she ran, knowing from the sounds behind her that she had not yet been missed. She lost one of her tiny, expensive shoes as she ran, and burrs and stones tore her small feet, but she paid no heed and kept running. Her crinolines impeded her long legs, yet she ran on.

Behind her, the sudden hue and cry told her she had been missed. Confusion and shots rang out, though she did not stop or look back. The startled pony jerked up, snorting. She wrapped her fingers in his mane and tried to mount. The pony reared in confusion, tossing her to the ground in a heap of torn petticoats.

17

And then they surrounded her. The big Appaloosa thundered by, and a strong arm reached out and swept her from the ground. She found herself gasping for breath against the big, scarred chest of Iron Knife. He cradled her effortlessly in his arms while the snorting stallion pranced. The horse's lunge threw her naked breasts against his buckskin shirt. She tried to recoil from the heat of his body, but he held her tightly.

"Don't fight me, Little One." He spoke perfect English, smiling with white, even teeth. "Don't you know Indian ponies mount from the right side? That's why he threw you!"

He looked deep into her eyes. "I have fought Angry Wolf and won you. Now, you are mine to do with as I please!"

Summer's mouth fell open. "You speak English and you have white blood!"

He smiled wryly at her. "My mother was stolen from a wagon train, and I spent five years in the white man's schools when we were recaptured by the Bluecoats!"

"You will help me?" she asked hopefully, "because I am white, like your mother—"

"I am Cheyenne like my father," he declared firmly, grasping her waist, "and I will treat you as a spoil of war, a prize from a raid!"

She knew she was no match for him, but she fought bravely anyway as the horse danced around and the other warriors laughed and hooted. Rain fell in a fine mist as the brave held both her small wrists in one big hand and reached for a rawhide thong to tie her hands behind her.

Completely helpless now, she could only lean against him while the stallion's lunging threw her soft breasts again and again against his hard chest. She was both humiliated and terrified as he took his buffalo robe and wrapped it about his wide shoulders, enclosing her in its warm folds. He shouted an order, and the group moved out.

His hands felt like fire on her bare skin under the robe, and she struggled weakly but was helpless to resist his exploring fingers with her hands tied behind her.

18

"Be still, woman!" he whispered. "A man may rightly feel that which belongs to him!"

She tried to spit at him and he cuffed her across the face, but very gently. Even she could see he was holding back the force of tense, powerful muscles.

He smiled down at her. "Soon I will make better use of that soft mouth," he chided, holding her firmly as the horse broke into a canter.

Trembling, Summer felt the heat and the hardness of every inch of his brown body as he pulled her tighter against him, and the mist became a steady downpour. He covered her face with the robe, and she was warm against his great chest. Hours passed, and her weariness and her wound made her doze in spite of herself.

It was near dusk when the band rode into an Indian camp. No one came out of the tepees in the rain, and the riders scattered, her own captor dismounting in front of a large tepee painted with dragonflies. Swinging her lightly from the pony, he carried her inside and dumped her unceremoniously on the floor while he knelt to build a fire in the fire pit. Finally he faced her, studying her heaving, naked breasts. Rain had soaked both their clothes as he'd brought her from the horse to the tepee. Summer struggled against her bonds, but she was helpless and she knew it. She tried to cry out, but his hand covered her mouth, muffling the sound. She paused and the hand moved slowly across her cheek, down her slender throat, and brushed oh so gently across one rose nipple. Her pulse raced unexpectedly. Her whole sexual experience consisted of one or two chaste kisses behind the palms at the annual Debutante's Ball. Her eyes held his, and it was he who looked away, pulled the big knife from his belt.

"Please don't kill me," she asked simply, knowing she couldn't stop him. He paused, the firelight gleaming on the blade.

19

"I will never hurt you, Little One," he promised with a shake of his head, "nor will anyone, as long as I draw breath." He reached, and with one lightning move, cut the bonds that bound her wrists behind her.

Summer crouched, ready to run past him.

"Not so fast, my frightened little deer," he said, smiling. "Now, you are going to repay me for saving you from having your throat cut. And I expect you to be very, very grateful!"

"You said you wouldn't hurt me!" she cried.

He shrugged. "What's one more man to a saloon girl? Do you think I do not recognize what you are? I said I wouldn't hurt you, I didn't say I wouldn't love you!"

Terrified, Summer stared up at him, knowing he was about to take her virginity.

Chapter Two

Hungrily, Iron Knife stared back at the half-naked blonde poised for flight in the middle of the tepee. Almost twenty-five winters had he seen, and in all those years never had he desired a woman so much as this one.

She shivered in her wet, gaudy dress and the movement brought him back to reality.

"I will get you dry clothes," he grunted, suddenly uncertain. It had been a long, long time since he had lain with a white woman. That red-headed whore had worn a scarlet dress, too.

The girl bristled, and her chin came up stubbornly. "I demand to see whoever is in charge! My name is Summer Priscilla Van Schuyler of *the* Boston Van Schuylers, and I demand to be returned to Fort Smith at once!"

Iron Knife smiled incredulously as he wiped the rain from his weathered face. What spirit she had, this Little One! Here she was, a helpless captive, miles from her own kind and within minutes of being mated, and she was making demands!

"Summer," he murmured, "a good name for one with hair the color of the white man's ripe wheat, eyes the color of Hiriutsiishi skies, the hot month you call July."

Memories came flooding back of the five years in a small Texas village. "I shall call you Summer Sky," he announced

21

dramatically, touching his own broad chest. "And I am Iron Knife, son of War Bonnet, once a great chief of our people."

"Then I demand to see this War Bonnet!" She tossed her mane of golden hair. "Maybe he has enough sense to know you just can't pull a Van Schuyler off a stage and get away with it! Why, Father will have Senator Wilson and half of President Buchanan's cabinet out looking for me!"

"My father is dead." He shook his head regretfully. "Killed by the hated Pawnee when I was a youth. And you, you will demand nothing!"

He grasped her shoulder roughly. "The council will no doubt meet tomorrow night to decide this issue. Until then, you are mine!"

She jerked from his grasp and he saw a flicker of fear in her blue eyes, replaced quickly by haughty anger. "Don't touch me!"

He shrugged. It would be a long, cool night and he had much experience with women. Before morning, he would have her gasping beneath him, digging her nails into his whip-scarred back. Her protests were lies. She could not be a virtuous woman, traveling alone, wearing that sensuous dress. He had spent five years with the Whites before his mother died, and he knew their customs. This Little One was either a whore or a dance-hall girl. The thought brought back a half-repressed memory of that other time and place, and the red weals on his back seemed to burn again as they had when he was but a boy of thirteen. . . .

"I will get you some dry clothes," he said again, abruptly banishing the memory as his hand reached up to touch his broken nose. The mob of white men would have killed him, he thought, had it not been for his brave mother holding them at bay with her shotgun. . . .

"Do not try to run, little Summer," he admonished from the tepee entry, "you are many miles from this place called Fort Smith, and deep inside the Indian Territory. It is rainy and almost dark outside, and no one here would help you, knowing you belong to me!"

He stepped outside and paused a moment, listening. The rain had stopped, and dusk spread over the camp. The camp crier rode around the circle of tepees, telling the news of the stage coach raid, the white captive. He called the men to Council tomorrow night to discuss this. Iron Knife yawned and sniffed the fresh, wet smells of the rain. The Cheyenne were far south and east of their usual track this year. They followed the great herds of buffalo that seemed fewer each season as the white man moved deeper and deeper into the Great Plains that the Cheyennes had roamed for generations. The ten great tribes of the Tsistsistas scattered farther and farther, dependent on much meat. But with the buffalo fewer, the warriors were raiding into eastern Indian territory to steal the fat cows and horses of the Five Civilized Tribes.

The camp was quiet now at dusk, the tepees arranged in a great, orderly circle, each opening facing to the east. In the inner circle of the Dog Soldiers' lodges, he heard casual talk and laughter. Somewhere, a dog barked. Roasting meat smells drifted from his uncle's lodge as he entered and nodded silently to his cousins, Two Arrows and Lance Bearer, who had stood ready to back him in the fight with Angry Wolf.

He addressed the plump wife of his father's brother. "Pony Woman, I have need of a dress and some very small moccasins and food." He gestured toward the cook pot that simmered over the fire pit. "When will my uncle be returning to camp from the Chiefs' Council?"

"In the morning." Pony Woman rushed to get the things he had requested. "Do you need medicine, too? Is the woman hurt?"

"Yes." He nodded. "Angry Wolf cut a small place on her arm. It is good you think of this."

She gathered up the things from her parfleche bag, and he took them and returned to his tepee.

The blond girl had collapsed in a heap on the floor, but she struggled to her feet as he entered and again tried to pull the

23

frayed cloth over her creamy breasts.

"Here, put this on," he ordered, holding out the buckskin dress as he set the small pot of broth by the fire.

She took the dress, hesitated. Then her little chin went up stubbornly. "Please step outside while I change."

He considered a moment, torn between admiration for her spirit and amazement at her arrogance. For a dance-hall girl, she seemed terribly spoiled and used to ordering people around.

"I will not step out," he decided, sitting down cross-legged. "The whole camp would laugh when they heard of Iron Knife's being ordered about. He shook his head. "No, I want to see what it is that I risked my life for this morning, whether what I have won is worth almost killing a fellow Dog Soldier for."

"Then I'll wear this wet dress all night!" Her eyes flashed, although he could see she was weary, and her arm was smeared with dried blood.

"You are my woman," he announced flatly, "and you will put on these dry clothes before you become sick. Do you want me to pull those wet things from your body?" He half rose from the floor, and she stepped backward, tears filling her eyes and dripping down the long lashes.

Iron Knife softened, remembering his own mother, Texanna, so much like this woman. But his hunger was stronger than his pity. Summer was his to enjoy, at least until the Council made another decision. With such a body as her soft curves hinted at, why should she be hesitant to let him gaze upon it? No doubt many white men had seen her nakedness, and she would not deny him because he was an Indian.

She looked at him a long, searching moment, then turned her back to him and began to change. The flickering shadows half hid, half revealed her loveliness as the torn dress and petticoats fell in a heap at her feet, and she pulled the buckskin dress over her head.

Iron Knife stared in wonderment. Even in the dim light, he was struck by the pale smoothness of her skin, the blond hair

24

hanging almost to her slim hips. He watched the fine legs, the curve of her soft, full breasts. His sudden intake of breath caused her to jerk the dress down to her thighs, and she whirled to face him.

"Are you satisfied?" she asked defiantly, and stepped out of the crumpled red dress.

"I am more than satisfied," he murmured, abruptly aware of his manhood under the skimpy loincloth. Slowly, he got to his feet, his dark eyes never leaving her pale blue ones.

"For such a prize, a man might be willing to kill a dozen brave warriors, even though he would be exiled by his people. Now I finally know what it was that made my father love a white girl, why no one else could ever replace her in his heart."

He pulled his own wet buckskin shirt off, hung it by the fire, revealing to her for the first time the two big scars on his chest from the ordeal of "hanging from the pole" that his Sioux brothers called the sun dance and his people called the Medicine Lodge ceremony. He half turned to reach the pot of broth, and felt her eyes on his scarred back.

"Long ago, some white men took a horse whip to me." He answered her unspoken question as he dipped the steaming, rich broth into two gourd containers he kept by the fire pit.

"Oh." She paused, but her tone revealed much sympathy, perhaps a feeling for all hurt things. "Why?" she asked. "Why would they do that?"

He left the question hanging on the air unanswered. *Because of a red-headed dance-hall girl in a scarlet dress*, he thought.

But he only thrust a gourd of food at her. "Here, eat!"

He watched her as she sat on the floor and drank the soup daintily. She obviously had not eaten in a long time, but she didn't gulp, he noticed. She had the manners of a fine lady. For a long time, he studied her soft, delicate hands and looked again at the torn dress in a heap on the floor. It was a whore's dress, but a fine lady's petticoat. He knew good lace from his mother, who had supported them both with her sewing after the Texas Rangers forced them to go back to the white family

25

who had lost her.

Summer's accent was strange, too, and he knew that she was not from any place he had ever been, and he did not know the whereabouts of this place she called Boston.

She finished the tasty broth and wordlessly returned the gourd to him. He set both gourds by the fire and reached out to take her hand. Immediately, she stiffened.

"Let me see your wound," he commanded, jerking her arm to him. "If I do not do something, you will get the sickness the whites call 'blood poisoning.'"

She relaxed and let him study the cut. He was keenly aware of the smell of the fire, the small movement of her breasts as she sighed.

His own hard hands sweated holding her small one. There had been many women to share his blankets, but none who he desired as he desired this one. Gently as his big hands could, he took a scrap of cloth from her torn dress and water from the water skin hanging from one of the tepee poles and washed the blood from her arm. Then, he treated it with maheskoe, the dried root of the red medicine so favored by his people. Perhaps tomorrow he had better call the medicine man with his spells and chants to make sure she healed well.

Now he clasped her fingers and slowly pulled her toward him.

She stiffened again. "If you touch me, I'll scream!" she threatened, her blue eyes flashing.

He grinned and fingered the big brass object he wore as an earring. It was a button from a cavalry officer's jacket. The bone whistle hanging from his neck was made from the wing of an eagle. All Dog Soldiers wore one.

"You cannot scream with my lips devouring yours." He chuckled. "Do you think there is any army of Bluecoats waiting outside to rescue you? Do you not know how many of them I have killed before we signed the peace treaty?"

She scrambled to her feet and tried to move toward the door. He held on to her arm. "If you run outside, away from the protection of my big blade," he patted the knife in his belt, "Angry Wolf and the others will catch you! Do you want me or all of them? Do not play the innocent with me! Iron Knife has been much with women, and I will fire your blood as no white man has ever done in the past."

He jumped up and jerked her roughly to her feet, holding her against him, reveling in the clean smell of her hair. "You are mine!" he whispered, feeling his heart pound in his great chest, feeling his manhood rise. "You are mine as my lance is mine! As my horse is mine!"

"How dare you!" She seethed as she struggled to pull away. "Do you know who I am? My father owns the biggest fleet of whaling ships on the Atlantic coast! He is very rich and will pay well to get me back unharmed! If you will send a ransom message to Fort Smith, he will send gold! A lot of gold!"

"I have no need of gold, I have need of you," he grunted, pulling her to him. "My body has much need of you!"

She clawed and fought him as his hot mouth claimed her cool, trembling lips, firing his blood as he forced her mouth open. He kissed her deeply as she made little whimpers of protest in her throat.

Her arms were pinned helplessly to her sides now with his iron grip but she struggled anyhow. He lifted her off her feet, bent her backward, and felt her heart pound as her firm breasts jutted against him, for she wore nothing under the buckskin shift.

"Do not fight me, Summer," he warned against her lips. "Do not feign innocence to tease me. I am wise to the way of white whores. I learned that bitter lesson many years ago. You should be proud that a mighty warrior like me has chosen you."

He swung her up lightly in his arms and moved toward the buffalo robe bed on the floor. "I will make love to you as no man ever has, and by morning you will never want to leave my side."

But now she wept softly, desperately, as he lowered her to

the soft fur. "Please, don't!" she wept. "Oh, no, please—"

He hesitated, not used to such protest.

"I've never had a man! Please, no, not like this!" Her bravery had finally collapsed, and she wept.

He had never had a woman weep before. They had all been eager to part their soft thighs to accept his throbbing manhood; even the red-haired whore. . . .

Still he was excited by the white girl's struggles and protests, and his Indian half urged him to take her passionately now just as he had dreamed of doing ever since he had first seen her on the prairie near the overturned stage. He did not believe her, of course, but his pride was stung that she was refusing him that which no doubt many white men before him had tasted.

"Do not try to fool me!" he protested. "You wear a whore's dress. Do not tell me you have never had a man."

"I traded for the dress," she wept, brushing back a blond lock. "I had run away. I knew they would be searching for me in my fine blue silk and bonnet, and I would arouse suspicion traveling alone. No one would notice a dance-hall girl traveling by herself, especially if they were all looking for a girl dressed in blue."

He knelt and put his big hand under her small chin, turning her face up to him. "How can you be a rich girl?" he challenged. "You wear no jewels."

"I sold them all in Fort Smith to a saloon keeper to get money for my stage passage." She wiped her eyes. "I told you I was running away!"

"Why would you run away?" He looked deep into her eyes.

"My father was angry with me. He was sending me to live with his uncle, the Reverend Harlow! I didn't want to go."

She was lying, of course, and he would not be taken in. He took her in his arms and she struggled only a little in her weariness, and he kissed her deeply again, exploring the warmth of her mouth. She could not be a virgin; she wore no *nihpihist*, the chastity belt of his people. But then, he remembered, white people did not use that thong tied around a

28

woman's waist, and going down between her thighs to protect their untouched women.

Perhaps she was chaste! The thought excited him even more, and as he kissed her he realized that she knew nothing or little of kissing or being kissed. He had a lot to teach her.

Very gently now, he cradled her in his strong arms as she trembled, and he buried his face in the yellow hair. The feel of her soft body brought back memories of this morning when he had seen her for the very first time, lifted her lightly to his stallion. He had thought of nothing else but possessing her completely all those long miles back to camp. He had known then, as he cradled her against his big chest, that at last he had found his woman. The one who would be to him like his right hand, like his beating heart was to him. This woman would possess his soul as he possessed her body. And finally she would carry on his lineage, bear many fine sons for him.

"Please, don't!" She twisted away from him, seemingly too weak to do much else.

The hunger in him was almost uncontrollable now. "Be still, woman," he commanded. "I shall be your first man and your last. I shall be very gentle and patient as I teach you, and you will want me, and moan my name in the darkness."

But she wept more loudly, and he pressed her face against his bare chest, trying to muffle her sobs. "Hush!" he whispered roughly. "The whole camp will hear you crying and think I love you badly or that I beat you!"

She stopped sobbing and looked up at him uncertainly. "Please don't rape me!" she begged.

Iron Knife winced at the word. He had not heard that white man's word since that whore accused him falsely. The trauma of the word's memory caused his manhood to go soft and his passion to fade. He reached up to wipe away a tear that overflowed the big, blue eyes and muttered silent, Cheyenne curses at his white heritage that could be so moved by a woman's tears. Regretfully, he pulled her buckskin dress back down over her thighs with hands that shook.

"I will not take you tonight," he announced. "I will wait until your hunger is as strong as my own. But do not tell the others. They would laugh at my softness!"

Summer pulled back and looked at him a long moment. "Would you help me get back to my people?"

He pushed her away roughly, and stood up. "I did not say that! The Council will decide your fate. Why should I do as you ask?"

He took the big blade from his belt, turning it over and over in his hands, remembering past battles against the whites, his thirst for revenge. The knife he had fashioned himself from the broken tip of a Bluecoat's saber after he had counted coup on the man . . .

"My father would give you a lot of money to return me." She stood up, too, caught his elbow. "I would be very grateful."

He shrugged her hand away. "I have no need of money and you are not grateful in the way I would wish." He nodded toward the bed, and angrily thrust the big blade back in his belt.

"You will not help me, then?" She sighed and sank slowly down on the buffalo robes.

"I did not say that, either!" He snapped, torn by his conflicting emotions. *I love you, Summer Sky,* he thought, gazing at her. *I have loved you since the first moment I saw you, and risked my life to save you. Now, you spurn me, and I care too much to take you by force. Until you come to me . . . until you come to me . . .*

"Then you're not going to rape me?" She sat on the rumpled bed and looked up at him with that direct gaze that was not seemly for a maiden. *She was headstrong,* he thought, *headstrong and untamed like a fine, wild filly that could be ruined by too rough handling. But, oh the passion she could arouse in a man, and all the fury of emotion that could be released if she could ever be tamed and mounted as she was born to be!*

"Here, lie down!" he commanded gruffly, afraid she would guess that he was the one who was a prisoner. He had captured

30

her body, but she held in thrall his *tasoom,* his soul. "Lie down!" he said again, "You are very tired and weak. In the morning, we will talk more of what will become of you."

She lay down hesitantly, the unspoken question in her eyes.

"No, Summer Sky," he answered softly, sitting cross-legged by the fire. "I will not take you by force. There is pride involved here and something else . . ."

His voice trailed off, and with sudden clarity the grizzled face of Jake Dallinger, the army scout, came to his mind. Jake Dallinger with his cruel whip. The white man's word, "rape" had brought back out all the old, half-forgotten memories like Mihn, the Cheyenne legendary monster arising out of the dark river. . . .

"Sleep now," he whispered to her, "Sleep and I will protect you all through the night." He patted his knife hilt. "No one will dare to touch the woman of Iron Knife."

He could see that she did not trust him, for she lay down on the buffalo robe but did not close her eyes, watching him intently as he squatted by the fire. She was very weary and weak from her wound. He watched her long eyelashes flutter as she tried to stay awake, but gradually they closed and she slept.

Iron Knife saw her tremble in the chill *Tonishi* night, that which whites called September. He watched the firelight flicker on the golden hair that tumbled over her small shoulders. No woman had ever made his blood run so hot. His hard hands clenched as he gently spread a buffalo fur over her, imagining how it would be under the cover holding her warmth against him.

He thought how it would feel to run his hands down to the warm wetness of her very being and taste her full, perfect breasts as she arched against him. He held his breath, imagining the feel of pumping his manseed into the deepest depth of her, his hard hands cupping her small hips as she wrapped her long, slender legs about him and begged for more against his lips.

Cursing himself for a soft fool, he stirred the fire and sat

31

cramped and cold on guard by her bed. Her beautiful face was at peace now, the light flickering on the soft mouth, the stubborn chin as she slept warm and safe by the fire. His gaze never left her face, his eyes unable to drink in enough of her. But finally, toward morning, he, too, dropped off into a troubled sleep.

They were both awakened at dawn by the stirring of the camp outside. Iron Knife stood and stretched, his muscles cramped and sore from his all-night vigil.

The blond girl looked up at him, puzzled, as if she did not know where she was. Then apprehension came into her eyes as she seemed to remember. "What will happen now?"

"I do not know," he answered truthfully, glad to see a hint of the old fire and spirit he remembered from yesterday morning. "The old chiefs will decide tonight. Are you hungry?"

She nodded imperially. "My father will see that you are rewarded for taking good care of me."

"You still do not seem to understand!" he snapped. "Your father's money, if indeed he has any, is worth less than nothing here. You are totally dependent on me. I can feed you, or let you starve, or beat you to death, and no one in this camp will protest or try to stop me."

She shrugged haughtily, and he thought it would be very hard for a man to break her spirit, and then wondered silently if he would desire her so much were she docile.

"Here. Let me see your wound."

She held out her arm and he gently unwrapped and inspected it. *It looked bad,* he thought. *There were now red, angry places spreading around the wound. He would get the medicine man to say special prayers and sing songs for her well-being. . . .*

He rewrapped the arm and said, "I will send Pony Woman to see after your needs." And with that he went outside.

Nonuno, the rainbow, hung in the clearing sky. The camp teemed with life: horses neighing, dogs barking, children running about between the tepees. He asked Pony Woman to look in on the captive, went by the medicine man's tepee and promised him a fine pony if he would do ceremonies later to help Summer. Then he walked down to the river the whites called the Arkansas and the Indians called the Arrow Point.

The Cheyenne were a clean people and there were many of them in the shallows, splashing. He wanted solitude, time to sort out his thoughts. So he chose a deep, clear pool around the bend, out of sight of the others. Under towering pines, he stripped the breechcloth from his hard body and dived in, relishing the chill of the early morning. For a few minutes, he gave himself over to the enjoyment of the water and then turned toward shore at a sound of footsteps.

Gray Dove, the beautiful Arapaho girl who had caused him so much trouble in the past, posed on a big boulder at the water's edge. Her ripe, brown body gleamed naked in the early morning light. She stood there turning about, displaying herself like a wanton.

He hissed in clipped Cheyenne. "Have you been eating the plant the whites call 'loco weed?' Someone will see you displaying yourself like a common whore!"

She laughed easily and dived into the water, surfacing near him.

"I wanted you to see again what it is that I have to offer." She tread water and looked up into his face. "I hunger for you, Iron Knife. I have always hungered for you since our two tribes, the Cheyenne and the Arapaho, have shared camp grounds. I have waited long for you to offer ponies to my father for me."

"Angry Wolf sent marriage ponies," he reminded her, unable to keep his eyes off her body, clearly visible in the clear water. "The ponies stood in front of your father's lodge two days before you finally sent them back."

She was standing now in the chest-deep water so close that

33

her large breasts brushed his chest. "I would not send back your marriage ponies," she murmured.

"I have told you before, Gray Dove, I do not want you for a wife! Why is it you turn down a brave warrior like Angry Wolf, and flaunt yourself before me in front of the whole camp? Angry Wolf and I were once friends before you made so much trouble between us."

She reached out and touched him beneath the water, and he could not control the rise of his manhood. Summer had built a fire in him last night that had not been quenched. Roughly, he pushed the Indian girl away.

She laughed knowingly. "So the pale blond captive that all the camp gossips about does not satisfy. I would satisfy you, I know from much experience all it takes to please a man's body!"

She moved in closer, found his hands, and placed them on her hips. "I am Arapaho. We do not make so much of chastity as the Cheyenne do. Let us go lie on the warm sand of the riverbank," she nodded toward the shore, "and please each other."

She pressed so close, he could feel the heat of her breasts against him in the cold water. "Tonight," she whispered, "tonight, tell the Council you have reconsidered; that you do not want the blonde one. Let them give her to Angry Wolf or trade her off to the Comanche. Give me a chance to make you forget you ever hungered for her."

"You have the morals of a wolf bitch!" He pushed her away and waded toward the shore. "You are evil, Gray Dove, and will always bring trouble to any man who desires you. I do not want you for my woman!"

Hurriedly, he jerked on his breechcloth and returned to camp, ignoring Gray Dove's calls behind him.

Inside the tepee, he marveled at Pony Woman's handiwork. Summer was fed and washed, her yellow hair done up in braids in the Indian manner. He took a long look, drinking her in. "You are very beautiful," he said simply.

34

She blushed at his words displaying proper maidenly modesty and touched his arm hesitantly. "I'm—I'm sorry I've been so rude when you have done so much for me! I want very much to go back to my people, to Fort Smith. Would you help me?"

Could he deny her anything? He had struggled with his feelings all night, and he was angry with himself that her touch set the blood in his temples pounding. *Could he let her go?* He wanted her very much, but not against her will.

Suddenly, her happiness meant much to him, and although it would tear the heart out of him to lose her, he would do whatever he could to make her happy. "I will speak your part before the Council," he answered stiffly, "then it is up to them."

The medicine man came by in the afternoon and inspected Summer's arm. He declared he would have to build a sweat lodge, purify himself, and go through other rituals before dealing with this. He would be back at dawn tomorrow.

Iron Knife spent the rest of the afternoon taking Summer about the camp, letting her look, letting the Cheyenne look at her. Now she seemed to feel safe in his presence and stayed close to his side. She did not seem to mind the women and children stopping to pat her yellow hair, inspect her white skin. She even stooped to play with a fat baby sitting in the door of its family's tepee. Only Gray Dove gazed hostilely at her, but Iron Knife shook his head warningly at the dark girl. "Be careful how you treat my woman!" he warned in Cheyenne.

Finally, a lavender and pale rose twilight descended. Drums pounded, calling the men to Council.

"It is time," he said, leading her toward the big Council tepee.

She took a deep breath, and he could see the apprehension in her eyes. "I will do my best for you," he promised gently, "but you should know some of our customs. Do not step between anyone and the fire, that is bad manners. Also, do not stare at the chiefs in that direct, impudent manner of yours. Keep your eyes downcast, and say nothing as befits a proper maiden. Do not sit cross-legged. Our women do not sit that way."

They passed a couple of Angry Wolf's friends and one called out to him in Cheyenne. The other said something also, and slapped his leg in laughter.

Iron Knife whirled, his hand on the hilt of the big blade and glared at the men, feeling the unaccustomed pangs of jealousy. The braves subsided into a respectful silence, and Iron Knife grabbed her arm and pulled her along with him as he walked.

"What did they say?" she asked, almost running to keep up with his long strides.

His eyes flashed and his mouth was a hard gash in his dark face. "I am offered a good lance and three ponies for you," he answered, "but Walking Man offers four ponies, a good blanket, and says I can sleep with you sometime when he is not using you!"

She looked over her shoulder uncertainly, and hurried to walk close by his side as if she sought his protection.

"Do Indians treat their women like that?"

"You are not one of our women," he retorted, gripping her hand as they walked. "Need I keep reminding you that you are only a captive slave? That means you cannot pick and choose your man as a Cheyenne woman would. Besides, our people value chastity, and yours is not assured since you dress like a whore and wear no protective rope!"

Her face flamed and he felt a twinge of guilt at this urge to lash out and hurt her. He did not need a *nihpihist* to know no man had touched Summer Sky. He had made his decision. If she would not have him, he did not want her around as a constant reminder. He would try to send her back to her people. Someday, in a faraway place, this Boston, a white man with much gold and a fine, silken bed would lay claim to what Iron Knife hungered for. . . .

They were at the big Council tepee now. A fire blazed in the center, and the sides were pulled up so that those not of the Council might still witness what was to take place from

36

the perimeter.

"Are they all chiefs?" Summer whispered.

"No, only those four old men over there," he gestured. "Each of the ten bands of the Cheyenne have four chiefs, plus there are four great chiefs overall. They are all elected to office for ten years, although sometimes they will be asked to serve a second term."

Iron Knife led her over and seated her at the edge of the circle where all might gaze at her. There were only men in the Council tent, but women and children peered beneath the raised side to follow the action. The four old chiefs sat in front of the fire. Drums beat a steady rhythm, calling the warriors in. Angry Wolf and those of yesterday's raid stood to one side, their arms folded resolutely across their chests. Two Arrows and Lance Bearer caught their cousin's eye, and nodded reassuringly. On the outlying fringe of the crowd, Gray Dove returned his stare and smiled archly.

He strode into the firelight, and stood there a long moment, knowing he looked magnificent in his finest buckskin shirt decorated with dyed porcupine quills. His black hair gleamed in the light, and the brass cavalry button and the bone whistle reflected the fire. He knew mens' eyes watched him in admiration because he had counted many coup in battle, and was one of the best hunters in the village.

Next time, he would be elected leader of his warrior band, Hotamitaniu, the Dog Soldiers, or even chief. He felt the hot glances of the maidens, more than one of whom had hinted that if he should wish to tie ponies in front of her father's tepee, they would not be turned down.

Then he squatted to one side, and waited for an old man to stand and announce the proceedings. He glanced at the four old chiefs. Two of them he could not be sure of. Old Blue Eagle, resplendent in his scalp shirt, was a friend to Angry Wolf. Clouds Above was his own uncle, and he wore a fine Pendleton blanket and a necklace of bear claws.

With much ceremony, the pipe was filled with tobacco and

kinnikinnik, the ground bark of red willow. Solemnly, it was offered to the sky, the ground, and the four directions as the chant was intoned. "Spirit Above, smoke. Spirit Below, smoke. Four cardinal points, smoke."

Then the pipe was passed around the circle following the sun's path, being passed right to left. After that, the discussion began.

First, the old men voiced an opinion or told what they knew, next the middle-aged warriors, finally, the younger ones. Later, when a decision had been reached, the camp crier would ride in a circle about the camp from east to south, to west, then north telling what decision the Council had made. The war chiefs, each a leader of a warrior bands such as the Dog Soldiers, the Fox, the Bowstrings, stood listening intently. Whatever the Council decided, it would be up to the leaders of those warrior groups to carry out the tribe's wishes.

Iron Knife's mind had wandered, watching Summer. Now he came back to the present because Two Arrows was speaking. ". . . we had been hunting and were led to the scene by shouts and confusion. My brother, Lance Bearer, my cousin, Iron Knife, and I, came upon Angry Wolf and his friends after they had already attacked the stage. There was much firewater being drunk. The blond captive is the only one left alive from the stage."

Clouds Above glared at Angry Wolf. "You and your friends dare to break Crookedhand Fitzpatrick's treaty that we signed seven years ago at Fort Laramie?"

Angry Wolf strode to the center of the circle. "Are our warriors like women that they fear the whites? I fear them not, and I care nothing for their treaty!"

He gestured. "We are becoming soft. Once on a raid such as this, no one would have called us to account like naughty children! With honor, we would have painted our faces black, and ridden into camp with the scalps hanging from a pole to show there had been a great victory with no loss of life. There would have been much feasting and dancing of the

38

scalp dance."

"Once long ago I felt the same," Clouds Above nodded, "but a chief looks first to the safety of his people, not to his own personal glory." He paused, and his voice seemed far away. "It is an uneasy peace, this, and sometimes broken, but the Cheyenne must try not to break it. That is what the whites want so they will have an excuse to destroy us. They are as plentiful as grains of sand. Forever, they push toward us, wanting more land for their plows to destroy, forever pushing us back so they can search for the yellow metal."

The old chief shook his head. "I see the future clearly and am powerless to stop it. My own grandsons will not ride free as I do now. Always, the whites will push and push until there is nowhere left to go!"

"Then, I say we fight!" Angry Wolf paced the circle. "Let us fight the white man!"

One of the other old chiefs, Scalp Taker, shook his head. "You speak with the fire and foolishness of youth. We all know why you hate the white man so much, and with good reason. Nine years ago, the whites brought the dreaded disease they call cholera into our midst. Almost half the Cheyenne people died and you were left with no family at all. We are powerless against the white peoples' sickness."

Clouds Above nodded. "Hear me say this, and remember it well: We have less to fear from the white man's guns than from his firewater and disease. When our people are destroyed, when they have lost their proud heritage completely, these two things will have done more to wipe us out than all the soldiers' bullets!"

There was a murmur of agreement from the crowd.

"Oh, great chiefs, hear me!" Iron Knife stood up. "I have earned the right to speak in this Council even though white blood runs in my veins. Have I not counted many coup on the enemies from the time I returned after my stay in the white town? From the time I was but thirteen until all the tribes gathered to sign the Great Treaty, I fought the white men as they fought me, neither giving quarter. But once we signed the treaty, I laid aside my anger, my thirst for revenge because it was important for the good of the People."

He paused and reached up to touch his earring. "Only once since then, when Sumner's soldiers attacked us, have I fought them. I say, let us live as best we can under the treaty, giving the Bluecoats no excuse to sweep down on us and drive us farther west until they push us off into that Great Ocean beyond Cheyenne territory."

He paused and gazed at Angry Wolf. "This is a great warrior and a good Dog Soldier, but there is a point where bravery must give way to discretion. The white man's firewater makes even brave men do foolish things. Let us lay aside our personal differences for the sake of the People."

There was a murmur of approval. He knew most of the camp gossiped about the bad blood between them over Gray Dove.

"But we have played a great joke," Angry Wolf injected. "We left arrows and bead work from our hated enemies, the Pawnees, at the stage wreck so the army would chase them. And the rain has washed out our ponies' track so we cannot be followed. The Pawnees break the treaty often enough when they aren't scouting for the soldiers, let them take the blame for this, too!"

Many of the others nodded in agreement. The Pawnees were a fierce and hated enemy. They killed War Bonnet, caused the death of Texanna and many other Cheyenne in raids over the years, and most of all, they had stolen the Cheyenne's sacred Medicine Arrows. That had been many years ago and the People thought of nothing else but getting the Arrows back. The friendly Sioux had gotten two of the four returned to the Cheyenne, but the Pawnee still had the others. The People made new ones, of course, but they seemed to lack the magic of the originals. The People were convinced their luck would continue to go downhill until the other two ancient and sacred Medicine Arrows were returned.

Old Blue Eagle studied the blond captive. "What of this

woman? Did not Angry Wolf capture her?"

Iron Knife nodded. "He captured her, but I fought him and won her. She asks to be returned to her people."

The old chief looked at him incredulously. "You know we cannot do that! Even now, the soldiers hunt the Pawnee for this raid on the stagecoach! Should this white woman be freed to go back to the fort, she not only would tell them the Cheyenne did it, she might even be able to lead them back here to our camp, endangering our women and children!"

"Angry Wolf should have given thought to all this before he filled his belly with firewater," Iron Knife said dryly. "The white woman tells me her father is very rich and important, and will pay much to get her returned."

Clouds Above shook his head. "That is even worse! If she is indeed the daughter of an important chief, the Bluecoats will not rest until they have found her, bringing death to our camp!"

"The woman no doubt lies," Iron Knife said quickly. "I do not think her father is a chief. Many saw the way she was dressed when she was taken off the stage. She is only a toy for men to play with in the white man's dance hall. No one will probably come looking for her at all."

Old Blue Eagle studied Summer keenly. "I think we should kill her," he said thoughtfully, "so there will be no chance the soldiers will find out. After all, she is the only one alive from the stage."

Scalp Taker injected, "Maybe we should trade her off to the Comanche to the south! They will enjoy her awhile and then sell her across the border. Mexicans would pay much for such a pale beauty for their whorehouses!"

Angry Wolf grinned wickedly. "I like Scalp Taker's idea. Let's trade her to the Comanche!"

There was a murmur of assent. Iron Knife's hand tightened on his knife. "I—I would never disobey the Council," he said grudgingly, "but my heart beats for this woman." He hesitated, not wanting to admit his weakness in front of the

41

whole tribe. "My manhood cannot stand the thought that any other man might mount her."

He looked deep into Summer's eyes, wondering if she realized he was begging for her life even though he spoke the soft musical words of the Cheyenne.

She had been sitting there demure, her eyes downcast as he had instructed her. But perhaps she saw the desperation in his eyes, and was now aware that things were going badly. Whatever made her do it, she suddenly scrambled to her feet and faced the four old chiefs.

"I don't know what you're saying!" she raged, "but I defy you! You hear? I defy you!"

A murmur ran through the crowd. It was unthinkable that a captive slave should speak in front of Council. Iron Knife stood frozen to the spot, horrified at her effrontery. But still, she paced and waved her arms and shouted, "How dare you think you can decide my fate! Who do you think you are! I will not sit here quietly and let you do as you will!"

She was magnificent, Iron Knife thought admiringly, *She might be sealing her doom, but this Council had never been treated to such a show of spirit from such a lovely, enraged woman.*

With sinking heart, he grabbed her and yanked her back down to her seat. The four old chiefs turned inquiring eyes to him and he hesitated a moment, then translated word for word.

"She defies us?" asked Old Blue Eagle.

"She defies you." Iron Knife shrugged. He might have lied about what she said, but there were a few in the crowd who spoke English. Anyway, there was no denying the intent behind the flashing eyes and the angry, soft mouth.

"We will now deliberate," Clouds Above announced. The four old chiefs pulled into a small group and talked for what seemed an eternity in quiet whispers.

Finally, Clouds Above stood and announced solemnly, "Angry Wolf and his friends have been guilty of breaking the treaty by attacking the stage. However, because firewater was involved, also because he thought to blame the hated Pawnee

42

and we do not think the soldiers will come here, we will be lenient."

He gestured toward the chiefs of each warrior group. "We declare *tuhkayats*, punishment will be inflicted for disobeying. The chiefs of the soldier bands will whip the guilty ones through the camp so that all may see the Cheyenne intends to stand by this treaty."

He turned and took a long look at Iron Knife and then at Summer. "The white girl can never return to her people for reasons already given, but we will not kill her. It would be a shame to waste such bravery as she has when she could produce such fiery chiefs."

He smiled ever so slightly at Iron Knife. "If my nephew yearns for this she-bobcat, the Council feels he has fought for and won her fairly. So, even though we think he will regret taking this woman to warm his bed, we give her to him to be his slave forever!"

Chapter Three

Summer couldn't understand the old man's words, but she knew a decision was being announced. She looked about the Council tepee and saw the nodding heads, the murmur of discussion among the men. Then the gathering broke up, some of the crowd leaving, some gathering in small groups, talking.

Iron Knife came over and took her hand, pulling her roughly to her feet. "You little fool!" he hissed, "it is unheard of to create a scene in front of the Council! It's a wonder they didn't vote to kill you!"

Summer let him pull her along the dark path from the meeting. Her arm began to throb and her head hurt. They passed a pretty Indian girl by a campfire, and she gave Summer such a murderous look that Summer shivered, wondering what she had done to merit such hate.

"Who was that?" she queried, trying to catch up to his long steps. It was hard to keep up. She felt weak and very tired.

He shrugged. "Only Gray Dove, an Arapaho girl. The Arapahos have been friends of the Cheyenne for many years and often camp with us."

He offered no further explanation. Summer's thoughts blurred as she struggled to keep up and she paused.

He turned and looked down at her. She could see the concern on his face by the light of the campfires. "You are ill?"

"No," she lied, not wanting anything to interfere with her goal. "When does the Council say I can go back to Fort Smith?"

Wordlessly, he put one big hand on her flushed forehead and frowned. Then he swiftly lifted her and carried her back to the tepee. He sat her gently on the buffalo robe bed and again put his hand on her forehead.

"When am I being sent back?" she persisted.

"Not right away," he murmured, not looking into her eyes. "Anyway, you are ill and couldn't travel all that distance now."

She nodded and did not press for more details. It was true. She did not feel well at all. She felt dizzy and her head pounded angrily.

He took her small face in his big hands and stared into her eyes. "You skin feels like fire," he muttered, "and your face is flushed! Let me see your arm!"

Dutifully, Summer held out her injured right arm and he unwrapped it and stared at the knife cut. She saw the look of concern cross his face, and understood why as she studied the arm herself. The wound looked raw and swollen and crooked red lines snaked from it across her white skin.

She looked up at him, suddenly frightened. "It's bad, isn't it?"

"No, not so bad," he answered soothingly. "I will go get the medicine man again and give him many presents. He will have spells and much magic to cure this."

He left the tepee and Summer tried not to look at the wound. If only she were back in her own four-poster bed in the big mansion on her father's estate. Dr. Morgan, the renowned surgeon, would be making a house call and solicitous maids would be scurrying about, bringing her tea, fluffing her down pillows.

She felt very, very warm now and the arm throbbed. Perspiration beaded on her upper lip and she lay down on the robe. It occurred to her that she might die here and no one back home would ever know what had happened to her.

No, she shook her blond head stubbornly, *she wasn't going to die, she was going to live.* When the Indians took her back to the fort she would be a dutiful daughter, and do as her father had ordered—at least until the scandal in Boston died down a little. . . .

Iron Knife returned, interrupting her thoughts and bringing with him the venerable old man carrying charms and herbs in a bag made of skunk skin.

Summer wondered for a moment if she should allow the old man to treat her again as he had this morning, and then realized she didn't have much choice. He seemed to be the only help available and she was feeling worse by the minute. The medicine man examined her arm, shook his head, and said something in his foreign tongue to Iron Knife. Iron Knife answered in Cheyenne, seemingly insistent. She watched the old man as he took little bunches of grasses and herbs and burned them in the fire pit, filling the air with a hazy, sweet smell. Then he began a singsong chant, shaking a gourd rattle all the while over Summer's arm.

Summer looked at Iron Knife questioningly.

"It is all right." He nodded. "Usually, the rites of purification and ceremony would take longer, and he would require a sweat lodge to be built near the river for you, but . . ."

His voice trailed off, and he looked away. Summer caught the implication. Her condition was too serious to delay for the usual ceremonies.

The medicine man spread white sage on the floor, and smoked the ceremonial pipe. He sang his chants and prayed, shaking his rattle over her. His lined old face seemed to blur in her vision.

"I'm—I'm very hot," she gasped, "burning hot." She hurt now, and the pain seemed to be spreading through her arm. She felt dizzy, too. Her thoughts seemed to jumble themselves. Dimly, she heard Iron Knife and the medicine man conferring in guttural Cheyenne. Then she was aware that the big savage took out his knife and laid it on a stone at the edge of the fire pit with the blade in the flame.

He knelt by her and whispered, "Little One, we have to do something about that wound. It must be purified, and fire is the only way!"

She only half-heard his words, not understanding anything in her fever. Her eyes flickered open and she saw the fat, old squaw enter the tepee, the one who had combed her hair and fed her this morning. The woman knelt to hold down Summer's feet. Iron Knife held down her left arm with his right hand. Then he very gently turned her face away so that she could not see what the medicine man was doing. She struggled and realized she was powerless. The medicine man was holding down her right arm.

Uncomprehending, she saw the big savage take his knife from the fire pit, its blade glowing in the semidarkness. He laid it on a stone near the old man and then, gently, he again turned her face away, holding her so that she could not look.

"I'm sorry, Little One," he murmured, "but this has to be done. I wish I could bear the pain for you."

Dimly, she was aware of the feel of his hand on her face, the weight on all her limbs. Then the hot blade hissed as it cut into the wound. Never had she known such agony! She screamed and bit his hand hard, aware of the taste of his blood. As she teetered on the ragged edge of unconsciousness, she remembered the scene at the stagecoach when the savages had captured her . . .

. . . *tell her what we will do to her pale body with fire and blade . . . fire and blade . . .*

They were torturing her to death, she thought in her pain, and looked up at Iron Knife as she drifted into complete oblivion.

"You—you promised you wouldn't hurt me." Her eyes accused him. She saw him wipe the blood from his bitten hand.

"It had to be done," he muttered, "but you will never be hurt again, Little One! I promise it!"

47

"I don't believe you!" she sobbed as she slipped into the blackness. Her last awareness was that he held her left hand and kissed the fingertips and her palm very, very gently.

She did not know how long the time was that she fainted, but when she awakened she was vaguely aware of him sitting dipping a cloth in water, wiping her face.

"Oh, that feels so good," Summer gasped. "I'm so hot!" She closed her burning eyes and enjoyed the feel of the cold water on her fevered face. He wiped her face and throat, down into the neck of the buckskin dress. Her mouth felt dry and fuzzy. She managed to open her cracked lips. "Thirsty," she managed to whisper, "water . . ."

He held a horn cup to her mouth. She gulped greedily and watched him through half-opened eyes as his big hands caressed her face and arms.

"Your touch is gentle," she whispered.

"With you, I shall always be gentle," he answered, sponging her face again. "Do you feel any better?"

"No," she gasped, "I am warmer than before. I—I feel worse!"

She could feel drops of perspiration running down her breasts, across her belly. She couldn't seem to keep her thoughts straight. She closed her eyes again, and in her fevered mind, she was a child once more, running through the summer heat at the big estate next door with her twin brother David's best friend, Austin. . . .

"It's so hot, Austin," she murmured aloud. "Say, why don't we have your cook make us some lemonade? The butler can serve it in the conservatory where the flowers bloom . . ."

She felt herself being lifted, something pulling at her clothes. Vaguely, she opened her eyes, trying to remember where she was and who this big, bronzed man was who pulled her dress off. "No, please don't!" Even in her delirium, she tried to cover herself modestly with her hands and struggled to push him away.

But he lifted her lightly as if handling a doll. "Don't fight

48

me, Summer," he said tersely, "I'm not going to hurt you. I've got to bring that fever down."

Weakly, she struggled while he stripped her naked and laid her back down on the soft fur. He was going to rape her, she knew, and she was too weak to do anything about it. She couldn't remember who he was or why she was here. There was something about a family quarrel because she had embarrassed the family . . . There had been a stagecoach . . .

"Hot. So hot . . ." she whispered and felt the big hands moving over her, wiping her fevered skin with the cold cloth. It felt good and she relaxed, quit struggling, letting his hands move over every inch of her. He sponged her hot skin with the cool water. With her eyes closed, she felt the cold cloth come down her throat, wipe each breast, continuing down the hollow of her belly, across each fevered thigh. From there, the cool massage worked down her long legs, even to the soles of her feet.

He did it again and again, starting with her perspiring face and working his way down every inch of her. Occasionally, he turned her over, sponging from her neck, down her back, across her slim hips, and down the soles of her feet.

It occurred to her that even though it felt wonderful, she shouldn't be allowing this to happen. She struggled again and tried to protest, but strong hands held her down.

"No, Summer, don't fight me," he ordered, "I'm not going to hurt you."

Once in the hours that passed, she looked up into his dark eyes as he sponged her face and saw the weariness and concern reflected there.

"Am—am I dying?" she asked.

He gathered her into his arms. "No! I won't let you die! All these lonely years I have waited for you to come along, and I won't let Heammawihio take you! I promise you will never walk the *Ekutsihimmiyo*, the Hanging Road to the sky, without me. The *seyan*, the place of death, will not receive you yet."

She felt safe then. Another human was watching after her

and cared what became of her. Time passed, and it was a blur of heat with the cool cloth wiping her body continuously. Once, she remembered a horn spoon between her lips and warm broth, and many times there was cold water poured between her cracked lips. Sometimes, she opened her eyes and saw the plump Indian woman in the tepee, and sometimes the old medicine man, but she knew, somehow, that Iron Knife never left her side.

Then, she was no longer hot, but cold. Her teeth chattered and she shivered uncontrollably. She dreamed of a sleigh ride behind one of her fine-blooded horses back home at Christmas time. She could almost feel the ermine-trimmed blue velvet bonnet and fox-fur muff. . . .

But when she opened her eyes, she was once again in a strange place, and a handsome, dark man was wrapping a fur robe around her naked body. The soft fur felt good against her skin. She lay there, watching as he built the fire to a roaring blaze and turned back to her.

"I'm cold," she whispered through trembling lips, "I'm so cold."

He stood looking down at her shivering body and seemed to make a decision. Abruptly, he began peeling his clothes off. Summer had never seen a naked man before. She shivered and stared up at the magnificent, bronzed male. He was wide of shoulder, and narrow at the waist and hip. His hard muscles rippled in the firelight, showing the whip scars on his back, the sun dance scars on his great chest.

She felt her face flush crimson as she looked away from the beauty of his maleness. She only half realized for a moment that the naked savage was crawling under the robe with her. "No!" She tried to push him away. "No!"

"You little fool!" he hissed, reaching out to pull her shivering body close to his warm, hard chest. "I'm trying to warm you! Lie still!" he commanded.

She struggled a moment longer, shaking, thinking she had never been so cold before. As she felt the heat from his big body, she instinctively pressed herself against him. She was only dimly aware now of both their nakedness, and the rightness or wrongness of it, only drawn to him like a flower to the warm sun.

She felt his arms go about her, cradling her blond head in the hollow of his dark shoulder. He half-covered her shivering form with his body and pulled her against him so that she could feel the maleness of him. Summer remained rigid a moment and then, relaxed in his arms and gloried in the warmth that slowly spread through her slender frame.

His big hands felt like fire as they massaged her back, her hips, returning circulation. It felt good, and since she was powerless to stop him anyhow, she sighed and almost enjoyed the feel of his hands as she drifted in and out of delirium.

Once, she imagined that his lips kissed the soft hollow of her throat, and she thought he trembled as he held her. But she was warm now and her arm no longer throbbed. For the first time in many hours, she was not in pain. Somehow she felt protected and secure even though she lay naked in his embrace.

Gradually, she dropped off into a deep, healing sleep.

When she finally awakened, Summer lay puzzled, looking about the tepee, trying to remember where she was and what had happened. The memories flooded back and suddenly she realized she lay naked with her long blond hair spread out over the hollow of Iron Knife's shoulder. One of his powerful arms lay possessively across her curved hip under the buffalo robe.

Horrified, she tried to scurry away from him and realized how weak and exhausted she was. He came out of his deep slumber with a start as she tried to crawl away. Putting his arm under his head, he watched her fumbling with the deerskin dress.

"Don't be so terrified," he assured her. "I didn't take you."

"How do I know that?" she sobbed, struggling with the dress.

51

"Do you think I could, and your body not know?"

He stood up slowly, and she blushed at the sight of his magnificent maleness. She paused, thinking. Of course he hadn't touched her. Even in her delirium, she knew she would have remembered being invaded by such a stallion.

He dressed silently and then turned to help her pull her dress down over her head and reexamined her arm. She looked with him, and realized that the swelling had gone. The arm was healing. Trying to stand up, she staggered. She would have fallen had he not caught her in his arms.

"I—I must have been ill a long time," she whispered.

"You were." He looked down at her, and she saw the weariness in his face, realized he had probably slept very little.

"Well, I'm very grateful to you," Summer said primly, trying not to recall the images of his naked body, the warmth of him against her. "When I get back to Fort Smith, my father will reward you."

He swore an oath and jerked away from her abruptly. "Do you think I did all that for money? I did it for you, Summer Sky, because you are my woman!"

"I am not your woman!" she snapped, stiffening. "You can't own me like you would a rifle or a horse. Anyway," she shrugged, "the whole idea is ridiculous! After all, I'm a Van Schuyler, and you're—"

"Just a dirty, worthless Indian," he raged, "not fit to touch a white woman! Even a white whore once rejected me this way, luring me into her bed, and then yelling 'rape,' because she was ashamed she had let a dirty half-breed touch her!"

Summer cowered before his rage. "I didn't mean—"

"I know what you meant!" He towered over her. "Twice now, I have saved your life, and yet you spurn me while calling the name of 'Austin' in your sickness. Is 'Austin' a rich white man, and does he kiss you without your protest as I have longed to?"

Before she could answer, he jerked her roughly into his arms, forcing her lips apart, kissing her deeply and thoroughly

52

in a way she had never been kissed before. For a split second, she swayed in his embrace, shaken at her own primitive response. Then she pulled away, bringing her hand up to strike him.

He caught her hand in a steel grip and glared back at her. She shivered as she realized what savage, brute strength was being held back by his sheer will. Abruptly, he freed her hand and turned away, leaning against a lodge pole by the fire pit.

Why, he's trembling! she thought, wondering.

"I didn't mean what you think," she said gently. "It isn't that you're Indian, but, you see, this is an impossible situation."

She went over and touched his arm. He brushed her away. "I meant I won't forget your kindness when I return to my own people."

He turned and looked at her, his face inscrutable. "Enough of this talk of leaving," he said brusquely. "You are too ill and weak to travel now."

"That's not true!" she protested, even though she had to sit down on the buffalo robe to keep her head from spinning. "I can ride just fine, and I'll be all right if I can just get back to the fort."

"Is the man 'Austin' waiting for you there? Are you Austin's woman?"

"What an impudent question." She tossed her head haughtily. "It's none of your business, but I was being sent to my uncle's family. He's the Reverend Harlow, a circuit rider outside Fort Smith. I had displeased my father, and he was angry with me."

Iron Knife nodded. "You are at the age when you should have a man. I would know how to deal with such an unbroken filly!"

"I do not intend to let you deal with me at all." Her blue eyes flashed fire. "And I am certainly not used to strangers being so nosy about my personal life!"

He smiled slowly at her. "After the last several days, I think

53

we are hardly strangers."

She felt the blood rush to her face at the memories, and she looked away. It occurred to Summer that it was foolish to make an enemy of the big savage. He was the only one in the encampment who might help her escape. She would do well to make a friend of him. With that thought, she moved closer to him, taking his big hand in her two small ones.

"I have treated you badly after you have done so much for me. But I will see you are rewarded when I go back."

The Indian brushed her hands away, and avoided her eyes. "We will discuss going back when you are stronger," he said.

Abruptly, there were sounds outside of a horse reining up, and a male voice called out in Indian. Iron Knife answered and one of his silent sentinels from the stage poked his head through the tepee opening. He eyed Summer curiously, then ignored her as he spoke with Iron Knife in Cheyenne. They talked a few moments and the other nodded and went outside.

"There is a hunt," Iron Knife announced to her. "Deer have been seen south of the camp and we are short on meat. Most of the men will be going." He gathered up his bow and lance.

"Are you leaving me here alone?" The thought frightened her. She didn't realize how much she had come to depend on him.

"Poor little white girl," he smiled sarcastically, "doesn't know whether to be more afraid of the big, dirty savage inside or the ones outside the tepee!"

Summer felt the color rush to her face. She didn't know the answer to that puzzle herself. Her feelings toward Iron Knife were becoming more and more confused all the time. . . .

"Will you be gone long?" she asked. Somehow, she didn't want him to leave. Even though she was a little afraid of him, she trusted him more than the others, and felt secure when he was nearby. The inside of this tepee had begun to feel like home to her, and she had no idea what dangers awaited her outside.

He finished gathering up his things before he answered. "I don't think we will be gone more than a few hours. You will be

54

safe enough. The women won't bother you, and all the men except the very old and the very young are going on the hunt. Everyone knows you are my woman, and would not dare harm you."

She started to argue that point again, and decided against it. "But what shall I do while you are gone?"

He shrugged. "You had better rest, for you are still very weak, but you can go outside if you feel well enough. A few of the women speak a little English. My uncle's wife, Pony Woman, is at the big lodge with the white buffalo painted on it." He gestured. "She will have food for you when you are hungry."

He paused in the doorway. "I will return with much meat, and there will be dancing and games. You will see that my people are not so bad to live with."

"But what of Fort Smith—?"

He hesitated. "We will discuss that later." Then he was gone, leaving her staring into the fire.

She realized suddenly just how weak she was and lay down and slept. It must have been several hours before she awakened and decided to venture outside. The weather was balmy for early autumn, but the sky was still cloudy from past rains.

Most of the Indian women smiled shyly at her, but shook their heads when she tried to speak English to them. She remembered what Iron Knife had said about the white buffalo tepee and found it, only a few yards away. A squat, plump squaw had a big buffalo skin pegged to the ground and was scraping it as Summer appeared. She smiled at Summer, and Summer remembered her from her illness.

"Ah, my nephew's woman!" She grinned at Summer. "Come! Sit! Eat!"

Summer smiled back at her warmth, thinking how much the plump little woman reminded her of Mrs. O'Malley, her personal maid; never mind the dark skin.

She sat down obediently, and watched the big hunk of meat slowly roasting over the open fire. The smell of it enforced her hunger.

Pony Woman cut off a big piece of the crisp meat, and handed it to her. It was delicious! Summer ate every bite, and licked her fingers. She smiled at the image of her mother's snooty music society and what they would say if they could see Summer eating like a savage with her bare hands, licking her fingers.

"Good." She motioned to Pony Woman, "Very good. Thank you." She shook her head when offered more, and tried to carry on a conversation with the woman, only to realize how little English Pony Woman spoke. When she got back to civilization, she would send some fine cloth and other things to Iron Knife's aunt for all her kindness.

Finally she gestured that she was going to leave and walk about the camp. Pony Woman nodded good-naturedly, and went back to scraping on the pegged-down buffalo hide.

A half dozen children and two straggly dogs trailed after her curiously as she toured the camp. Impulsively, she held out her arms to one fat, naked toddler and he ran to her, chattering happily. The others, now bold, moved closer to her like shy, silent deer. She smiled at them and tried to start a conversation, but none seemed to speak English. They simply stared at her. Summer liked children, and it occurred to her that these had probably never seen any candy. She decided she would purchase a whole barrel of pepermint sticks, and have them sent to the children if they had candy at Fort Smith.

A girl no older than Summer came out of a tepee, and smiling shyly at her, said something in Cheyenne to the baby in Summer's arms. It struggled to get down and ran on unsteady legs to its mother. Reluctantly, Summer watched it disappear inside and walked on. The other children trailed after her. She stopped and let the curious and more bold touch her white skin and knelt so a little girl could stroke her blond hair. Summer moved on and the children, tiring of her, finally ran off to play. She could hear them running and laughing around the camp.

As she passed one tepee, a girl looked out at her—the same

pretty girl who had given her such a hateful look the night of the Council meeting.

"You are Iron Knife's woman." The girl glared coldly at her. "I, Gray Dove, wish to speak with you," she said in English, indicating the inside of her lodge with a nod of her head.

Summer sat down on a buffalo robe and studied the girl, seeing hostility and raw hate in the other's eyes.

"You speak good English," Summer ventured, wondering what the girl wanted of her.

"I learn much from the white men at the trading posts, and the bluecoats I have met." She smiled archly. "White men have taught me many things."

Summer said nothing. Her eyes caught the other's bold ones and held.

The Indian girl looked away first. "You are wanting to go back to Fort Smith?" she asked.

"Of course I intend to go back." Summer nodded. "Iron Knife will take me when he returns from hunting."

"Did he say that?" Gray Dove sneered.

"Well, yes," she began uncertainly. Had he promised to take her back to the fort? She thought he had. "Of course, he's taking me back," she retorted firmly.

"I wouldn't be too sure of that!" The Indian girl grinned wickedly. "But I might help you get back to your people."

"Why would you want to do that?" Summer queried, "I can tell you don't like me. Why would you want to help me?"

Gray Dove seemed to tremble with suppressed rage. "I'm not doing it for you, I'm doing it for myself. At night, you are sleeping in the arms of the man I love! He sees nothing but you, speaks of nothing but you! You are like the black widow spider, devouring his very being! No wonder the Cheyenne word for 'spider' and 'white' is the same word, *veho*. The whole camp gossips that Iron Knife is devoured and bewitched by the *veho* squaw! They all laugh at me because I want so much to be his woman, and he takes you instead!"

Summer felt her face burn. "I am not his woman," she

57

stammered. "Nothing has happened between us."

"You lie!" The other seethed, moving to glare into Summer's eyes. "He has hardly left your side for three days! Do you deny that you have been sleeping naked in his arms?"

"I deny nothing." Summer tossed her head in patrician anger. "But you have no need to be jealous of me. I have no interest in Iron Knife."

"Then you are a bigger fool than I thought. He is a Dog Soldier, the bravest of the brave! He is one of the select four who carries the *hotamtsit*, the honored dog rope. Did you not see it hanging in his tepee?"

Summer frowned, remembering. There was some sort of long, decorated cord hanging in the lodge. It had not occurred to her that it held significance. . . .

She shrugged. "I do not want him."

"Well, I do! I have always wanted him, and I thought he might be softening his heart toward me until you came along!" She made a threatening gesture. "I have waited a long time to lie in his arms, and I will not lose him to a soft, *veho* squaw!"

Summer felt her own eyes flash. Spirit and fire lay near the surface of her own serene, civilized exterior.

"Do not threaten me for nothing," she said firmly. "I do not want to be Iron Knife's woman. I only want to return to my own people. If you would help me, it would clear the way for you with him and I would see that you get a nice reward."

The other's eyes glistened with greed. "Reward? You mean, money? White man's money for ribbons and jewelry?"

"White man's money for ribbons and jewelry," Summer repeated.

Gray Dove's pretty face softened hopefully. "You speak the truth?"

Summer nodded. "If you don't believe me, I could wait for Iron Knife to take me when he returns from the hunt, but that might be many hours. I would like to go as soon as possible."

The Indian girl laughed cruelly. "Did he say he would take you to the fort? In that case, he has lied to you, White Girl, because he fears your rejection. He could not let you leave even if he wanted to. Because of the Council's decision you will only be able to leave if I help you."

Summer felt her heart sink, and knew suddenly what she had suspected all along when she could not get a firm commitment from the warrior. "What—what did the Council actually decide?" she asked.

Gray Dove smiled, obviously enjoying Summer's discomfort. "So he did not tell you. I thought as much! He did not tell you that the old chiefs had forbidden him to let you go? The Council is afraid you will bring back the bluecoats for revenge. As it is, the army must think you dead or is searching the Pawnee camps for you!"

Summer's spirit despaired both at the news and something else. *Was it because she had trusted him, and he had lied to her?* Anger surged in her breast, anger mixed with disillusionment. There had been, almost, a feeling for him that was now washed away by a rage both cold and hot and a need for action. She did not want to know, but somehow she must.

"What else did the Council say that night?"

Gray Dove glared back at her jealously. "They have given you to Iron Knife to warm his bed. They said he should sire great chiefs by you. Do you not understand, White Girl? They handed you over like a blanket or a pony. They said you were to be his slave forever!"

Chapter Four

Summer stared back at her a long moment, realization dawning slowly. She knew the girl spoke the truth from the way Iron Knife had avoided her eyes, her questions. He had lied to her all along, never intending to let her go. Even now, he must be laughing with the other warriors at her expense. She gritted her teeth, thinking how she had almost begun to trust him. She had been betrayed, and she was furious. She decided then and there she would run away even if it cost her life.

Gray Dove smiled, obviously enjoying her disillusionment. "And now, White Girl, I will help you escape!"

"Are you not bound by the Council's decision also?"

The Indian girl shrugged. "It is of no matter to me what the old chiefs of the Cheyenne decide; I have little respect for traditions. Yes, I would be in great trouble if they found out I helped you escape."

Her mouth hardened into a grim line. "They would force me into exile, maybe even kill me. But I would rather be dead than to see you with my love every day, know that on chilly nights, you are wrapped in his arms while he whispers endearments and plants his son in your belly. It is worth any risk to me to get you out of this camp."

"I do not intend to be a brood mare for his sons!" Summer retorted, fixing that stubborn, direct gaze of hers on the other.

60

"You are such a fool, White Girl. Do you not realize he is big and strong enough to take you any moment he decides to? Do you think he will ask whether you wish to carry his son or no?"

Summer shivered involuntarily, remembering the powerful, sinewy muscles held back by sheer willpower when she had foolishly tried to slap his face. Even the most gentlemanly white man might have struck her for her insult. Yet, that great, savage animal had held himself in check. But Gray Dove was right; he could overpower her and take her body any time he wished, so it was imperative that she escape as soon as possible.

She faced the Indian girl. "I do not trust you, but it seems I don't have much choice. I will have to accept your help since no one else will dare go up against Iron Knife and the Council." She held out her hand in friendship. "I give you my word I will not bring the soldiers back to take revenge on this camp, and my father will send you much gold and trade goods."

But the Indian girl brushed her hand away contemptuously. "I know you will not bring the bluecoats here, *veho* squaw. I help through no friendship for you, only wishing to get you out of here and out of his heart. Perhaps when you are gone with your pale eyes and yellow hair, perhaps he will look again and reconsider. I would be proud to produce sons for this great Dog Soldier."

A fleeting image crossed Summer's mind, disturbing her thoughts. For a long moment, she saw an image of the voluptuous dark girl lying naked beneath the warrior, and the thought gnawed at her mind. Already, she had begun to think a bit possessively about the man, and the idea of the other in his arms made her frown. An unaccustomed emotion filled her, and it almost felt like jealousy.

Then she dismissed that ridiculous thought with a toss of her blond head. "Gray Dove, what is your plan?"

The other smiled. "For a long moment, I thought you were about to reconsider; that you did not want to leave him. In that case, I would have been obliged to think of another way to get rid of you; perhaps an accident along the trail somewhere as we

61

move the camp!"

Summer glared back, lifting her stubborn chin. "I am not so easy and soft an enemy as you might think should you want to try. But I care not if you end up in his blankets! After all, he has lied to me and plotted to keep me here against my will!"

"He has also fought for you and saved your life when you nearly died from the knife wound," Gray Dove answered jealously. "Would he care so much for me!"

"He doesn't really care about me," Summer retorted. "I am only a captive to humiliate! A blond plaything for him to rape!"

"If that were all, he would have already done that a hundred times and passed you on to his friends for their enjoyment."

Summer admitted grudgingly to herself that this was true. "It doesn't matter," she answered hotly. "I only want to get away from here; away from him and we are wasting valuable time! Obviously, he will not help me escape, so I will take my chances with you! What is your plan?"

"I will get a pony and some food for you, and we will meet in a few minutes in that clump of cottonwood trees behind that little rise by the river. Do you know the one I mean?"

Summer nodded as she glanced cautiously out the tepee opening. "Yes, I saw it this morning. I will sneak out of camp and meet you there soon."

"Make sure no one sees you," the other cautioned. "The Council must never know I helped you, and no one must see us together. I will meet you at the cottonwood grove."

Summer didn't answer as she slipped away from the lodge. She crept stealthily outside the large circle of the camp and paused to see if she had been noticed. But the camp dozed quietly under the cloudy sky, the only sound a pony snorting and stamping its feet. The smell of a campfire's smoke drifted on the still air. For a second, she regretted leaving this quiet, simple existence, this carefree way of life. How much more complicated and dull her life had been in Boston, and now she would be leaving all this excitement and adventure and returning to her staid mansion. Maybe she would go ahead and marry Austin Shaw as her family wished, thus uniting two great fortunes. She sighed as she thought of Austin and crept along through the tall grass toward the meeting place.

Without meaning to, she suddenly wondered how Austin looked nude, and her face flushed as she remembered another man's body, naked and virile. She experienced confused, mixed feelings as she thought of the Indian. She didn't understand the way her pulse raced when their eyes met, and she didn't like the helpless, overpowering feelings she felt when he touched her. Men had always danced like puppets to her whims, especially Austin, and yes, even her brother David, and most of the time, her stern, unsmiling father. She had a sudden feeling the big brave would never bend to her whims, in fact, would expect her to bend to his. And even worse, she had the uneasy feeling that he could make her happy to do so.

She shrugged off those crazy, disturbing thoughts as she crept through the tall brush to the rendezvous. Suppose Gray Dove had betrayed her and had men waiting at the meeting place to capture her? No, the girl wouldn't dare do that. She wanted Summer out of camp, and not only the Council but Iron Knife would be angry if he knew.

Breathlessly, she reached the meeting place and flung herself down on the grass. She was still weak from her wound and the resulting infection. It occurred to her it would be a very difficult trip back to the fort, but she seemed to have no other choice. If she could make it part way, perhaps she might run across an army patrol along the eastern border of the Indian Territory and she would be safe.

She heard a sound, and froze against the ground like a frightened quail. "Gray Dove, is that you?"

In answer, the dark girl appeared leading a straggly roan pony and carrying a small rawhide bag. "I managed to get some pemmican," she said, "and a few dried plums from my own lodge."

"You might have gotten me a better horse," Summer snapped, looking over the old, thin roan.

63

Gray Dove shrugged. "A better horse would have been missed sooner out of the herd. As it is, no one will start a search for this one when it doesn't turn up." She held the pony's bridle as Summer grasped the animal's mane, and mindful of the last time, mounted from the right side.

The Indian girl handed up the small bag of food. "The nearest fort is still Fort Smith," she said. "Fort Coffee has been closed for a long time, and the army closed Fort Gibson last year." She pointed to the horizon. "Ride that direction and by nightfall you should be within eyesight of the fort."

"That direction?" Summer hiked the deerskin shift up as she sat the horse, exposing slim, bare thighs. "I would have sworn when we came in the other night, we came from the right, not straight ahead."

"No. No!" The other jerked the horse's head back around in the direction she had indicated. "You are confused, White Girl, the fort lies straight ahead, about one day's ride."

Summer hesitated. *Was she confused?* Two hundred years of sailors' blood ran in her veins on her father's side, and she had always had a good sense of direction. Her instinct told her civilization lay off to the right, not straight ahead, but maybe she was wrong. After all, it had been cloudy that day as it still was now, so she would get no help from the sun. Certainly, if the sky cleared tonight and she still hadn't reached the fort, she was smart enough to follow the stars. Besides, it was to the Indian girl's advantage to make sure Summer got back to the fort.

The other must have read her thoughts. "It would be stupid of me not to send you the right way. After all, I will only collect the reward if you are returned to your father."

Gathering up the reins, Summer moved out in the direction the dark girl pointed.

"Do not tarry, White Girl!" the other called after her. "The men will be returning from the hunt soon and you will have lost your one chance to escape!"

The thought speeded Summer into action as she ceased

64

staring up into the cloudy sky, still trying to decide time and direction. "Thank you for helping me," she called back over her shoulder as she dug her tiny, moccasined feet into the pony's sides. "Slip into the fort soon and collect your reward, and tell Iron Knife—" She let her voice trail off, knowing Gray Dove could not pass on a message without betraying her part in the escape and she wasn't sure the girl would pass on the message anyway. *What was there to say to him?* She struggled with the thought a moment, remembering his passion, his tenderness.

Then with a resolute jerk of her stubborn chin, she turned her back on the sullen Indian girl and rode away into the forest.

For several hours, she rode hard, stopping occasionally to rest the pony and listen for sounds of pursuit behind her, but heard nothing. Her mouth felt dry and her pulse hammered as she tried not to think what punishment the Indians might hand down if they caught her escaping, and what they might do to Gray Dove for helping her. But then, the Arapaho girl was too shrewd to get caught. Just once, she imagined how Iron Knife would react, how his face would look when he returned to find her gone. But she dismissed that thought from her mind.

Autumn leaves swirled about her as she rode, making crisp, crackling sounds under the roan's hooves. Even heart-shaped leaves of the native redbuds were turning red and gold, and wildflowers scented the still air. A gray Scissortail Flycatcher passed overhead, its long tail feathers fluttering. Great, green clumps of mistletoe clung to giant trees along the trail.

In the path ahead lay a mound of earth teeming with millions of large, red ants. The pony shied and snorted a warning. Summer reined him around the crawling mass, staring down as she passed at a hapless caterpillar that had fallen from a tree branch to the anthill. It writhed in obvious agony as the giant ants attacked it, tearing it to pieces. Summer shuddered and urged the pony forward, around the bend toward the sound of rushing water.

Up around the bend in the path was a clearing, several paths leading in different directions. Through the clearing ran a creek, flooding now because of all the recent rains, although this part of the forest looked tinder dry. Foam floated along the creek's edge and then was carried swiftly downstream to a rapids she could see in the distance.

She let the roan pony thrust its muzzle in the cold water and dismounted herself to drink from the still eddy pool and splash her perspiring face. The weather still waxed cloudy and humid, but it looked like it might finally clear. A promise of autumn was definitely in the air. Her heart gradually ceased pounding as she realized that no one pursued. She began to think toward the future, how she would deal with her angry father, and that stern uncle.

Realizing abruptly how hungry and weak she was, she took out the small bag of pemmican and ate greedily of the delicious mixture of dried meat, tallow, and pounded choke-cherries. She paused as she thought she heard a crackle of leaves back along the path from whence she had come. *Gray Dove*, she thought, little prickles of fear going up her back. *Would Gray Dove double cross her, follow and try to kill Summer along the trail to the fort?*

Why would Gray Dove bother? She reminded herself again. After all, the Arapaho girl had admitted she wanted Summer out of the camp, away from Iron Knife, and Summer was riding away as fast as she could. That should satisfy the jealous Indian girl.

She listened intently for another sound, then laughed silently at herself, thinking her imagination ran wild. She was almost safe now; only a few more hours and she would ride into the fort.

The straggly pony munched grass peacefully as she knelt once more by the eddy pool. One more drink and she would be on her way. Summer dipped her small hand into the icy water and stared down at her own reflection, studying how thin and tired she looked. So much had happened in less than a week and she would never be the same again, no matter how far from this savage land she ran. The wild country was in her blood now and she wouldn't forget it even as she looked out over the rooftops and well-manicured lawns of the big city. And it wasn't only the land . . .

Despite herself, a face came to her mind, a bronzed weather-beaten face with a broken nose and strong features. Annoyed with herself, she swirled her fingers in the water to wipe out the thought and looked down again at her own image.

Abruptly, there was another reflection in the water, a face behind her. It was a broad, pock-marked face with grinning, yellow teeth. In cold, unbelieving horror, she stared at the image and then sprang to her feet and ran for her pony.

Angry Wolf caught her arm as she ran past him, and held her in an iron grip as she struggled and screamed.

"So, White Bitch, we meet again!" he hissed as he pulled her to him. "Only this time, there is no half-breed bastard to save you or even my own men to share you with!"

"Let go of me!" she shrieked, clawing at him.

"Scream all you wish!" he said, laughing, twisting her arm behind her painfully as he pulled her up against him. "There is no one to hear you and no one is likely to!"

She could smell the reek of his sweat and she recoiled from his clammy skin.

"You will not mind the smell of me when I am through with you, Yellow Hair! You will beg to be allowed to kiss my sweat away if only I will stop hurting you!"

"If you hurt me, you will regret it," Summer challenged as she turned her direct, stubborn gaze upon him. "Even now, a soldier patrol from the fort might cross this area and find us."

"Not likely." He laughed cruelly and she recoiled from his hot, fetid breath. "Gray Dove told me she had sent you off in the wrong direction. You little fool, you are even farther from the fort than before, you are riding *notum*, due north when the fort is southeast!"

For a long heartbeat, Summer paused, knowing what he said must be true. The Indian girl had betrayed her, sending her off to become lost in the woods, knowing she would never find the fort. To insure that, Gray Dove had sent Angry Wolf after her to kill her.

He had his hot mouth on hers now, forcing her lips open. She freed one hand and clawed his face.

He swore a white man's oath and struck her, knocking her half-conscious to the ground.

"This time," he promised, "you are going to pay for that, and Iron Knife will not be here to stop me! Because of you both, me and my followers have been whipped through the camp like misbehaving puppies. You have brought disgrace on me and now you will pay for that. I only wish that son of a white whore could be here to see what I do to his woman!"

Dimly, Summer was aware of being dragged across the clearing. Her own blood from her cut lips ran sticky sweet in her mouth. Still, she put up a valiant struggle for such a small woman. She felt him slam her against the ground as he reached for small broken branches. The squat Indian knelt with his full weight against her chest, bruising her soft breasts with his bulky body as he held her down.

He pulled rawhide thongs from his belt, reaching for the stakes he had picked up. "Now, I have plans for you!"

She felt him wrap a thong about her wrist, secure it to a stake as he pounded it into the ground, using a flat rock for a hammer. In moments, he was doing the same with her other wrist and both ankles. Despite her struggles, Summer found herself spread-eagled and helpless, staked out in the dirt like a trussed animal.

Smiling, Angry Wolf took out his knife and leaned over her. Almost leisurely, he slit the deerskin shift from throat to hem and tossed it aside, exposing her ripe naked body.

He took several deep breaths as he eyed her. "You are more beautiful than I imagined," he muttered. "I am going to do everything I ever dreamed of doing to a helpless captive and no one will stop me!"

Summer renewed her struggles as his dirty hands ran roughly down her skin, touching her breasts, roughly pinching her tender thighs. He grabbed her throat and forced her mouth open with his clammy lips and she gagged on the taste of his mouth. She tried to bite him and he jerked back, laughing a little.

"You have spirit! I like a woman with spirit! There is more passion to them."

She spat at him then, catching him full in the face, and he stopped laughing and slapped her repeatedly until her ears rang.

"I can bite, too, White Bitch! And I can teach you not to spit!"

He bit her soft lips, her breasts, and her thighs while she cried out, "Iron Knife would kill you for this!"

"Yes, he would!" The man nodded, wiping her blood from his mouth as she struggled helplessly against her bonds. "But Iron Knife is not here to stop me! You were a fool to run away from his protection, leaving a trail a blind man could follow! Your big brave is still out on the hunt with the others. I came back early and Gray Dove told me what had happened, how you had overpowered her and stolen a horse! She knew I could easily track you and kill you if a wolf or a stray Pawnee didn't get you first!"

"Iron Knife will come looking for me!" she gasped, writhing under his exploring hands.

"Of course he will! But by then, I will have had my fill of you, and your dead lips won't tell him what man has mounted you! He'll think the Pawnee's were here."

He twisted his hand in her blond hair and looked earnestly into her face. "I think I have wanted you even more than I ever thought I wanted Gray Dove. Let us betray them both! Accept me willingly and I will let you live!" He bent to kiss her. "Even now, my humiliated friends make plans to leave the camp, go off to join other outlawed Dog Soldiers. I told them to pack my

69

tepee, and I would join up with them on the trail if I were not back in camp by morning."

He tried to kiss her. "I wanted to make sure I had plenty of time to enjoy you without anyone looking for us. Accept me as your man, and we will go with the outlaw Dog Soldiers. You will sleep in my arms, and your tepee will always have plenty of meat for I am a good hunter."

"Never!" Summer spat at him again. "I would rather be dead than to be your woman!"

"Then so you shall be! It is your own choosing!" He twisted his hands in her hair, forcing her to look into his face. "If you will not take me willingly, it is also good to take you unwillingly, force my body into yours! I will enjoy you all afternoon and then you are going to beg and plead in your pain as I let you slowly die! It will be exciting to hear you whine and cry as I take my blade to you!"

Summer gritted her teeth as his hands roamed over her body. "There is nothing you can do that will make me cry and plead for mercy!"

"Is there not?" He reached into his belt for his short quirt. "Have you noticed all Dog Soldiers carry one of these as well as the eagle whistle?" He touched the object hanging from a thong about his thick neck. "I have welts on my back because of you! How do you think it feels to be whipped? How do you think it will feel to have my lash cut across your soft breasts? Maybe the smell of your blood will draw a wolf later tonight, maybe even a bobcat. Maybe I will leave you alive but staked out helpless! How would you like a big bobcat for a deadly lover?"

He was insane, she thought, *to be so cruel, and yet perhaps she could still bargain with him.* "If you will help me get back to the fort," she tested her bonds as she spoke, "I will see that you get a lot of money! My father is a great chief and would pay much for my return! You would be an important man among your people with such wealth, and they would need never know where it came from. Even Gray Dove would be impressed!"

70

He seemed to think it over, then grimaced. "What good is money to a dead man? The Council would whip me for daring to go against their wishes or probably banish me from the tribe! And I would never live to impress Gray Dove! Iron Knife would kill me for daring to touch his woman!"

"I wouldn't tell him! I promise I wouldn't!"

He seemed to make a final decision. "No, you won't tell him, Golden Hair, because you will never leave here to get the chance! The gamble isn't worth it to me, knowing that the half-breed would hunt me the rest of my life. I would always have to look over my shoulder, awaiting his blade in my back. You can be only an afternoon's entertainment for me, but what an entertainment that will be!" He slapped his quirt thoughtfully against his bare leg, and stared down at her naked body, writhing against her bonds.

He wore only a skimpy loincloth, and she watched his manhood rise against its brief covering as he ran his tongue over his wounded lips. She was more angry than frightened, and she struggled to keep her lips from trembling. If she kept a cool head, she might survive yet.

The brave stared down at her, thinking. "I have an even better idea, White Bitch! Did you see the red ants back along the trail?" He gestured behind him.

For the first time, Summer panicked, feeling cold terror as she recalled the writhing caterpillar. She forgot that she had boasted she would not beg. "No, please, you wouldn't—" Her voice trailed off in a sob.

He guffawed cruelly. "So now it is 'please?' Maybe you would even take me willingly? It is too late for you to beg me now! I have decided when I am finished to share you with the ants! I saw a wild bee tree a few hundred yards off the trail, and I think I will rob the bees of their honey. When I am done with you, I am going to smear your white body with its sweetness!"

"Please, no!" Summer whimpered. "Please, not the ants! Let us talk about this!"

"Talk, all we have done is talk! I am tired of your voice in my

71

ears. You have had your chance to talk!" He took a small rag and stuffed it into her mouth. "I am going to put a stick in the hinge of your jaw and pour the sticky sweet down your throat!" He trailed the tips of his quirt down the length of her silken belly. "Let us see if my tiny red brothers can thrill you deep in your woman's vessel! See if their kiss is fierce on your tender tongue!"

She wept in protest and fought against the bonds, but he only laughed. "I think I shall go get the honey right now, and have it here where you can see it while I make love to you!" The thought seemed to please him as he trailed the quirt across her full breasts. "I wonder just how many minutes it will take a million ants to follow a honey trail from their mound to your staked-out body?"

He laughed again and led his paint horse into the forest, out of sight.

As his footsteps faded down the path, Summer struggled with all her strength to pull the stakes from the ground. If she could only get one arm loose, she could untie the other bonds. Breathless and trembling, she choked on the dirty gag and closed her eyes. What should she do? Maybe she would yet have a chance to convince him she would make love to him willingly. He might untie her, and if she could get her hand on that knife in his belt . . .

She thought she heard a footstep, and a big hand touched her face ever so gently. She would have known that touch anywhere. Her eyes blinked open to look up into Iron Knife's angry face. She saw his dark eyes glitter in hate at the bruises and teeth marks on her skin.

"Whoever did this will not live to see the sun set!" he muttered as his blade flashed and he cut her ankles and one arm free. He reached to cut the other rawhide thong that bound her, intent only on her.

She saw Angry Wolf loom up suddenly behind him, and she tried to warn her rescuer though she still had the gag in her mouth. But he must have seen her eyes widen as he half-turned to meet the challenge.

The squat, heavier brave caught him off balance and knocked him down, the big blade falling from Iron Knife's hand just out of Summer's reach. She saw his head hit an outcrop of rock as he fell and the two rolled over and over. Then they stumbled to their feet, facing each other warily.

Iron Knife gestured toward Summer, still pinned by one wrist. "You have tried to violate my woman, you whelp of a coyote! For this, you will surely die!"

"Brave talk for one who stands before me empty-handed, no knife, no quirt," the other sneered, pulling his quirt slowly from his belt, hefting his knife in his other hand.

Summer saw her big brave glance toward his horse. His quirt hung from the saddle, his knife lay on the ground just out of Summer's reach. Angry Wolf crouched between him and the weapons and now smiled slowly.

"We shall see who will die! I have been whipped through the camp by the leaders of the seven warrior groups! Never have I felt such humiliation! I want you to know the taste of a lash!"

He whipped his quirt against the ground. "Always I have lived in your shadow before the Council of Chiefs. Always the people follow you, listen to your words so you will be chosen next time they pick a chief. My friends and I will go off to join the outlaw Dog Soldier band. When the people see our bravery, they will sing songs of us around the campfires, and Gray Dove will look on me with new eyes!"

Iron Knife did not answer as he backed slowly toward the swollen creek. He moved as if injured, and Summer saw the blood well up scarlet over one eye where he had hit a rock when he fell. He wiped the blood from his brown face and gestured. "Let us talk of this, brother Dog Soldier!"

"Talk! You are as bad as your woman about wanting to talk!" He gestured disdainfully. "Sing your death chant, Iron Knife, son of a white whore! And then with your dying eyes, you will see me mount your woman! Because of you, I have been spurned by mine!"

The big warrior backed slowly into the swirling water as Angry Wolf advanced on him with knife and quirt.

Summer reached for the knife on the ground just out of her reach. She tried to pull the last stake out of the soil that pinned her wrist, but she was too weak. The rope would have to be cut. She clawed the dirt, reaching, reaching.

Iron Knife glanced at her in wordless appeal, the scarlet blood running down his bronzed face and into the water. She couldn't do it, but she *must* do it! Again, she clawed the dirt, straining toward the knife. The rawhide thong bit into her wrist as she struggled toward the weapon. Blood seeped under the rope as she reached and threw her weight against the rawhide. If she had not had a gag in her mouth, she might have cried out from the pain.

Once more, she strained, and then she had the knife by the tip of the blade! For a long, heart-stopping moment, it almost tumbled away from her, but she had it! Quickly, she cut the remaining rope from her wrist, and took the gag from her mouth. Now she crouched, knife in hand, watching the two in the knee-deep, swirling water. So intent was Angry Wolf on his injured quarry that he never turned to look behind him. He quirted the other across the face, and Iron Knife grabbed the lash. But it dropped into the swift water, and was swept away.

The other laughed in triumph. "So now, it is only we two with no Council or tribe to back you up. I have dreamed of this moment! Your heart is about to take my blade, and then I will finish off your woman, and no one will ever know what happened to either of you!"

"You know it is a terrible tabu of the Cheyenne to commit murder among our own! You would be exiled for four years and my cousins would seek revenge!"

Angry Wolf shrugged. "As I said, they will never know! Since you will both be missing, they may think you have dishonored your people and returned to the white civilization to live with your woman!"

Behind him, on the bank, Summer hesitated with the dagger

in her hand and looked toward the Appaloosa stallion grazing nearby. Why should she care what happened to either of the men? All she had to do was let them fight it out to the death while she took the swiftest horse and fled. She knew which direction to take now, and she did not think either man could catch her if she rode the fine stallion. What did it matter which man was killed? Why should she care about the wounded Dog Soldier? And yet . . .

Even as she turned toward the horse, she stopped and looked back to the battle in the water. Iron Knife would surely lose. He was at a clear disadvantage, wounded and weaponless, as the other moved in for the kill.

In that moment, the squat Indian lunged, cutting the other a glancing blow on the shoulder. They meshed, struggling in the racing water, churning it to bloody foam like two great stags in an age-old battle. Iron Knife hung on valiantly but his opponent, using his heavier weight, took him to his knees in the boiling current.

As she watched in growing horror, Angry Wolf dropped the knife, but lifted a rock from the bottom and struck the other a glancing blow. Iron Knife staggered, seemed to slip on the slick bottom. He went down in the foaming water, and the squat Dog Soldier had him by the throat, holding him under, drowning him.

This was her last chance to run for the horses, she knew that. In another minute or so, her attacker would be finished with his murder and coming after her. Still, she hesitated. Her head told her to run, but her heart told her something else. Without even realizing it, she ran for the water, her hand still clutching the dagger.

Angry Wolf had his back to her, intent on murder. She was almost upon him, running lightly and unencumbered by clothes across the sand. Summer was in the water before he seemed to hear her. His hands let go of Iron Knife's throat as he turned abruptly to face her.

He made a futile grab, but her anger made her swift. As he

75

lunged, she dodged his arm and plunged the knife deep into his chest, then jerked it free.

His mouth opened in disbelief and fear spread across his face. He gave a weak cry as he staggered, the scarlet stain spreading down his chest into the water. He made a threatening gesture, then clutched at his fatal wound as he fell backward into the current and was swept away.

Summer stared in shock, the bloody knife hanging limply from her numb fingers. She had killed a man!

Iron Knife staggered to her side, still choking and coughing from the water. Together, they watched a long moment as the body washed down the stream and on over the rapid.

She looked up at him and then at the bloody knife in her hand, suddenly feeling very faint. "I—I owed you that," she said simply, and swayed on her feet. *But deep in her heart, she knew she lied. That wasn't the reason she had done it.*

Quickly, he caught her in his arms, and lifted her as she collapsed, carrying her to the shore. The sun came out from behind the clouds in sudden brilliance as the warrior stood on the sand and cradled her gently in his powerful arms, looking down at her.

Summer stared at the bloody knife in her limp fingers that now draped across his broad shoulders. It occurred to her that it was still not to late for her to stab him in the back and run away, freeing herself from the Indians forever. She need only take his horse and head for the fort. No one need ever know what had happened here. She could keep the secret.

For a long moment, he looked deep into her eyes as the sun warmed them. Finally, he spoke. "Will you now kill me with my own knife, Summer Sky?"

Her mouth dropped open at his question and at the realization that he made no move to protect himself. Her fingers unclenched, and the dagger clattered harmlessly to the ground behind him.

"I might have killed you!" she whispered.

He still held her naked, wet body swinging lightly from his

strong arms. "I was willing to bet my life that you wouldn't!"

"You're a reckless fool!" she challenged. "Why were you so sure? I didn't know myself for a moment what I would do!"

"I knew, my Summer Sky! I knew the moment you came into the water to save me instead of running for the horses!"

She could only look dumbly up into his eyes, her emotions a tangle. He bent his head, and his lips brushed hers, light as a butterfly's wing caressing a flower. It was a hesitant kiss. He seemed almost awaiting her command to pull back. He seemed to expect her rejection which would be swiftly followed by the sting of her hand across his scarred face.

She was surprised by his hesitancy, this bold savage who had tasted her lips with such assurance in the past. And this, perhaps, triggered her own reaction. She seemed to have no control over her own body as she felt her arms reach around his sinewy neck. Her soft hands pulled his bronzed, bleeding face down to hers, and she kissed him in a way that she did not know she knew.

He started in surprise as, instinctively, her mouth explored his deeply, thoroughly. Then, he was all man, crushing her to him as she still swung in his embrace.

She wasn't sure what would happen next, but she knew he would let her decide.

Or would he?

Chapter Five

Had her actions unleashed a wild thing she couldn't control?
She trembled, torn by mixed emotions as he carried her clear of
the water and laid her gently on the hot sand.

He looked down at her from his great height with dark,
smoldering eyes, and the sun was not so warm to her damp skin
as the fire of his gaze.

Without a word, he pulled off the wet buckskin shirt and
leggings and draped them over a bush to dry. He turned back to
stare at her again, a virile animal, clad only in a brief loincloth.
The eagle bone whistle still dangled around his neck and the
sun reflected off the cavalry button earring and the sheen of
his muscles.

She was not ashamed of her nakedness as once she had been,
responding with a primitive savageness of her own, glorying in
his appreciative glance.

"You are the most beautiful woman I have ever seen,
Summer, and I have seen many!" he said as he strode to his
horse. She felt her skin burn with a blush as she raised on one
elbow, watching him dig in his saddlebags, tossing aside the
useless quirt.

He came back to her with a small vial of ointment, and swore
under his breath, white man's swear words, as he examined her
injuries. She felt his hard hands stroke her skin with

suppressed fury as he rubbed the soothing medication on her wounds.

"You have been hurt too many times already," he muttered through clenched teeth, "and I keep promising that no one will ever hurt you again!"

"This wasn't your fault," she quieted him, his anger terrible to see. Summer took the ointment from his hands, and rubbed it into the cut above his eye and the small wound on his shoulder. He lay down on the warm sand beside her, and his eyes closed as she touched him gently. Her fine hands caressed the ropy muscles of his chest, and as she touched the sun dance scars, his big hand caught her wrist and held her as his eyes opened and looked intently into hers.

She was acutely aware of the power of him; the hand that clasped her wrist could just as easily break her back. She stiffened for a long, tense moment, but his grasp did not hurt her and, somehow, she was not afraid.

"Let go of me," she ordered softly, but he did not. His eyes bore hotly into hers as he held her wrist.

"You ran away from me," he accused.

She shrugged. "I wanted to go back to my own people so I simply stole a horse and went." She would not complicate things by telling him of Gray Dove's part in all this; about her sending the now dead brave out to track her down and make sure she never made it back to the fort.

"If I had not followed, you would have been violated and dead by now. I seem to spend much time protecting you." He let go of her wrist, and reached up to touch a long, blond curl that cascaded down her neck near her bare breast.

She shuddered, thinking of Angry Wolf. "Was I going in the wrong direction? He said I was." Summer was keenly aware of his fingers playing with her hair, lightly brushing her skin, but she did not move away.

He nodded. "You were going north, not southeast," he answered. "I would have thought you had a better sense of direction than that. If Angry Wolf hadn't caught up with you,

79

you still wouldn't have made it back to your people. There is nothing the way you were headed but wilderness and wild animals. You would have died or been captured by another tribe's scouting party."

"Would you have cared?"

His hand paused in its stroking, and he hesitated as if loath to admit it. "Does a man care if his heart is torn from his body?"

Automatically, she reached out and touched his lips with the tips of her fingers, very much aware of his rising manhood under the skimpy loincloth. She knew he breathed deeper and heavier as his fingers moved nearer her breast.

He wanted her badly, she knew that, as a woman always knows. It was a part of her own primitive heritage that money and generations of civilized blue blood could not erase.

Could she barter for her freedom? "If I let you make love to me, will you let me go back to the fort?"

Swearing violently, he rose to his knees, his hard hands grasping her soft shoulders. "Do you bargain with me like a common whore?" he raged. "Toying with me, realizing that I could take you by force this very minute as I could have taken you any time these past few days?"

She had pushed him too far, and she was frightened, feeling his fingers dig into her shoulders. But she raised her stubborn chin in that direct, unsettling gaze and looked straight into his eyes. "You don't want me that way," she whispered, "otherwise, you would have already taken me!"

His fingers unclenched, leaving small red marks on her flesh from the pressure. "Am I such a fool that it shows in my face?" He looked away sharply. "Never have I let a woman humiliate me in the way you have done."

But she persisted, turning his face back to hers with her fingertips. "If I love you willingly, will you let me go?"

"Is the thought of me so terrible that you would sacrifice your virginity to escape my embrace forever?" He caught her hand, turned it up, and kissed the palm. "There is nothing to keep me from saying 'yes' and then going back on my word after I have claimed your body."

She looked up at him earnestly. "You would not trick me that way. Somehow, I know it." But she wasn't quite sure what she would do if he offered to exchange freedom for violating her maidenhood.

"Summer, I cannot lie to you," he said softly, kissing her fingertips, "I would do anything to make you happy, even set you free. But the Council has forbidden it, thinking you will bring the soldiers back for a terrible revenge on our camp. I feared to tell you, knowing you would be wild with anger."

He kissed her hand again. "Accepting you from the Council to warm my bed was the best I could do for you. There were some who wanted to kill you or trade you off to the Comanche."

"But you knew I would realize sooner or later that you weren't going to allow me to leave. What did you expect to gain by the delay?"

He hesitated. "I thought that if I kept you long enough, you might come to care for me, and if not . . ."

He paused and his voice trailed off.

"And if not . . . ?" she prompted.

"If not, I love you enough for both of us. If you cannot care for me, it is almost enough to have you near, to be able to look at you. I guess I know now that you could never care about me. I'm not white enough or rich enough." He let go of her hand, and his gaze seared into hers. "But know this, Little One, no man, white or brown, will ever love you as I do!"

His eyes asked an unspoken question and she hesitated, not sure of the answer herself.

She was sure that no man, not even Austin Shaw, had ever offered such deathless devotion. But how did she feel herself about the man crouched on his knees facing her?

A woman can give her virginity but once, whether she be a rich heiress or a poor serving maid. Many men had hungered for and courted Summer Priscilla Van Schuyler—men rich and

81

powerful, men who loved her with varying degrees of adoration. She had held back, slow in making her choice, knowing she could give the precious gift but once. *Until now*, it dawned on her, *until now, just now, never had she met a man she wanted to share love with.*

"Summer?" His dark eyes asked what his lips did not.

If she said "no," would he take her anyhow? Did she want to say "no?" She hesitated, fighting her rising flood of emotions. This was her decision to make; he was awaiting some signal from her.

She knew then that this was the man and this the time; the moment she had waited for all her life. There were no consequences, no thought of right or wrong or tomorrow. *There was only this moment and this man . . . her man . . .*

Her heart, not her conscience, made the final decision for her. Emotion guided her. Almost without realizing it, she made the gesture she knew he had been waiting for. Very slowly, she held out her arms to him, and that was all he needed. He crushed her against his massive chest, fell with her to the hot sand.

"Summer . . . Little One . . ."

"Yes!" she murmured. "Oh, yes!"

His lips brushed her eyelids and the pulsing hollow of her throat. His strong fingers tangled in her blond mane, arching her body against the white sand as his mouth sought hers. She had never been kissed like that, his probing tongue invading her mouth as he whispered feverish endearments.

She kissed him back with a surging passion that surprised her, returning his kisses in a way that again she did not know she knew.

"Dearest!" she gasped. "My dearest!"

She ran her hands down his muscled back, touching the whip welts tenderly. The taste of his mouth was sweet on hers.

His warm breath caressed her ear as he breathed against her hair. She felt his heart thudding against her, his male hardness rising. Her hand went down to explore, glorying in the size and

82

strength of his passion.

Summer moaned aloud as his lips brushed her ear, nibbled at the lobe, and his mouth came back to reclaim hers. She marveled at his gentle savagery. His kisses were hard, but not violent. She felt his lips travel down her throat to her breast, and she gasped in sudden pleasure at the unaccustomed feel of a man's mouth on her taut nipple. Her hands locked behind his head, willing him never to leave that fount of ecstasy. But he pulled away, to the other breast, and then down between them to the soft hollow of her belly.

Instinctively, she knew what she hungered for, and she spread her legs, stripping the loincloth from his magnificent maleness as she pulled him toward her. She trembled as she felt his lips caress her inner thighs, but she wanted more. She tried to pull him to her, but he hesitated on his elbows, looking down into her eyes.

"Why—why do you wait?" she gasped. She must have him now, this moment. This was what she had been born for, so that this warrior could pump his seed into her waiting vessel.

Still, he hesitated, his face troubled. "Little One, I am built very big! You are a virgin—"

"I'm *your* virgin!" she breathed against his lips.

"But I have promised you will never be hurt again!" he protested.

"Hurt me!" she begged as she kissed him deeply. "Hurt me as I want to be hurt!"

His hands cupped her small hips as he entered her sweetness. Summer moaned at the feel of him surging within her, and tried to pull him deeper into her very being. She could feel him holding back, testing her maidenhood, not giving her his full length.

She was like a wild thing in her newfound passion, wrapping her long legs about him, digging her nails into his lean hips.

"Easy, Summer!" he gasped into her ear. "Take it easy! I'm trying not to hurt you, but I cannot help myself with you doing that!"

In answer, she pulled him down harder, wanting all of him, all he had to give, surprising herself with her capacity for passion.

"More!" she demanded. "Don't hold back! I—I want you!"

He took control of the situation then, not holding back any longer, driving hard and deep against her maidenhood. She dug her nails into his back, gasping with animal delight as his big hands tilted her small hips up so that he could give her his full length.

"Summer," he whispered as he kissed her, "are you coming with me?"

For a moment, she did not understand what he meant, knowing so little about love, not knowing there could be more than this new excitement. But then he clasped her to him and shuddered, emptying himself into her. She could feel the throb of him right to the core of her being. She was almost frightened, not understanding as her own body shuddered, tightening its hold on him. And then it was almost like dying— a little death, a wonderful death. She felt she floated in a sweet blackness for endless seconds and then she began to weep as her body slowly returned to life.

He kissed the tears from her eyes. "I have hurt you," he said regretfully, trying to move off her belly.

But she kept him a prisoner of her slim legs, and tightened her arms about his neck. "No, you haven't hurt me!" she wept. "It's just that I never felt anything like that before! It felt— wonderful." She reached up to touch his bronzed face.

But he disengaged himself and rolled over on his side, cradling her blond head on his broad shoulder. "You are truly my woman now, Summer Sky, and God help the man who even looks at you as if he would share your deep sweetness!"

She felt safe and contented lying there in his arms. "I think I will never want any man but you."

"You say that now because I am your first, and I think, no matter what they say, women never quite forget their first man, but someday . . ."—his voice trailed off as his callused hand brushed the soft skin of her cheek—"someday, my love, I think you will regret this, giving yourself to a penniless savage by a creek in the wilderness when most women drive a much harder bargain."

"No, never!" she retorted hotly. "I won't regret it! I love you like I never knew love could be!"

"Even if you lie, I am content with that for now," he whispered as he tightened his protective embrace. "But it will come! You will regret this, even hate me, wanting to return to your own world to lie on a silken bed in the arms of a rich white man."

"Would you care?" she teased.

"Given the chance, I would kill him," he promised simply, and looking into his eyes she knew he meant it.

A frown crossed his face as he remembered. "Has not a man already died today over possession of your body?" The thought seemed to disturb him, and he rose and walked over to pick up his knife from the creek bank, staring at the rushing water. "Once we were friends, but he seemed determined to die. Murder is a terrible tabu of my people."

Summer scrambled to her feet. "He would have killed you without regrets if I hadn't gotten there first."

"Yes, he would have." The warrior nodded, and stooped to wash the knife in the stream, stuck it in his belt. "It was more than you or even Gray Dove that came between our friendship. I think it was my white blood. Ever since his family was wiped out by the epidemic, he was ruled by mad hate, almost as if he wanted to die."

She didn't answer and he turned and studied her gravely. "Our folk hero, Sweet Medicine, warned our people to stay away from the whites many, many years ago. He said they would bring nothing but death and unhappiness to us!"

Summer ran to him, and pressed her naked body into his arms. "And have I brought you unhappiness, my dearest?"

He kissed her cheek thoughtfully. "I think you will before you are done taking possession of my heart. I think this will be

85

a bittersweet love that will make me wish I had never seen you on the grass by the stage. Already, you take captive my thoughts, my emotions. Sometimes, I cannot remember who is supposed to be the slave, and who the master."

"I am your slave; my body knows that!" She molded herself against the hard planes of his body, and felt his manhood rising again against her belly. "I will never knowingly bring you heartache, nor trouble to your people."

He held her close, murmuring, "I wish I could know it were so, just as I wish I had time to take you again here on the sand, but we must be going before darkness catches us too far from the camp."

The brave pushed her from him reluctantly, and reached for the clothes on the bush. He put on the leggings himself, and seemed to consider a moment. "Since your dress is cut to shreds, my shirt will have to do for you."

He handed her the fringed leather and she slipped it over her head, enjoying the soft, warm feel of the skin against her own.

"What do you think?" she asked.

He laughed softly as he surveyed her in the oversized shirt. Its hem hung below her small bottom, the long sleeves hid her hands.

She looked at him, thinking of the afternoon, the dead man. "What will happen now?"

A frown replaced the smile. "I do not know," he answered. "Murder among our people is so rare."

"It wasn't murder, it was self-defense!"

"I am afraid the Council will not see it that way. I was supposed to become a chief at the next tribal election, replacing my uncle, Clouds Above. A chief is supposed to think only of his people. He is not supposed to care or take revenge should another man steal his woman. Nothing should be in his mind but the safety of his tribe. I shall be exiled for this, me and all my relatives who want to go with me, share my banishment. It is almost a death sentence since it is almost impossible to survive in the wilderness alone."

"Must you tell the Council?"

"Summer, I must," he answered with a nod of his head. "It is the honorable thing to do and a man without honor is hollow inside. His *tasoom*, his soul, is dead."

Frightened, she faced him. "You are forgetting that you didn't kill him; I did! What will the Council do to a white slave who has caused the death of a Dog Soldier?"

She saw him blanch under his dark skin, and thought she knew the answer.

"I won't tell the Council you were involved. I'll take the blame myself!" he retorted.

"That is no less a lie; a smear on your honor. Sooner or later in the questioning, one of us will slip up, and they will find out I did it. Dearest"—she took one of his hands in both of hers— "we don't have to go back to the camp, we could go to the fort. We could spend our lives together among my people."

"So the truth comes out!" he said savagely. "And once at the fort, I would be hanged for daring to touch a white woman, and you would go back to Boston!"

"Will you never trust me?" she implored, looking up into his face. "I mean it, we could live together among the whites."

He grimaced bitterly. "And if you spoke the truth, and did not leave me, what would I do in the white civilization, Little One? Should I sit at a desk and handle papers, imprisoned behind glass windows? I, who can scarcely read and write and like the wind blowing wild and free in my face? Should I sweat behind a plow, scarring Mother Earth's breast like those cloddish men who cross our land in endless wagon trains? I know nothing, care nothing for farming."

"You must have some skills—"

"Of course I do!" He shook off her imploring hands impatiently. "I can bring down a great, charging buffalo bull with a single arrow. I can cut a man's throat so swiftly he has no time to cry out!"

"You could be a scout for the army—"

"And lead the bluecoats to ambush and kill my own

people?" His face hardened. "The man I have reason to hate most in this world was an army scout! No, little Summer, I cannot live in your world, so you must live in mine! Even if I wanted to, the whites would not accept me, would ridicule and mistreat you as they did my mother for accepting the love of a savage. I told you that you would regret becoming my woman, and it has started already!"

"No, never!" She flung herself into his arms. "I have been waiting for you always, waiting for you to come into my life. Waiting for you to take me in your arms, only I didn't know it until this afternoon. I am complete now, fulfilled! Could I ride off to the fort this moment without you, I would not go!"

He held her so close, she could feel his heart pounding. "Would I had the courage to test your words, and see if indeed you would choose me over your own kind."

He looked deep into her eyes as if trying to gauge her sincerity. "A white woman's lies once almost cost me my life, and I have been wary ever since. I find the whites lie often— their false words seem to come very easy on their tongues."

"I do not lie about my feelings for you!" *Only time*, she thought, *only time would prove to him how much she really cared*. His scars were much deeper than the ones on his back. "To show you how much I care for you, I am willing to go back and face the Council, tell them that I killed Angry Wolf and why. Then let them do what they will!"

She had reached him, she knew, and now maybe he trusted her a little. She did not yet possess his whole soul, his complete trust. But she would someday; she would. For a long moment, she was tempted to tell him of her involvement with Gray Dove, that the jealous Arapaho girl had ultimately caused Angry Wolf's death. Then she reconsidered. She had a score to settle with Gray Dove but she determined to settle it herself. If she told Iron Knife, there was no telling what he would do to the Indian girl in his anger and it would make even more trouble for him. No, Summer would deal with that trouble-maker herself and spare her love the danger of involvement.

He held her close, and she could feel his fingers move nervously on her back. "I am afraid of the Council's decision, not for myself, but for you. Their word is not absolute law, but they mirror tribal opinion and you would not get much sympathy."

Thunder rumbled in the distance and Summer glanced up with trepidation at the sudden jagged flash of lightning. The forest was tinder dry, she thought, feeling the leaves crackle under her feet. All that rain had fallen to the west of here. She watched Iron Knife's face as he stared at the three horses.

There was a long moment of silence and finally he seemed to decide. "What I am going to do is not honorable for a Cheyenne warrior, but I must do it."

He strode over, took the bridles from her roan pony and Angry Wolf's paint, spooked them so they ran off into the woods. Then he hid the bridles in the deep leaves. As she watched, he hid everything—her torn dress, the stakes. Then he took a small branch and dusted away all footprints, all signs of this afternoon's struggle.

She watched him. "What are you doing?"

"Listen to me, Summer. Listen carefully! We have seen nothing of Angry Wolf should anyone ask. Understand? Nothing!"

He held out his hand to her. "Those ponies will join a wild horse herd that grazes just past the forest, and there is nobody to prove murder."

She took his outstretched hand. "I understand." She nodded.

"You went picking berries for my supper and became lost in the forest. You had no thought of disobeying the Council and running away," he commanded firmly.

Had she ever intended to run away? The afternoon seemed a long, long time ago, a million years ago, before she had become a woman. She missed her family and regretted that they would never know what happened to her, but given a choice between them and her man, she had already made her decision. All that was lacking now was that he believe how much she cared. But that would take time. She was willing to wait.

"Are you listening, Summer?" His voice brought her back to cold reality. "Since you were lost picking berries, it was very lucky I came along and found you."

She looked up at him and she was no taller than his great chest. "I know this deception goes against everything you believe, that you do this only for me. Your honor means a great deal to you, doesn't it?"

She felt him hesitate, then kiss her forehead. "Not as much as you do," he said simply. His arms went around her and she watched lightning jagged against the darkening sky. His Appaloosa snorted nervously.

She gloried in the hard feel of his body as she leaned against him, remembering the first time he had held her when she had been trussed and terrified. She would never have met him had it not been for a drunken Dog Soldier who was now dead.

The dead man's image came to her mind and she shuddered. "Will they send search parties for Angry Wolf?"

"Some will look, mostly his followers. But when they do not find him, they will think the bluecoats or Pawnee got him. He wasn't very popular among our people; no one will mourn him much."

Lightning flashed silver and gold through the green pines and the wind came up quick and chill.

"We should go back now," he murmured, "there is going to be a bad storm."

Almost in answer, lightning arced overhead and the static electricity created seemed to electrify the air around them.

She saw the concern on his face as they both looked up at the great flashes of white and angry yellow against the growing purple storm clouds.

"It's going to be a bad one," he said, "and with this part of the forest dry as dust, we'll be lucky if the lightning doesn't start a fire—"

Summer never heard the rest of his words. Loud, rolling peals of thunder drowned him out. The terrifying crash of sound that accompanied the next flash came suddenly, too suddenly to make a move although Iron Knife tried.

A jagged flash cut across the darkening sky like a broken piece of glass and hit a dry, dead pine not a hundred yards from the pair. Instantly, the bitter scent of sulphur, of fire, stung Summer's nostrils.

"The horse!" Iron Knife shouted a warning as he ran toward the stallion.

The Appaloosa reared and whinnied in panic at the booms of thunder, the sudden smell of smoke in the air. For a split second, she stood frozen to the spot, unable to move as the horse reared again, breaking its reins.

Iron Knife grabbed for the broken, trailing reins as the horse reared again and backed away. He missed the grab by inches as the terrified, snorting animal slung its head wildly, seeming to realize for the first time that it was free. Thunder clapped again and the stallion neighed in terror and bolted.

Iron Knife ran after the animal even as Summer forced herself to move and tried to help by heading off the Appaloosa.

Iron Knife called out. "Here, boy! Come back, Spotted Blanket!"

It was too late. Even as Summer ran forward, trying to help recapture the mount, the horse neighed in panic and galloped off.

Summer and Iron Knife ran after the animal as he raced in the direction of the wild herd on the prairie outside the forest miles away.

She had a sinking, desolate feeling as they both stumbled to a halt in the middle of the woods and looked after the disappearing horse. It was immediately lost to view among the tall pines.

Iron Knife gasped for air. "We are afoot," he gasped, "and—"

"Iron Knife, look!" Summer whirled to look behind her as she smelled the spreading, acrid smoke.

The gigantic bolt of lightning had done more damage than making the horse bolt. With their attention on the stallion, they hadn't noticed the fire.

Summer looked around, realizing in sudden horror that they were trapped in the midst of flames!

Chapter Six

For a moment, Summer gaped with unbelieving eyes at the scarlet and orange flames gobbling the paper dry brush and trees around them. A sudden rush of air as hot as the furnaces of hell made her choke on the thick smoke.

Iron Knife reacted first.

"The bolt of lightning hit a dead tree," he shouted. "We've got to get out of here fast or be trapped!"

Hypnotized by the hungry flames licking through the trees, Summer only stared in fascination. She felt the heat blowing toward her on the mounting breeze, coughed as the smoke stung her lungs.

Iron Knife grabbed her hand and whirled her around. "Come on, Little One, run!" The river is a couple of miles behind us! We've got to get there!"

She took his hand but he had to drag her to get her feet running. *A couple of miles. It was so far . . .*

The crimson and yellow flames already climbed the trunks of nearby pines like reckless, naughty children.

"Come on, Summer," he urged, "the wind's picking up! We're going to have to run for our lives!"

Gripping his hand tightly, she began to run through the forest toward the river. In places, the trees were too close, the underbrush too thick, and he had to let go of her hand so that she stumbled forward alone. The brush and thorns cut her bare legs, but she was glad for the soft moccasins as she fled through the forest. The pine needles and dead leaves were spongy under her step and she shuddered, thinking how this volatile carpet would blaze beneath her feet if she couldn't outrun the flames.

Her lungs already hurt with the exertion and the heat as her lover caught her hand again and ran on, half-dragging her as his long legs easily outdistanced her shorter ones.

He stopped. "Summer, you have to run faster, the fire is gaining on us!"

She leaned against a big pine, choking and coughing. "I—I can't run any faster!" she gasped. "My legs are too short and I'm not used to running. Boston ladies don't ever walk. They take a carriage."

"I'm fresh out of carriages." He smiled thinly but she saw the desperation in his eyes and realized she was holding him back. Without her, he could make it easily.

He had her hand again, urging her forward. She could hardly see where she ran, stumbling blindly through the thick acrid smoke as he dragged her along. Behind them, the roaring of the fire devouring the forest around them grew deafening. It was almost as if some terrible giant were slowly chewing up the landscape.

She stumbled and fell and he lifted her to her feet, pulled her resisting body forward. "You've got to run, Little One, the fire will catch us!"

Her feet were unsteady and weariness descended on her as she answered his urging. Even though her rebel body resisted her mind's command, she moved forward because he demanded it. Her mouth felt dry and sour as she tasted the bitter smoke rolling past her.

He loosed her hand and ran slightly ahead of her, obviously looking over the terrain, trying to find short cuts and easier paths through the trees.

"This way, Summer," he called and gestured. "There's an old deer trail down through here and I think it will be easier for you—"

The rest of his words were lost in the roar of the flames as he turned and ran ahead, scouting out the path.

He was right, this trail was a little easier, she thought with a sigh of relief as she ran on, concentrating on his muscular, brown back moving just ahead of her through the trees.

Her lungs seemed to be on fire with the suffocating fumes and the effort of running but she knew she must keep moving even though her soft, exhausted body was threatening to fail her.

You can do it, Summer, you've got to do it, she admonished herself as her valiant little heart pumped hard, speeding the blood through her tired body, her aching legs. She wouldn't think about how far it was to the river, the only body of water deep and wide enough to offer protection against the red wall of flames.

The hot wind blew against her sweating back. She could feel the heat of the fire gaining on her. The deerskin shirt of his that she wore was binding but offered some protection from the sparks and embers that blew on the wind behind her. She shuddered to think what would have already happened if she had been wearing the cheap, red satin dress she had worn only a few days ago. A human torch, she thought as she ran, trying not to think how the red satin would go up, how the yellow hair would flame.

Behind her, she could hear the pine needle carpet burning. Iron Knife paused ahead of her, gestured frantically. "This way, Little One, it's shorter!" He turned and ran on, scouting out an easier trail.

They were both running too slowly, she realized with a sob as she glanced over her shoulder at the massive wall of flame. He could make it without her but he might not, burdened down by a weak, stumbling girl. She would not cause his death by delaying him, she vowed, tripping with weariness as she ran.

Summer Van Schuyler was no quitter. She would run until the fire overtook her or she was unable to force her tired legs to move by sheer grit and willpower.

The wind picked up, pushing the fire faster. Over her shoulder, she saw the scarlet monster relentlessly stalking her. It climbed every tree it came to, uncertain at first, then faster and faster when it realized it could.

Birds flew in a rush out of each tree as the flames climbed, chattering and calling as they flew about, disoriented by the fire. Some flew ahead of the racing monster. Some, in a whirl of confused wings, flew directly into the heart of the inferno. Those were gone in a sudden flash of burning feathers, their frightened calls cut off as they fell toward the ground, wings on fire.

It was a horrid sight. Summer wanted to scream out at the obscenity, the agony of life caught in this trap, but she could do nothing but run on. She kept her eyes on his broad shoulders moving ahead of her as he scouted out the trail.

He looked back over his shoulder and she gave him an encouraging smile.

"I'm doing fine," she lied, panting. "We'll make the river, all right."

She was past believing that. She was past anything except putting one foot ahead of the other, knowing that if she fell, he would return for her and be caught in the inferno himself. It seemed she had been running forever now as she stumbled, her lungs on fire with the effort of it. Somewhere ahead lay the life-saving river, but she had lost track of time and distance. She was only aware of the fire behind her, the pain of her lungs and aching legs as she ran.

Now, she was acutely sensitive of other sounds in the woods besides the roaring flames—the small cries of doomed wildlife that fled along with the humans. Everything that still lived in the forest was trying to make it to the water.

A frightened cottontail rabbit dashed past her, its small puff of a tail on fire, and as she stared in horror, it fell on the path

96

before her and died in a sudden burst of flame. Immediately, the dry leaves beneath the tiny body ignited and she dodged past the small funeral pyre, the new outbreak.

Deer scampered past her, hardly seeming to see the humans as they ran instinctively toward the river somewhere up ahead.

A black bear, then a panther, brushed her, paying no heed to her or each other as they loped ahead of the flames. None of the racing animals seemed to see or react to each other. A stag dashed along beside the bear and the panther, rabbits brushed against running bobcats. All concentrated only on the universal enemy.

Behind her, she still heard squeals of protest by tiny, chattering squirrels trapped in the treetops by the flames already eating at the trunks of the tall oaks. She glanced upward. Some of the little fox squirrels moved from tree to tree through the upper branches, staying ahead of the fire. Others, too terrified to think clearly, retreated to the refuge of their nests built of tree branches and roasted alive there as the fire trapped them.

Over her own agonized breathing, she could hear the protesting bird calls as jays, scissortails, and hawks took to the air. Some flew toward the river and the trees on the other side. Others, disoriented, flew right into the flames.

Summer tripped, went to her knees.

Ahead, Iron Knife turned back toward her. "Little One, you must run! We aren't that far from the river now!"

He waved in frantic, encouraging gestures as he ran toward her. "Summer, look out!"

Wearily, she raised her head, glanced up to see what it was he saw, what his frantic voice and hands warned her of.

A tall pine nearby, flames burning through its base, swayed and trembled, even as she stared up in disbelieving horror toward the sky.

Iron Knife dashed toward her. "Summer, run!"

She tried. For a split second, she stared at the leaning giant pine, realized it was going to fall. Her brain sent signals to her exhausted legs and she attempted to flee.

She almost made it. Even as she turned and ran, the big tree came down with a reverberating crash. Her world was a sudden forest of heavily scented pine boughs. She wondered as she lay on the ground whether she were dead.

Iron Knife hacked savagely with his big blade at the limbs covering her. "Summer! Little One! Are you all right?"

"I—I think so." She took mental inventory of her body as he fought his way through the pine branches to her side. "I think I'm okay. Wait—"

"What is it?" He knelt, looked anxiously into her eyes as he gathered her into his strong arms.

"My ankle's caught!" She pulled frantically on her left leg, unwilling to believe what her mind had comprehended.

"Let me help you to your feet."

She could tell by his eyes he didn't believe it either, didn't want to believe it. He tried to lift her and she whimpered.

"No, it's true!" She looked into his eyes, the terror growing on her. To be trapped in the fire was a death sentence. "I—I can feel a limb across my left ankle."

She saw the unspeakable horror in his eyes as they both looked toward the spreading flames of the tree's trunk. The fire was chewing its way greedily the length of the giant pine. In a few minutes, it would spread to the smaller limbs, to the one that held her prisoner.

Iron Knife hacked through the pine needles with his big knife down to her feet. When he turned back to look at her, she read her death sentence in his tortured eyes.

"Summer, I—I can't cut through this limb, it's too big, almost as big around as my arm! I could cut through it maybe if I had a lot of time . . ." His voice trailed off and he did not finish.

Time, she thought when she glanced at the wall of red flames blowing toward them. *Time was the one thing they didn't have.*

He bent now, wrapping his arms around the limb. "If I can lift it just an inch or two so you can pull your foot out . . ."

Sweat stood out on his bare chest as he struggled and strained. The limb didn't move at all.

His face grew frantic as he looked back toward the flames moving up the trunk, the wall of fire blowing through the forest toward them. She saw the reflection of the flames in his dark eyes as he tried again.

"Pull, Summer! If I can just move it a fraction of an inch, you can pull your foot out!" His great muscles bulged and strained, sweat broke out all over his smooth brown body as he struggled with the weight of the tree.

Summer pulled on her foot, but she only felt the scrape of raw skin stinging, and she knew then she wasn't going to be able to free herself.

"It's no use!" she gasped. "You'll have to think of something else!"

There was nothing else; they both knew it. But he would not quit. She could feel the heat of the flames moving closer, taste the grit of the ashes floating on the air. She saw blood on his hands as he struggled with the pine bough, fought its rough bark for possession of Summer's body.

For a moment, calm returned to her soul as she faced the inevitability of death. Only a few short hours ago, she had finally found what life was all about when she had discovered love.

Had it only been a few short hours? She stared at the moving flames, coughed from the heat and black smoke as she watched her love struggle to move the tree. All her life, she had been searching for love. Now that she had finally found it, was she going to lose it along with her life and his, too?

But the fire need not take him, she thought abruptly. He was free to escape if only he would. Her lover could live and she was going to give him that chance.

"Iron Knife, go on!" she urged. "You can make it to the river! Your legs are long and swift! Go on! Go without me!"

He paused, came back up the trunk to her, bloody scratches on his big body from the rough bark. He looked at her as if he didn't comprehend what she was saying.

"Go on? Without you? Never!"

She reached up to embrace him. "Yes, love, there's no point in both of us dying because you can't free me. If you love me, go on to the river. Live for both of us!"

"No," he answered defiantly. "I've only just found you. I won't live without you. If you die, I want to die, too!"

"But the fire . . ." Her voice trailed off. They both stared at the moving flames. At that moment, a deer dashed by, it's coat in flames. It fell near them, kicking and writhing in agony until it was totally consumed.

Iron Knife took her face in his two hands, looked down at her. Summer closed her eyes, remembering the deer, imagining how it would feel to burn alive as the fire flashed up the trunk of the fallen tree, reaching her feet first . . .

"Go on, Iron Knife," she whispered, determined to save him but not wanting to die alone. Her long blond hair, she thought, would go up like a torch, and she would be a mass of red flames for a few seconds before death took her.

"No," he said again, and she wasn't sure if it was sweat or tears running down his rugged bronze face, "I won't leave you, Little One, now that I've finally found you. If need be, we'll die together!"

He took her in his powerful arms, kissing her forehead gently. She gloried in the feel of him, remembering the warm sand of the creek. If she must die, this was the way she wanted to go, held in the protection of his big arms the way he had held her only this afternoon, so many lifetimes ago.

But she would not permit herself that luxury. Even as his lips brushed hers gently, the fire moved closer and she knew what she had to do. The flames were consuming the big pine now. In only a minute or so more, it would be at her feet.

Reluctantly, she tore herself from his grasp. "You must go!" she urged. "For you to die is useless when your people need you so. The truth is—I—I never really cared for you. I regret my passion already. I—I would try to go back to my people if

100

you freed me."

She saw the sudden pain as she mentioned his people, saw him react to the lie that she didn't want him. Only those two things could hit the most vulnerable depth of his heart and she knew it.

"Even if you lied to me, I—I can't leave you to die like this, Summer, all alone, in agony. . . ."

"Your people need you. I don't. I never really did. You—you were only a moment's pleasure, a prize for a rich white girl." She lied, pushing him away. His life was more important to her than her own. She would do whatever it took to save him. "Go on, you dirty heathen, run!"

His face was a mask of agony, of indecision. "I—I can't Little One. I can't leave you to die this terrible death alone, no matter whether what you say is true!"

She could feel the fire's hot breath now. The smoke was so thick, she could hardly see him as he knelt by her.

And then, she knew what the answer was as she looked at the big knife in his belt.

"Don't let the fire get me, Iron Knife," she urged, gripping his hands with the intensity of her plea. "You're skilled with the blade. You could end my life instantly."

He jumped back, startled. "No! I couldn't do that!"

"You can! You must!" Tears came to her eyes. She reached out, jerked the gleaming dagger from his belt, tried to press it into his unwilling hand.

"No!" He dropped the knife as if it were a poisonous snake. "That I can never do!"

She looked deep into his eyes, pleading with her own. "Can you leave me here to die in slow agony like the deer? Your blade is razor sharp, and it would be over in a flash for me. Is that not better than roasting slowly while I scream in pain?"

Summer saw that the logic had touched his heart, although she saw the conflict of the terrible choice in his dark eyes. Very slowly, he leaned over, picked up the knife. As he looked deep into her eyes, she saw the love and torture of the decision on

101

his features.

The terrible heat became almost unbearable on her tender skin as the fire moved up the trunk. She only had another minute or two.

She reached up to him almost in prayer. "If I mean anything to you, save me from this terrible death."

He bent over to kiss her. She tasted the salt of tears on his rugged face.

Summer wiped a stray tear off his high cheekbone. "Make it swift," she murmured, and bit her lips to hold back her vow of eternal love.

Taking a deep breath and closing her eyes, she offered up her slender neck for his expert kill. *I wonder if it will hurt*, she thought, then steeled herself for the slash of the blade across her throat.

She heard the agony of his breathing over the roar of the fire as it moved toward her. A stray spark lit on her skin and she brushed it away hurriedly. Only a moment more and the pine boughs around her would be aflame.

"Quickly!" she commanded without opening her eyes. "Quickly, if you love me! Then save yourself, go back to your people, and forget me!"

She waited for his action. Slowly, she opened her eyes and looked up at him. He stood poised with the knife high, ready to bring it down across her slender throat. And when she looked into his face, she saw agony as he looked back at her.

"I must try to lift the tree one more time," he decided as he ran to grasp the trunk. "Part of it has burned away. Maybe that might lighten it a few pounds!"

"Iron Knife! There isn't time!" she protested in vain, watching him as he grasped the trunk. "You will be trapped by the fire yourself! Kill me, and flee while there's still time!"

But he seemed to pay her no heed as he threw his weight into the mighty effort. The sparks from the fire were showering down on him and he winced as he struggled.

She watched his huge muscles bulge and strain with the

effort. Sweat ran down his great body as he lifted. Near her head, a spark set the grass aflame. She beat it out with her bare hands.

And still, he struggled with the effort to lift the tree.

She had to save him! "Run, dear one, the fire is upon us! Save yourself!"

The heat from the flames began to scorch her tender skin and she coughed and strangled on the smoke. *Only a few seconds and the flames will envelop us both,* she thought wildly. She called out in protest to Iron Knife, urging him again to give her a quick, merciful death and run for the river.

If he heard her, he ignored her, for he gave no sign except that his head went back and he called out, "Great Heammawihio, look down upon me now and give me strength as you once gave Sampson in the Black Book my mother read to me! Please, Heammawihio!"

With that, he gave it one more try, and she knew he was putting everything he had into a last great effort because there was no time for more.

For a split second, the giant Indian's powerful muscles bulged and rippled with the effort as the straining sinews stood out in his neck and legs. Sweat ran off him in trickles of pain as he lifted.

Summer glanced at the moving wall of flame.

"You can't do it, dearest! Give up and save yourself!"

His strength was going into his lift and she saw him mouth the words, *not without you . . . both or none . . .*

Sparks from the advancing flames fell around her in a shower of heat as the fire moved up the trunk closer to the man. He was surely being scorched by the proximity of the fire, she thought in terror as he struggled with the burning tree.

It was too late, she thought, too late for either of them. They were both going to burn alive and she screamed at him, urging him again to save himself. Even as she did, his muscles quivered with his mighty effort and she felt the tree move.

Hardly daring to hope, she held her breath and watched him

103

lift and strain.

Summer glanced at the flames around them. "Oh, dear God, help him," she prayed. "Don't let him die for me!"

In that instant, the burning part of the trunk fell away, making the weight lighter, and the tree moved just a fraction. Not much, only a scant inch or so, but it was enough. She could feel the weight lift off her imprisoned ankle and she pulled her leg free, scraping the skin raw as she managed to crawl out from under the big branch. She was free!

Summer struggled to her feet as Iron Knife ran to her and grasped her hand.

His eyes said everything as he half-dragged her. "We'll make it now, Little One! Run! We can still make it to the river!"

She started forward and staggered, almost fell except that he caught her in his strong arms. "My ankle!" she wept in bitter disappointment. "I think it's badly sprained! I can't walk! You must go on without me!"

But he swung her up in his arms. "Little One, do you think I went through all this only to lose you now? I'll carry you if I have to!"

And suiting action to the word, he started to run.

Looking over his shoulder, she saw the place where she had lain trapped burst into flames and shuddered at the image that came to her mind. Scarlet, angry flames consumed the whole pine tree. Then, the greedy fire moved relentlessly forward, pushed by the strong, rising wind.

She held on to Iron Knife's neck as he ran with her in his arms, but she felt the quivering in his exhausted muscles. All his strength and energy had gone into lifting the tree off her leg and there was not much left to make it another mile to the river carrying her weight.

The flames were moving too fast, Summer realized as she buried her face against his chest so she couldn't see. They weren't going to make it after all his effort. She could feel his great heart pounding against her face with the effort. At least they would die in each other's arms, she thought.

She kissed his shoulder gently and closed her eyes as he labored with the effort of his running. The fire was gaining on them. She didn't want to see the wall of flames when it caught them.

"My love," she whispered against his neck. "Oh, my love! We aren't going to make it after all, but we'll die in each other's arms!"

Chapter Seven

Summer sobbed against his neck as the hopeless realization swept over her. "Leave me behind, dear one," she wept. "You might make it to the river alone but you'll never make it carrying me!"

His breathing grew labored as his great chest sought air. "Hush, Little One," he gasped, "we'll either make it together or die together!"

She tried to protest again and struggled in his arms. But he no longer answered her as he stumbled forward, both of them choking on the black smoke as the line of fire moved behind them.

She could see the river ahead now, near and yet so very far. *Too far,* she thought as she looked over his shoulder at the relentless flames blowing after them. She felt the trembling of his lithe muscles, the falter of his long gait as Iron Knife moved, knew he was almost to the limit of his endurance.

Ahead of them lay the rocky banks and shining water of the Arkansas. Frantic animals—deer, bobcat, panthers, rabbits—scampered past them and into the lifesaving water.

How strange, she thought, almost in a daze, the animals ignored each other as they crowded into the stream. Large and small, predators and vegetarians, all waded about side by side in the water without trouble. They were all too intent on the great fire.

The blaze gained on the man. Summer could feel the heat blowing behind them. She hid her face against his big shoulder, shielding her tender skin from the heat. The trees thinned out on the landscape to open prairie and the fire ran along behind the running man like a molten river of scarlet, flowing over the dry grass, the small bushes.

She had never thought before about the sounds of a fire, the labored breathing of those struggling to make it. Behind her, she heard frantic calls and sounds of desperate animals running. Some staggered with exhaustion and finally fell, kicking frantically, too tired to keep up the pace. The greedy fire consumed them as it raced forward.

The deafening roar of the fire almost drowned out the labored breathing of the man carrying her as he stumbled, going to his knees.

She fought to get out of his arms. "You can't make it with me weight!" she screamed. "Leave me behind and go on!"

She saw his hand coming as he clipped her across the jaw and she collapsed, only half-conscious.

Vaguely, she heard his gasp, "Sorry, Summer Sky, I had to do that!" Then he threw her across his wide shoulder, staggered to his feet, and ran on.

Overhead, she was dimly aware of thunderheads gathering, the distant rumble of thunder. *It was going to rain*, she thought, *but not in time; not in time.*

Dear God, she prayed silently, can't you see us? Can't you help us?

She prayed silently, feeling the tears running down her dazed face as she felt the man stumble, go to his knees again. It seemed to take him a long moment to struggle to his feet.

The last of the animals who had survived ran past them and into the water only a few hundred feet ahead.

She heard the rumble of thunder again and looked up. The angry clouds built jade green behind the red and yellow flames. They weren't going to make it, she thought as Iron Knife staggered forward, unless . . .

Summer prayed harder than she ever had before and as she did, she thought she felt the wind shift. For a long moment, she thought it was her hope and imagination and yet . . .

"The wind," she gasped. "The storm is causing it to shift. It's no longer blowing toward us; it's blowing the opposite direction!"

Iron Knife paused and swung around to look. "You're right, Summer," his exhausted voice held new hope, "the fire is blowing back toward itself. We're going to make it after all!"

They wouldn't have made it otherwise, she thought as she closed her eyes to return thanks. The last few yards, Iron Knife stumbled forward at a walk.

Then, she came alert suddenly as he waded into the cold water with her in his arms. She laughed in delight at the feel of the waves lapping at her smudged, scorched skin. Animals surrounded them, small eyes and ears peeking out from the surface and they seemed to look curiously at this human who laughed out loud. All turned to watch the great wall of fire that faltered only a few hundred feet from the edge of the river and started to consume itself as the shifting wind blew it back.

Iron Knife carried her out deeper and she floated free and put her arms around his sinewy neck, reveling in the exuberance of being alive when she had resigned herself to death.

She looked up into his tired face. "You were about to give your life for me even though I had lied and told you I didn't love you, didn't want you. Why?"

He shrugged as he kissed her forehead. "Because at the last moment, when it looked like we would die together back there in the forest, you called me 'dear' and 'dear one.' I knew then that you lied to try to make me leave you behind. But I do seem to spend a lot of time saving you, Summer. It makes me think the great god, Heammawihio, doesn't really want me to have you and someday will cease playing with me and take you away forever."

She winced at the thought. "We are meant to be one. Somehow, whatever happens, we are fated to spend the rest of our lives together."

His face saddened. "I wish I could be sure of that. My mother felt the same way."

They turned to watch the fire. From a great red outlaw monster, it was rapidly dwindling to an impotent cannibal dwarf. It fed on itself and barely moved across the sparse grass near the water's edge.

Iron Knife turned toward the other bank. "I know a cozy nook almost like a cave under a rocky ledge on the far side of the river. There's a shallow place up around the bend where we can cross."

He took her hand and led her as the animals watched them with curious eyes. The flames were dying fast, Summer thought, and the coming rain would drown out the remnant quickly.

Thunder rumbled again and the air was cool on her wet body as they stumbled out of the water onto the far bank. A few giant drops of rain splattered on the river, making small, rainbow pools that widened across the surface.

Iron Knife started to lift her again as they staggered out onto the bank, but Summer protested with a stubborn shake of her head. "Give me a little assistance and I can make it," she said.

He looked as if he might argue the point with her, then shrugged as he mumbled something about her strong will. He put one strong arm under hers and half-supported, half-carried her as she hobbled across the ground on the sprained ankle.

The ledge was not so very far from the water but it seemed a long way to Summer as she gritted her teeth and limped. It really was a cozy lair under an overhanging rock with a view of the river.

With a tired sigh, she collapsed on the layer of soft scented pine needles.

He looked down at her tenderly. "You need to get out of that wet shirt."

She looked down at his oversized buckskin she still wore, and with no shame, pulled it over her head and hung it on a rocky outcrop in their cave.

She felt no shame at her nakedness or the way his eyes appraised her nude, ripe body.

Slowly, he took off his wet breechcloth and fringed pants and hung them to dry next to her shirt. Then he settled himself next to her on the pine-scented bed with a tired sigh.

Summer leaned back against the rock, watching the occasional raindrop hitting the grass at the front of the cave. "We made it, love, I really didn't think we would."

He put one big finger under her chin, turned her small, heart-shaped face up to his. "I told you we would make it together, or die together."

She caught his hand with her small one and kissed his fingertips. "I wish I could find a new way to say how much I love you."

His hands reached out and pulled her against him. "My English isn't good enough to find the words I need for this moment."

But there were no words needed between them as they embraced and watched the fire sputtering on the far side of the river. It was hard to believe the weak, orange sparks were great walls of red flame only minutes before.

Summer frowned. "I wonder what happened to your horse?"

He shook his head. "Spotted Blanket is the smartest horse I ever owned. He either made it out onto the prairie where the wild horses graze safely, or he swam the river like we did. Sooner or later, I will find him or he will return to the village. They will send out a search party when he comes in without me."

Iron Knife stopped to examine her ankle, his big hands gently touching the swollen, discolored sprain.

She bit her lip and winced as he moved it. "I don't think I can walk all the way back to the village."

"No matter," he said. "We are both too exhausted to do any traveling and it is going to storm."

She glanced up at the thunderheads still building on the horizon as another raindrop spattered on the rock outside their lair.

Iron Knife stood up and she realized again what a marvelous physical specimen he was as she studied his nude body. *It was almost like having their own little Garden of Eden,* she thought, looking down at her own nakedness. A few short days ago, she could never have imagined being caught up in a romantic adventure such as this.

He stretched his rippling muscles and looked outside. "It will be raining hard in a few minutes and we will need a campfire as the rain brings a cool breeze. Also, we must have food." He stepped out to the cave's entrance. "I must go back across the river."

"No, don't leave me!" She reached up to grasp his fingers.

He squeezed her hand, then disengaged his own. "I must, Summer. I will have to make several trips, but I'll bring back a burning stick so we can have a campfire."

"Where will you find food?"

"One of those deer or rabbits that didn't survive will provide us with plenty of delicious roasted meat."

So saying, he strode away. She watched anxiously as he crossed the river and was soon swimming back with a burning branch held over his head. Within minutes, he had a merry fire crackling under the ledge to warm her trembling, naked body. Then he returned to the smoldering remnants of the forest fire and brought back a haunch of venison.

The animals that had survived the fire left the river now; some crossing to the far side, others scattering into the unburned areas to the south of the forest.

Iron Knife just managed to crawl under the shelter of the ledge and flop down beside the campfire as the rain commenced. They gobbled the delicious meat, licking their fingers and putting small morsels in each other's mouths as

111

they sat by the warm fire and watched the sky break open. The rain came down hard.

Over on the other side, the forest fire was out, an occasional wisp of smoke or a tiny pink tongue of flame licking weakly at the blackened underbrush. The cold rain fell among the blackened skeletons of burned trees and she stared, shuddered to think how close she and her love had come to being burned alive.

But this was not the time to think of that, she thought with a contented sigh as she ate the last of the meat and lay down next to the fire with him. It seemed they were the only two people in the whole universe. Summer was filled with calm satisfaction. The soft, scented pine needles made a velvet bed beneath her naked skin. There could be nothing more wonderful in life than this, she thought.

She smiled at him. "I would be happy to stay here forever, just the two of us."

He grinned. "Like the white man's story of Adam and Eve?"

"You know our story of the world's beginning?"

He nodded, reaching out to stroke her hair. "The only people who were kind to my mother and me when we lived among the whites was an old minister and his wife. He told me the Cheyenne believe that all the world was water and a great duck swam to the bottom and brought mud up in his bill over and over until land was formed."

She closed her eyes, loving the feel of his hands stroking her hair. "And the People?"

"The People lived under the ground and came up to the light. We have stories of another time when the Cheyenne lived far from here, had no horses and grew corn."

"Grew corn?"

"We lost the corn and could grow it no more. It is part of our legends like that of Ehyophstah."

"Who is that?" She brushed her fingertips across the dark rosette of his nipple.

"The Yellow-haired Woman Who Brought the Buffalo to

our People. When my father first saw Texanna, he had never seen a woman with light hair and pale skin. He thought she was the magic woman of the legends and, entranced, he stole her from the wagon train." Iron Knife caught her small hand with his big one, looked into her eyes intently.

She thought how big and callused his hand was, covering her small one. "The People cannot live without the buffalo, can they?"

He shook his head. "When the time comes that we lose the buffalo," he answered, his eyes growing more smoldering, "we lose everything, our freedom, our way of life." His free hand stroked gently along her rib cage as the rain poured down outside. "I would like to make love to you, Summer, but you are too hurt, too exhausted—"

"Try me," she smirked impishly, reaching up to pull his face down to hers.

"Lay still and let me amuse you, then," he whispered and she lay back with a sigh. She shook her damp hair so it spread out like a pale halo around her and closed her eyes.

She felt him move to her feet. "I'm going to kiss every inch of you," he whispered and she felt him pick up one of her small feet in his two big hands. His lips were light as butterfly wings against the sole of her foot as he kissed it, moved slowly up her swollen ankle, her leg.

Now she felt his warm, moist lips leaving a velvet touch on her thigh and she started to protest. "Not there, you surely aren't going to kiss me there!"

"I said every inch of you," he murmured and she felt his breath warm on her inner thigh, gasped in surprise at the eager way her body responded to the touch of his lips.

His fingers followed his lips, gently spreading her legs apart, stroking, caressing.

She protested at the idea. "You shouldn't . . . really shouldn't . . ."

But his fingers stroked in a manner that excited her in a way she had never felt and she couldn't bring herself to try to make

113

him stop.

As if she could, she thought, half-opening her eyes to study the lithe, bronze naked body of the man who touched her. She was a small plaything in his big arms. No, she was queen and he was a slave, commanded to amuse and satisfy her on threat of death.

The fire crackled and the rain beat down outside, but they were safe in their own little world of love.

She felt his fingers stroking her silken insides and she knew she should make him stop but she found her body responding to his light touch. Her thighs spread themselves, her body arching up for the caress of his hand.

Her nipples hardened with desire and his free hand came up to stroke her full breasts as his other hand touched deeper and deeper.

It was a world of touch sensation, she thought with a sigh as she breathed deeper, her body tightening with tension as his hands and mouth loved her. His lips were everywhere as he had promised, sucking, kissing, caressing.

His lips were on her ear. "Now, you stroke me, Summer, caress me as I have loved you."

She felt her face burn at the thought but she did as she was commanded, running her hands over his hard lean body, across his flat belly.

He caught her hand, moved it to his chest. "You know where I want you to touch me," he murmured.

His nipples grew hard under her fingertips as she touched, bent her mouth to kiss them.

She heard the sudden intake of his breath, felt the tension of his big body. His hand caught hers again, bringing it down between his legs. "Touch me, Summer," he commanded. "Make me want you more."

Her hand held his manhood. It was hard and throbbing in her grasp as she stroked him rhythmically. His fingers went deep inside her, stroking her velvet wetness. His mouth nibbled her breasts and she arched herself, urging him to nip her swollen nipples with his teeth.

She was caught up in a frenzy of desire, wanting him to take her breasts deep in his mouth, suck them and delight them with his tongue. Summer felt the virile seed of the man seeping on her hand as he slowly spread her thighs.

She looked up at him with half-closed eyes, gasping with her need as she reached up to him.

"I love you," he whispered as he came to her and took her in his arms.

She accepted him deep within herself and moaned aloud as she felt him hard and throbbing with life at the very core of her being.

He made love to her very gently, his hands stroking her long hair, his lips soft on her face, her eyelids.

She reached up to embrace his strong body, feeling the muscles bunch under her feathery touch. The power and the size of the man still astounded her and the wonder of it was the way he responded to her desires, eager to please her.

She whimpered and tensed and his breath brushed her ear. "Not yet!" he commanded. "Not yet, Little One! Make it last and last . . ."

She tried to obey him but could not. Her body had a mind of its own, trembling with desire and eagerness. She fought to hold back as he commanded, but every nerve fiber seemed to be on fire, her senses reacting to his touch, his taste, the man smell of him.

She opened her lips, taking his tongue deep in her mouth as her body took his manhood, relishing the warm, moist invasion of him, the total domination of his maleness. She was swept by a frenzy of desire, her small hands running up and down his naked body, fighting to keep from clawing him, pulled him even deeper. She could feel him throbbing in the very core of her, pulsating and swelling with the life he was surging to place within.

She was not going to be able to wait for him, she thought with regret, feeling the trembling beginning deep in the very soul of her being. The trembling became strong convulsions of desire and her small hands gripped his hard hips as her body gripped his maleness. She kissed his lips and felt his hands covering, squeezing her breasts as he drove hard and deep into her.

"I—I can't stop," she whispered as she surrendered to the tidal wave of pleasure that was sweeping her along on its crest.

"Don't stop. Come with me," he gasped. Then she felt his body hesitate, shudder deep inside her. For a split second, she was aware of the way her eager body seized his, eager for the seed he was placing deep where she wanted it, needed it.

The tidal wave swept her along helplessly. She couldn't stop it, didn't want to stop it. The intensity of the feeling swept her under and she was gasping like a drowning victim, holding on to the man in her arms.

"It's all right, Summer," he whispered. "Let it take you . . ."

And she relaxed and gave way to the urges of her body, floating on the tidal wave as it crashed against the shores of her consciousness. They seemed caught in time as he gave up his lifeseed and she accepted it willingly, hungrily.

It was a sensation she didn't want to give up, the passion of the crashing waves, but slowly it was receding, leaving her flung on a distant beach. She wondered for a moment where she was. Her eyes flickered open and she realized he held her against his heart very tightly. She could feel her breast pressing against his beating heart, her own rhythmic pulse. She heard his gentle breathing, felt the fine dew of perspiration on his bronze skin.

She looked into his eyes. Only moments before, they had been burning and intense. Now they were soft pools, reflecting her own image back at her because of the flickering fire against the twilight outside.

She smiled and reached up to touch his cheek. "I see me in your eyes," she murmured.

"Do you see me also in your heart?" he asked earnestly as if suddenly aware that it might be too good to last. His big hand

116

cupped her small face ever so gently as if he were afraid she was a ghost that would disappear if he loved her too deeply.

"You know I do." She said, smiling, reaching her arms up around his neck, remembering how he had refused to leave her behind in the forest, even to save his own life. He still lay within her and she didn't want him to move.

He frowned slightly. "You say it so easily," he said, "and yet I'm afraid you will never be quite mine, never all mine as I want you to be." His hand touched her face. "You *mistai*, you magic thing, who are you?"

Her face wrinkled in puzzlement. "I don't understand what you mean. I am Summer Priscilla Van Schuyler; you know that."

"If the day ever comes that you are really mine completely," he murmured, "you will give me a different answer."

His words troubled her because she did not understand what he meant. But she did not want to think about the future as she snuggled into his embrace. "Let's talk no more of this." She kissed the edge of his mouth. "We have each other and this moment and that is enough for me."

He held her as if he would never let her go. "If it is enough for you, it will have to be enough for me, too," he answered. "But I want more, probably more than you are willing to give, maybe more than you are able to give."

"I don't understand . . ." Her voice trailed off sleepily as she stared with drooping eyelids into the campfire while the rain poured down outside their snug lair. There seemed to be no one else in the universe except the two of them and she had never felt so safe and secure.

He moved from within her, cuddled her close against his chest with her head on his arm. As she drifted off to sleep, she felt his heart beating against her bare breast, his lips brushing her face. The last thing she remembered was the steady sound of rain outside as she slept locked in his arms.

*   *   *

117

When her eyes flickered open, she could see dawn in the east with its pale lavender and rosy hues. She sat up abruptly; realized she was alone.

Frightened and suddenly vulnerable, she crossed her hands over her nakedness, her long hair draped down to cover her full breasts. Had he abandoned her? What would she do? How would she survive? Summer looked down at her ankle, still slightly swollen, but much better. Still, it would be tender to walk on. But where would she walk to? She had no idea where she was in the wilderness.

The small fire barely burned, its ashes pale pink and gray in the morning light. The rain had ceased.

She craned her head, looking for the rugged, bronzed face. "Iron Knife?" she called. "Where are you?"

He wouldn't have risked his life yesterday to save her and then abandoned her, common sense told her that. Still, her heart beat faster and she felt uneasy as she peered through the green trees around her, already turning gold and orange in the coming autumn.

"Iron Knife?" she called again.

She heard a sound and he came into view around a giant boulder leading the Appaloosa stallion. "Hush, Little One." He put his finger to his lips in warning. "If there were any enemies in the area, do you not think they would be drawn to the sound of a woman's voice calling out in English?"

She felt a rush of relief, got up to throw herself into his arms. "I didn't think of that. I was afraid you were gone, never coming back."

He touched the tip of her nose lightly. "Now you sound like me, Summer. Why do we both worry so about losing each other?"

"Because this much happiness can't possibly last," she answered in a rush of emotion as she hugged him to her. "Because both our civilizations frown on our love and they are bound to separate us sooner or later."

He put his arm around her shoulders and looked intently

into her eyes. "When they do that, it will be because I am dead and unable to stop them. Remember that, Summer, they will never take you from me except for that reason."

His words reassured her and she limped over to pat the horse's soft, velvet nose. "Where did you find Spotted Blanket?"

He also patted the horse. "Like I told you, he had swum across the river and was grazing not too far from here. He came running right up to me."

He went over, stoked the fire, reached up to touch her shirt still hanging on the ledge, then tossed it to her. "Can you make it by yourself to the edge of the river to wash and clean up?"

She nodded and slipped the shift over her head.

He strode over and took a plump rabbit off his saddle. "I managed to catch this in a snare made of vines and I've picked some berries and some wild black walnuts. When you come back from the river, we'll eat."

It was a great morning, she thought, shaking back her hair as she limped down to the water to wash up. Raindrops glimmered on wildflowers, each a rainbow of color as the sun touched it. Wild plants had turned lush green overnight from the rain and a doe drinking from the river looked up in startled surprise and bounded away. It all contrasted starkly with the blackened skeletons of the forest on the other side.

Yes, it was a great morning, she thought again as she splashed her face. Yesterday, she had discovered love and survived certain death. She thought how great it was to be alive as she limped back and settled herself by the small fire.

They shared the fat rabbit he roasted and ate the berries. She licked her fingers and smirked at him. "If only the Beacon Hill ladies of Boston could see me now, they'd be scandalized."

His eyes gazed tenderly at her as he leaned back on his elbows. "Because you slept naked in my arms all night?"

"That too." She giggled. "But the idea of eating with my hands and licking my fingers! Why, they couldn't imagine how much fun this can all be. All these years, I haven't been living;

119

I've been merely existing. Like most women, I've been too afraid of life to really live! I never really had any fun before."

His face was suddenly serious. "Is that all I am to you, 'fun?' I can just see you someday sitting in your fine home, entertaining your friends with the story of your escapade among the savages while they hang on your every word and thrill with the horror of it all."

She grew serious as she turned to watch the stallion munching grass contentedly. "I'm not ever going back," she said with finality, "not unless I can take you with me. I don't even want to go back to your village." She turned to look at him appealingly. "Can't we just stay out here by ourselves forever?"

He broke off a straw, trailed it down her face to her full lips. "You know we can't live out here alone. Why do you say that?"

She sighed, brushed away the straw as it tickled her skin. "Because of last night," she answered. "Because I can't get enough of you and don't want to share you with anyone."

His eyes were hot and intense as they swept over her. "You don't have to share me with anyone. As long as I feel you want me, I'll never again make love to another woman."

She looked deep into his eyes. "You'll not take a second wife as the Cheyenne do?"

"I couldn't satisfy two women if the other wanted me as you did last night."

"I want you now," she whispered and felt the flush creep up her neck and she glanced away, shame-faced.

"Take off your shift," he ordered.

"Now?" she looked at him. "But we just last night—"

"Your wanting me feeds my own desire," he answered, "and I find suddenly that I ache for you again. Take off that shift or shall I grab you and rape you as I would a captive?"

"I'm your captive, your Cheyenne captive," she answered. Summer pulled the deerskin shift slowly over her head and stood naked for his appraisal.

120

She saw his eyes darken with urgency and desire. "We both know differently, but I shall humor you," he said as his eyes studied her ripe body. "Turn slowly around, slave, and let me enjoy looking at that which gives your master so much pleasure."

She had a sudden fantasy of being a slave girl on an auction block being put up for bids. Taking a deep breath so that her firm breasts jutted out, she pivoted slowly, favoring her sore ankle.

He leaned back on his elbows, frankly appraising her naked body. She could see the pulse pounding in his neck and the heightened color of his face. "Now, come here, slave girl," he commanded. "Your master wants you."

She stood looking down at him, liking the way he studied her. "Do I please you?" she asked coquettishly.

"You know you do." He reached up, caught her hand, and pulled her down on top of him. "You're going to be dessert after breakfast," he murmured against her lips.

"Whites don't have dessert after breakfast," she answered primly as she closed her eyes.

"I had you after supper, remember?" He nibbled the corner of her mouth. "We are going to make our own rules from now on. We will have each other any time we feel like it; we will look into each other's eyes and be unashamed to say it."

"Say what?" She sat astride his body, leaning back on her hands, blatantly teasing him with her arched breasts.

"You know what I want you to say, you small, sly vixen." His mouth bent to nuzzle her breasts. "Say it!" he commanded.

She threw her head back and gasped with pleasure, her long hair trailing across his legs. "I—I desire you, master. Your Cheyenne captive wants your body ever so much!"

His hands were on her thighs now and she could feel his manhood rising hard against her velvet softness.

His big hands grasped her small waist, pulling her toward him. "Lock your legs around my waist," he whispered.

He must have seen the surprise in her eyes, the sudden flush

121

of her face at the idea. "I can take you deeper this way," he commanded. "And that's what you want, to be taken even deeper than before."

"Oh, yes!" she sighed, moving so that he entered her as her legs went around his waist. His arms went around her body, stroking her back as his mouth opened, encouraged her to put her small pink tongue within as he sucked gently. Her arms went around him, touching the whip scars on his back as she pressed against him, rubbing her breasts against his chest. She loved the hard friction of his chest against her sensitive nipples.

Her tongue was deep between his lips, wanting to go deeper as he plunged into her.

His hands were beneath her naked bottom, stroking, caressing, pinching.

And then her need was so great she could think of nothing else but plunging her tongue deep in his sucking mouth, grinding her body down on the pulsating dagger that impaled her womanhood. A great, shuddering spasm swept over her thoughts, her emotions, her mind. Her body was in charge, unashamedly answering its own primitive needs as any female in a savage wilderness.

Her body exploded in spasms of fulfillment and they clung to each other as she felt him tense and release within her. Time stood suspended.

When it was finally over, she clung to him, sobbing softly. "I—I don't know why I'm crying," she sobbed. "I—I don't know why."

He held her so tightly she almost couldn't breathe as he kissed her tears away. "Many women have wept in my arms," he admitted. "It is a sign of complete surrender."

She was abruptly jealous at the images that came to her mind and she jerked away from him and stood up. "You reduce me to a begging, weeping female, like a mare of your large herd, rubbing herself against a stallion."

He stood up, pulled her against him roughly. "I said there would be no others for me anymore as long as you want me to be your man. This stallion is here to service you any time you want him."

"I—I feel ashamed to admit my body needs you." She tried to pull away but his arms held her tightly against him as his lips brushed hers.

"You're my woman, Summer. I want you to desire me with nothing held back. I want to see your hunger for me in your eyes, have you come to me desiring my body while throwing all your inhibitions away. This is a once in a lifetime passion for us both!"

"I love you so much," she whispered, kissing him again. "I want this to last forever. . . ."

"It will last as long as both of us love each other equally." He kissed her mouth and sighed. "And now, Little One, we really must go back. Everyone will wonder where we are since they surely saw the smoke of the forest fire. My uncle's family will worry that I am hurt or dead."

As she dressed, he kicked dirt over the small fire, made ready to leave. He mounted the big stallion and pulled her up to ride behind him.

She put her arms around his slim waist and felt his lean hips against the vee of her thighs as she sat close to him. She leaned against his naked back, rubbing her breasts against him as they started off.

Iron Knife chuckled. "Don't do that," he chided. "We really must get back to the village."

They rode back along the path through the woods that she had taken yesterday. Summer pressed her face against his broad back, liking the male smell and warmth of his brown flesh.

Yesterday, I was a naive, silly girl, she thought. *Today, I am a woman. I have been taken by a stallion of a man who loves me as passionately as I love him. My man will mate me until I am heavy with the son he desires and then give me another, and another . . .*

They rode the rest of the way in silence, but Summer sensed

123

something was wrong as they finally arrived in camp late in the afternoon and dismounted in front of the tepee. Pony Woman scurried up to them and Summer felt the old aunt's sharp eyes take in everything—the torn clothes, the wounds of yesterday.

Pony Woman gave the familiar Indian greeting, *"Hou!"* and then launched into a flood of hurried Cheyenne.

Summer watched Iron Knife frown at the woman's words and he asked several questions in the Indian tongue before turning to her.

"There is yet more trouble," he said to Summer. "Some think the old chiefs have gone too far. Those who have been whipped and some of the other young hotheads who itch to fight the whites are making plans to ride out of the camp tomorrow morning."

He gestured toward the lodge. "Wait for me. I must discuss this with my uncle and the others. They hope to dissuade the angry ones so they will not leave."

"Don't you want to put on a shirt first?" Summer asked in English, knowing the old woman's eyes saw what Summer wore, saw the scratches and wounds on Iron Knife's bare chest.

Without a word, he went inside and came out wearing fringed buckskin, hiding all the marks and bruises except for the cut over his eye.

She reached up to touch the cut and spoke again in English. "You were hunting deer yesterday with the others, remember? I think you fell during your hunt and cut your face."

His eyes caressed her and the look told her more than words ever could. "I think you are right," he said, gesturing. "Now, wait inside for me."

She nodded and limped into the lodge as he left in long strides, his fat little aunt running to keep up with him.

It was more than an hour before he returned, and in the meantime she had built a fire in the fire pit and roasted a haunch of deer he had hung up from yesterday's hunt.

Summer shared it with him when he returned, his face dark

and angry as storm clouds. She remembered now what Angry Wolf had said to her about the Dog Soldiers leaving and thought she had forgotten to tell Iron Knife about it. It hadn't seemed important at the time. Now, judging from his angry face, it must be very important.

After they finished eating, she gathered up the scraps to toss to the many rangy dogs that hung around the encampment.

"Is the news so bad?" she asked finally.

"It is much as I feared," he sighed, settling himself to gaze into the fire. "The peace-talkers can do nothing with them. Some young braves have been waiting for just such an excuse as this to ride out. Not all the Dog Soldiers are going, but those who do take some of the others from many warrior societies."

Summer frowned. "Where will they go?"

"They will join up with the old renegade band that roams, claiming no allegiance to either the north or the south bands of Cheyenne. This group goes back twenty years to the time when Porcupine Bear was banished for murdering Little Creek and took his outlaw Dog Soldiers with him into exile."

She paused, thinking how close to banishment they were themselves. "Does it really matter if they go?"

"Of course it matters," he answered irritably. "Our great people as a group are growing weaker all the time. It is enough that we are already split into two groups, following the great north and south herds of buffalo without the renegade Dog Soldiers forming their own militant band."

She watched his high cheekbones in the firelight, willing herself not to reach out and caress his face, knowing this was not the time for it. "Do the outlaw Dog Soldiers cause much trouble for the tribes?"

He nodded, staring into the fire, "They will not abide by the treaties or listen to the council of the old chiefs. They think they are a law unto themselves so they do as they please, attack wagon trains, raid the white farms and settlements. Then the stupid bluecoats, not knowing one Indian from another, retaliate against the peaceful groups."

"Can you not explain to the soldier colonels about the renegades and that the chiefs cannot control them?"

"The soldiers want to kill Indians. The great White Father in Washington orders them to kill Indians whenever there is a raid. We cannot get them to listen when we try to explain. Sometimes, we fight even if we do not want to."

A thought came to her with sudden clarity. "You yourself have fought the soldiers even though you speak peace?"

He nodded slowly, his mind seemingly far away. "Two years ago, the outlaw Hotamitaniu were raiding up and down the Smoky Hill, the Republican, and the Platte rivers. The whites sent a bluecoat chief they call 'Bull o' the Woods' to hunt them down."

"That's Colonel Sumner of the first Cavalry." Summer brightened. "I met him at a political dinner my father gave several years ago."

He did not seem to hear her as he sat lost in the memory. "It was the very hot month, *Hiriutsiishi*, the Time of the Rutting Buffalo, last year that the troops finally stumbled on this band. We were camped on Solomon's Fork, hunting buffalo, when our scouts brought word that the soldiers were coming. We knew nothing of the Dog Soldier raids, but we knew mounted cavalry meant trouble for any Indian in the area."

She watched his mouth tighten. "Why did the Cheyenne not flee the place?"

"Many of us argued for it; we did not want trouble with the soldiers. We only want to live and hunt in peace. But some of the younger men care nothing for Crooked Hand Fitzpatrick's treaty; they called us frightened women."

He paused, remembering. "Two medicine men, Gray Beard and White Bull, said they had a strong magic that would make the whites' bullets useless against us. Our men grew excited about this magic of having bullets strike harmless against our bodies. We were also very tired of always running, always being blamed for something we did not do!"

Summer frowned. "Surely with your background among the

126

whites, you must have realized that this was superstitious nonsense. There is no magic that protects against bullets."

He raised his scarred face slowly and looked at her. "No, I did not believe it at first. But how could I ride away and leave my friends to fight alone? One who owns the *Hotamtsit*, the Dog Rope, is expected to die in battle."

Summer's eyes turned toward the long strip of buffalo hide, scarcely as wide as a man's hand that hung from a lodge pole. It was ten or twelve feet long and ornamented with feathers and porcupine quills done in bright red and yellow native dyes. A sharp, red-painted stake hung from one end. What was it Gray Dove had said? *The bravest of the brave . . . only four Dog Soldiers in the society wore this badge of honor.*

She prompted. "And then?"

"It was very hot," he recalled softly. "The sun reflected off the soldiers' buttons and spears of the *nutqui*, our warriors. There were hundreds of them, less of us, strung out in two opposing lines. I remember the salty taste in my mouth and, most of all, the sudden stillness just before the attack. Then the stillness was broken by the cries of a wheeling hawk, our young men singing their war songs, and the jingle of the bluecoats' spurs."

He took the big knife from his belt, turned it over and over in his hands, and she knew he was remembering something that must have happened to him personally. . . .

She started to reach out to him, to take him out of the memory, and then hesitated as he continued.

"Even *I* began to believe in the medicine men." He laughed bitterly. "My Indian half is often at odds with my white half. We charged toward the soldiers, confident that their bullets would do us no harm. But a smart officer had heard of our medicine. One of them yelled an order and they drew sabers instead and charged us. The iron knives were like mirrors reflecting the sun.

He looked ruefully down at the weapon in his hands. "Our leaders had warned us the magic medicine was no good against anything but bullets. There was fierce fighting and some killed on both sides." His hand went up to touch the cavalry button earring. "I counted coup that day several times and was given a new name. Before that day, I had been called Falling Star because I was born on the Night The Stars Fell."

"The famous meteor shower in the autumn of 1833!" she exclaimed with excitement. "And I read of the cavalry charge last year!" Summer remembered the incident then. It had been only a small item in the back of the Boston papers. *"Biggest Charge With Drawn Sabers in the History of the Cavalry,"* she recalled the headline.

The man shuddered. "Yes, we fought because we had to, but it was not a good day. Finally, we fled like frightened children. Our medicine was bad and there were too many of the soldiers. But some did not live to see the sun set." He stuck the knife back in his belt with finality.

Summer reached out to touch his arm, then stood up. "I know you are not a coward, not a frightened child. You are one of the bravest of the brave. Tell me of the Dog Soldiers."

He stood and took her in his arms. "We help with the ceremony of the Sacred Arrows, and in the northern band with the Sacred Buffalo Hat. We also help when moving the camp."

His arms tightened around her and she felt the tension of him, knew he was holding back something, did not intend to tell her of the dog rope.

She prompted. "Is there not more?"

He kissed her forehead, not looking into her eyes. "Why worry yourself about that?"

She pressed her face against the buckskin of his hard, scarred chest, reveling in the warmth and male scent of him. "Tell me the main duty of a Dog Soldier," she persisted.

She felt him hesitate, his lips brushing her hair before he spoke. "I suppose you will have to know sooner or later. Since so many are leaving, the duty will fall heavily on those who stay. We are the ones who follow the column when the band is on the move. In case of attack, we provide the rear guard action."

"Which means?" Her heart sank at what she suddenly knew. *The bravest of the brave . . .*

"Which means, if the band is being pursued by enemies, the Dog Soldiers must hold their ground, try to delay the enemy while the rest of the tribe escapes."

She felt the tears come and she turned away so he wouldn't see them on her cheeks, but she couldn't stop her voice from shaking. "In other words, you are a 'suicide' society!"

She would not ask about the brightly decorated band. Somehow, she knew it belonged to this terrible ritual of holding their battle line at all costs.

He came up behind her, put his hands gently on her shoulders. "I do not know this white word, 'suicide.' But if it means will the Dog Soldier sacrifice himself in a delaying action to protect the retreat of the old ones, of his women and children, the answer is 'yes'!"

She drew in her breath sharply and he raised her hair, kissed the back of her neck. "What happens to the clan and the whole tribe is important, what happens to the individual warrior is not if he dies bravely. Our women will wail and cut themselves for him and stories will be told of his exploits around the campfires for many generations. Thus it is, thus it has always been."

She could not bring herself to answer and he kissed the back of her neck again. "I expect nothing more, Little One, except that I might find a woman who would love me as I love her the few short years I live. I have never hoped that I would live to enjoy the luxury of warming my old bones by my grandsons' campfire."

She whirled in his arms, turned her tear-stained face up to him. "Don't say that! We will both live to be very, very old together."

He shook his head regretfully and bent to kiss her quivering

129

lips. "Can you not see the whites are closing in on us from all sides? They are the ones who will end our history, not our old enemies, the Pawnee and the Crow. Although I do my best to keep my people on the peace road, I know it cannot last; the whites will not let it."

He wiped a tear from her face with a gentle finger. "I already know, Summer, that I will not live to be an old man, any more than my father did. I have done the ceremony of the badger and I believe I saw my fate. But if I can only be granted a few more years by Heammawihio, the Great God Above, I shall die happy if I can spend those few years with you in my arms!"

"No!" she protested, kissing him, blocking out the words she didn't want to hear. She had waited all her life for this man and she would not give him up easily. Tomorrow might bring all sorts of turmoil and hardship, but tonight, this long, chill night, he was hers alone.

Her fervent kiss seemed to flame him as a prairie fire takes dry buffalo grass. He moaned as his hands pawed at the long shirt that she still wore, pushing it up so his hot hands could cup her hips.

She felt his manhood rising against her belly as his mouth forced itself inside hers.

Her hands clasped his neck, pulling his face down to hers. Her soul cried out for him to enter her again as he had done the moment he had first awakened her to ecstasy on the hot sand of the riverbank and again by a small campfire in a hidden lair.

Everything else could wait for the troubled dawn, but now all that mattered was the way he lifted her easily and carried her to the soft buffalo robes; the way the firelight flickered on his face in the darkness.

"Summer, my little love . . ."

"My dearest, take me now . . . please take me . . ."

And the prairie fire roared through both of them, wild and untamed and uncontrolled.

Chapter Eight

He made love to her all night. Finally, as the fire became only glowing ashes, they were both sated. He dropped off to sleep in her embrace, not waking until nearly dawn. The renegade Dog Soldiers rode out a little past daybreak. Outside his tepee, Iron Knife put his arm protectively around Summer's shoulders and frowned as he watched the sullen group riding through the camp. It wasn't a big group, he realized as he counted the men, a half-dozen Dog Soldiers who had accompanied Angry Wolf on the ill-fated stagecoach raid. But unfortunately, one of those was an important brave, Black Badger, an owner of the *Hotamsit*, the Dog Rope.

Squeezing Summer's hand, he watched the ponies dragging the travois through the mud in the early morning chill. He had not told Summer of the responsibilities of the owner of the Dog Rope, but she had guessed part of it. This was one of the reasons he did not expect to live to be an old man. He and his *nahnih*, Lance Bearer, had often discussed its burdens. The fourth rope had been in the possession of another man who had died only a few days ago of an old wound and no one had yet taken that *Hotamtsit*.

Summer interrupted his troubled thoughts with a question. "Are they all Dog Soldiers?"

"No, that one carrying the crooked lance is a Himoweyuhkis, an Elk-horn Scraper. Those two with their matched scarlet shields are Mahohewas, Red Shields."

In all, he counted silently, there were probably not more than a dozen warriors and their families leaving with their big dogs and their ponies dragging travois. But the Tsistsistas needed every warrior should they have to go into a major battle.

Then they were gone, disappearing through the golden and green trees in the early autumn mist. Their women with their cradleboards on their backs walked behind the loaded travois, the young children running alongside the horses, shouting in excitement as the dogs barked.

He noted someone had packed up Angry Wolf's things and taken them along, no doubt expecting the missing warrior would join them later on the Republican or the Smoky Hill rivers where the outlaw Dog Soldiers camped.

He said nothing as the group faded from view and he and Summer reentered their tepee.

"You were thinking of Angry Wolf, weren't you?" she asked.

"No," he lied, "I was only thinking how heavy the responsibility must be on the old chiefs this morning. We cannot afford to lose a dozen good men; our enemies are too many!"

She took his hand. "When you are chief, you will know just what to do and your people will prosper because of it."

He smiled thinly at her. He would not tell her he could never be a chief now. He had broken a terrible tabu of his people and it would bring bad medicine to them and disaster to himself if he dared to accept the post.

So he only shook his head and sat down before the fire pit. "I do not think I want to be chief," he sighed. "There is much responsibility and it is a thankless job."

"You can't mean that!" she declared. "It is a great honor, and since you understand the white world, you could help your people in the future."

"Maybe I was too long in the white man's world to think like an Indian." He looked up at her. "A chief of the Cheyenne is supposed to think of nothing but his people. He is required to put away all his jealousies and hatreds and put the welfare of the tribe ahead of his own personal feelings and emotions."

"Which means?"

"Which means, Little One, that like the owner of a scalp shirt, a chief must not involve himself in fights or arguments in the camp, show any jealousy, or take revenge even if some brave should steal his woman."

Her mouth dropped open. "You mean, if some other warrior desire me and stole me away, you couldn't do anything about it?"

He smiled as he stood up, taking her in his arms, reveling in the clean smell of her hair. "No, I would have to let him keep you and not even accept gifts from him for the offense as another man might. To fight over the possession of a woman is supposed to be beneath the dignity of a chief. They say if a dog dares lift his leg on a chief's tepee, he must pretend not to see as he ignores anything that stands between him and his duty."

She looked up into his eyes and he was hypnotized as always by their pale blue depths. "You would let another man take me without protest?"

Automatically, his hand went to the big knife in his belt. "I would gut him like a buffalo for even looking at you," he warned, pulling her against him. "Jealousy is not an Indian emotion, but a white one. As I have said, my Indian half is often at war with my white blood."

Her lips brushed the underside of his chin. "Do you really care so much for me?"

"You know I do," he said softly. "And I humiliate myself by telling you how much I care. Do not ever take advantage of me, Summer Sky, and make me regret loving you as I never before loved a woman." He knew his eyes flashed a warning. "You hold my *tasoom*, my soul, like a small, trembling bird in your hand. Do not crush it with thoughtlessness or faithlessness,

Little One, for you alone can hurt me as no Pawnee or bluecoat soldier ever could!"

"I will never, never hurt you, dear," she promised as she stood on tiptoe to kiss him.

"I should marry you in the manner of my people," he whispered against her lips. "If I tied many ponies in front of your father's lodge, would that rich chief accept them?"

Summer laughed. "I can just imagine what Silas Van Schuyler would say if Evans, the butler, reported there were ponies and blankets on the doorstep."

Roughly he pushed her away. "You laugh at my expense, thinking me an ignorant savage!"

"No, dear." She caught his arm. "I'm not laughing at you. It's just that the whites do things differently, in case you've forgotten. I would marry you in the Cheyenne manner, but also I would like to be married in the white man's way."

He studied her intently, wishing he could believe she cared for him as much as he did for her. "You would marry me in the church if you could? You would say you wish to be my woman in front of all the whites?"

"Yes." She nodded. "If it were possible, I would stand in front of all the whites in their legal ceremony and tell everyone how proud I am to be your woman."

"But you are already my woman," he reminded her as he took her in his arms and kissed the soft hollow of her throat. "We cannot go to the white town and do as you want. The men would take you away as they did my mother and if you protested, they would say you had gone insane and threaten you with the asylum as they threatened her."

The years among the whites came back to him in a painful rush and the scars on his back seemed to burn again as they had that night when the saloon girl was killed and he remembered how dangerous it was to trust any white.

"I know I am already yours," she said patiently, "but I would still like the white man's words said over us."

"No!" He dismissed the idea with a shake of his head. "My

father took Texanna in an Indian ceremony. They never had the white man's words said over them, but no two people ever loved each other so much—"

"Until now." She interrupted, kissing the underside of his jaw.

"Until now," he agreed, crushing her against his chest, vowing silently never to let her go.

Later that day he took her around the camp, introducing her to people, trying to teach her a little language. Pony Woman volunteered to help her learn the intricate bead and porcupine quill work the Cheyenne were well known for and he left her in the care of his aunt for a while.

Even his *nehyo*, Clouds Above, nodded approvingly as they met in Iron Knife's tepee later to share a pipe.

"It is good you finally take a woman, my nephew." He nodded. "But I wish you had chosen one of our own maidens. You have taken so long in choosing, half the girls in camp were turning down marriage ponies, hoping you might be thinking of making an offer to their fathers."

Iron Knife stared into the fire. "Perhaps I am too much like War Bonnet and only light hair and eyes like blue mountain pools can set my heart on fire."

He felt the old man's eyes on him. "Yes, you are much like my older brother," he admitted as he smoked. "He looked like you but his skin was much darker. The white Texas girl's blood flows also in your veins. She brought War Bonnet much heartache, you know."

"She also brought him love like he had never known," Iron Knife gently reminded the old man.

"Perhaps," the old man admitted as his nephew blew smoke toward the sky. "But I am afraid you are going to find dealing with the white man's world more difficult than merely sleeping with one of their women. They rape ours constantly but they are furious if we touch one of theirs! I warned my brother to amuse himself with the white girl a little while but not to let her take his heart. I told him to take a Cheyenne wife, but he

135

wouldn't listen."

"My mother would never have left him if the Texas Rangers hadn't carried us off while War Bonnet and the rest of you were away from the camp. She was big with child so she couldn't run and I was no help in defending her. Several times she tried to run away and come back to my father until the whites threatened to lock her away and put me and the baby sister in an orphanage."

His uncle looked at him in curiosity. "What does that word mean?"

Iron Knife shrugged. "I know only that it was such a terrible place that Texanna stopped trying to run away. She said it was a bad place where children go who have no parents or anyone to care for them." He wondered again what had ever happened to the baby sister. He and his mother had left the sick child behind with their only friends, the man of God, the night the pair fled Fandango forever.

Clouds Above made a noise of surprise. "Why do they need this 'orphanage' place? Do not the whites take a second or third wife when a warrior is killed so that a woman and her children do not go hungry?"

"No, I know it seems strange, but they think it wrong to take more than one wife at a time."

"No wonder then they must build a place to put these homeless children." His uncle snorted and passed him the pipe. "Although your father never took a second wife, even though he must have known she was gone forever, he only lived alone and grieved for her. I have never seen a man so under the magic spell of a female as he was about that girl he called the Golden One, or any man so happy as when he finally found out where she was and led the raiding party to bring you both out."

"And I know, at last, how he felt," Iron Knife admitted softly as he smoked. "I will never take another wife, either. I want none but Summer Sky."

The old warrior shook his head. "We are a warrior nation.

So often a man falls in battle and there is some wailing female who must be taken as wife by some brave."

"That is true," Iron Knife said thoughtfully, "and I suppose we could never explain to the whites our habit of the second and third wife often being sisters of the first."

Clouds Above seemed to study him keenly. "Does your woman have a younger sister for you to take as second wife?"

He shrugged. "I think she has mentioned one, a very young child. But it does not matter. I will marry only this one."

He watched the pungent smoke drift in the dim light of the tepee, wondering when Summer would return from her lessons with Pony Woman. He grew increasingly impatient with his uncle and sometimes the Indian ways. The old man had not merely come to smoke, he knew. There was some business on his mind but it was not polite to rush right to the point as the white man did. He wondered if this were the reason the whites sometimes called the Indians "lazy," because they were well mannered enough to take the time for first the food, then the smoking and the long conversations before finally coming to the point. He wondered when his uncle would finally get around to it.

"You may not think so now," his uncle suggested, "but when this wife has a baby at her breast, you will need another wife, for you will not dare mount her for fear of getting her again with child. If that happens, her milk will not flow, starving the child she already has. That is another reason our men take a second wife."

"I will face that when the time comes. I want no other woman." He tried not to sound too short, wondering why the old man had come. He couldn't be representing some hopeful girl, for it was always a respected member of the groom's family who called on the girl's relatives. Maybe he was only making polite conversation until he was ready to bring up whatever it was he had on his mind.

He took another puff of the pipe and passed it over. "You only took two wives," he reminded his uncle gently, "and

137

these last few years, you have had only one."

Clouds Above accepted the pipe and drew deeply. "When Pony Woman's older sister was taken by the white's cholera, I decided one wife was plenty for me. And anyway," he conceded, "I am an old man now and my blood doesn't run as hot as it once did. If you insist on keeping this white girl, you should quickly get her with child so you may have sons to bring meat to your lodge when you are too old to hunt anymore."

Would the old man never get to the point? "My woman is eager to produce fine, strong sons for me," he said in the soft, muscial Cheyenne tongue.

"Just make sure they are *your* sons!" his uncle admonished. "The white women have very loose morals and do not wear the *nihpihist* to assure their purity. She might already be carrying the seed of some white man."

He very nearly lost his temper. "My woman is chaste!" he defended her hotly. "When first I took her, there was a scarlet stain. I would wager my life she would allow no man but me between her thighs!"

Clouds Above frowned and passed the pipe back. "I think you care for this woman too much," he grumbled. "More even than you care for your own people. Do not let this small female blind you to your duty."

"I am afraid it is already too late, my uncle," he admitted as he smoked. "She has taken complete control of my heart and mind, pushing everything else out. Nothing matters to me anymore like this slight, yellow-haired one."

The old chief snorted in derision. "I thought you had greatness in you but I see you suffer the same weakness as your father! What difference would it make anyway if you took a brown wife and used this small one for a second if you must keep her? When you are old, you will realize that there is not much difference between women after all. It is good to have one like it is good to have a pony or a fine lance; any of them can warm a man's robes at night and produce sons for him. A chief's first duty is to his people."

So here it was, finally.

"You are thinking of giving up your chief's position, Uncle?"

"I am growing old and weary of the responsibility. Great trials lie ahead of us, I feel it in my bones. I thought to offer your name to the Council to replace me instead of my son, Lance Bearer."

"My cousin would make a fine chief."

"True," the old man nodded. "And someday I know he will step into that place. But right now, he is younger than you and lacks your judgment and reputation as a warrior. The men would not follow him as readily as they would you."

All his life, he had waited for this moment to have his name offered as chief, to follow in his father's footsteps. But it would be bad medicine for the tribe for him to accept after being involved in a killing.

"I—I cannot," he said.

"Nonsense! You cannot think that much of this white woman. Take a Cheyenne wife and you will easily be accepted as chief and our people need you."

"My father had a white wife," he reminded his uncle.

"Your father was already a great chief before he ever took Texanna. He had led many successful raiding parties as he was doing that time down in Texas against the Comanche when he stole her from a wagon train. You have not proven yourself to that extent and some might grumble at accepting a chief with a white wife."

"There are many reasons I cannot accept the chief's place," Iron Knife said regretfully, knowing he dare not tell. His uncle, being the great chief he was, would have to put the Cheyenne tabus ahead of family ties. He would have to let the old man think what he would. "Uncle, I cannot give up this white girl. Perhaps I haven't got the makings of a chief, for I do not think I could put my duty ahead of her welfare if I had to choose between the two."

Clouds Above's eyes widened in disbelief. "You turn down

139

the chance over a mere woman?"

He had wanted it so long because he knew he could help the People; but now, it could never be.

"Tell the Chief's Council that I am honored but I will not accept. When all the bands gather next summer for the Medicine Lodge sun dance, I hope to see Lance Bearer has accepted this honor."

The other sighed and smoked a long time. Neither of them said anything and Iron Knife wished he could confide in his uncle. But Clouds Above put his people first, always, and he would feel duty bound to send his own nephew into exile.

Finally the old man stood. "It will be as you wish, my nephew. Only you know why you feel called upon to turn this down."

He looked at Iron Knife sadly. Iron Knife's heart went out to his uncle as he noticed for the first time how gray the old man's hair had become under the hammered silver coin hair decorations and otter fur bands that bound his braids. The bear claws from the fierce animal he had killed in his younger days glistened around his neck as he pulled the Pendleton blanket around his stooped shoulders. He handed the pipe to Iron Knife and started out of the tepee, then turned and came back. "I almost forgot I had another reason for coming."

"Yes?"

"My younger son, Two Arrows, wants to marry Pretty Flower Woman."

Iron Knife smiled. "This I have been expecting for over a year. You wish me to take the gifts to the girl's family?"

The chief nodded. "They will be much impressed if a well known Dog Soldier such as you represents his cousin."

"Two Arrows is fast becoming a great warrior in his own right like his father."

Clouds Above said modestly, "Your praise is too great and we are undeserving."

"It is good that a great chief is modest about his many coups, but I am honored to be asked by you to perform this service."

140

He clapped his uncle on the back. "I was wondering if that pair would marry before we left for our winter camp in the Big Timbers."

"My son is tired of sleeping alone and it will be cold this winter in the mountain country." The old man smiled in spite of himself. "We are prepared to give ten of our very best ponies, three fine blankets, two iron pots, a mirror, and a large pile of beads from the traders' store."

Iron Knife nodded, impressed. "That is a fine bride gift! I know her father, Fierce Bear, will be honored to merge the two families. I will come for the gifts as soon as I am dressed in my best."

Clouds Above paused in the doorway. "I will tell Two Arrows."

He was gone then, leaving Iron Knife holding the ceremonial pipe. The stone for the pipe came from only one small area in Minnesota traditionally owned by the Sioux who traded the soft stone to the other tribes so that they might smoke. He knew the white men called the stone Catlinite after some man who painted Indian pictures. As he put the pipe away, he studied its plain design. The Sioux designs were always more elaborate.

Summer entered the tepee, interrupting his thoughts. "What was it your uncle wanted, my husband?"

"I am not your husband yet!" he teased, gathering her into his arms.

"In every way but ceremony." She looked up at him. "Did your uncle's visit concern me?"

"Of course not!" he said, looking away. He could not lie to her when he looked into those blue eyes. "It did not concern you in the least and, anyway, it is not proper for a woman to inquire into the business of men."

"You sound exactly like my father," she bristled. "He always thinks women should be seen and not heard!"

"There have been some honored women among the Cheyenne," he answered. "Some have even ridden in war

141

parties and several of the soldier societies accept them as members although the Dog Soldiers do not." He reached out for her. "But since you cannot handle a lance or bow, I think you should do what you do best, which is take care of your man and come to my blankets whenever I feel the need for you—which will be often."

He felt the pulse quicken in her throat as his lips brushed her neck and she asked. "Is that time now?"

He smiled as he gently pushed her away. "I think I have created a monster like the Mihn in the deep water of the lakes and rivers. Do you think this warrior has nothing to do but quench your fires?"

She looked up at him coquettishly. "It was you who ignited the flame!"

"I will extinguish it later." He smiled at her. "Right now, I have promised to be the go-between for a marriage for Two Arrows."

"You are helping to arrange a marriage?" Summer clapped her hands with evident glee. "When will the wedding be?"

"Probably in the next several days if her father accepts the gifts and I have no reason to think he won't. I have watched my cousin mooning over Pretty Flower Woman for many months now."

She looked puzzled. "Does every Cheyenne woman's name end in the word 'woman'?"

"Yes, but don't ask me why. It just does."

"Are they engaged?"

He shrugged. "I don't know that word. But for more than a year now, I have seen my cousin grab at her sleeve whenever she passed to get her attention. Always, he seemed to be standing outside her tepee, awaiting his turn with the other young braves to stand under the cover of her shawl and flirt with her."

Summer smiled. "Courting is much the same, isn't it, no matter the culture?"

Iron Knife laughed. "I suppose! My cousin plays the love

142

flute long and late into the night and has even paid one of the *heemaneh,* the half men-half women who are such good love talkers, to speak to her for him."

"Will there be feasting and dancing?"

"Of course! No culture seems to be able to put on a wedding without feasting and dancing. Now I must get ready to go and you should be practicing what Pony Woman has taught you."

She frowned. "I sew well enough that I think I will finally be able to do the fancy bead work, but I am having a hard time with the language. So few of these people speak English and, also, some of the customs and tabus confuse me."

He took her small face in his two big hands and turned it upward by putting his thumbs under her jaw. "These are your people now, Little One, and you will have to learn their language and their customs. What is it the Black Holy book of the whites says? 'Where you go I shall go and your tepee shall be my tepee'?"

"I shall try harder," she promised, turning her head slightly so she kissed the hand that held her face. "If your people will accept me, I will learn their talk and customs."

"They will accept you, Summer Sky, if in your heart you truly accept them. You will need the friendship of the women when we leave for the Big Timber country to winter near Bent's Fort in the territory whites call the 'Rockies.'"

A shadow seemed to cross her face. "Will we never see white people again?"

"So the regret begins so soon!" he said bitterly.

"No, it is not regret," she denied, but the doubt remained in his heart.

"There are sometimes a few whites around Bent's Fort," he answered as he released her. "I have met the one called Jim Bridger there and the Bents themselves are married to Cheyenne women. In fact, George Bent's wife is niece to the peace chief, Black Kettle."

"Do you have white friends there, too?"

"Maybe my old friend, Kit Carson, the one we call 'the Rope

143

Thrower.' He has taken a Cheyenne woman in the past and he sometimes works as a hunter to provide meat for the fort."

"When will we be leaving?"

"In a few days." He decided not to tell her more, afraid she might be plotting to run away from him. Much as he yearned to, he was afraid to trust her declaration of love, afraid she didn't really love him as he loved her and he would do anything to keep her. Even though she swore she cared for him, in the still, small hours of the night, doubts returned to haunt him that she might change her mind if given a choice.

Dressed in his finest and wearing all the trappings of a well-known warrior and wealthy man of many ponies, he tied the gray eagle coup feathers and hammered silver coins in his black hair. Iron Knife placed many strings of the antique blue pony beads around his neck from the old days of the traders and he put on numerous brass bracelets to go with the brass cavalry button earring. His soft skin shirt and moccasins were adorned with the tiny seed beads and fine quill work. The beads and quills had been obtained by trading with the white men and the northern tribes.

He gathered the gifts from his uncle and walked with great dignity across the camp, leading the ten ponies. *He must be careful to keep Summer away from the fort when they moved up to the Big Timber country*, he thought. Some trapper might question her and she might ask for help in returning to her people. He knew it was selfish of him, but he couldn't let her go. He loved her too much. And yet he wanted her happiness more than anything, which caused great conflict in his mind. Maybe someday, she would love him enough that she wouldn't want to run away. Until then, he would hold her a captive.

He felt many eyes upon him as he marched solemnly across the camp toward Fierce Bear's lodge. He knew the gossip of the marriage offer flashed like wildfire through the village. He tied the ponies before the lodge and stacked the other gifts there.

"My *nahnih*, Two Arrows, wants Pretty Flower Woman for his wife," he announced loudly before turning to leave with

144

great dignity. He could feel Pretty Flower Woman's eyes on his back and knew the family discussion would have begun before he had even turned to walk away. The offer was mostly ceremony, seldom did the Cheyenne try to force their daughters to marry men the girls did not want. In that case, the girl would sometimes elope with the man of her choice or, if thwarted, had been known to hang herself.

"But what if the ponies aren't accepted?" Summer asked later as they discussed his role in this offer.

"They will be accepted," he promised her, stroking her yellow hair. "That is why *I* delivered the ponies because my uncle thought her family would be more impressed and as the father of the groom he couldn't make the offer himself. Usually, though, the ponies are taken by some elderly person of the family but ours seems to have none left. Anyway, the marriage is a foregone conclusion. The whole camp has been watching this love bloom since sun dance season before last. My cousin has worn a path in the dirt following her when she goes to the river for water. Have you not heard his flute at night among the others as the young men serenade their sweethearts?"

She smiled. "I have heard the flutes, but I didn't realize they were being played for sweethearts."

"Do not white men do much the same? Are we such savages, then?"

Her face colored. "I suppose men in love do many of the same things, no matter their color. When will we know if Two Arrows is being accepted?"

"The ponies are tied in front of her father's lodge now. If the marriage is welcome, her family will take the horses away and put them with their own ponies. It is bad manners to let them stand more than a few hours without being accepted. In fact, that almost never happens, for a brave would not humiliate himself by offering ponies he did not think in advance would be accepted." He thought for a moment of Gray Dove. It was cruel of her not to let Angry Wolf know in advance that she was not interested in his offer and thus spare him the humiliation and laughter of the whole camp. *Because of a girl, he and the man had become enemies. Finally it had led to this killing that stopped Iron Knife from becoming chief.*

"A penny for your thoughts," she said, placing her small hand over his big one.

"What?" he asked, puzzled.

"You know, it's a white man's saying that doesn't mean anything. You seemed so far away for a moment, I wanted to bring you back to me."

"I wasn't thinking anything," he said, turning over his big hand so her small one lay in his palm. "I was thinking of the wedding."

"Will it be soon?"

"Probably tomorrow or the next day. Indians see no point in long waits now that the offer has been made. We want to leave soon for our winter camp. Almost never do we come this far south and east but the buffalo on the western plains seem fewer this year. There are deer over in the pine and blackjack forest of this area and, besides, we delight in stealing ponies from the Cherokees and Creek tribes who live around here. They are soft victims to raid because they have walked the white man's road too long and even keep black slaves."

"But aren't there millions of buffalo? Enough to feed the tribes forever?"

"Maybe." He brought her hand up to his mouth and kissed her fingertips. "Motsiiu, Sweet Medicine, our folk hero, warned us to stay away from the whites and to guard our Sacred Arrows, the *Mahuts*, and the Buffalo Hat, *Issiwun*, from danger. If these two religious talismans were safe, the Cheyenne would have good medicine. We have had two of the arrows stolen by the Pawnee and had to make new ones to replace them but they lack the magic of the originals and we seem to be having a lot of bad luck."

"And the Buffalo Hat?"

"It is still safe at this moment. But we protect it carefully, for legend says when it is damaged or desecrated the buffalo will disappear and the Cheyenne will be caught up in a whirlwind of bad luck."

The wedding of Two Arrows and Pretty Flower Woman took place the next afternoon. Gifts equal to those first offered were sent by the bride's family to the groom's. Then the bride, dressed in her finest, was placed on a horse and led to her father-in-law's tepee while her mother brought up the rear, carrying gifts. Male members of Two Arrow's family placed the bride on a blanket and carried her into the tepee.

Later that day, a new tepee for the couple was erected near the bride's parents, but the groom had to remember not to break the tabu of never speaking to his mother-in-law. A great feast was prepared from meat killed by the groom's family, and as darkness fell there was much dancing and eating around the great campfire in the center of the lodges.

Iron Knife sat with his friends, his woman serving them choice portions. As she served his friends dutifully, she winked at him and he had a hard time keeping a straight face.

Children ran through the crowd, playing and chasing each other. Women stood in small groups, gossiping as women will. He noted with relief that they all seemed friendly to Summer Sky as she tried hard to converse in their language. Only Gray Dove glared at her without speaking and turned to walk away in the darkness. Annoyed at the Arapaho girl, he thought about it and decided to say nothing. Sooner or later, she would realize that she could never replace the white girl in his affections.

The drums started now and Summer came over to sit by him but he did not touch her. He longed to pull her close, but it would not look seemly for a warrior to show how much he cared for a captive.

She leaned close and her laughter drifted over the sound of song and drum. "Isn't this fun?"

"It isn't so very different from a white wedding I once

attended as a child in Texas," he said, smiling. "Lot's of proud relatives, food and gifts and a shy bride and groom waiting to slip away the first chance they get." He nodded toward the newlyweds standing at the edge of the circle.

"Tell me," Summer whispered and her mouth was so close to his ear he could feel her warm breath. "Does Pretty Flower Woman wear one of those—well, you know!" She blushed and did not continue.

"*Nihpihist?* Of course she does and she doesn't have to take it off tonight if she doesn't want to."

"But won't Two Arrows force her to take it off? After all, he's bought her with the ponies and gifts—"

"You really do think we are savages, don't you?" He frowned at her. "Two Arrows didn't buy her. Those things were gifts. Are there no gifts at a white wedding?"

"Of course." She nodded.

"And a Cheyenne woman retains ownership of her own property and ponies even after she marries, while in the white world, I understand the man owns and controls everything his wife has."

"I suppose that's true."

"As for the chastity belt, Pretty Flower Woman will decide when she is going to take it off and give herself to her husband. She may want to wear it for several weeks as they become better acquainted. Isn't that better than the brutal, legal rape that so often takes place a few hours after a white wedding?"

She looked at him thoughtfully. "Maybe you are right. Maybe it is my people who lag behind and are savages."

Summer Sky seemed lost in quiet contemplation so he turned back to visit with his friends. The dancing started and women were pulling men out to dance the slow, rhythmic beat in the big circle lit only by the giant fire. Summer disappeared but Iron Knife hadn't noticed until he looked up and saw the hunger on several male faces.

Following their hot gaze, he turned and saw Summer dancing all by herself in the semidarkness, oblivious to those around her. The firelight glowed dim where she danced, but it played on her long blond hair which she had shaken loose; now it hung free down her back almost to her hips. Swaying to the savage beat of the drum, she reminded him of a sexual fertility goddess.

Her curved hips writhed and the deerskin shift strained taut against the nipples of her full breasts. he could see the silhouette of her sensuous figure as she danced and swayed in the flickering light. The sudden hardness in his groin told him his body understood her message.

Quickly glancing around, he realized her dancing was being noticed by other men. He could see their hot eyes coveting her body. He was jealous and angry as he got up and walked over to grab her arm.

"What do you think you're doing, making such a spectacle of yourself?"

She looked up at him in obvious confusion. "I wanted to dance and I didn't know if I would be welcome in the circle. Over here by myself, I didn't think anyone would notice me—"

"Notice you!" He gestured toward the men. "Every warrior here has noticed you! You tease their manhood like some white dance hall girl!"

"What would you know of dance hall girls?" she flung back.

"I was once almost whipped to death for killing one!" he blurted out without thinking and he stopped short as he saw the blue eyes widen in horror.

For a long moment, they faced each other and then she turned and fled into the darkness, away from the fire.

"Summer!" he called. "Summer!"

But she was gone.

Chapter Nine

"Summer, wait!"

He was going to tell her he was innocent, that he hadn't killed the red-haired woman but knew who did.

Regretfully, he stared after her. She was too upset to listen to reason now and he was not sure what he would say to her later.

No one in camp knew what had caused his terrible scars except his family, just as no one knew of the little sister left behind in Texas the terrible night Iron Knife and Texanna had fled for their lives. Texanna would be dead in less than a year, his father the year after. By then, the little sister had been with the whites too long to ever adjust to the hard life of the Cheyenne.

Iron Knife frowned regretfully. If Cimarron were still alive, she would be grown by now and probably still down in the town of Fandango.

If only, he thought with regret, *if only he and Texanna had not been out picking berries that day along the Red River when the Texas Rangers spotted them. If only his father or some of the other warriors had been at the scene instead of out hunting, he and his mother would not have been captured.*

He thought tenderly of Texanna. His white mother had been big with child and unable to flee when the white men spied them among the wild blackberry bushes. He might have gotten away himself but he had been unwilling to run because he loved his mother more than his own life. Nor could he have faced his father and admitted the Rangers had taken her while he ran like a cowardly coyote to save himself. So the Texans captured them both.

Iron Knife had been called Falling Star in those days because he was born in the month of *Hikomini*, the freezing moon that the whites called November during 1833. Whatever the whites called it, the Indians would always remember that time as The Night the Stars Fell.

He was eight years old when the Rangers captured the two and took them, kicking and struggling, back across the Red River into Texas.

For a few hours, he hoped his father could follow the tracks, but the warriors were off hunting buffalo and a heavy rain began a few hours after the capture. Even a keen tracker like War Bonnet could not follow a trail that was washed away by pouring rain.

He remembered now how terrified of the whites the boy Falling Star had been and how Texanna had fought and begged to be allowed to return to the Cheyenne.

Even now, he could remember the jubilation of the Rangers as they looked at Texanna and said over and over: "Cynthia Ann Parker."

Texanna had shaken her head. "Please believe me," she begged the Big Chief of the Rangers, "I am not that girl you seek. My name used to be Texanna Heinrich and I was taken from a north Texas wagon train in the spring of 1832 by the Cheyenne chief, War Bonnet."

The captain chewed one end of his mustache as he looked at her, then toward the defiant son. "Looks like the savage didn't waste no time enjoying you."

Young Falling Star caught the leering look, the obscenity of his meaning as he struggled against the ropes that bound him. He spoke the little English his mother had taught him. "My father will come after us and kill you for this!"

Texanna shook her head at him warningly as the Texans jeered his threats.

But her head was held high and proud as she spoke to the Ranger leader. "Yes, I am War Bonnet's woman," she said, "and this is his only son. Please let us return to our people."

There was another man, a dark, handsome Spaniard, and his eyes were full of sympathy. "*Si*, the señora's right, Captain. She obviously isn't Cynthia Parker and she wants to go back to the Indians. I hate the idea of taking her against her will—"

"Are you loco like she is, Durango? Even if she isn't the Parker girl, you can see she's white and there may be a reward out from her family—"

"The white family usually doesn't want the woman back in these circumstances." The Spaniard nodded toward Falling Star and Texanna's bulging belly.

The captain tipped his hat back with the barrel of his pistol. "Wal, now, Diego de Durango, that ain't rightly our problem, I reckon. Let's let her folks make that decision. She might want to stay in civilization once she has a chance to think about it. It turns my stomach to think of handing a pretty gal like that back over to the Injuns for some brown buck to mount—"

"Watch your mouth, hombre." The Spaniard's eyes flashed. "I don't like the word 'Injun.'"

The other laughed good-naturedly as he holstered his pistol. "Sorry about that, Durango. I plum forgot you were with the Rangers yourself when they overran the Comanche camp down on the Brazos and rescued a pretty Cheyenne girl. Heard you got a baby by her."

Falling Star watched the Spaniard's mouth. It was a hard, grim mouth like a scar on his handsome face. "That girl is now my legal wife." He emphasized his words as if he were fighting to hold his temper. "And my son is legal heir to my ranching empire."

"No offense, señor," the captain said with a quick grin as they rode along. "It's just that not many men marry Injun

152

girls, and as much as you like Injuns, I'm surprised you ever joined up with us. If I had a fine ranch like yours, I wouldn't ride with the Rangers."

Maybe only Falling Star saw the anger and the finality in the Spaniard's eyes as he nodded. "You're right, hombre. I feel less and less that I belong with the Rangers. *Sí*, I've realized it for a long time. I think I'll go back to the Triple D and raise fine cattle and horses and watch my son grow up. But first, I'll ride along and see that this girl is returned to her white family safely." He looked around at the rough frontiersmen. "Some of your men might think because she would take on a Cheyenne, she's fair game for anyone."

It took many days riding, but at last they approached the small Texas village.

Durango reined up on the edge of town and turned to the captain. "You sent a rider with a message so the family would be prepared?"

The man chewed his mustache and did not meet Durango's eyes. "I sent word we was bringing in a girl who called herself Texanna Heinrich. I didn't say anything else, well, about, you know . . ." He glared at Falling Star.

Durango frowned at him. "Holy Mother of God!" He swore softly in Spanish. "This is cruel for everyone concerned," he muttered. "The family should have been warned."

The captain shrugged. "How do you tell a family something like this?" He nodded toward Falling Star and Texanna's bulging belly. "You were right. I wish we hadn't brought her in now. No self-respecting family would want her back and no white man will accept an Injun buck's leavin's."

Durango hit him then. Even the boy was surprised at the way the Spaniard's fist flew out and caught the Ranger's chin. The captain flew sideways off his startled horse and hit the dirt like a sack of cornmeal.

Durango's eyes were soft with sympathy as he looked into

153

Falling Star's. He tipped his hat to Texanna as the Ranger stumbled to his feet. "Señora, I'm very sorry for my part in this, forgive me."

And he turned and rode off to the southeast as the Ranger rubbed his chin and remounted.

The group rode down Main Street. Iron Knife winced even now, remembering as he stared into the darkness after Summer Sky. Even now, he was not sure he could share that pain with her. It had been afternoon and the whole town had turned out for the occasion. People lined Main Street and a small band played loudly if slightly off-key. There were banners hanging everywhere. The boy could not read but he looked over at his mother's drawn face as she read them and saw her silently mouth the words: Welcome Back, Texanna! Texanna, Our Heroine!

There was a rotund man standing out in front of the crowd who strutted as if he felt he were important.

Falling Star heard the captain mutter, "The mayor of the town, no doubt. This is going to be worse than I thought. They even got a brass band and decked out the town like the Fourth of July!"

The group rode down Main Street while the band played and people cheered. Then, gradually, they seemed to see the boy, the condition of the drawn, tense woman. The cheers faded and the music trailed off uncertainly. Falling Star looked into hostile, closed faces and heard the murmur of the crowd. He didn't have to speak very good English to understand the remarks. The anger and contempt of the voices told him everything.

"My Gawd, a half-breed Injun kid!"

"Will you look! She's—she's expecting a baby!"

"How could she? With an Injun, I mean?"

The boy glanced over at his mother who sat her horse with quiet, calm dignity and ignored the curious stares.

The pompous mayor stepped forward uncertainly as the horses stopped. The blondish woman standing next to him took

154

one look at Texanna, clutched the arm of the elderly, frail man next to her. Then the woman shrieked and fainted dead away.

"Give her some air!" the crowd yelled even as they clustered around the fallen woman while the mayor looked from her to the Rangers, and over to Texanna.

"Well, what did you expect?" an irate, stiff-backed woman said to another as they fanned the unconscious one vigorously. "After all, how would you like to have waited twelve years to find your sister and have her come back in the family way and have a half-breed boy with her!"

The mayor stepped forward and stuck his thumbs in his bright vest as he confronted the Rangers.

"I am Ransford J. Longworth," he huffed and the red veins stood out around his long nose. "That is my poor wife, Carolina, who has just fainted from the shock!" He gestured wildly. "Land o' Goshen, why didn't you warn us about—about this?" He nodded toward the boy and Texanna's swollen stomach.

The boy watched his mother's eyes as they searched the crowd, looked down at the elderly man kneeling beside the fainting woman. "Father?" she said.

But the withered man glared at her with revulsion and hate. "Ach, whore!" he spat out in a foreign accent. "Slut! We thought of you as our pure Joan of Arc sacrificing herself to save the wagon train. We thought of you as the dead saint of Fandango!"

One tear made a crooked trail down Texanna's face. "I'm sorry you're disappointed I'm alive! I'm sorry to destroy your shining image. I am only a woman after all with feet of clay like any poor mortal."

She looked around the crowd. "Where are my brothers?"

Longworth shifted his bulk and looked back at his wife who was now sitting up in the middle of the street, sobbing and obviously enjoying being the center of attention, the object of sympathetic glances.

The man fiddled with the heavy gold watch chain across his

155

paunchy stomach. "Miss Heinrich, I'm your brother-in-law, and your brothers . . ."

Falling Star heard the ripple of whispers through the crowd. "Poor thing, she's been gone so long she doesn't even know both her brothers are dead."

The boy saw the pain on his mother's face as the words reached her.

Longworth fumbled with his watch and studied its face rather than meet her eyes. "Your big brother Joe died at a place called the Alamo only four years after you were stolen by the Indians."

"And my young brother Danny?"

The crowd was very quiet now, hostile, but quiet. Only the blond woman sobbed loudly to keep the attention of the crowd on herself.

The mayor sighed. "Danny was executed by the Mexicans in the terrible black bean lottery after the Meir expedition two years ago."

Texanna's face crumpled. "Danny," she wept. "Oh, not my favorite, Danny!"

The boy looked up to see a horse galloping madly into town from the other direction, and as it reached them a man slid off and ran toward them.

"Gawd Almighty!" the man drawled as he ran up to Texanna's horse. "I came as soon as I heard you had been found, and . . ."

The man's voice trailed off, disbelief mirrored on his ugly, bearded face as he stared up at the woman, his mouth hanging open. He was a big man, dressed in rough, frontier-style clothes. His western hat was pulled down over his eyes, and a silver filigreed whip hung on his belt.

When he spoke again, his voice was an angry, accusing drawl. "Texanna, how could you? How could you have let one of them savage stallions—?"

He didn't get to finish his sentence. Texanna lashed out suddenly with the ends of her reins, catching the big man

156

across the face.

"How dare you! How dare you scold me, Jake Dallinger!" She looked out across the crowd in outraged dignity. "How dare any of you disapprove of me! Don't you remember? The war party demanded a hostage or they would wipe out the whole wagon train. How quickly you forget! I gave myself up to save your worthless necks and this is your gratitude!"

Falling Star glanced around the circle, saw them look away, ashamed. It was true what she said. He could tell by the way people kicked the dust in guilt and the crowd began to drift away to their homes.

He watched a man reach up and rip down a banner, then someone helped him pull down another. They threw them in the street and as people mounted up and rode away, the departing horses trod on the banners, grinding them into the dust.

The boy listened to the muttering of the crowd as they drifted away. "Well, yes, she did go out to the Injuns when they demanded it or they'd kill us all, but she didn't have to sleep with them. She could have done what any self-respecting white woman would have done; she could have committed suicide."

"Poor Carolina Longworth! Her so high-class and caring of what everyone thinks. I'll bet she wishes they'd never found her sister."

"Wouldn't you under the circumstances?"

Even the sister got to her feet, and assisted by her husband and father stood looking around uncertainly. The bent, gnarled father turned away with finality.

The man called Jake wiped the blood away where Texanna had lashed him. "Missy," he drawled, "I reckon you're upset, but if you'd consider marryin' me, I'd forgive you for—well, you know."

He looked over at Falling Star and the boy felt instant dislike for the man, knowing the scout did not want him.

"Forgive me?" Texanna threw back her head and laughed

157

heartily while tears ran down her face. "Forgive me! How kind of you to overlook my loving a Cheyenne chief who's twice the man you'll ever be!"

The wind picked up a banner out of the dust of the almost deserted street and blew it toward them, spooking the horses.

Welcome Home, Texanna.

So the miserable life in the town of Fandango had begun, Iron Knife remembered now with a sigh. Carolina Longworth did what she considered "her Christian duty" in finding the two a small shack on the edge of town. Then the family ignored them pointedly. Only Pastor Schmidt and his wife were kind to Texanna and her half-breed son.

Texanna had inherited the nimble fingers of her father, an expert tailor who was now too crippled by age to sew. She supported herself and her son by making clothes for the women of Fandango. For the most part, the townspeople avoided the two except when they needed sewing done.

The white man named Jake Dallinger came to the house only one more time in the next five years and the boy was not sure what happened that night but Ransford Longworth had been in the parlor when the boy went to bed. He was awakened by loud, angry words and had peeked around the door to see his mother confronting the army scout. Texanna and he had backed Jake out of the shack with weapons.

Falling Star remembered the night the new baby was born. Not even the town doctor came. The minister's wife delivered the baby while the pastor sat with the boy. Aunt Carolina had been conspicuous by her absence. As she told everyone in town later, someone had to uphold the morals of the family and she didn't want anyone to think she approved of her fallen sister by associating with her. Texanna shrugged when she heard that gossip and retorted that Carolina was neither in charge of family nor town morals. She might think she was, but no one had voted her that position.

Texanna looked down proudly at the pretty girl child crying wildly in her arms. "She has a loud, lusty voice," she said, smiling. "I will call her Cimarron, which means 'wild one' in Spanish."

Falling Star reached out to touch the small fist and it promptly closed on his finger. "With a cry like that, 'Wild One' is a good name." He nodded. "Father will like that."

Tears came to Texanna's eyes and she buried her face against the tiny head. "I don't know what to do, how to find the Cheyenne again," she sobbed. "There's so much wilderness and if they catch us trying to escape, they'll say I'm loco, send me to an asylum, and you children to some terrible orphanage."

He reached out to pat her hand. "Someday, Mother," he assured her, "someday, either Father will track us down or I will be big enough to rescue us all. We'll wait for that day."

So life went on for the small family for the next five years. Then, one fateful afternoon, when he was thirteen, a saloon girl had lured him up to her room. He had known then that the boys at school had said the girl belonged to the big army scout, that she slept with men and gave Jake the money.

Iron Knife sighed now, remembering. It had happened in the late afternoon, and before midnight his back would be scarred forever and his brave mother facing down a lynch mob with a shotgun. . . .

He could remember vividly the events of that one day and night as if it had happened this morning although it was a long time ago. . . .

He was unhappy among the whites because the adults called him "Injun bastard" and the other children at the one-room school teased and mistreated him. But he was big for his age, almost as big as some full-grown men and he had fought all the boys and whipped them so that they no longer teased him. They ignored him.

He remembered now that it had been a hot Friday afternoon and he was walking home alone as always from the school. His

159

path led past the back door of the saloon. A smiling, red-haired woman in a scarlet dress had come out the door and called to him.

"Say, you're Texanna's son, ain't you? Why don't you come in for a minute? There ain't nobody here but me right now. I been watching you walk past here for weeks."

The only white woman who ever smiled at him was his mother, so he shyly followed the girl inside where she took him up to her room and gave him white sugar, which was rare and expensive. It was all his mother could do to provide the bare necessities with her sewing and there was no money left for fancy things. He hunted with his bow, of course, and tried to find work on the surrounding ranches. No one would hire an Indian even though he was bigger and stronger than most grown men.

He remembered even now the taste of the gritty sweet and the woman's smile, both were so rare to him. He knew the other boys at school laughed about this woman. It was said she would let men mate her if they gave her money. The boys also said the scout, Jake Dallinger, claimed this woman as his own when he was in town and sometimes brought men to sleep with her and made her give him most of the money the men paid her.

Now the saloon woman stood very close to him, so close he could see that her neck was dirty and smell the strong reek of her perfume.

"My name's Kate," she said, and she moved closer, running her hand across his big shoulders and he didn't move since he was not sure what she wanted.

"Have you ever had a woman?" she asked finally.

He shook his head, feeling foolish and embarrassed and wanting to run away. But she was stroking his arm in a manner that excited him as nothing had ever excited him.

He thought of what the boys had said.

"I—I have no money," he admitted.

She threw back her head and laughed and he realized that her lips and cheeks were smeared with red color like scarlet war paint.

"You been talkin' to the men, ain't you? Believe it or not, I don't always do it for money! Sometimes, I see a good-looking man and get to thinkin' about how it'd be and invite him up. Have you really never had a woman?"

He bent his head feeling very young and stupid, wondering why she asked such a naive question. No, of course he had not yet had a woman. He'd been too young for the captive women the warriors occasionally took. And a brave could not take a proper wife until he had proved himself on the hunt and accumulated enough property on the warpath to offer gifts to the girl's family. No Cheyenne girl would think of removing her protective string and letting a man mate her unless he went through the appropriate offer and marriage ceremony.

The dance-hall girl put her hands in the open neck of his shirt. "You look a lot younger up close than I thought you was from a distance, but you're sure built like a man."

Her fingers stroked his skin lightly, unbuttoned his shirt. "I like the idea you never had a woman before. Well, I'm gonna teach you about women, my young warrior," she whispered.

He stood there dumbly, afraid and embarrassed, ready to run. Yet not quite sure of what she expected if he stayed.

By now, she had his shirt off and was running her fingertips across his nipples.

She took off the red dress and posed for him a long moment, then slowly removed her stockings and the rest. She was flabby and heavier than he would have wanted in his first woman, but still she seemed very desirable to him with her pale skin and the way her full breasts jutted against his chest.

To his surprise, his man's thing came erect and hard and he felt an unaccustomed ache in his groin. All he could think of now was topping her as he had seen war parties do with captive women.

Kate stepped back and looked him up and down with appreciation in her eyes.

"Now, that's more like it!" she purred as she came to him

161

and pulled his face down to hers to kiss. He would always remember the reek of cheap perfume and the taste of whiskey on her lips.

Instinctively, his hands came up to pull her against him, for he was more a man than a boy. His arms held her tightly as he kissed her and she moaned against his mouth and pulled him toward the dirty, rumpled bed.

With his superior strength, he grabbed her and almost threw her on the bed, fumbling in his eagerness to mount her. But she resisted his attempts to open her thighs.

"Take it easy, my young brave," she whispered, kissing him, "you're not gonna get it off that quick like the animals who pay me for it!" She kissed the corner of his mouth. "I'm gonna teach you how to love a woman and make her like it! I'm gonna teach you what I want you to know from the best whore this side of the Mississippi. Then you'll always know how to please a woman!"

And Kate did teach him, he remembered with gentle affection. It was a long time that day before she would let him enter her and by then he was aching with his need for release and she was whimpering and gasping. Even now, he remembered the smell of her perfume as he finally took his first woman and became a man. He remembered how he had ground himself against her, trying to plunge even deeper as she made grunting noises and dug her sharp nails into his muscled back.

She locked her legs about his lithe body and arched her breasts against him and he could feel her deep sweetness locking on him as she came.

Finally, she released him and looked up at him. "You're better than I dreamed you would be," she whispered, "and virile enough and young enough to give me all I want. You drop by often, you hear? Just make sure that bum of a scout ain't around when you show up. He'd be madder'n hell if he caught me givin' it away, especially to an Injun!"

He was eager to take her again and she was eager to have him.

162

He remembered now that they were locked in each other's arms, intent only on the pleasure of their union, when, abruptly, there was someone else in the room.

He heard the door fling open and a cry of outrage as the big scout strode to the bed, jerking him up and slamming him across the face with a stick of stove wood as Jake threw him to the floor.

"You rotten Injun bastard!" Jake screamed as he beat him about the head. "It ain't enough that your old man took Texanna from me, now I catch his bastard son toppin' my fancy woman! Gawd almighty! I'm gonna kill both of you for this!"

Iron Knife winced even now, remembering the pain as the big scout slammed him hard against the wall and he could feel the blood from his broken nose and torn face dripping down his naked body.

He could remember the shrill shriek of the woman as Jake Dallinger uncoiled the big drover's whip he always carried.

The woman backed away. "The kid was rapin' me, Jake, honest he was! You know I wouldn't let no Injun touch me, no matter how much he paid! You know that!"

Jake slapped the woman hard and the boy struggled to his feet. He knew he should help the woman, but he was no match for the big, hard-muscled scout and he had no weapons, while the bearded man had a knife and the giant whip. He swayed on his feet, fighting off unconsciousness while the man beat her.

Weakly, he managed to grab his clothes and stagger out the door toward home. Behind him, he could still hear the woman screaming, "It was rape! Honest to God, the kid was rapin' me!"

He did not think he would ever manage to put on his pants and crawl home. Falling Star was almost unconscious when Texanna found him in the yard. He remembered his mother washing the blood off his face and dragging him into the house.

It was dark when the mob of drunken cowboys led by Jake Dallinger came with their torches. Kate had been found brutally raped and murdered, they said, and the mob dragged the boy away to tie him up in the town square to whip him. . . .

Jake Dallinger, he thought, grinding his teeth. *Jake Dallinger and his whip.* . . .

That had been twelve years ago, he thought now as he stood staring into the darkness after Summer. He had never trusted another white woman after that or even told anyone outside his own family how he came by the terrible scars. He had never meant to tell Summer any of his past, and now he had blurted some of his secrets to her. Sometimes he was more white than stoic Indian after all.

His thoughts were interrupted by a small boy who ran up to him, speaking Cheyenne so rapidly he could not understand all the child said.

"Stop and tell me again more slowly." He smiled gently at the boy.

The child glanced wildly behind him.

"Come quickly, great warrior!" he shouted, gesturing. "Your woman fights with the bad Arapaho girl and I think one is going to kill the other!"

Chapter Ten

Humiliated by Iron Knife and horrified at his confession about the murder of the dance hall girl, Summer fled blindly through the darkness toward the tepee. A shadow loomed across her path, someone blocking her way. She hesitated, her heart pounding as she recognized the voluptuous form.

Gray Dove put her hands on her hips and smiled. The full harvest moon lit her features. "Where are you going, White Girl?"

"None of your business!" Summer retorted. "Get out of my way! I know now you are my enemy and that you lied to me, sending me into a trap and trying to get me killed!"

"Have you told Iron Knife about our little bargain?"

"No!" Summer said. "I intend to deal with you myself and don't need his help in this. No doubt he would do something terrible to you for tricking me and sending Angry Wolf to kill me!"

"Speaking of Angry Wolf," the other glared back at her, "he has not been seen since that afternoon. I wondered what has happened to him?"

"Maybe he has gone off with the renegade Dog Soldiers!"

"Has he now? And no doubt, up at the Dog Soldier camps on the Republican and Smoky Hill rivers, they think he changed his mind and decided to stay here."

"Perhaps a Pawnee war party—"

The other snorted derisively. "Not likely, although I've heard rumors that Pawnee have been sighted a few days north of here."

Summer tried to shake her head casually. "Perhaps the forest fire . . . anyway, what is all that to me? I know nothing of Angry Wolf."

"Do you not?" The dark girl peered threateningly into her face. "I say that you do know what happened to him. That somehow, as he was trailing you, you caught him by surprise and killed him."

Now it was Summer's turn to snort in disbelief. "No one would ever believe that. I am not strong enough or clever enough to kill a fierce Dog Soldier."

Gray Dove gave her a long, searching look. "No, you aren't. Not unless you had some help." She seemed to be thinking aloud. "I saw you coming back to camp riding double with Iron Knife."

Summer felt her pulse quicken. "Surely you can't think he has anything to do with the disappearance."

"He is strong and clever enough to kill the other. He must have been involved."

Summer's heart hammered, wanting to protect him even if he had murdered the saloon girl. "But you can't tell the Council or anyone else what you suspect without revealing your part in the plot."

The dark girl glared at her in fury. "You are right, of course! If I could put all the blame on you, I would have already gone to the old chiefs, but I will not endanger Iron Knife or reveal that I was involved. I love him too much to see him banished from the camp over his minor, passing fling with a captive."

"I'm not a minor fling!" Summer argued. "He is serious about me. He intends to marry me!"

"Does he? I have not heard any such announcement. I think he only plays with you. But should he really think of marrying you, I will kill you or get you out of this camp somehow.

Perhaps I will yet think of a way to blame you for Angry Wolf's death without involving either myself or the man I love!"

Summer's stubborn streak came out and she stuck out her chin. "You will never get me out of this camp. Do you hear? Never! I have changed my mind and have fallen in love with Iron Knife. I will stay with the tribe and be his woman forever! It will be me sleeping in his arms at night and bearing his children, do you hear? It will be me! Never you!"

Gray Dove attacked her in a sudden fury and they went down screaming and clawing in the dirt. The area had been deserted until now, but as they fought Summer saw sleepy heads poking out of tepees to see what the noise was about. Furious with the sly Indian girl who had caused her so much trouble and struck the first blow, Summer was past caring that they were drawing a crowd. She clawed and fought in a way that belied her genteel upbringing and she saw surprise in the other's eyes.

"I'll teach you to hit me!" Summer shrieked, giving the other girl a good whack.

Over and over in the dirt they rolled while they scratched and bit. A growing crowd surrounded them.

"White bitch!" Gray Dove spat at her. "When I finish with you, you will be so ugly and scratched up, he won't want you and will send you away!"

"Look out for your own face!" Summer warned as she slapped the other. She pushed the Indian girl down in the dirt and sat on top of her, pulling the black braids.

Abruptly, she felt strong arms around her, lifting her off the Arapaho girl but she went right on kicking and fighting. "Let go of me!" she yelled. "Let go of me!"

"Stop! Stop all this!" his deep voice ordered. "What's happening here anyway?"

She looked up into Iron Knife's surprised face as she struggled and he lifted her lightly off the ground.

"The white girl started it!" Gray Dove sobbed as she scrambled to her feet. "I was just walking past her and she

167

wanted to argue and she finally hit me!"

"Well, Summer Sky?" He put her on her feet.

She hesitated, unwilling to discuss it in front of the crowd of Indians. "Send them away!" she pleaded.

For answer, he turned and gave a curt command in Cheyenne and the people drifted back to their tepees or the big campfire.

"Now, Gray Dove," he said in English, "I'm warning you to stay away from Summer or I will see you run out of this camp. I know you well enough to know you must have done something to start this!"

The girl started to say something as she brushed her disarrayed hair back and obviously thought better of it. With an arrogant shrug, she turned and walked off.

"Now," he commanded Summer, "I want to talk to you, you little vixen!" He took her arm and steered her to the top of a nearby rise covered with a grove of blackjack oak.

He sounded stern, but she saw his white teeth flash a smile as they reached the hill. "You shouldn't tangle with Gray Dove. She's mean and she outweighs you."

"I gave as good as I got!" she answered proudly as she sat down on the grass in the bright moonlight. "If you hadn't come to her rescue, I would have yanked her bald-headed by now!"

"You know, I believe you would have at that! Maybe I underestimated you, Summer Sky!" He laughed and sat down himself against the rough bark of a tree. "What was that fight about, anyway?"

"You mostly." She ran a finger down a small scratch on her face and decided not to tell him the rest. What good would it do to worry him about what the Indian girl suspected about Angry Wolf? And she could never tell him of Gray Dove's involvement in her escape because then he would realize a third person had reason to know the dead brave had followed Summer. He would worry that Gray Dove would tell and Summer was sure she wouldn't. The Arapaho girl cared too much for Iron Knife to report him to the Council.

"Gray Dove thinks I should step out of the picture so she can have you."

He sighed. "I have never been anything but honest with the Arapaho girl when she talked of marriage. I think she is too much a whore to be true to any man anyway."

"Have you made love to her as you have to me?"

"What kind of a question is that?"

"The kind every woman asks about a rival or wants to ask," she said jealously.

He reached out and took her hand in his. "I have made love to many women, Summer. Surely you realized that?"

She felt tears well up in her eyes. "No, I suppose I didn't think of it since you were my first man. I thought what we had was special."

"It is, Summer, it is!" He kissed her fingertips. "I have made love to many women but I have never been in love with them as I am with you."

She felt the need for reassurance. "Did you make love to the dance hall girl?"

His face became a cold, inscrutable mask. "Yes, I made love to her. She was my first woman, since you insist on discussing that which does not concern you. I did not kill her. I was almost whipped to death because they *thought* I had killed her."

She caught the pain in his cold eyes. "And that is what happened to your back?"

He nodded very slowly and she knew he had never discussed that with anyone. "Yes, they whipped me." His voice was low and angry. "They whipped me and hung me up like a dog in the town square where everyone could see my humiliation. The man most involved would not have stopped until he killed me but my mother came to my rescue with a shotgun." He sighed and leaned back against the tree. "That night, Texanna and I fled the white village forever, leaving behind my sick little sister who was too ill to travel. We wouldn't have made it if War Bonnet and his small raiding party hadn't ridden in to grab us up off the street at the very last minute."

"Your mother was a white captive like me?"

"Yes. My father, War Bonnet, stole her from a Texas wagon train. He was down there warring against the Comanche."

She knew from the tone of his voice he was revealing painful things that he had never discussed with anyone before.

"Texanna must have loved him very much," she whispered. "And did he love her, too?"

"He loved her so much that he never took a second wife."

Summer thought a minute, puzzled. "But if they loved each other, why had she left him in the first place to go back to the whites?"

"She didn't leave willingly. I was a small boy and the band was camped near the Red River. Most of the men were gone hunting when the Texas Rangers rode in and recaptured us. She fought like a she-bobcat but she was heavy with the baby that was due soon and the white men took us away by force."

"Did you both never try later to escape?"

"We tried." He sighed tiredly. "But all during that next five years, we never made it. I might have made it alone but I wouldn't leave her behind to deal with the hostile whites by herself. Her family decided she had gone insane from living with the Indians and threatened to put her an asylum and her children in the orphanage. After that, Texanna quit trying until the night we ran for our lives after the whipping."

There was a long silence and Summer could read by the pain of his face that he was reliving all the hurt and humiliation of his miserable life in civilization.

". . . she was wearing a red dress," he muttered.

"Who?"

"The dance-hall girl." He shook his head as if to do away with the memory. "It was almost exactly like the one you had on when I took you from the wrecked stage that morning."

Things became suddenly clear to her. "And you thought I was that same kind of woman, one who sleeps with men for money?"

170

He nodded and looked into her eyes. "I knew from living with the whites that only whores and easy women wore a dress like that. Where did you get it, anyway?"

She smiled. "I traded for it in Fort Smith. I knew everyone would be on the lookout for a rich girl dressed all in blue so I traded with a dance-hall girl. Then I sold all my jewelry to get enough for my passage to San Francisco. Father had not given me much money to start with. I think he knew I might run away."

"You had a reason for going to this place called San Francisco?"

"No," she said, smiling. "I don't know a soul there. It just seemed like it was far away enough that Uncle Jack—"

"Who is this 'Uncle Jack'?"

"A relative. One of those very strict preachers. Father was trying to get me out of Boston for a while until the gossip died down and he thought Uncle Jack was a logical choice. The old man was due to pick me up in Fort Smith the next morning, but I caught the 3:30 a.m. stage out instead."

"You did something to anger your father?"

"My goodness, did I ever! It started out as a small protest over suffrage for women."

"What?" His face showed his puzzlement.

"You know, the right for women to vote!"

He laughed heartily. "You must think me a fool! Even having had only five years in the white school, I know that women cannot vote."

"That's exactly what I mean!" she snapped. "I had been reading the *Lily*, the suffragette newspaper, and decided I should do my part. So I organized and led the other girls from Miss Priddy's Academy to demonstrate for women's rights at the Boston State House."

"This alone angered your father enough to send you away from the family?"

"I'm afraid there's more." She giggled in spite of herself. "Someone at the capitol called the police and they came to talk to us, rather condescendingly, I might add. The police sergeant told us to behave like well-brought-up young ladies and go home. When I decided they weren't going to take us seriously, I lost my temper and hit the sergeant over the head with my parasol.

"Parasol?"

She smiled at the memory. "That's an umbrella. Then the other girls followed my lead and started hitting the police and screaming. To make a long story short, they hauled us all off to jail. All that is but Maude Peabody. She had chained herself to a door and forgot to bring along the key."

Iron Knife looked at her in disbelief. "You spent time in the white man's jail? No wonder your father was angry!"

"That wasn't what made him the maddest!" Summer chuckled at the memory. "We were out within an hour, as soon as Father could reach his lawyer. That is, everyone but Maude who was still back at the State House, chained to the door while the police tried to cut the chain. What made him furious was that someone notified the newspapers and the reporters were at the jail when Father arrived."

"I can imagine a great chief was not happy at having the story in the newspapers."

"Well, I think more than that, Father thought he had enough power to keep it out of the press, but he didn't after all. It was spread over the front pages and Father was furious, especially when the papers told about the bloomers."

"'Bloomers'?" He looked confused. "What is this word, 'bloomers'?"

She blushed in spite of herself. "It's a type of ladies' undergarment, sort of like pants with lace on them, and they show under a shorter than usual skirt."

He looked so serious that Summer had to smile. "'Bloomers' seems a strange name for ladies' undergarments."

"They are named for Amelia Bloomer, the famous suffragette, and have become the badge of protest by those of us who fight for women's rights!" Summer felt a trace of

172

sadness now as she remembered the scene that night at the supper table, her father raging as always, her bratty little sister, Angela, looking pleased and smug that Summer was in trouble. Summer's twin brother, David, had tried to come to her defense and been shouted down.

Her mother had said nothing as always, but Summer sensed that she was secretly amused and delighted at Summer's defiance. Priscilla Van Schuyler hardly ever said anything anymore, going about lost in a fog of sherry and laudanum. She had always been almost a remote stranger to all the children. Priscilla seemed to prefer her self-induced haze, almost as if living in the real world hurt too much.

"And then what happened, Summer?" Iron Knife's voice brought her back to the present.

"That's about it, I'm afraid." She shrugged. "He put me and my maid, Mrs. O'Malley, on a train to St. Joe and we came the rest of the way by stage. He said I could come home in six months or a year, when people in Boston quit laughing at our family. I bought Mrs. O'Malley a good bottle of sherry. Being Irish, she's quite fond of a wee nip. When she passed out, I grabbed a bag and ran. You know the rest of it."

"And now you will never go back to Boston in six months or even six years," he whispered, snuggling her closer to him.

"No, I will stay here forever," she agreed, putting her face against the hard muscles of his great chest and looking toward the camp.

It was mostly quiet now, for the hour was late, but she could see the great campfire and hear the drumbeat pounding for the few remaining dancers.

Somewhere, far away, a coyote howled in the autumn air and the stars hung like bits of glass in the velvet night. It was very warm for early fall, she thought as she smelled the crushed grass beneath them and held her beloved close. In all the world, there was noplace she would rather be tonight; no one she would rather be with.

"Summer, what are you thinking?" His breath was warm on

173

her ear. "Are you regretting getting on that stage? Regretting me?"

"Never!" she declared. "Never!" As if to reinforce her words, she turned her face up to his and he kissed her closed eyelids ever so gently and then moved his lips down her face to her mouth. She opened willingly as he caressed its depths with his own and then she probed the velvet of his mouth deeply even as his manhood had probed the first time he took her.

His tongue went to flick the inside of her ear and she shivered uncontrollably. "Do you like that, Little One? Tonight, I am going to teach you many things and take a long, long time to love you!"

She felt a surge of eager wetness between her thighs and reached out to clasp his manhood with her hand.

"Not yet!" He pulled away from her. "After all, we have all night and there is more to it than that!"

"You're right. We really do have all the time in the world," she gasped. She stood, and looking around to see that they were alone, pulled the deerskin shift off over her head. She stood there naked in the warm moonlight, partially covered by her long, blond hair hanging free almost to her hips. The moonlight gleamed on her proud, jutting breasts, but her flat belly shone concave and shadowy as did the soft place below.

He didn't move from his place against the tree but she felt his hungry gaze on her body. "You were so eager to dance before," he whispered. "Dance for me now—me alone now that no other man can see you!"

"Here? Now?"

"Yes, now!" he ordered. "You are, after all, my captive, my plaything. Entertain me now by dancing!"

Summer hesitated a long moment, listening to the steady beat of the far-off drums and then the rhythm became her pulse and she began to dance. In her imagination, she was a harem slave girl, ordered to please her master and, instinctively, she knew how.

There on a hillside in the moonlight she danced naked and unashamed, writhing and turning to the distant beat. She thrust her inviting breasts at him, moved her hands slowly down her thighs to tantalize him, sending a message of hot, savage blood calling out to his. Civilization was only a thin veneer she had stripped away with her clothing. Deep down, she was as savage as her mother's English ancestors, dancing a ritual mating dance in the heart of a dark, Druid forest.

Rhythmically, she moved, swinging her hips at him, shaking her long hair so that it caught the silvery gleam of the moon, luring a man with her ripe body.

She might be his captive but she could enslave any man, and she knew it as she heard him breathe heavier. She danced closer, cupping her hands over her breasts, then reaching for him. Sweat broke out on his forehead as she twisted and writhed before him.

"Now, you dance with me," she urged, holding out her hands to him. He stood slowly, not taking his eyes from her body. Pulling off the shirt and leggings, he stood before her clad only in a brief loincloth.

Taking his hand, she pulled him out of the shadows and almost hypnotically he began to move to the slow drumbeat.

"I want to see your body as you see mine," she whispered and moved close to pull away the loincloth and tossed it to one side. " Now, dance with me!"

They danced without touching, only caressing each other's body with their eyes. She reveled in the sight of his nakedness, his broad shoulders, narrow hips, and prominent manhood. He wore nothing but the gleaming earring and the eagle bone whistle. Summer gloried in his powerful, rippling muscles and the way his maleness paid tribute to the eroticism of her moves. It was a primitive mating ritual and she danced with abandon, making him hunger for her as she did for him. She knew she would only be sated when his thrusting dagger filled her aching void.

Reaching out to touch his erect hardness, she stepped

175

backward out of his reach as he grabbed for her. She danced closer, touching his hard nipples and brushing her fingers lightly across the sun dance scars.

"Enough! I can't stand any more!" He jerked her to him roughly and tangled one hand in her hair. He crushed her against him and his mouth forced itself inside hers.

She dug her nails in his chest and his other hand went to her small bottom and pulled her even closer. His hardness thrust at her belly and he tried to lift her from her feet so he could take her standing. But she guessed his intent and broke away from him, laughing coquettishly as she ran from him. "I think I have changed my mind!" she laughed as she ran.

But he ran after her, caught her, whirled her around. "You will not tease me like that!" he ordered, kissing her wildly. "I will have you now if I have to take you by force!"

"I don't think you can!" She struggled, but not too hard. Her blood ran hot tonight and she wanted to be taken violently and conquered while she fought him.

She didn't fight long. With his superior strength, he lifted her clear off the ground and his lips found the hollow of her throat and then, as she arched backward over his arms, his mouth went to her breasts. She could not stop from crying out at the feel of that hot, moist caress.

Gradually, they both slid to the ground and she clasped his head to her nipple as she felt the soft cushion of the grass beneath her. She gasped in pleasure as his mouth went to her navel and then down one thigh. She could feel his hands forcing her thighs apart.

"I must kiss the font of all my pleasure," she heard him whisper as his breath felt warm against the triangle at the top of her legs.

"You shouldn't!" she protested. "You really shouldn't kiss me there!" She was still uneasy with the idea and tried to pull away from him. But she was helpless on her back against his superior strength as he spread her legs.

"Put your hands behind your head!" he ordered harshly.

176

"You are my captive and I will do as I will with you and you will not try to stop me!"

Numbly, she obeyed, knowing he could force her obedience by sheer strength and she put her hands above her head and let him do as he would. When his warm lips touched her most secret place, she whimpered and her hands gripped the grass above her head and she could not stop her eager body from arching itself against the moistness of his searching mouth.

She felt him forcing her thighs even further apart and she forgot about everything but the sensation of the blade of his warm tongue sliding home in her scabbard. She was one quivering nerve as she gave in to the feel of his lips and she had to bite her own to keep back the moan of satisfaction and excitement as she came. It seemed a long time that she drifted in an almost unconscious state and when she finally opened her eyes, he was looking down.

"Have I satisfied you, Little One?"

She was embarrassed. "You know you have."

"I want to hear you say it," he demanded.

"Yes!" She almost screamed it. "You have more than satisfied me, you have made me writhe in hunger like I never knew existed and then sated me!"

As he looked down into her eyes she could see the veins standing out in his neck and feel the unfulfilled throbbing with each heartbeat of his maleness against her leg.

Summer reached up to touch one of his hard nipples and he gasped.

"And now, I will satisfy you!" she declared and her small teeth lightly bit his chest.

"You are a yellow-haired witch," he moaned aloud. "A dream creature like the Mihn, pulling men under in the bottomless lakes!"

"Then relax and enjoy being taken to your doom," she whispered. "You may have had many women, but none of them can have loved you with the passion I am going to give you!"

177

She sat up and pushed him down onto his back, and then she leaned over and kissed both edges of his mouth. Her hair trailed across him as she sat up and stroked his scarred face and chest with feather-light touches of her fingers.

His hands came up, trying to pull her down on his chest but she shook them off. "No," she protested, "this time you are the slave and must lie there and let me do as I will with you."

Obediently, he slid his hands to his sides as he humored her. But she felt him tremble all over with the effort of keeping his hands off her. She knew that no doubt those same big hands had broken men's backs, strangled the life from those far more powerful than she. Summer felt heady with the power of her sexuality, heady with the way she could control this giant, dominant male.

Her lips caressed the hard, flat belly and he stirred restlessly.

"Be still!" she ordered. "I'm not through. I'm going to make you ache with wanting me, until you think you can't stand it anymore!"

"I've passed that point!" He sounded tense.

"But I haven't made you want me as much as I intend to," she whispered as her mouth moved down his taut belly. The male scent of him excited her and she did something she would have thought almost unthinkable only a few minutes before: she kissed his manhood.

Summer was suddenly transported back in time and she was a priestess in old Egypt, worshiping at the shrine of the eternal male phallus. What she did, she did instinctively now that she had been freed from her straitlaced Victorian upbringing. This was her man and it was her right to love him as she chose and there was nothing right or wrong. The female in her seemed to know exactly what to do although she had been so lately a virgin.

Her mouth caressed him, teasing him with her warm tongue, tasting the saltiness of him. He was hers now—all hers, for she had kissed all his body.

He began to thrust upward with his strong hips, still keeping his hands clenched on the grass as she had ordered.

"Please, Summer!" he gasped. "I can't take any more of this. Please—!"

And with that plea, she gripped his thighs and took him deep in her mouth, feeling his seed surge as he thrust upward and his hands came up to grasp her face to his groin.

For a long moment, he surged and she tasted the wonder of the slightly salty lifeseed and she had never loved him so much.

Finally, he lay still, breathing heavily and she sat up and looked down at him, knowing no other woman had ever given him so much pleasure.

He rose on one elbow and pulled her up to lie beside him and he looked with tenderness into her face. "You are truly magic!" he murmured, kissing her hair. "How can a virgin make such a love slave of a man? You have to be bewitched, for you hold my heart hostage."

"No, I am the captive, remember? And you have taught me love in a way I never even knew existed."

He pulled her to him in an embrace that crushed her. "I will never let you go even if you want to leave! I swear I have never made love like this to another woman; never even knew it could be so good! I have given you my *tasoom*, the deepest, most tender part of my heart. I don't think I could let you go, no matter what!"

"I will never leave you, my dearest," she promised, kissing the hard planes of his face. "You must learn to trust me for I will never, never hurt you!"

"I think if you did, I would kill you for it!" His voice had a hard, uncertain edge. "If you think you could lie in the arms of another man and laugh at the savage you had toyed with—"

She kissed his mouth to stop his words and felt very small and fragile in his arms that could so easily crush her, but she was not afraid. "I will never leave you," she said again. "And when you finally believe me and trust me, our love will be even better."

For a few minutes, they lay in each other's embrace. Then

179

Iron Knife sat up regretful. "We must return to camp."

He stood and helped her to her feet while she yawned sleepily. He tugged her shift on for her and caressed her with his hard hands as he pulled it down her body. She helped dress him, too, touching and stroking him as she helped him put on his clothes.

Finally, they started down the path to the village. But she tripped in the darkness and would have fallen had he not reached out and caught her. Then he swung her up in his arms and started off in long, easy strides.

"I can walk!" she protested sleepily, resting her face against his chest.

"You didn't seem to be doing a very good job of it." He grinned down at her with white, even teeth. Carelessly, she brushed her mouth against his nipple as he carried her.

His arms tightened on her. "Stop that," he commanded, "or we will spend all night on this hillside!"

She obeyed and let him carry her through the now quiet camp. Only a horse snorted and stamped its hooves as they settled down in the warm buffalo furs and he drifted off to sleep clasped in her arms. But she lay sleepless a long time, wondering at this conflict within her between the militant feminist and the purring female who surrendered everything to rejoice in being dominated by this uncivilized male animal.

Perhaps what she had been battling against all this time was the unfair treatment of soft, civilized white men who could force her to do their bidding but never make her pleased to yield. Iron Knife adored her; she had no reason to rebel anymore. She was fulfilled and satisfied as she drifted off to sleep. She was not Priscilla, her mother, being afraid and dominated. Summer could stand as an equal with her man and it was a wonderful, free feeling.

It was the next morning that more trouble came to the camp. Summer and Iron Knife sat in front of their tepee. Dogs

180

barked, people shouted. There was a flurry of noise and confusion as a group of short, very fierce-looking Indians rode into the encampment. Summer stared at the group and especially at the white man who rode with them. He was dressed Mexican-style and he looked rough and evil. The man stared back at her, tipping his sombrero in a leering grin. She realized then that part of his right ear was gone. The remainder's edge looked ragged as if it had been chewed off in a fight.

Iron Knife sat beside her, repairing arrows as the men rode past.

Summer stared at the riders with a tremor of dislike, thinking some of them were the darkest, most savage Indians she had ever seen. "Who are they?"

"Comanche and their allies, the Kiowa." Iron Knife paused and looked at the group. "Some of their leaders are coming in from Tejas, which the whites call Texas. They have fought the Texans without pause for many years. Now that Texas is part of the United States, they war against the United States, too."

Fascinated, as if she had just seen a poisonous snake, Summer studied the swarthy man who rode with the Comanche. He dressed like a Spanish vaquero with a wicked knife stuck in his belt. Looking back at her as she stared after him, he tipped his sombrero again and smiled widely. *His teeth were sharp and prominent like a lobo wolf's,* Summer thought uneasily. She felt a shiver of warning go up her back.

He wants me, she thought as she reached out and put her hand on Iron Knife's arm for reassurance. *That man looks at me like he already imagines raping me.* She made a quick decision to stay away from him while he was in camp.

The man twisted in his saddle to keep his eyes on her and ran his tongue over his lips in an obscene manner. His eyes seemed to strip the clothes from her body.

Whoever he was, she thought with a shudder, *he had rape on his mind; her rape.*

Chapter Eleven

Iron Knife felt her small hand tighten on his bronzed arm. They both looked after the group riding down through the tepees.

She bit her lip. "That man, he looks white. Why does he ride with the Comanche?"

"Comanchero." Iron Knife's lip curled in distaste. "That is the one they call 'El Lobo,' the wolf. He leads the Comanchero out of their stronghold in the Sangre de Cristo mountains west of Texas."

They watched the men riding down the line of tepees toward the Council lodge.

"Comanchero?" she questioned. "Is he Indian? He looks Spanish."

Iron Knife stared after the group as they dismounted, dislike and disdain in his tone. "Comancheros are sometimes Spanish, outlaw Anglos, mixed bloods of every kind. Scum and bandits, that's what they are. They have traded with the Texas tribes for many years now, supplying weapons, bullets in exchange for stolen horses, cattle, women."

Her pale blue eyes widened in surprise. "Women?"

He nodded. "They'll take children, too. The Comanche take captives on raids and trade them to the Comanchero."

"What do the Comanchero do with the captives?" She

182

looked like a small, curious child as she watched the men talking to some of the Cheyenne men in front of the Council tepee. In the background, he heard the camp crier riding about, announcing the visitors.

"Some of them are ransomed if the families can raise the money. The Comancheros sell others to the Mexican silver mines to use as slaves. The pretty ones end up in whorehouses or someone like El Lobo keeps an occasional one for himself."

Summer shuddered. "What a horrible thought."

He put his big hand over her small one. "I never told you everything that was discussed at Council the night your fate was decided. Some thought we should trade you to the Comanche to be sold off to the Mexicans for use in a whorehouse."

She looked at him. "Would you have let them do that?"

He studied her tenderly. "Did you not see my hand go to my knife that night? I was ready to fight my way out of that Council and take you with me." He smiled mischievously. "But maybe you would have been one of the lucky ones. Instead of ending up in a whorehouse, you might have become the mistress of a powerful Comanchero like El Lobo."

Summer wrinkled her nose. "Him! He looks filthy! I'll bet he even smells bad."

Iron Knife laughed as he stood up and stretched. "You will never have to get close enough to find out. They will only be in camp a few hours. There is disagreement among the Comanche and Kiowa whether to try to make a treaty with the whites or keep fighting them. Probably they want to see what their allies, the Cheyenne and Arapaho, think."

He put away the arrows he had been repairing. "All the warriors will be expected to put on their best and come to the meeting."

"The women are not invited, as usual?"

He pulled her to her feet, slapped her rump as men do to a woman whose body is familiar to them, liking the feel of her bottom. "You can sit and peek under the edge of the tepee if

183

you wish, if you don't mind watching a bunch of old men smoke and beat around the bush for hours. It's not polite to get right to the point at a Council meeting."

She giggled and rolled her eyes. "No, thanks. It's going to be a hot day for late September, and I don't think I want to sit in the heat when I don't speak enough Indian or border Spanish to follow what's going on. You tell me about it later. I think I'll go down to the river and swim."

"Don't go by yourself," he warned. "You never know what will happen out here in the wilderness."

"Okay," she agreed as she ambled off toward Pony Woman's tepee.

Iron Knife called after her wistfully. "What you're doing sounds like more fun. As soon as the meeting's over, I'll join you in the water. There's a private little nook around the bend where we could spend the rest of the afternoon."

She turned around and laughed, still walking backward. "Don't you ever think of anything else?"

He winked at her. "Do you?"

With a sigh, he went inside to dress for the Council meeting. He was not looking forward to sitting through the Council with their fierce, southern allies. The warlike braves could only be here for one reason.

He was right, of course, he thought wearily as he sat cross-legged with the others in the big tepee watching the old men smoke. As the discussion began in border Spanish and sign language, Iron Knife fought an impulse to yawn. It wasn't polite to get right to the point and the old ones wanted to remember every battle they had all fought together as allies since they had made peace with each other in 1840.

Frowning slightly, he studied the swarthy Comanchero who sat cross-legged next to the Kiowa leader, Aperian Crow. *He shouldn't be here*, Iron Knife thought as the pipe was passed toward the Spaniard, *he is not Indian, not even in his heart*.

184

"Wait!" Old Blue Eagle made a dissenting motion and the pipe paused in the hands of old Bull Hump, the Comanche. Disapproval etched itself on the old Cheyenne's face. "This white." He nodded toward the Comanchero. "This hombre is not Indian, he should not be allowed to smoke."

"I deal with your allies a long time," the man protested. "They share their food and women slaves with me."

"But you are not Indian," Clouds Above said, "and we do not trust you."

The swarthy Spaniard glared at Iron Knife. "I see a half-breed in the Council meeting. Am I not as welcome to smoke the pipe as he?"

Scalp Taker frowned. "We have never thought of the one you mention as white. In his heart, he is as Cheyenne as any man of us."

Iron Knife gritted his teeth and stood up, anger and indignation in his soul.

The chiefs nodded at him, giving him permission to speak.

"My father was the great chief, War Bonnet," he retorted with a scornful curl of his lip, "and I am a Dog Soldier, a carrier of the *Hotamtsit*. How dare you question my right to sit in this Council! We have a right to question you because you sell out your own kind for money. I say you are no better than the carrion Pawnee and Crow who work as scouts for the bluecoats, accepting white man's money in exchange for leading the soldiers to Indian villages!"

He heard murmurs of agreement among the others and many heads nodded as Iron Knife sat down.

Old Blue Eagle spoke. "What the brave Dog Soldier says is true. A man who would sell out his own kind for profit is a man without a soul, a man who is evil." He looked toward the visiting Comanche and Kiowa chiefs. "Why did you bring this Comanchero among us?"

Old Bull Hump shook his gray braids. "I would not have brought him, for, like you, I trust him little."

Little Buffalo, the Comanche with the reputation for a

185

ruthless hatred of whites, stood now and touched his chest. "I brought this man with us. We have come to talk with our Cheyenne and Arapaho brothers about uniting to attack the whites although not all Comanche want to take the war trail." He looked scornfully toward old Bull Hump.

The fierce Kiowa leader, Aperian Crow, spoke. "If you decide to join us in fighting, the Comanchero will be useful in supplying weapons and bullets as he has in the past. He asked to come along, smelling out profit as a buzzard sniffs rotten meat. But the Cheyenne are right." He gestured. "This is a meeting for Indians." He looked toward El Lobo. "I say the Comanchero should wait outside, since he will have no part in the decision-making."

Little Buffalo nodded in agreement. "I have no love for the Comanchero. Any man who would sell weapons to kill his own people is beneath contempt, but useful, nevertheless. Since I brought him, I now say to him, 'Go wait without and amuse yourself. If we reach an agreement needing your services, we will call you back in.'"

The Comanchero stood up, anger dark on his face and went outside the Council tepee.

Iron Knife sighed as the pipe began its rounds again. The Comanche and Kiowa were wasting their time here, he thought. The Cheyenne who wanted to fight had gone off to join the renegade Dog Soldiers and he knew the rest of the clan felt the same way as old Bull Hump. They wanted no more trouble with the white soldiers who were itching to attack Indians. The Cheyenne only wanted to be left in peace.

His mind had wandered and now came back to the discussions. Aperian Crow had stood and was speaking. ". . . because we have always fought the Texans and Mexicans," he said, "and probably always will, since they hunger to own all of the land west and even our Sacred Mountains near the river they call the Red. Now, the Texans have made peace with the Great White Father whose tepee is in that place called Washington. I do not understand exactly what has happened, but somehow the Texans are no longer a separate people but part of the tribes of the United States."

He sat down and the hot-blooded Comanche leader, Little Buffalo, said: "We hear rumbles of news sometimes from the Comancheros and the traders. They say, soon the whites may fight among themselves over whether any of them will be allowed to own the black people. If this should happen, it would be a good time for the Indians to start their own war against all whites. If the soldiers are busy in the east fighting each other, there will be few of them on the plains to keep us from reclaiming our land."

Old Bull Hump stood as the younger man sat down. For a long moment, there was no sound save the crackle of the Council fire as all waited respectfully for that great old chief to speak. "All here know my reputation. I have fought the whites for many years. When they write their history, my name will be mentioned many times." He paused and looked around into each face. "Each man here knows my many coups and scalp counts. But I say, even if the whites do fight each other over the black people, we still cannot win. My clan is tired; many have died. I have come along to hear the talks, but I tell you now I will not lead my people on any more war parties."

He hesitated so long that no one was quite sure if he was finished.

"What are the Great Chief Bull Hump's intentions?" Clouds Above asked politely.

"My clan has been invited to meet with the soldier chief for a peace parlay here in the Indian Territory at the springs near the stream the whites call Rush Creek. Even now, my band awaits me there while visiting and trading with the Wichita village nearby. I say 'no' to war. I will go back to my band and await the coming of the soldier chief." He spoke with tired finality as he sat down.

Aperian Crow rose to speak again, goading the Cheyenne and Arapaho to join him on the war path, but Iron Knife knew before the discussion was over that the Kiowa was wasting his time and the Comanchero would make no weapons sales here. Those two leaders might continue to fight the whites, but Iron Knife's people only wanted to keep their peace treaty and be left alone to hunt and live in dignity.

His mind strayed as the discussion neared its ending. It was sweltering in the Council tepee and his mind went again to Summer and he smiled slightly, thinking of her laughing and splashing in the cool river, thinking of joining her in the secluded nook to swim and make love. . . .

As Summer had turned and walked away from Iron Knife, she had not really minded that she could not attend the Council. The day was warm for late September and she would really rather play in the water. Walking down to see if Pony Woman wanted to accompany her to the river, she felt so lighthearted, she actually skipped a few steps. The freedom of the Indian encampment was unbelievable to her.

If Summer had been in Boston on a lazy afternoon like this, she thought, she would have been wearing a whalebone corset cinching her waist so tightly she could hardly breathe. In addition, there would have been long pantaloons, a corset cover, numerous petticoats, and tight shoes. Her afternoon would have been spent doing needlework, playing the harp, or returning a social call on other young ladies as bored and idle as she was herself. The most exciting happening would be class at Miss Priddy's stuffy school or riding in an open carriage around Boston, carefully escorted, of course. She had done a lot of shopping because it was something for a rich girl to do, although she cared little for clothes and possessions. There were no sports available to a debutante that were acceptable except walking, riding sidesaddle, or the occasional society ball.

Last year, she had tried to go to work in Father's business and the scene that ensued almost put him in the hospital. Respectable women did not work, he informed her icily, and he would be laughed out of Boston society if Summer came to that male enclave of his office and attempted to work in his business. Unfortunate widows and unmarried ladies generally took the charity of a brother or married sister to survive. If they were educated, they might be lucky enough to land a spot as a governess. Loftily, Summer informed him that all would change when women got the vote. His outraged shouting could be heard all the way out to the front sidewalk, or so the family coachman told her later.

Yes, it was a relief to have the freedom of the Indian encampment, Summer thought as she went to find Iron Knife's aunt. She found her but that chubby lady made it plain by gestures that she was curious to sit beside the Council tepee and watch the proceedings. Pretty Flower Woman, Two Arrows' new wife was scraping a hide to make a new dress and shook her head about going to the river. Not knowing who else to ask, Summer went down to the river alone and watched several women and children playing in the shallows. Her ankle still hurt a little and she favored it when she walked. Summer found the private little nook she thought Iron Knife had mentioned. It was secluded with no one else close by. She took off her buckskin shift, hung it over a limb, and waded naked out into the blue water. Its surface was placid and reflected her image like a mirror.

Summer played like a child in the shallows, enjoying the feel of the cool water on her hot skin, the scent of towering pines and wildflowers. Bright butterflies rose up as the breeze stirred the flowers and bird calls echoed through the rocky hills. It was a bright day, a day all gold and green and blue.

She played in the water a long time, lost in the naughty thrill of being naked, splashing about in the shallows like a small, sleek otter. She must get Iron Knife to teach her to swim, she thought regretfully. None of the women she knew in Boston could swim. The cumbersome costumes they wore to protect their modesty precluded such activity.

A long time passed before she noticed the sun was high in the heavens and all the women and children had gradually left the area.

Yawning, Summer stood up near the bank. it was only knee-deep there and she splashed with her toes, oblivious to her own nakedness since there was no one to see her.

Summer decided that she would go lay on the warm sand until that tiresome Council meeting was over and Iron Knife joined her. She had done all her work until tomorrow when she was supposed to help Pony Woman and Pretty Flower Woman make pemmican.

She paused, apprehension stealing over her. She felt a strange feeling of being watched. It had been foolish of her to stay at the river when there was no one else nearby. Iron Knife had cautioned her and she had ignored his warning. She would fetch her shift, she decided, and get herself back to the village until Iron Knife could accompany her.

But as she started up out of the water, a man stepped out of the woods, the Comanchero of this morning. He leered at her as he stepped over, grabbed her dress, and held it up triumphantly.

"*Bueno dias, señorita.*" His pointed teeth smiled in a wolfish grin as he walked toward her. "*No habla español?* Do you speak English or Comanche?" He spoke a curious mixture of border Spanish and pidgin English. Summer didn't answer as she tried to cover herself with her hands and backed slowly to the edge of the water.

"Please, señor," she pleaded. "My dress—"

He wadded the dress, tossed it to one side as he advanced toward the water. "Come here, *puta*. Whore," he hissed. "You can't be much if you're livin' with the Injuns, letting every red hombre top you."

"Get away from me," she warned, backing deeper into the water.

"You want money?" He held up coins. "I have ribbons, trinkets in my saddlebags."

"My man will come if I scream—"

He threw his head back and laughed. "Señorita, I know Injuns well. I've spent my life among them, *comprende?* If I offer your man a little whiskey, some ammunition, maybe a rifle in exchange for an hour with you, he'll be eager to share you." The man moved even closer and Summer backed waist-deep into the water. She looked frantically behind her, afraid to go any deeper.

The man was up to his boot tops in the water now, motioning invitingly to her. "*Sí*, come out. Make your own deal with me. Why should you not get the gifts for your favors instead of me giving them to your man? *Comprende?*"

He scowled, pulling at his chewed ear. "If I have to get wet to get you, you'll regret it!"

Summer felt the current pulling at her naked body. She was deep as she could go without being able to swim and the short, powerful man was wading out to her.

"Come here, *puta*, you whore," he swore. "You're ruining my good disposition that I should have to get wet to reach you, but perhaps hard to reach fruit is the sweetest, *sí?*"

Summer wished now with all her heart that she had listened to Iron Knife. But she had expected this Comanchero to sit through the council meeting, too. If she did scream, would anyone hear her over the usual noise of the camp?

Summer couldn't get to shore without getting past him and he seemed to sense this.

"Come, sweet one," he coaxed. "Maybe I will trade your man out of you and take you with me. I have a hideout with a hundred men at my command up in the hills of New Mexico. You could be my woman."

"No." She shook her head and the blond hair trailed in the water. "No, I will stay with the man I have."

"Stubborn bitch," he swore and let loose a string of oaths in Spanish as he spat in the river. He glided even closer through the water and she thought suddenly of a deadly water moccasin snake slipping through the current.

She couldn't move any farther back. The sluggish river

current was already tugging at her bare body. But if she stayed where she was, he would reach her in seconds. Clumsily, she struck out, trying to swim around him in a wide circle.

But he laughed easily as he reached, caught her wrist, and started back toward shore. She struggled and fought him as he dragged her toward land and he turned and forced her head under water.

She came up choking and coughing and he laughed, showing gleaming, sharp teeth. "You got too much spirit, *puta* whore! El Lobo likes his women docile as sheep. You need the fight taken out of you and I'm just the hombre to do it!"

Summer strangled on the water, without enough air to scream as he dragged her into the shallows, twisted her hands behind her back.

He grinned down at her, water dripping from his clothes. "I told you you'd be sorry if I had to get wet, gringo bitch. Now, I'll show you how to make a woman docile. When I get through with you, you'll be glad to lay on that beach and take my weight without a whimper just so I won't hold you under again."

Realizing what he intended to do, she struggled, tried to cry out for help. It was a long way to the village, she thought with sudden clarity, and she might not be heard over all the noise of barking dogs and playing children.

Even as he stood dripping in the ankle-deep water, he suddenly hooked his foot behind her slim legs, tripped her so that she fell backward. As she went down on her back, he moved her imprisoned wrists above her head and fell heavily atop her.

By lifting her head, she could keep her face above water, but otherwise she was helpless. His weight prevented her from moving and his strong grip held her wrists pinned above her head against the sand of the river bottom.

His face loomed close to hers and she could smell the stench of garlic and rotten teeth as he bent to kiss her. She struggled and tried to bite him, wincing from the sharp conchos and metal of his belt on her bare skin.

192

He smiled. "You've got more spirit than I thought, *señorita*. This is gonna be mucho fun." He reached with one big hand to touch her forehead and applied pressure. With horror, she felt him gradually submerging her face.

Her straining neck was no match for his brute strength as he forced her head backward. He was going to drown her in ankle-deep water! In panic, she fought to get out from under him, lift her face out of the river. She felt the cold water splashing against her cheeks, her nose. Then, he had the back of her head against the river bottom and she felt the water covering her face completely.

In cold horror, she fought to get back up to the life-giving air, but through the cold water she could see his evil face laughing with delight. Summer gasped and choked in panic, straining all her muscles to get out from under him.

After a long moment, he took his hand off her face and she managed to raise her head up out of the water although it lapped around her cheekbones. Summer gasped for air, choking and coughing while he laughed.

"See, white whore, when you struggle or try to scream, your head gets submerged again. You think I won't drown you? *Sí*, I would." He nodded. "I wouldn't even mind taking you dead. A dead female is mucho docile. I know, I've done it before."

He was crazy, Summer thought in desperation. Why hadn't she listened to Iron Knife about coming to the river alone?

"Listen," she gasped. "Let's get up on shore and make love. It would be better than this."

He didn't move, leering down at her as he lay on her. She was struggling to breathe with his dead weight on her naked body.

The dirty Spaniard was enjoying tormenting her, she realized suddenly as his hand moved slowly toward her forehead again. The thought came to her that he was becoming sexually aroused from scaring and torturing her. She stared up in horror at the hand coming down toward her face.

"No!" she protested, trying to free her hands from above her head, arching against him in protest. "Let me up! My man will kill you for this!"

"You said the wrong thing, white bitch. *Comprende?*" and his expression was mean and ugly. "I know Injuns. I'll give him a few trinkets from my trade goods and he'll let me use you any way I want. Now, submit!"

But Summer struggled again, trying to escape his crushing weight on her small body and looked up to see his hand descending relentlessly. She did her best to keep her face above water but his fingers were on her forehead again and he was forcing her head back, under the water so that her nostrils were barely covered. Desperately, Summer tried to hold her breath, but the pressure of his hand never let up. Finally, she had to take a breath and her nose and mouth filled with water. Never had she known such panic! He was drowning her and she was helpless to save herself.

Finally, he moved his hand and she managed to get her face to the surface again, gulping air in great gasps.

She could see the evil delight gleaming in his eyes and remembered suddenly catching her young sister pulling the wings off flies at the music-room window. Her sister had worn just such an expression.

The Comanchero's swarthy face was very close to hers now and he whispered, "I think I might want to take you from behind, bitch. Do you realize I could drown you in only an inch of water as I mount you with both my hands on the back of your head?"

He would do it, too. She knew that now, looking into the crazed face only inches from her own. Her neck ached with the strain of holding her head up out of the water and she could hardly breathe from the heavy weight of him across her. She tried to wiggle her fingers pinned in the mud above her head and realized her arms were going to sleep with the circulation cut off as it was.

"Please!" she managed to gasp. "I'll let you do anything you want if we get up on the riverbank."

"Anything?" She could see the cruel ideas lurking behind

the wolfish eyes. Lord help the poor Texas ranch women who had fallen into his hands on raids!

"Anything," she whimpered, trying hard to hide her anger and appear as docile as he wanted.

He laughed and stood up, jerking her to her feet. "I didn't think you wanted to die! Maybe I might give you enough pleasure that you will want to accompany El Lobo back to the Sangre de Cristo mountains, *sí?*"

"Maybe," she managed to say as he dragged her toward the shore. *He was going to have to kill her first before she let him rape her,* she thought with stubborn determination. Summer was buying time for herself, hoping against hope that someone might come down to the water and go for help. She wanted it so desperately, she imagined she saw Pretty Flower Woman watching from behind a tree. *Terror does strange things to the mind,* she thought desperately, because when she looked again she saw nothing.

El Lobo dragged her dripping and coughing up on the beach and took her in his arms, running his big, dirty hands up and down her naked back. She could feel the heat of his hard manhood against her bare belly as he reached to unbutton his pants.

"I'm gonna take a quick sample, *señorita,* without ever taking my clothes off. If you're as good as you look, I'll trade you away from your Injun. I might not even make you service my men at the stronghold; just me alone."

His wet, slimy mouth was on hers, forcing her lips apart as she still gasped for air and one of his callused hands cupped her breast, squeezing cruelly.

Summer relaxed in his arms a moment, trying not to retch on the taste of his filthy mouth exploring hers, his hands running freely over her soft skin.

If he would just let down his guard . . .

It was now or never! She pretended to respond to his lust, molded her body against his dripping wet clothes. His body relaxed its guard a little as he enjoyed the kiss. This was her one chance and she took it. In a quick, desperate move, Summer brought her knee up, caught him in the groin. As he moaned and turned loose of her to grasp himself, she broke away and started to run. She didn't quite make it.

The Comanchero swore viciously in Spanish as he reached out, caught her arm. "You bitch!" he swore. "You conniving bitch! I'll make you wish you had never done that!"

She tried to scream but he had his hand clasped over her mouth again, dragging her to the water. She fought with everything she had, knowing this time he was going to drown her and rape her dead body. But she weighed less than half his weight and she was like a broken doll in his grasp as he dragged her into the ankle-deep water.

"Now, *puta!*" he swore. "I told you I'd do this. Didn't you believe me?"

He threw her down on her belly in the shallow water, knelt with one big hand on the small of her back, and threw his full weight on it so she couldn't get away.

"Aha! *señorita.*" He laughed gleefully. "I'm gonna put one boot on the back of your neck and put your face in that mud. After I hold you under a few more times, it'll take the fight out of you, no? And if not, I will enjoy you every bit as much unconscious or dead!"

She could feel his big boot on the back of her neck now. Her own terrified face reflected back at her in the dark water only inches from her nostrils with his ugly face looming in the background.

His boot came down on her neck with his weight behind it and her own horrified image came up to meet her. She could feel the rough grit of the sand bottom on her tender cheek as he pushed her face under and she fought in terror to free herself.

It seemed an eternity that she struggled and fought, feeling his hand on the small of her back, his boot on her neck as he pressed her face against the river bottom. She held her breath as long as she could before she had to breathe in and the water rushed into her mouth and nose.

196

Never had she known such terror! Just as she was blacking out, he took his foot off her neck and she managed to raise up on her elbows, gasping and strangling as the life-giving air rushed into her heaving lungs.

Summer tried to scream out but was too spent to give more than a weak cry.

The man moved to mount her from behind. "And now, you bitch, I'm gonna take you like a wolf takes a bitch in heat and you're gonna lay on your belly and take it without a whimper. *Comprende?*"

Summer took another breath of air, almost too exhausted to struggle now. It was all she could do to lie on her belly, raising up on her elbows as the man lay his great weight across her hips. She could feel his hot, hard manhood against her naked bottom as he spread his length along her back.

His clumsy hands reached around to grasp her full breasts and squeeze. "I like something to hang on to when I take a ride," he chuckled close to her ear as he prepared to enter her.

She was determined not to submit to him if she had to die for it! As he rose up on his knees to come into her, Summer struggled, again determined to fight her way out from under him. If she could ever break free and make it to the village . . .

She couldn't even get out from under him. He gripped her breasts so cruelly, she cried out and his mouth was on her ear, biting at the lobe. "Give up, whore. I'm gonna take you, and for this I teach you a lesson, *si?*"

His hands moved to the back of her head as he positioned himself again. "I'm gonna hold your head under while I'm enjoying you! If my pleasure lasts too long, you may be dead by the time I let up."

She was a scant inch from the water again, fighting to keep her face up as he positioned himself to take her from behind. She could feel him forcing her legs apart, panting with the pleasure and expectation of enjoying her.

She was too tired, too weak to fight any longer, her aching body told her as he forced her face toward the water. It would

197

be so much easier just to give up and die. *Drowning was probably an easy death*, she thought as he pushed her face into the water again. *Just relax and breathe in and in seconds blackness will overcome me and I'll be past terror, past pain, past anything but oblivion.* But her spirit refused to give up. Even as he pushed her head under, she came up out of the water fighting while he swore and struck at her.

"Iron Knife!" she managed to scream as she realized she was going to die. "Iron Knife, where are you?"

Chapter Twelve

And suddenly he was there, charging across the shallow water like an enraged buffalo bull, grasping El Lobo by the arm, throwing him to one side.

The Indian was a tanned, avenging angel to her dazed eyes. She struggled up out of the water and heard his angry swear words. Then he lifted her dripping and gasping and carried her to the bank. Summer saw Pretty Flower Woman's anxious face peering down at her as the Indian girl covered Summer with the buckskin shift.

Pretty Flower Woman looked worried. "I came down for water, saw what was happening, and went for help."

Summer smiled gratefully at the girl. Around her, Indians were running from all directions.

But Summer's eyes searched anxiously for only one face, one pair of eyes. "Iron Knife," she gasped as she looked up into his face that was dark with fury, "I—I knew you'd come when I needed you most!"

Iron Knife studied Summer's pale, bruised face as he grasped the hilt of his big knife hard and turned toward the Comanchero who stood staring at him, his dripping clothes making a puddle on the dry sand of the riverbank.

"You greasy son of a Mexican whore!" Iron Knife crouched and drew his blade. "For this, I kill you!"

"Now, wait *uno momento. Comprende?*" The man made placating gestures with his dirty hands. "I didn't hurt her none, I was just teasin' her a little, huh, hombre? Listen, I've got a lot of trade goods with me. I'll buy her from you and you can pick up another girl next time you go on a raid."

"No!" Iron Knife moved toward him as a circle of curious Indians formed. "My woman isn't for sale and I'm going to gut you for the insult!"

The Comanchero backed away slowly. "*Sí,* I understand. You don't want to sell her. Tell you what, El Lobo is a generous man." He smiled and his wolfish teeth gleamed in his swarthy face. "I give you a good rifle, even some firewater just to use her a couple of hours this afternoon before we leave the camp. Now that's fair enough, isn't it?"

Iron Knife had never felt such anger as he glared at the man and looked over to where Summer Sky shivered and coughed, holding the deerskin shift up against her bruised breasts. Even from here, he could see scratch marks and wounds on her fair skin.

"You Mexican bastard, make ready to die!" He swore, and the veins stood out in anger and throbbed in his neck. "I'm going to spill your guts all over this riverbank!"

He hefted the big knife from one hand to the other easily and saw sudden fear in the squint eyes as the Comanchero reached for his own long blade.

El Lobo looked around the circle of faces desperately. "No fair, *amigo,* these are all your friends." He gestured toward the circle of faces. "If I kill you and then they all attack me, I'm up against a stacked deck, no?"

Iron Knife looked around the circle. The old chiefs had joined the growing crowd along with the visiting Comanche and Kiowas. His own cousins moved in behind the Mexican but Iron Knife shook his head warningly at them.

"I want no help, no interference," he ordered everyone.

"To me alone belongs the pleasure of spilling his guts upon the ground and rubbing his face in them while he dies!"

Scalp Taker nodded in agreement and spoke in a mixture of broken Spanish, Cheyenne, and sign language. "So much trouble over a woman! But young blood runs forever hot. This is between them over this blond one."

The old Cheyenne turned toward the Comanche and Kiowa chiefs. "Is this acceptable to you?"

Bull Hump shrugged. "The Comanchero means nothing to us except that we trade with him sometimes. Let the two young stallions fight for the white girl and no one else interfere."

Little Buffalo and Aperian Crow nodded in agreement as did the other chiefs.

The Kiowa, Aperian Crow, raised an eyebrow as he folded his arms. "This provides an interesting entertainment. The Comanchero has always made big boasts about his bravery. I'll wager a new blanket on his chances. And if he wins, I may try to buy the girl from El Lobo myself."

Iron Knife started to protest, realized the others were nodding in agreement with the Kiowa as bets were wagered. It seemed simple enough to all the watching men. Like any wild herd, the male who won got the privilege of mating the female. He could do nothing but agree. But he didn't intend to lose.

Glancing over at Summer, he realized by her strickened face that she had finally comprehended what was about to happen, that she was the prize in a fight to the death.

The Comanchero was shorter but heavy and perhaps more powerful, Iron Knife thought as he watched the man pull out his own wicked dagger, heft it in his hand.

The man seemed self-assured now and he sneered. "Okay, hombre, I'm the challenged one so I get to choose the way we fight. You know the Rio Grande way of dueling?"

Iron Knife felt his stomach lurch. He had never fought Rio Grande style, but judging from the sudden cockiness of the other, El Lobo had.

Iron Knife could not back down now and only spilling this

man's blood would cool his anger. "I have lived among the whites, I know how it is done. Yes, I will fight you this way."

He saw the sudden frown on his uncle's stern countenance and the worry on his cousins' faces. An excited murmur ran through the crowd as those who knew the method of dueling whispered it to the others.

Even Summer glanced around, obviously picking up the bits and pieces of Cheyenne words.

"No!" she protested, staggering to her feet as she clutched the buckskin shift around her naked body. "No! I won't let you—"

"You can't stop me," Iron Knife said quietly, his anger still making the cords stand out on his neck as he looked at her bruises. She ran to him, clutched him imploringly.

"No!" she wept. "I don't want you to risk your life over me!"

She clung to him and he looked over her head at his aunt, signaled her with his eyes. Pony Woman came over, unclasped Summer's hands, and dragged her kicking and fighting to the edge of the big circle.

Old Blue Eagle walked with much pomp to the center of the circle, a strip of rawhide in his hands. "Come forward, both of you!"

Iron Knife took one more look at the weeping, injured girl to fuel his anger as he stalked to the center. The Comanchero came to the old chief's other side. Blue Eagle commanded, "Your left wrists!" Both men slowly extended their left arms, each holding his wicked blade in his right hand.

Blue Eagle bound the two men's wrists together securely with the rawhide strip. "This is a fight to the death," he announced to the crowd. "The winner cuts himself loose from the other's dead body and takes the girl!"

A murmur ran through the crowd and Iron Knife knew what they were all thinking by looking around the circle of worried faces. On horseback, armed with a bow and lance, a Cheyenne Dog Soldier had no equal in the world. But afoot, armed with a weapon more familiar to the Spanish, Iron Knife was at a distinct disadvantage.

Iron Knife felt a quiver of excitement and danger run over him as he studied the old scars on El Lobo's arms and face. No wonder he had chosen these rules. Iron Knife voiced his thoughts impulsively. "You have fought this way many times?"

The other threw back his head and laughed as the old chief finished binding the two together, tested the rope for sturdiness. "You betcha, you loco red hombre! I've killed four men in cantinas this way and cut the ears off three more!"

A murmur ran through the crowd as Bull Hump and Little Buffalo translated his Spanish boasts so that the crowd could understand him.

Blue Eagle held each of their right hands in his hands so neither could make a sudden first lunge. "Are you ready?"

Both nodded eagerly. On the sidelines, Summer struggled in plump Pony Woman's arms and tried to protest.

Pony Woman frowned and held on to her. "Be quiet, white girl. You humiliate my nephew with your protests. Besides, when men fight, they pay no heed to women's cries."

A hush fell over the crowd as the old chief disengaged slowly from the pair, backed to the edge of the circle. Now the two faced each other in a fighting stance, big, sharp blades in each right hand, the length of their two left arms between them.

Nervously, Iron Knife hefted the knife in his hand. The sun glinted off the bright blade, momentarily blinding him as he took the measure of the other. Very slowly, they moved in a tight circle, tightly bound at the left wrists.

He could see by the other's frown that he was taking Iron Knife's measure also and not liking the odds. They circled warily, each with his knife ready. It was a war of nerves and a man who was easily panicked could be hurried into making the first move, slashing in too fast and getting sliced open by an opponent with steady nerves.

Iron Knife felt slightly unsure of himself, never having

fought this white man's way before. He did not feel easy about being tied to an opponent so that he could not dodge and attack, using his lightning reflexes to best advantage.

The sun reflected off his blade again and he glanced past his opponent's shoulder and saw a dragonfly hovering in the background over a wildflower. Steel cold calm descended on his being because his spirit animal had sent a sign. When the right moment came, the dragonfly would tell him what to do; help him. He sent a silent prayer of thanks toward the spirits as he moved with renewed confidence. *The dragonfly*, he thought. *It will tell me.*

But the other caught him unaware, jerking suddenly on the tied wrists and with powerful muscles pulled Iron Knife off balance and to his knees.

Using his own great strength, Iron Knife recovered quickly, jerking the man about and dodging as the other flashed in for the kill and missed, but left a bloody cut along Iron Knife's ribs.

Summer screamed and there was a murmur through the crowd as the opponent drew first blood.

The Comanchero leered triumphantly. "This is going to be easier than I thought! I should have wagered more than just the mating of your female!"

The Spaniard was goading Iron Knife. He could feel the anger rising in him, struggled to keep his calm. A man enraged is a man too quick to attack, too eager to think straight.

Iron Knife smiled in challenge, feeling the warm blood dripping down his naked body from the cut. "You greasy, one-eared offal." He raised an eyebrow archly. "You cross between the lowest *puta* and a mangy, rabid coyote!"

The other's face flushed dark red and his eyes blinked rapidly as he swore in Spanish. "I'll kill you for that, Injun, do you understand? Then I'll slice your ears off and your woman's, too. What I intend to enjoy on her, she don't need ears for."

The Comanchero was roaring mad. It was visible in the way

his nostrils flared and the way he charged in recklessly. Iron Knife sidestepped easily and cut the Spaniard's arm open to the bone as they gripped each other's knife hands and struggled for supremacy.

The other roared in pain and rage like a wounded bear and jerked hard on his own left wrist, taking Iron Knife off center with sheer strength. Iron Knife fought for balance but went to one knee and threw his right arm up to ward off the other's downward thrust. They poised thus a long, heart-stopping moment as they struggled before Iron Knife managed to throw the other's knife arm away from him and the other lost his balance and went down slashing. The momentum of his fall took Iron Knife down with him and they meshed and rolled over and over in the circle.

He heard Summer's cry of warning and threw his hand up in time to grip the other's wrist. His opponent used sheer weight to battle to the top.

Sweat dripped from both of them and dust clung to their bodies. The Comanchero laughed viciously as he tried to bring his knife down for the kill. The pain of the long cut on Iron Knife's ribs stung as sweat and dust covered the raw flesh. His life was slowly draining out of him through the slash. If he didn't finish this soon, he would lose consciousness and his life. He could smell the rotten breath and the rank sweat of the Spaniard as they struggled.

Gritting his teeth, Iron Knife held the other's knife wrist and the man's warm blood ran down both their arms. The other grinned down at him. "Think! You red bastard, you son of a white whore who would mate with even the cannibal Tonkawa, think how tonight I will enjoy lying between the legs of your woman while you lie here on the sand with your spilled guts crawling with blue flies!"

White-hot anger at the image gave Iron Knife new strength and he jerked suddenly on the other's arm and flipped him over his head. For a split second, they scrambled in the dust, each jerking on his left wrist to throw the other off balance and slashing with his right hand. Iron Knife could taste bitter fear and revulsion at the image the Comanchero drew of Summer's fate. Dirt and sweat ran down his rugged face and into his grimacing mouth as they struggled to their feet and crouched again in a fighting stance.

He was dizzy and faint from the heat of the autumn sun that shone like a gold coin in the pale blue sky and the loss of the carmine blood that slowly dripped down his side.

The other's arm showed white bone where Iron Knife had slashed it open. Both men's blood dripped between their feet, making mud for the combatants to slip in.

They feinted slowly, cautiously, each realizing they were both tired, both almost to the end of their endurance. There were only one or two good moves left in either of them, Iron Knife thought, taking a deep breath as they circled warily. He knew now why the Comanchero had wanted to fight this way. *He was the best with a blade Iron Knife had ever challenged; maybe even better than himself.*

But Iron Knife knew he had one thing in his favor, one thing that gave him extra strength and purpose the other didn't have. Iron Knife glanced at the sobbing blond girl. Iron Knife was fighting for love; to protect his woman. The other fought for lust and the sheer joy of murder. The first gave Iron Knife a spiritual advantage. But he was tiring fast, he knew, even faster than the Comanchero. He jerked El Lobo off his feet and they rolled over and over again, then staggered slowly to their feet.

Iron Knife knew from the black shadows that kept blurring images in his vision that he was near to unconsciousness. He only had another minute or two, maybe one or two good strokes left in his weakening arm before he collapsed into blackness. He was running out of time. If he didn't kill the Mexican in the next minute, he would collapse from lack of blood and never awaken again.

The Comanchero knew it too. He leered triumphantly toward Summer. "I may gut you so you'll die slow, hombre. *Comprende?* I want you to see me cut your woman's ears off!"

Dimly, Iron Knife saw the dragonfly floating slowly outside the circle, its green and gold gauze wings reflecting as it lit on a bright red wildflower. Was it a spirit animal or was it his father returning to help him? The light reflected off the luminous wings again. *Reflection. The sun shone off his blade like a mirror and he knew, he finally knew what the spirit had tried to tell him from the first moment he had seen it.*

Iron Knife thanked the spirits silently again as he smiled triumphantly. "You Mexican dog," he said. "You have just pronounced your own sentence!" And with that, he gave the rallying cry of the Dog Soldier, the high-pitched shriek that sounded like a savage, half-wild ghost or phantom wolf. As he did, he turned his blade so that it caught the sunlight, reflected in the Comanchero's eyes, temporarily blinding him. In split-second reflex, the Mexican half-closed his eyes, threw his hand up to shield his vision from the blinding dazzle. But Iron Knife took advantage of the moment, jerked the man off-balance, and as El Lobo went down on his back, Iron Knife kicked the Comanchero's knife out of his hand and out of the circle.

"You pronounced the punishment!" Iron Knife swore as his razor-sharp knife flashed.

The man screamed in pain and protest as Iron Knife cut off his good ear and held the bloody blade to the man's throat.

There was a long moment of silence broken only by the Spaniard's whimpering as the man lay on his back, his left hand pinned above his head by Iron Knife's left hand. His own weapon lay out on the edge of the circle while Iron Knife's bloody blade was held against the jugular vein of his dirty throat.

As the man whimpered, Iron Knife looked to the old chiefs for directions. The Comanche, Bull Hump, nodded. "You have won fair. Kill him and cut yourself loose from his body!"

The others nodded in agreement as the Comanchero looked around the circle, his eyes pleading like a terrified cur dog. "Please, hombre, I beg you for my life—"

Iron Knife spat in his face. "My woman begged. Did you

show her mercy?"

The Comanchero sobbed now, writhing under the edge of the sharp blade. He was so terrified, he wet himself and Iron Knife wrinkled his nose at the strong smell of urine.

The other men laughed in satisfaction and a murmur ran through the crowd. "You have cut off his ear, brave warrior. Now cut his throat while he dirties himself like a papoose!"

"Yes," someone else shouted. "We want to see him flop around like a headless bird as his lifeblood makes mud beneath him!"

But Iron Knife turned to look toward Summer. "It is your choice. What say you?"

He heard her gasp, saw her strickened face. But he knew her heart, knew what she would say.

"Turn him loose," she said so softly that he knew she spoke only to him. "Turn him loose. Spill no coward's blood on my behalf!"

Iron Knife nodded, and with one lightning stroke cut the band that bound him to the other. The Comanchero stumbled to his feet, holding on to the side of his head that dripped scarlet blood down his dirty neck.

Iron Knife wiped his knife on the sand, stuck it back in his belt as he swayed to his feet. "The generosity of Summer Sky gives back your life," he said. "Now, come no more to the Hevataniu Cheyenne!"

Clouds Above turned to Little Buffalo. "The Comanche are satisfied?"

The other nodded as he looked at the sobbing Mexican. "I have nothing but disdain for the Comancheros. We would not mix with them at all if we didn't need the guns and powder they trade us."

Aperian Crow agreed. "I have just lost a good blanket from betting on the wrong man. But the enjoyment of watching your Dog Soldier wield his blade was worth the price. Now the Kiowa and Little Buffalo's Comanche return to the area of our Sacred Mountains near the Red River to plan our next attack. We are sorry the Cheyenne and Arapaho will not forget the treaty and join us against the whites."

Bull Hump shook his head. "You are taking the wrong path. Better you should join my clan as we meet with the soldier chief to talk peace."

But Little Buffalo scowled. "I hope you will not regret it. I do not trust the whites so my clan will keep fighting them."

Aperian Crow motioned toward the sobbing, moaning Comanchero and sneered. "Someone put this whipped, wetting puppy on his horse so we may leave."

Iron Knife swayed on his feet and Summer broke loose from Pony Woman's grasp and ran to him, her shift sliding down her body so that she was almost nude as she pressed herself into his arms.

He could feel her trembling as he gently pulled the shift up to protect her modesty. "It's okay, Little One." He swayed on his feet, feeling very weak. Together, they watched the Comanche and Kiowa throw the bleeding, whimpering Comanchero across his saddle and they prepared to ride out.

"Summer," he said, swaying slightly. "I—I think . . ."

He couldn't finish the sentence because things were starting to spin around him and Two Arrows stepped forward, caught him in his arms, motioned for Lance Bearer. With Summer hovering anxiously at his side, the two carried him in and lay him down in his tepee.

It was pleasant to lie on the soft fur bed and watch his woman scurry about, bringing him cool water, bandaging his wound.

She peered anxiously into his face as her small hands caressed his face with a cool, wet cloth. "Are you all right?"

He smiled up at her. "Yes," he said, "my spirit animal or perhaps my father brought me the answer."

She paused and frowned. "I'm afraid I don't understand."

Her hair had dried in the heat of the day and now, as she leaned over him, a small wisp of it brushed his bare chest and he reached up and cupped her full breast possessively. "Summer Priscilla Van Schuyler would never understand," he said. "She would only laugh at my superstition.

Maybe someday . . ."

She bent over and kissed him very, very gently.

The kiss lasted a long moment and when she pulled back, he didn't take his hand from her breast. "I'm too weak to make love to you, Summer. But I would like for you to make love to me if you would. *Ne-mehotatse.*" He said the Cheyenne words for "I love you."

"I love you, too. *Ne-mehotatse,*" she whispered in her faltering Cheyenne. Her fingers brushed his skin as she touched his nipples. "I will adore you in a way that you will never forget tonight, my love, and you will only lay there and enjoy what my talented lips and hands can do for you."

He relaxed with a tired sigh, closing his eyes as he felt her stroke him, touch him tenderly. Her lips covered his and when he reached for her, she dodged his hands. "No," she ordered. "Lay still and let me show the victor how much the captive appreciates your fighting for her."

He felt a rising excitement in spite of his weariness as her lips moved over his body. "How long do you plan to keep up this exquisite torture?" he murmured, gazing up at her with half-closed eyes.

Her lips brushed his eyelids. "Until you drop off to sleep, my love, and I lie naked in your embrace."

"That might take all night," he whispered, gasping at the exquisite pleasure her seeking mouth was producing in him.

"I've got all night." Her warm breath sent delicious shivers across his skin as her kiss caressed him.

It was not going to be a long night at all, he thought, feeling his pulse beat in a rising crescendo. They would both be too eager to make it last. Even though he was wounded and tired, he could enjoy lying passively, letting her make love to him.

He was asleep moments after she finished. He only faintly remembered her curling up nude in the curve of his shoulder as he dropped off into a deep, healing sleep.

*   *   *

210

Days blended together into golden and scarlet early autumn warmth. But it was the cool, ebony nights he relished most; nights just made for soft fur beds, love, and passion. His wound gradually healed and he spent his time hunting, visiting with his friends and helping with plans to move the camp to the Rockies. Every spare moment, he spent with Summer in his arms. Having finally found her, he couldn't get enough of her.

But it ended abruptly one cool morning just before dawn when he was awakened by sudden noise and confusion outside.

Summer sat up, trying to pull the soft fur around her lush bare body. "What's happening?" she asked.

But Iron Knife was already on his feet, hastily pulling on his clothes. "I'm not sure, but judging from all the confusion, I think it may mean trouble."

Dogs barked frantically outside and voices yelled and shouted in the general confusion as he hastily pulled on his moccasins. Now he paused to listen to the old camp crier riding through the camp calling out the news.

Summer frowned. "What is he saying?" she asked. "I don't understand many of his words, but I know he's saying something about 'dead' and 'enemy.'"

Iron Knife hushed her with a wave of his hand as he listened intently, feeling his spirits sink as he realized the message.

Summer caught his arm. "You're in no shape to go out there. You were in a fight only days ago, remember?"

He shrugged her hand off. "Only a small scratch compared to some wounds I've survived. I've got to get to my uncle. The chiefs will be calling the warriors into Council."

She bit her lip and looked up at him as he paused in the tepee doorway. "It's trouble, isn't it?"

He nodded. "A lot of trouble. The crier says the Pawnee have attacked the Hofnowa band of our people in a surprise raid and slaughtered many! Yes, this means plenty of trouble, Little One!"

Chapter Thirteen

Iron Knife walked across the camp toward the Council lodge for the hastily called meeting. *Ohahyaa!* What a great tragedy, this attack on one of the smaller, poorest band of Cheyenne.

A light frost shimmered on the ground he crossed. It was now the moon of *Seine*, that which the whites called October, the time when the water begins to freeze along the edges of the streams.

The people of the Hofnowa still straggled into camp, their women weeping. Only a few warriors were without a wound. Even their ponies were sore-footed and limping. Iron Knife's people, the Hevataniu, mingled with the newcomers, offering food and assistance.

Today the warriors of both groups would meet to decide whether to go to war against the offending Pawnee. Entering the Council tepee, Iron Knife nodded to friends as he went to sit beside his *nahnih*, his cousins. He was careful not to cross between the old chiefs and the fire as he sat cross-legged beside Lance Bearer. His thoughts were in turmoil, knowing that as a warrior he should be eager to take the war trail. But as a man, he longed for the peace and contentment of the winter camp in the Big Timbers where he could leisurely visit with old friends and hunt as it pleased him. But most of all, he thought of all the cold, snowy days and nights curled up before the fire pit with his golden-haired woman. He frowned, thinking he must be growing old, yet knowing it was the love of the white girl who had changed him.

The Hevatanius' four old chiefs sat once again in regal splendor and with them now sat the three surviving chiefs of the Hofnowa. The fourth had been killed in the attack on their camp. Iron Knife remembered seeing his wailing women as he came to Council, their legs and faces covered with dried blood where they had slashed themselves in mourning.

The old chiefs began the ceremony of the pipe, offering it as always to the God Above and Below and the *Nivstanivoo*, the Four Cardinal Points. All were extremely careful how they handled the pipe as it was passed around the chiefs, for it was unlucky to touch the stem against anything. The chiefs wore their best ceremonial dress from Scalp Taker and Blue Eagle's scalp shirts decorated with the hair of their enemies to his own *nehyo*, Clouds Above, in his fine blanket and bear claws.

One of the visiting chiefs wore a magnificent war bonnet much like his father's.

His uncle spoke. "Our friends and relatives north of here have been attacked, as most of you know. Chief Coyote Man will tell of it."

Clouds Above sat back down in great dignity and the other chief in the war bonnet stood and regarded them stoically. Iron Knife thought with admiration that Coyote Man's war bonnet was the finest he had ever seen, except for his father's. It was made of gray eagle feathers, the best regarded of the three breeds of eagle they knew. Those were finest, of course, because it was assured that the wearer of gray eagle feathers was protected against bullets and arrows. Each feather advertised an important coup in the warrior's life and this bonnet's long tail of feathers reached almost to the ground.

After a long pause for drama, the old man began. "Brothers of the Tsistsistas, my heart is sad." He spoke softly but the sound carried throughout the tepee, for the men scarcely breathed, so intent were they on his words. The only sound was the crackling of the fire and, outside, the keening of a bereaved woman. "A little more than two days ago," the chief said solemnly, "we were attacked north of here by that traditional enemy of our people, the Skidi Pawnee. They caught us asleep in our blankets and killed many, including women and children."

Heads nodded and a slight murmur went around the big circle. Iron Knife grimaced, thinking of the Skidi. First, they had caused the death of his mother and, a decade ago, a party of them had killed his father and taken the war bonnet. Most unthinkable was the fact that more than two decades ago, they had stolen the Cheyenne's Sacred Medicine Arrows.

"It is not only that the Pawnee often war on us along with their allies, the Crows, the Shoshoni, and the Ute. Worse than that is the fact they often scout for bluecoat white soldiers and thus help drive us and our old friends, the Arapaho and the Sioux, from our traditional hunting and camping grounds."

There was a long silence as all the men considered this unspeakable sin, that Indian should help the white against other Indians.

Clouds Above stood and spoke in the silence. "We all know this is true." He nodded. "But the Pawnee are our enemies for a more terrible reason! They alone have stolen our sacred talisman! I was there the day that it happened. The arrows were being carried ahead of us into battle by Bull, the great Medicine Man. They were tied to a lance and a Pawnee managed to grab the lance and we fled the field in panic because of what Sweet Medicine had warned us about losing these holy objects. Our folk hero was right, of course, we have had bad luck continually since we lost the arrows. Only the intervention of our friends, the Sioux, managed to get two of the arrows returned to us and while we have made two new ones to replace the two the Pawnee did not give back, the new seem to lack the good medicine of the originals."

Coyote Man folded his arms and nodded in agreement. "The leader of the Skidi that attacked the Hofnowa played a major role in the taking of the Sacred Arrows. He has also killed many of our braves." He held his arms out for emphasis. "Warriors of the Hevataniu, I come to ask you to take the pipe and join us in going after the Pawnee band and its leader, Kiri-kuruks!"

Kiri-kuruks, the Pawnee word for Bear's Eyes. Iron Knife's anger at the name almost made him jump to his feet and disrupt the proceedings, an unthinkable action. *Bear's Eyes.* The name brought back all the horrible memories.

Lance Bearer must have felt him tense, for he reached out and grabbed his arm to keep him down. "You dare not interrupt the proceedings!" he whispered through clenched teeth although there was already murmuring among the gathering as the men glanced toward Iron Knife to see his reaction at the name.

"That is the ugly dog who killed my father and no doubt still has his war bonnet!"

"I have heard this," Two Arrows whispered. "I have heard my father speak of the day when Bear's Eyes and his braves killed his older brother."

Numb with shock and anger, Iron Knife slumped back down in the circle as the memories came flooding back. He was a youth again and it was his very first battle. His two cousins had been too young to fight. The Cheyenne had been outnumbered and surrounded but they had fought bravely anyhow.

Even now, when he closed his eyes, he could see the shaved head and the roached hair of the Pawnee braves and the ugly face of Bear's Eyes. Even the Cheyenne had heard the story of this man who had looked into the eyes of the terrible grizzly that had mauled and nearly torn his face away after he wounded it with a lance. It had left a terrible, livid scar, making the man's mouth pull up in a strange, mirthless grin and his left eyelid droop.

A mist came into Iron Knife's eyes and he could recall his dying father's warm body in his young arms as Iron Knife tried to stop the scarlet blood that pumped from the lance wound in his father's chest.

Bear's Eyes had counted coup on his father, grabbed the war bonnet, and was about to scalp the dying man when Iron Knife galloped up. As though it had happened yesterday, he could smell the sweet, sticky blood that poured warm over his hands as he tried to staunch the wound. War Bonnet had died in his son's arms even as Clouds Above had rallied the warriors and led a counterattack, chasing the Pawnee from the scene. All these years Iron Knife had lusted for revenge and the chance to retrieve his father's headgear. Now finally this chance was here and he was torn by inner strife. Why had they not stumbled on the Skidi trail last year or even a month ago, before a small, blond girl had come into his life and made him think love was more important to a man's life than the war trail?

Coyote Man held up the ceremonial pipe. "I come to ask you to take the pipe and join us in this revenge! You are as saddened as I over the loss of the arrows! Many of you have lost friends and relatives over the years to Bear's Eyes and his band. Now is the time for your blades to taste their blood! Smoke! And by doing so, pledge to join us on this war party!"

As he sat down, an excited buzz rose as men discussed with their friends whether or not they would smoke. Iron Knife looked around at the others, caught in his indecision. He had waited ten years for this chance and now it was like ashes in his mouth as he looked at the excited men around him. While he should be thinking of taking coups and avenging his father, all he could see in his mind's eye was a small, heart-shaped face and large blue eyes overflowing with tears as he rode away.

Clouds Above took the pipe and held it a long moment. The noise died a sudden death as he looked around. "I will smoke!" he announced solemnly. "I promise to ride against these traitors to all red men; these stealers of the arrows, these killers of my brother!" He took several puffs from the red clay pipe.

A member of the Fox Soldier band stood up. "I will not smoke!" he announced. "Not because I am afraid, for you all

216

know my battle coups, but because I think the time is wrong. We should gather all the ten bands and renew the Sacred Arrows to give good medicine to this venture before we take to the warpath."

He sat down and another man stood. "My friend, Lone Beaver, speaks true. We talk of war when what we should be doing is moving our camp tomorrow out of this hostile territory. I will feel safer when we are up in our winter hunting grounds among the Bents on the Arrow Point River, that which the whites call the Arkansas. The Bents are married among our people and it is a good place to be."

The man sat down and a murmur ran through the crowd again.

Clouds Above nodded gravely. "Everything that has been said is true! We are far to the south and east of our usual buffalo plains hunting deer, for the buffalo seem more scarce this year and we delight in harassing the civilized tribes and stealing their ponies. Also, it is true that we do not have the time at this season to gather in the ten bands and go through the Sacred Arrows Renewal. However, I will take the war trail, for who knows when we shall cross the path of Bear's Eyes again? But let each man examine his own *tasoom*, deciding for himself whether to smoke or no."

Iron Knife held his breath and watched the pipe being passed gravely from man to man. Some smoked. Some held it a long moment, considering what his own medicine told him, and with a sigh passed it on, unsmoked. Torn by indecision, he watched the pipe being passed to each of his cousins in turn and they both smoked.

It was placed in his two hands and he stared down at it, the scent of pungent tobacco and *kinnikinnik* drifting to his nostrils. He could feel all eyes turned toward him expectantly because they knew that Bear's Eyes had killed his father.

The Hotamitaniu, the Cheyenne Dog Soldier, was reared expecting to be killed on the battlefield. It was known that he who held the Dog Rope was certain to die against the tribes'

217

enemies. He knew it when he took that badge of courage. From his first faltering step, Iron Knife had been told that to die in defense of his people was glorious. And yet, life was very sweet and precious to him now that the small blonde had come into his life.

He hesitated, looking around the expectant faces and saw his uncle frown, perplexed. Iron Knife must smoke, he knew that. No matter what his heart told him he must ride to avenge his father or he and all his family would be laughed at and he would be unwelcome around many campfires.

For a moment, he wavered, regretting the fact that men could not live in peace and then he looked at the grim face of his uncle and thought of his father's agonizing death. The grinning, misshapened face of Kiri-kuruks came to his mind, laughing as the Pawnee rode away.

Very slowly, Iron Knife raised the pipe and smoked it. *In his mind, love warred against duty but he had sworn by duty first.*

His hand trembled ever so slightly as he passed the pipe on and he nodded to his uncle who smiled back in proud satisfaction. The pipe slowly made its rounds and he tried not to think of Summer Sky as he watched it being passed from man to man.

At last, the meeting broke up. More than half had smoked and it was a war party of about thirty or forty men that Coyote Man and Clouds Above would lead tomorrow.

In angry resignation, he thought of the Sacred Arrows as he walked away, not wanting to talk to any of the other warriors. Legend said that when something terrible had happened like murder or was about to happen to the tribe, the arrows themselves would warn them. When next opened for viewing, the shafts of the Sacred Arrows would be stained with blood. He shivered, thinking of Angry Wolf, and wondered if this were true.

He dreaded the discussion with Summer that was sure to come and hoped he might not have to tell her until he was almost ready to ride out in the morning. Sometimes, he thought with trepidation, it was easier for a man to face an armed enemy than an angry woman.

It was apparent she had heard the rumors by the anxious way she confronted him. "Some of the women say men might be riding out against the Pawnee."

He tried to avoid the unspoken question in her eyes. "A war party will be riding out at dawn tomorrow," he said impassively.

"The women are uneasy that there will not be time to renew the Sacred Arrows first." She sounded frightened.

He held his hands out to the fire. "It would take several weeks or more to send out messengers to the other eight bands."

Summer looked puzzled. "Would they not come?"

"They would come," he assured her from the fireside. "No one would dare risk the resulting bad luck by refusing to attend. Besides, the soldier societies are empowered to force attendance if need be by burning lodges and killing horses."

She came over to the fire. "Would it take a long time for the Renewal?"

"Only four days for the actual ceremony," he answered, and the arrows themselves will be put on display outside the Renewal tepee the morning of the fifth day. Four is the magic number of our people. But it takes time to build the shelter for the soldier bands who participate and the special renewal tepee. Some fear to wait, for we might lose the Pawnees' trail. The snows will be coming soon and it will be no time for war."

He took one of her hands, pulling her down beside him at the fire. *How could he tell her he was riding away at dawn tomorrow, possibly to be killed?*

She squeezed his hand absently. "What do these magic arrows look like?"

"Two of them are painted red and are called the Buffalo Arrows and symbolize the procurement of food. The other two are painted black and are called the Man Arrows and represent war and victory over our enemies." He talked in great detail, trying to head off the question that he didn't want to answer.

She looked at him eagerly. "I can hardly wait to see these Sacred Arrows!"

"Summer—" He paused, looking down at her small hand in his big one. "When the arrows are finally displayed on the morning of the fifth day, the Buffalo Arrows pointing upward and the Man Arrows pointing downward, no woman will be allowed to look on them."

"What?" She looked amazed and annoyed. "I think the women should picket the whole proceedings in protest!"

He laughed in spite of himself. "Sometimes one cannot change tradition and custom quickly. Protesting and great noise only build resentment and anger and steel the heart against change. Your protesters would do better to work quietly for change as even a steady drip of water gradually wears down the hardest stone. Anyway, I will not be taking part in any future Renewals myself for fear of bringing bad medicine down on my people."

She leaned her head against his shoulder. "Because of Angry Wolf?"

He nodded and sniffed the clean scent of her hair and knew she was worth all the trouble she had brought him. No, he would not tell her the legend of the blood on the arrows. Perhaps there was no truth in it and, anyway, it might be a year or two before anyone pledged another Renewal. It was not an annual event like the sun dance.

Her hair brushed his chin as she turned to look up at him. "But you are not thinking of going on this war party?"

It sounded more as if she were asking for reassurance than questioning his intent and this was the moment he had dreaded facing even more than the lances of the Pawnee.

He hesitated. "Summer, I must go. Please try to understand—"

"Why must you?" She sounded more wounded than angry as she scrambled to her feet. "Let the warriors of that other band see to their own revenge!"

220

"I must go!" he repeated stubbornly as he stood and looked at her. "The leader of the Skidi is Bear's Eyes, the man who took the arrows many years ago, who is responsible for Texanna's death, and ten years ago murdered my father!"

She looked at him, sympathy in her eyes. "But that was a long time ago," she said. "Does revenge mean so much to you?"

Not as much as you do, he thought. But aloud, he said, "Do not the whites ever war for revenge or honor?"

"Men everywhere are the same!" Her eyes flashed in anger. "Women of any color would fight only to protect their homes and young ones!"

In the silence, they faced each other like combatants, and in the quiet, he could hear the wailing of a Hofnowa widow.

He nodded toward the sound. "That band has just had their women raped, their babies murdered in their cradleboards," he reminded her. "If we do not retaliate, the Skidi may hit this camp next!"

He saw her shudder and her eyes pleaded with him. "Let someone else go on this war party! I fear for you and do not want you to go."

"And I do not want to go, Summer Sky!" He pulled her to him and looked down into her eyes. "Since I found you, life has become very dear to me! No more do I look forward to dying in battle on some distant prairie with the animals scattering my bones about."

"Then don't go! What good is honor to a dead man? To a widow?" She put her arms around his neck and he felt her press her soft body against him. "If you care about me like you say you do, don't go!"

He could feel her nipples through the deerskin as she pressed against his chest and he drew in his breath sharply.

"Little One," he whispered. "Do not try to tempt me to break my pledge and disgrace myself and my father's memory. I have already smoked the pipe and committed myself."

She jerked away from him. "If you care nothing for

221

yourself," she raged, "what of me? What is to become of me if you are killed?"

This had been the major doubt that had plagued him all along—not his own future but hers. "Perhaps the old chiefs will reconsider your return to your people," he answered. "If not, maybe Two Arrows would take you for his second wife or even Lance Bearer—"

"You would hand me over to another to warm his blankets?" Her eyes flashed in fury. "I thought you couldn't bear the idea of any other man touching me?"

He tried to reach out to her but she shrugged his hand away. "Do not white widows often remarry?"

"You sound as if you are almost certain you will be killed!" she raged. "If you try to give me to another, I'll hang myself like the young squaws do when they are disappointed in love."

He grabbed her, putting his thumbs under her jaw, forcing her to look up at him. "I get sick at the thought of another man touching you," he whispered savagely, "but the Tsistsistas have held their land because they were willing to fight for it and we are a nation of warriors. We expect to lose many men in battle. If men did not take a second or third wife, widows and children would starve, yet the whites think us uncivilized—"

"I will kill myself before I will warm the blankets of another man!" Tears overflowed her eyes and ran down her face on to his hands.

He felt such frustration and helpless anger that he almost could have strangled her while he stood with his hands on her soft neck. He was caught between his love and his duty. There was no easy way out for him and she seemed determined to make it even harder.

Angrily, he released his hold and paced the tepee. "What would you have me do, then? I can think of no other alternatives! Even if I could convince the old chiefs to let you go, I'm afraid the whites wouldn't want you back. Do you think any white man, even this 'Austin,' would take you to wife now that I have stolen your virginity?"

"You didn't steal it, I gave it to you willingly."

"I told you that day you might regret it," he reminded her gently.

"I regret it already," she wept angrily, "for I thought you loved me and now I find you don't!"

Roughly, he jerked her to him. "Do not do this to me, Summer Sky! Do not make me choose between you and my people! I love you like I have loved no other woman, but a man must put his honor and duty first!"

He tried to gather her into his arms, but she slapped his face.

"I hate you!" she cried as she fought him.

Fury overwhelmed him and he flung her from him onto the buffalo robes. "No woman has ever dared to do what you have just done!" he seethed. "And only one man still lives who has struck my face in insult! If you were anyone else, I would have killed you by now!"

She only answered by sobbing wildly.

"Even if I return, I am going to speak to the old chiefs about sending you back to your people since you obviously don't belong with mine. I was a fool to think love could bridge the chasm between our two civilizations!" He turned on his heel and went out to make ready for the war party, leaving her sobbing on the buffalo robes.

That afternoon, he saw Coyote Man and Clouds Above taking a pipe to the medicine man to ask his prayers and help against the enemy. Then they took a sweat in the sweat lodge to purify themselves. The leaders cut off little pieces of their skin and offered them as sacrifices, leaving them under the traditional buffalo skull that always guarded the entrance to the sweat lodge.

In the evening, those who were going on the war party marched around the circle of tepees, singing wolf songs. Some of the women relatives accompanied them, but of course Summer still wept in their tepee and did not go. As the warriors stopped in front of each lodge to sing, the owners came out and presented members of the war party with small gifts for luck such as tobacco and arrows.

Late that night, he lay sleepless and alone, for Summer had taken her blankets and crawled over on the other side of the fire pit by herself.

He found himself not only angry and sad but puzzled. He wondered what white men did when their women became angry and moved out of their beds? He wondered if they ignored the situation or begged? Not knowing how to deal with the small blonde, he lay there sleepless and listened to her weep and muttered silent curses.

Hours passed and he had never been so miserable. The same small girl who could give him heaven could also take him down to hell.

Finally, he stood and looked at the back she turned toward him. "Summer?"

She didn't answer but he was sure she was not asleep. "Come back to my blankets where you belong. I'm cold without you."

"I don't care," she answered peevishly. "I'm cold, too! Tomorrow night, you'll probably have a Pawnee captive and she can warm your bed!"

He had taken all he was going to take from his love. He decided to ignore the last remark as he stood looking down at her.

"If I'm cold and you're cold, too, it's time to put an end to this foolishness." So saying, he scooped her up, blankets and all, before she had any hint of his action and carried her back to his bed.

But she fought him as he put her down and snuggled in beside her. "I won't sleep with you! I hate you!"

"I don't hate you, I love you!" he whispered as he pulled her cold body next to his.

She struggled but not too hard as he ran his warm hands up under her shift. "Let go of me!"

He didn't let go. Instead, he pulled her more tightly against him so he could warm her with his big body.

"Don't fight me, Summer," he whispered. "I want to feel

you in my arms one last time so I will have the memory to take with me if I should die on this raid."

She gave a strangled cry and then clung to him, shaking with sobs. "I can't bear to let you go! We have so little time before dawn."

"Hush, Little One." He kissed the tears from her cheeks and stroked the yellow hair. "Whatever time is left we can use to make memories that will last us both forever if need be."

He ran his callused, hard hands over her soft, chilled skin, stroking every inch of her, even the soles of her small feet as he warmed her with his touch. And when he stroked her breasts in light, featherlike touches, he felt her nipples harden and grow taut under his palms.

She whispered, "I need you. Take me!"

He took her ever so gently, not so much in lust but as a promise and a fulfillment of his devotion. When he got her up to the Big Timber country he would marry her, he decided. He was almost sure of her love now and he had never loved another woman so much. Still, he lay sleepless most of the night with Summer in his arms and felt her small body shaking with sobs after she thought he slept.

Long before dawn, he was up, gathering his weapons and his father's *howan*, the dream shield, from its tripod outside the tepee. He stripped to nothing but a breechcloth and moccasins for the coming battle although he took along his buffalo robe cloak if the unpredictable weather should turn cold.

Some warriors took more than one pony, but he trusted none to carry him into battle but the big Appaloosa. It had been given to him by a chief of the Nez Perce, that tribe who bred those special horses in the faraway Washington valley of the Palouse River. Once in his wanderings, he had been there and saved the chief's small son's life. There was probably not another horse colored like this one far and wide on the buffalo plains.

He patted the stallion fondly as he tied a small parfleche of pemmican behind the light, Indian saddle in case they should not find game along the way.

Now, as the first pink streaks of dawn fingered the sky, he painted the symbols on the bay war pony with white clay. He drew zigzag marks down its front legs to make it swift as lightning and dragonflies along its flanks, for it had been his father's spirit animal and was his, too. A dragonfly was hard to see and hard to catch as it moved. Then he made hand prints on the bay Appaloosa's shoulders to signify he had ridden down men in battle and killed them in hand-to-hand combat. Next he bound up the stallion's tail for war as was the custom.

Last, he hung a Pawnee scalp from the pony's bridle and made ready for its final magic with the strong, gray medicine, *Sihyainoeisseeo*. Very carefully, he rubbed a little of the powder on the soles of the Appaloosa's four hooves and blew a little of the dust between its ears to make it enduring and long-winded.

Summer helped him paint himself but her fingers trembled so that as he looked at his reflection in a brass pot, he saw the black lightning marks on his face were a bit crooked. The black paint for the lightning marks and the dragonflies was made from the charcoal of a tree that had been set afire by lightning. Yellow clay composed the color for the hail marks on his body to represent the power of the thunder. On his head, he wore the straight-up chaplet of raven feathers that along with the eagle bone whistle and the quirt were the mark of a Dog Soldier.

At last, he was ready. He gathered his weapons and the Dog Rope. Around him, other men were mounting up and already the leaders were riding out toward the north as the sun began its rise.

There was only one thing left to do, and after that no woman might touch him until he had returned from battle. He went inside the tepee where Summer Sky stood. She was trying so very hard, he realized as he took her in his arms and saw her mouth quiver. She laid her face against his chest and although

226

she made no sound, she shook in his embrace and he felt the salty wetness of her tears against his skin.

"I want you to come outside with me," he said and he struggled to keep his own voice firm. "I want you to stand with the other women and see me leave and you will be proud like the Cheyenne and not weep."

"I—I can't!" she gulped.

"All right," he agreed quietly. "Then I will leave you here, for now I must make my final medicine, and after that no woman may touch me."

She reached up and pulled his face down to hers and kissed him fiercely. "I will come outside. You will have no need to be ashamed of my behavior!"

He had never loved her so much as he did in that moment that she steeled herself and came outside to see him off although he saw her hands clench into fists to hold her composure.

Now he took the magic powder, *Sihyainoeisseeo*, and rubbed it over his whole body to make him invincible and protect him from arrows and lances. And from that moment, no woman might touch him until after the battle; to do so nullified the good medicine of the powder.

Fitting his father's dream shield on his arm and the Dog Rope over his shoulder, he mounted the Appaloosa and looked down at Summer. "Be ready for a scalp dance when your warrior returns," he said brusquely, for he could not touch her or say what he wanted to say with people around.

Her stubborn little chin came up and she looked about proudly and no Cheyenne brave would have been ashamed to call her his own. "I await your return," she said with great dignity and perhaps only he noted that her chin quivered.

Resolutely he wheeled the stallion and joined his cousins as they rode north to fight the Pawnee.

Chapter Fourteen

Iron Knife wore his buffalo robe pulled around him with the head hanging on the left, the tail to the right in the Cheyenne manner. He joined his cousins to ride out, shivering a little, knowing it was not just the cold that made him do so. Later on in the day, the weather might be relentlessly hot as was so common in the Indian Territory. He shivered with anticipation and excitement. Gray Dove worked over a pegged-down buffalo skin as he rode past her and she called out, "Kill many Pawnee so we may have a scalp dance when you return!"

He gave her the barest nod of acknowledgment to show her he had heard, but did not smile. His thoughts were only on the small, brave blonde standing with the other women of his family as the trio rode out.

It was a long day. According to custom the war party might not eat or drink the first day until the sun went down. His mouth felt dry and sour and his head ached as he rode beside his cousins. He could not keep his mind from the ceremony of the badger. The ancient, powerful ceremony was seldom performed because the medicine was so great, the tribe feared it.

Once several years ago, he had taken part for he yearned to see his own future and what he had seen was not good. The men had ceremoniously killed a badger, ripping open its belly to allow blood to collect in the visceral cavity. Then they had laid it on a bed of white sage on its back with the head pointed east. The next morning, those who dared had walked naked with unbraided hair past the dead animal, looking at their reflections in the pool of congealed blood.

It was said a man could see his future this way. If a man saw his reflection staring back at him with wrinkled skin and gray hair, he would know he would live to be an old man. If the reflection's eyes were shut and the face shriveled, he knew he would die of disease. Iron Knife had hesitated and looked, seeing his reflection young and covered with blood and knew he would die in battle.

No man told another what he had seen although those who saw themselves dying young were often downcast and sorry they had looked into the future. Iron Knife had conflicting emotions about it. Since he knew his fate, he had decided to live life to the fullest.

He sighed as he rode, shifting his weight on the big horse. He had not told Summer of the badger for he was half-afraid she would laugh at the idea and he believed it so strongly. He wondered if this was the raid that would see his death and he was tempted to turn around and go back.

Perhaps the ceremony was foolishness like some of the other ideas, such as never speaking to your mother-in-law and not pointing a knife at a wolf while on a war party. Deep in his heart, his white half told him that many of the old tabus were nonsense, and yet his Indian half was afraid to test them. The constant conflict often brought turmoil into his life.

The sun beat down on them relentlessly as they moved north. It was unseasonably warm for autumn and the dream shield hung heavy on his arm. The shield was fringed around the edges with the feathers of gray eagles and sandhill cranes with bear claws sewn to the four cardinal points of the circle. In the middle was a large painting of a dragonfly because this insect was great medicine, darting about, hard to see, hard to capture or kill.

The shield had held special significance for his father, War Bonnet. Between the wings of the dragonfly was painted one small, bluebonnet flower to represent *Tejas*, Texas. That wild area south of here had been the scene of many successful horse raids before the Cheyenne had made peace with the Comanche. He knew there was some other significance of the bluebonnet to the fierce chief and he thought now of his mother, the girl stolen from a north Texas wagon train; the girl with bright blue eyes. The day after his father's death, he had a dream vision that the dragonfly should be his spirit animal, too.

On this war journey, the Cheyenne brought a *moinuenuiten*, a horse doctor, with them as many war parties did. He was to do the magic in order to protect the ponies and care for them should any be wounded in battle. Iron Knife could see him riding ahead in the long line as they moved through the sparse number of trees turning gold before the coming onslaught of cold weather. The sumac bushes grew fiery red as always at this time of year.

As they rode toward the Kansas plains, the landscape became more flat with tall bluestem and prairie grasses moving in the breeze like an emerald ocean. He felt at home on the bare prairie because it was more like the usual buffalo plains of the Tsistsistas.

The *Hotamtsit* chafed his body and he could feel the sweat under it as he looked down at the narrow, bright band decorated with feathers and porcupine quills. It was draped over his right shoulder and under his left arm. The rest of its ten-foot-length he carried over his arm. He tried not to look at the red-painted wooden stake tied to the end of the Dog Rope and hoped he would not be called upon to use it. He had used it before and thought nothing of it. But life seemed much more precious to him now, and he regretted that long-ago decision to accept the honor that had been offered to him because of his past bravery in action. Perhaps he should consider giving it up to a younger man.

*   *   *

230

It seemed a lifetime before the war party finally camped at sunset by a muddy stream shaded by a small grove of cottonwood trees. He felt almost faint with hunger and he dismounted. He was a big man and his body needed much nourishment. But even now, he might not rush to the stream and slake his burning thirst because of custom.

He licked his dry lips in anticipation, waiting for the young Sihivikotumsh who carried the leather water dipper at the end of a pole. The water was offered first to the leaders of the party, and then the boy worked his way down the line offering it to each in turn. The water was slightly muddy and tepid, but Iron Knife drank deep, letting it run down his chin. The pole was stuck in the ground until the next time it was needed.

Once Iron Knife himself had carried the *histahhevikuts*, as it was considered lucky to be the one to carry it on his first war party, even though it was a great deal of trouble.

The fire was built, and the work of readying the camp fell to the young boys and novice warriors. Iron Knife settled himself by the fireside with his cousins as befitted a brave of many coups. He waited for the boys to cook several quail and rabbits that had been killed that afternoon. Another man had shot a straggling buffalo, and Iron Knife watched pieces of it being dropped into a hide cooking-pot where the water was brought to a boil by dropping hot stones into the water. As carrier of a dream shield, he must take care not to eat of the heart.

The leaders of the party must not break the tabu of skinning or cutting up any animal that the party might have killed before battle. The leaders were forbidden to eat certain parts of the buffalo such as the head, the tongue, or the hump until after they had killed an enemy in the coming fight.

Iron Knife sat next to his cousins and ate, licking his fingers. The stewed meat tasted delicious to one who had been all day without food.

The war party leaders must not help themselves to food, another of the endless tabus, so they sat with great dignity and waited for the young boys to offer the meat. And all made sure they did not eat the forbidden parts of the animal.

Finally, after they had eaten, old Coyote Man took out the ceremonial pipe that the leader always carried and lit it. He offered it to the God Above and Below and the Four Cardinal Points before the men solemnly smoked and sang ceremonial songs. Then the old warriors gave the novices advice about the coming battle.

Iron Knife and his cousins had a few minutes to visit by themselves around the fire before wrapping themselves in their robes for sleep. He looked at both of them fondly. They were the brothers he had never had. Lance Bearer was several years older and taller than his brother. He was the son of Clouds Above's first wife, Pony Woman's sister, who had died in the cholera outbreak the whites had brought them in 1849.

Two Arrows was shorter, more lighthearted, and friendly like his mother. Both had the handsome, high-cheekboned look of the Cheyenne.

"I want you both to promise me something," he told them. They nodded gravely.

"If I am killed in this coming battle," he said, looking from one to the other, "promise me that you will go to your father and the old chiefs and see if you can prevail on them to let my woman return to her people."

He saw them exchange disapproving glances. "Why do you not ask our father yourself?" Two Arrows nodded to where the old man sat in Council with the other war leaders.

"Now is not the time." Iron Knife shook his head. "The old chiefs think only of tomorrow's problems and, besides, if I live, no one will have to ask them anything. If I do not, and they will not release her, I want one of you to take her."

Lance Bearer frowned. "I think it bad medicine to talk death before a battle."

"That may be so, but I cannot go into this raid with an easy heart if I thought Summer Sky would not have a warm place to sleep and food in her belly."

Two Arrows sighed. "I want no other but Pretty Flower Woman, but if need be I would take your woman."

232

"If something should happen to either of you, I promise to look after your women." Lance Bearer nodded. "Although, that trio of daughters old Coyote Man brought into camp with him has quickened my heart."

Iron Knife laughed in spite of himself. "If you should take all three of those girls to wife, you would have to give up the war trail, for you would not have strength enough to lift a lance!"

The other smiled only slightly, for he was a somber young man, bowed down with the responsibility of the Dog Rope. "Two of the four Dog Ropes are supposed to be carried by unmarried men," Lance Bearer said. "But if you are actually going to marry the white woman, you will take the place of the man who died a few weeks ago. I have been thinking of marrying myself and giving up the *Hotamtsit*."

"It is a great responsibility," Iron Knife agreed, staring into the fire. He was not thinking of battle or the *Hotamtsit*, he was thinking of Summer Sky.

Later, as Iron Knife curled up on the ground in his warm robe and looked at the stars, he thought of the *ekutsihimmiyo*, the Hanging Road to the Stars the whites called the Milky Way. His people believed that dead warriors rode dream horses through the endless skies and he wondered about his father and whether he would soon be joining him on his forever ride. He heard the faint song of the war party leader as the man sang a spirit song for the coming fight. Finally, he dropped off to sleep, but he awakened in the night, reaching automatically for a small body that was not there.

Several days passed as they rode north with their scouts, known as "wolves," scouting miles ahead of them, looking for some sign of the enemy. It was not hard to track the Pawnee. People and horses must have water, and there were only a few creeks on the arid Kansas plain where water was to be found. Late one afternoon, the scouts came galloping back, howling excitedly to show they had spotted the enemy.

Iron Knife's heart beat faster as he helped build a quick ceremonial mound of dirt and then joined the half-circle of warriors dismounted to sit around the little mound. The scouts rode in and circled them five times before sitting down across the mound from the war party.

His pulse quickened as Coyote Man offered the scouts the ceremonial pipe, saying, "What you report must be true."

The scouts smoked solemnly to pledge that what they were about to report was indeed the truth.

"We have seen the enemy camp not more than two hours' ride north of here. We know it is Bear's Eyes' band. We recognize some of the horses grazing there as ponies stolen from our Hofnowa when we were raided a few days ago."

After the report was completed, the group sang the war song the Shaman had given them before they left their own camp.

It was a somber group as each man checked over his horse and equipment, contemplated his own medicine and future. They awaited that hour before dawn when they would attack.

The youngest braves were in a great state of excitement as they moved nearer to the Pawnee so they would be ready for the attack. Many were hoping for their first coup and the older warriors told stories of earlier fights. Iron Knife watched them, feeling old and tired. He did not feel the thrill of the coming battle, but then it was not new to him, for he had counted many coup.

Killing an enemy was admired, and scalping gave tangible evidence of the kill. But to count coup, touch the enemy with a stick or the bare hand, was even better for it showed raw courage and that was what the Cheyenne admired most. The Cheyenne allowed three coups to be counted on the same enemy, the Arapaho, four. Thus, in a battle where the two friendly tribes both fought, seven coups could conceivably be counted on the same man. A Cheyenne warrior was allowed one feather for each coup, so a man wearing a long-tailed war bonnet such as Coyote Man's showed evidence of many fights.

Perhaps an hour before dawn, the *moinuenuiten*, the horse doctor, accepted a ceremonial pipe from the war party leaders and walked up and down over the Cheyenne pony track as he sang a spirit song to protect the horses from danger in the coming fight.

Iron Knife made a silent appeal to Heammawihio to strengthen his shield made from the thick neck hide of the buffalo bull. Just before dawn, they moved as silently as the *mistai* that the whites called "ghosts."

They sneaked up on the camp sentries and cut their throats so quietly the men slid from their ponies without making the slightest outcry to alarm the Pawnee.

Taking a deep breath of anticipation, Iron Knife put his big knife back in his belt. The men crept into the sleeping camp. It would be a great insult to the enemy to steal their best ponies right out from under their noses and the best ponies were kept tied in front of their owner's tepees. Once they got the finest ponies safely away, the men would attack the sleeping camp.

One particularly fine chestnut mare caught Iron Knife's eyes as he moved silently through the tepees. She was tied before a large tepee painted with signs of the Lance Knife Society.

He reached up to grab her muzzle and keep her from nickering a friendly welcome. She had a fine head and soft, intelligent eyes and the starlight reflected off the white star on her forehead and her four white stockings. *Here,* he thought, *was a gift worthy of his woman.* He cut the mare's tether, led her quietly out of camp, and remounted his stallion.

The others were remounted now and ready to ride out, but a dog barked somewhere in the camp, and then another, raising the alarm.

Pawnee warriors ran out half-dressed from the surrounding

tepees, shouting warnings and grabbing up the horses that were left. There were many Pawnee, Iron Knife realized, many more than they had been expecting!

His heart pounded with excitement as the Cheyenne sped away with their captured horses, the Pawnee in hot pursuit. The sun showed just the slightest rose tinge to the eastern sky as they galloped, the Pawnee shouting behind them.

Exhilarated, Iron Knife hung onto the rope of the little mare as he urged his mount onward and the big stallion easily outdistanced the other horses.

There was a place the Cheyenne had planned for a trap in case the Pawnee should pursue them—a gully less than a mile from here where they could shoot arrows from the safety of its protected banks.

Close to him rode Lance Bearer. The others were strung out with the enemy only a few hundred yards behind the last Cheyenne.

The excitement of the coming battle made him tingle all over and he could smell his own sweat and that of the lathered horses as they raced toward the gully.

The churning dirt clung to his sweaty skin. He looked back and realized the Pawnee were gaining on the stragglers. The enemy would overtake the slowest of the braves before they could reach the safety of the gully, he realized with a sinking heart. If someone didn't make a move to stop this retreat, all would be lost. Someone was going to have to make a stand, a battle line to rally the retreating warriors right here on the open plains.

He wheeled his snorting mount around, looking for Lance Bearer in the drifting dust. There was only one way to stop the retreat and hold the ground and this was the old, old tradition of the *hotamtsit*.

For a split second he hesitated, seeing Summer's face in his mind and not wanting to lay down his life for the others. He rode far out in front of the pack and could easily run away and leave them to their fate. Resolutely, he gritted his teeth and reined in the dancing stallion while the little mare snorted at the end of her rope. He was the bravest of the brave and now he must show he was worthy of the badge of bravery that he carried.

Jumping from the rearing stallion, he slipped the decorated hide band over his right shoulder and under his left arm and took the wooden stake in his hand. He hesitated only a moment before driving the stake into the ground with his war club. The Cheyenne raced past him although he could tell by the shouts that old Coyote Man and Clouds Above were trying vainly to rally the warriors.

Glancing over a few hundred feet, he saw Lance Bearer dismounting and doing the same as he did while the stragglers of the Cheyenne thundered between the two men on the ground.

Here they were, literally pinned to the spot by the ten foot bands. Here they would stay, pledged to fight to the death holding this line or unto victory, which was the meaning of the Dog Rope that only four men held.

Now that he and his cousin had actually driven the stakes into the ground, there was only one thing besides either victory or death that could free them from their pledge. That was if some Cheyenne managed to ride back and hit them with his quirt, literally driving them from the field of battle.

The Cheyenne all galloped past him now and he and his cousin, small figures on the flat plain, faced the oncoming Pawnee. They both blew their bone whistles defiantly, hoping to put heart into the retreating warriors.

On this spot I will die! he thought proudly, wiping the vision of a small, heart-shaped face from his mind so he would no longer be tempted to pull the stake and retreat, thus branding himself as a coward forever.

His hand hesitated as he thought of her, and then his fingers fitted an arrow to his bow and his old habits took over as he instinctively readied himself and faced the enemy, ready to kill or be killed.

With his great strength, he pulled the bow and a brave in the oncoming Pawnee line clutched his chest and screamed, sliding from his pony which galloped onward. Iron Knife's stallion snorted behind him, unwilling to flee the scene without him and the little mare nickered nervously. *If he were to be killed,* he thought grimly, *a Pawnee brave would be riding his fine horse.* That alone made him angry enough to give him nerves of steel as he faced the charging enemy.

The sun was up but the dawn was cold. Still, he could feel the sweat under the Dog Rope across his scarred back as he loosed another arrow and took down another man. Glancing sideways, he saw his cousin at the end of his ceremonial rope, shooting arrows with cold accuracy.

Ohohyaa! They would both die on this spot! he thought with little emotion as he and the other used their bows with deadly aim and blew their whistles in challenge. The thought came to his mind that he still had time to mount and outride the oncoming enemy and his white half yearned to do just that. But in his heart, he knew he was more Cheyenne than white and he would go down like the Dog Soldier he was. *War Bonnet would have been proud,* he thought as he used his last arrow and made ready to defend himself against the shouting horde riding toward him with only his lance, war club, and knife.

Then abruptly, he saw him, the Pawnee chief he had so much reason to hate. Cold fury took over and there were no more thoughts of regret or running away. In the line moving toward him was Bear's Eyes, Kiri-kuruks.

He had not seen the big Skidi brave in all these ten years, but his horrible, scarred face would have marked him anywhere—the mouth pulled up, the left eyelid drooping from the grizzly claws across his cheek that had almost torn his face away. Bear's Eyes wore the traditional roached hair style of his people. He looked heavier than Iron Knife remembered and he wondered if the Skidi had grown soft from years of easy living, scouting for the soldiers.

The Pawnee were very close now, so close he could see the

grins on some of their faces as they made ready to ride down the two Dog Soldiers and trample them into the dust.

Iron Knife's heart hammered with excitement and he shook with the fury of revenge. If he could slay the man who had killed his father, he would not mind if he died this morning. For this moment, he had been trained since a baby and ingrained with the thought that this was the most glorious way to die.

Around the campfire of the Cheyenne, they would tell his story over and over and he dared not think of the tears in the eyes of Summer Sky. Instead, he braced himself for the coming charge of the horses that were only a few hundred feet away.

Then the retreating war party rallied! He could hear Two Arrows, Clouds Above, and old Coyote Man behind him as they shouted cries of challenge, reining their horses around to come back against the superior force. He heard them shouting as they galloped back, made bold by the show of courage of the two gallant Dog Soldiers. The braves were returning to help hold the battle line that the two lonely figures had made by digging in and pledging to retreat no farther!

Now he braced himself to take the charge that was so close, he could almost feel the warm breath of the snorting horses. The Cheyenne were thundering in behind him, returning with renewed spirit to the fray. He had a sudden glimmer of hope that maybe, just maybe he might live to see his golden-haired woman again!

The Cheyenne galloped in and met the Pawnee line at the exact instant the oncoming enemy reached the two warriors of the Dog Ropes. For a moment, as they all struggled and fought in the confusion of whirling dust and shouting men, Iron Knife was not sure who was winning or losing. He heard ponies scream in agony as lances gutted them and their riders shrieked, too, as they were caught under the falling horses.

Coughing, he tasted the grit in his mouth as the dust churned and he could feel the fine particles sticking to the sweat of his straining muscles. He heard the metallic clang of metal on metal as men met in hand-to-hand combat and sometimes the dull thud and scream as a lance buried itself in soft flesh.

Confusion reigned around him. He swung his war club against an enemy skull and touched the man to count coup, then threw up his shield in time to protect himself from a thrown lance.

The warm, sweet smell of blood and lathered horses smote his nostrils as he fought. He dodged a rearing, whinnying horse as a tomahawk buried in its chest and it went down kicking and struggling.

The dust cleared an instant and he recognized Two Arrows nearby holding off two Pawnee. The fine war bonnet of Coyote Man glistened in the early morning light. His uncle, Clouds Above, fought like a charging buffalo bull and Iron Knife felt proud to claim the bloodline of the aging warrior.

Then he saw Bear's Eyes before him, rearing up his pony and sliding off to confront him.

"Cheyenne wolf whelp!" he snarled as he moved in with his war club ready. "Today, you shall be left here as food for crows!"

Iron Knife glared back in unspeakable fury as he reached for his knife. The ugly face brought memories flooding back of Texanna, of the day his father had died in his arms because of this Pawnee. He thought of all the disasters that had befallen his people because of the stealing of the Sacred Arrows and he thirsted for revenge.

"No! It is your day to die, Pawnee dog!" he shouted. "I have vowed your death on both the bodies of my mother and my father, War Bonnet, and no one shall count first coup on you today but me!"

As they crouched facing each other, Iron Knife realized the man was every bit as tall as he and heavier. Already, the paunch of middle age, soft living, and rich food from hanging around the forts showed in the Pawnee's build. Still he was a fierce and powerful man, an enemy to be reckoned with.

They meshed, and Iron Knife threw up his shield arm to

protect himself as the other's war club came down to split his skull. But it struck instead on the tough, bull hide shield and glanced off. As they locked in mortal combat, Iron Knife was thrown off balance by the Dog Rope that held him to this spot. The stress and pull on the stake brought it up out of the ground and he stumbled at the sudden release.

Now he could move and dodge and that put him on an equal footing with his adversary. Shouting triumphantly, he moved warily toward the other. He thought of nothing now but his revenge, spilling the blood of his old enemy and counting coup on his dead body. Around them, the heated battle raged and ponies snorted and stumbled, men fought and screamed.

Bear's Eyes brought the war club down again but this time Iron Knife did not move fast enough and he felt the blinding impact as the weapon caught a glancing blow on the side of his head, knocking his raven feather bonnet away. For a moment, he could not see or hear and he felt blood running warm and sticky down his head. He saw the Pawnee only as a dim shadow before him but he swung his own war club and Bear's Eyes grabbed his arm and twisted it, throwing him to one side as the weapon clattered to the ground.

He hung onto his knife with his other hand but it was not as deadly a weapon as the war club and the other knew it. Dimly in his ringing ears came the voice of the Pawnee laughing triumphantly. "And now I kill you, Cheyenne carrion, and leave you for the scavengers!"

Iron Knife dodged away, shaking his head vainly to clear it and his vision gradually improved.

The Skidi reached out and grabbed the trailing Dog Rope, using the sharp wooden stake as a weapon. But Iron Knife was his old self now. He was too quick for the big, paunchy Pawnee as Iron Knife reached out and wrapped the hide band around the other's legs, tripping him.

They were on the ground, fighting and struggling, each holding the other's hand. Iron Knife had his big blade but the other had a war club and each kept the other from using the

241

weapon as they rolled over and over in the dust. They rolled right under the hooves of fighting, plunging ponies as the din of battle raged around them.

A Pawnee screamed and fell from his horse in agony, grabbing at the lance that impaled him. He fell almost on the struggling pair.

Iron Knife glanced over and saw Two Arrows and Lance Bearer fighting bravely side by side against three Skidi warriors and he knew he had to finish this and go to the aid of his cousins.

But now he fought for his own life again as Bear's Eyes came down with his war club and Iron Knife slammed the man's wrist against his knee and the weapon clattered away. He raised his own knife but the Skidi twisted his arm and the big knife fell to the ground between his feet.

Bear's Eyes' fingers gripped his throat, and the ugly face smiled as he tightened his grip, slowly choking the life from him. Iron Knife tried to break the hold as he stared into the livid, scarred face but the heavier man was forcing him to his knees. He pulled at the man's fingers as he gasped for breath and the Pawnee forced him down on his back on the ground.

Iron Knife started to black out. He realized it with a frenzy as he tried to break the choke-hold. He gasped for air and his throat seemed to be on fire as the torn face grinned at his struggles.

His knife! Could he reach his knife? Somewhere on the ground near his head lay the big blade. Iron Knife fumbled above his head, feeling across the grass for the weapon. The Pawnee seemed blind to anything now but the death grip he locked on Iron Knife's throat.

Frantically, he felt in the dirt behind his head, gasping for air, knowing his vision was fast fading into blackness. It seemed inevitable that his scalp would hang tonight from the Pawnee's lodge pole.

He grasped the sharp blade by the handle! But he wasn't sure he could achieve the effort it took to raise its suddenly heavy weight as he began to drift into unconsciousness. Then as he began to pass out and give up, he saw a small, pale face in his mind and he couldn't die, he couldn't leave her!

With superhuman effort, he willed himself back to consciousness and found the strength to raise the knife. His vision cleared in that split second and he saw the other's eyes widen in surprise as the Pawnee saw the knife for the first time in his mad dog rage.

The blade flashed in the sun as it started downward. The Pawnee tried to loose his hold on Iron Knife's throat in time to grab the knife but his fingers were locked and his eyes shone in terror as he seemed to realize that fact.

Bear's Eyes screamed in panic and he turned loose of Iron Knife's throat but it was already too late. The blade flashed downward burying in the man's chest to the hilt.

The Pawnee stumbled to his feet, grabbing at the handle of the dagger and he almost looked bewildered by the bright blood pumping out between his fingers. He stood thus only a moment, the blood running through his hands and dripping to the dirt before he gasped and fell, crashing like a great tree that has finally been cut down.

With a shrill cry of victory, Iron Knife touched the man with his bare hand and shouted, "Oh, *Haih!* I am the first to count coup on this enemy!"

Then he retrieved his weapons and ran to help his embattled cousins, counting coup on another Pawnee as he fought his way across the ground.

But the tide of battle was clearly turning. The Pawnee who still could were fleeing the field, chased by victorious Cheyenne. In another minute, it had become a complete route, with the Skidi escaping before the smaller force.

They shouted insults after the fleeing losers and some mounted up to chase them. The rest stopped to take scalps and look to see how their own friends fared.

In stunned relief, Iron Knife looked around and realized though there were a few minor wounds, the Cheyenne had not had a single man killed.

He helped Lance Bearer pull his pin from the ground as they stared after the escaping Pawnee who weren't even stopping at their camp but were joining their women in running across the plains.

Coyote Man approached Iron Knife. "Our men were frightened and fleeing before the superior force. You two gave them heart to ride back into the fray. Your names will be long remembered and stories told around the campfires of your exploits."

Iron Knife smiled modestly. "We only did our duty, oh, chief of the Hofnowa."

Clouds Above rode up and spat on the dead body of the Skidi chief and looked at Iron Knife proudly. "You have avenged my brother," he said. "I have long awaited this day. Now let us ride into the Pawnee camp and reclaim what those worthless dogs have stolen from our people."

The Pawnee still fled across the prairie. The war party did not pursue them but rode into the camp and looted it as victors have always done. From the tepee where he had taken the chestnut mare, Iron Knife found his father's war bonnet very carefully put away in a parfleche box. He recognized it as his father's immediately because along the band that held the eagle feathers were dragonflies to protect the wearer and on the front-most dragonfly, a tiny bluebonnet flower shone on its back.

His eyes misted as he stroked the feathers, remembering vividly both his parents and all the joy and pain of his youth. Long ago, he had vowed revenge and determined that someday he would reclaim his father's war bonnet. Now he could hardly believe that after all these years, it belonged to his family again.

They looked throughout the camp for the Sacred Arrows, and not finding them decided the Pawnee had made good their threat to destroy the magic objects.

The Tsistsistas regrouped, and gathering up all the Pawnee horses, they headed back south, driving the great herd before them.

The trip back was so much easier than the trip up now that the battle was over and in spite of a few minor wounds, no Cheyenne had been killed. Iron Knife was joyous, for he had done all he had set out to do in retrieving the war bonnet and slaying his old enemy. Also, he would be a rich man from his share of the captured ponies. The little mare ran freely along next to his big Appaloosa and his heart sang since he had found not only a suitable mount for his woman but also a mate for Spotted Blanket.

When they returned, there would be a triumphant scalp dance and his woman could proudly wear the new coup stripes painted on her arm or across her light hair to boast of her man's brave deeds.

There did not seem to be any dispute this time over whom the various coups belonged to as he had occasionally seen in the past. If that had happened, a meeting would have been called when they returned to camp. Each man who claimed a disputed coup would have to swear he spoke the truth about his claim while touching a specially painted buffalo skull placed with a rifle and four arrows representing the Sacred Ones. No one would think of lying as he took this oath, for if he did he would surely die.

The war party had found the enemy sooner than expected so they were returning several days before the camp would be expecting their return. It was important to them to make a triumphant entry. For this reason, when they had ridden close enough to their Cheyenne camp to hear the dogs barking on the other side of the ridge, they camped for the night and made ready to march through the camp in a victory parade at dawn.

They had won the right to paint the war robes, so they mixed animal blood with soot until they had a black paint to draw the designs on the buffalo robe each man carried. According to custom, a man who already owned a war robe received the honor of sewing the wolfskin trim around the edges for decoration.

With burnt willow branches, they made charcoal to paint their faces black to advertise that they had won a great victory without losing a single man in battle.

At dawn, they put on their finest battle gear and made ready to surprise the people. First the war party leaders rode in to the just-awakening camp, followed by those who carried the scalps at the end of poles. Those who had shown unusual bravery rode behind them, ahead of the regular lines of warriors. Now they all galloped in, yelling and shouting and beating their drums so the people would come out to meet them. The village gathered to greet the returning men, everyone waving and shouting happily.

His heart thrilled with the jubilant welcome as he rode in with his face blackened, and women ran out to meet him, trilling victory songs. But his eyes looked only for one person, and when he found her he saw no one else in the noisy confusion of the crowd.

It was all he could do to keep from throwing himself from his horse and scooping her up in his arms when he saw her anxious face. But that was not fitting for a great warrior, so he fought the urge and sat his horse straight and proud. He rode around the victory circle of the tepees.

When he dismounted, his eyes sought hers. While he did not take her in his arms, he could think of nothing else but how he would love her that night to make up to them both for all the long, lonely nights they had been apart.

Chapter Fifteen

Gray Dove watched the Cheyenne war party ride out of camp to raid the Pawnee. Some of the Arapaho braves had joined them, but, as was not unusual, her father and two older brothers were too drunk to even stand up. She felt a surge of contempt for the Arapaho men in general. Occasionally, a Cheyenne brave married an Arapaho girl but never the other way around. *And no wonder,* she sighed. *How could an Arapaho man compete with the spectacle of a Cheyenne Fox or Bowstring Soldier or especially with a Dog Soldier in full battle gear?*

She paused in scraping the pegged-down buffalo hide to watch Iron Knife join his cousins and ride out in a whirl of dust. Her heart leaped as always at the sight of his fine, muscular body, almost naked now except for a brief loincloth and moccasins and the buffalo robe he carried. His brass earring and the bone whistle shone in the dawn's light and on his head he wore the "straight up" chaplet of raven feathers that marked the Dog Soldier. He wore nothing else save the yellow and black war paint on his rippling chest and high cheekbones.

Her heart ached with hope as he turned in his saddle to look back. Then she realized he wasn't looking toward her but at that pale blond bitch he had brought into the camp a few days ago.

Jealousy constricted her throat as she saw the look that passed between the two. She was furious that she hadn't managed to get rid of the white girl or even give her a good thrashing the night of Two Arrows' wedding. All these years she had turned down several marriage offers, hoping Iron Knife would bring ponies to her drunken father, and now she knew he never would.

The thought choked off her breath and she paused with the elk horn scraper in her hand and stared at his departing back.

"Kill many Pawnee so that we may have a scalp dance when you return!" she called after him. She knew that they were going after Bear's Eyes and she gritted her teeth in fury, wishing she were a man so she might go with them as her father should be doing to avenge her mother. She had never told anyone in this camp all that had happened that day of her mother's death; she had not even mentioned Bear's Eyes' name. But now, she remembered with a special hate and hoped the war party brought back prisoners so she could enjoy torturing them. It wasn't likely, though. The Cheyenne seldom took men prisoners and when they did they killed them without enjoying the primitive pleasures of torture. As for the women, they often took them and children and made them members of the tribe.

She stared after the departing war party and Iron Knife on his unusual stallion. It rolled its china eyes at her as it looked back and she thought again that she had never seen a horse colored this way with a white rump and big red dots across it. The horse alone was enough to make him the target of any enemy, for there were few such stallions on the plains and every man would want it. Gray Dove looked after him wistfully long after he had faded into the red sumac along the edge of the woods.

Turning, she saw the white girl moving away with Pony Woman and Pretty Flower Woman. She could hear only bits of the conversation but it was enough to know they obviously liked the white girl and were teaching her the language and

248

4 FREE BOOKS

FREE BOOKS

TO GET YOUR 4 FREE BOOKS WORTH $18.00 — MAIL IN THE FREE BOOK CERTIFICATE T O D A Y

Fill in the Free Book Certificate below, and we'll send your FREE BOOKS to you as soon as we receive it.

If the certificate is missing below, write to: Zebra Home Subscription Service, Inc., P.O. Box 5214, 120 Brighton Road, Clifton, New Jersey 07015-5214.

FREE BOOK CERTIFICATE

4 FREE BOOKS

ZEBRA HOME SUBSCRIPTION SERVICE, INC.

YES! Please start my subscription to Zebra Historical Romances and send me my first 4 books absolutely FREE. I understand that each month I may preview four new Zebra Historical Romances free for 10 days. If I'm not satisfied with them, I may return the four books within 10 days and owe nothing. Otherwise, I will pay the low preferred subscriber's price of just $3.75 each; a total of $15.00, *a savings off the publisher's price of $3.00.* I may return any shipment and I may cancel this subscription at any time. There is no obligation to buy any shipment and there are no shipping, handling or other hidden charges. Regardless of what I decide, the four free books are mine to keep.

NAME

ADDRESS _____ APT _____

CITY _____ STATE _____ ZIP _____

( )
TELEPHONE

SIGNATURE _____
(if under 18, parent or guardian must sign)

Terms, offer and prices subject to change without notice. Subscription subject to acceptance by Zebra Books. Zebra Books reserves the right to reject any order or cancel any subscription.

GET
FOUR
FREE
BOOKS
(AN $18.00 VALUE)

talking of the *Meenoistst*, the quilling society that only the most skillful women might join.

She took her anger and frustration out on the pegged-down hide, rubbing in a mixture of brains, fat, and soapwort to soften it. The Indians all traded the tanned hides to the whites for things they wanted or needed. *She didn't like hard work*, she thought. She would like to live like the rich white woman with people to fetch and carry for them. As she labored over the hide, she thought of other hides that she and her mother had been taking to the fort near the Platte River to trade.

Yes, she knew Bear's Eyes and his Lance Knife warriors, she thought grimly. Ten long years ago on a prairie many miles north of here, his raiding party had come on the little group of Arapaho unexpectedly. Even now, she could remember every detail as though it had happened yesterday . . .

She was fourteen years old that year and she walked beside her pretty mother who rode the finest, swiftest pony in the group. Her father's homely, pregnant second wife rode an old nag that pulled the travois loaded with hides to trade.

"Mother, will we be at the fort soon?" she grumbled. "I'm tired of walking!"

"Oh, Gray Dove, you are so lazy," her mother said, laughing. "We are several hours from the fort yet. Here." She handed over the cradleboard with the plump, brown baby. "See if you can get your little brother to stop crying."

Reluctantly, she took the cradleboard and looked into the baby's eyes jealously. When her mother wasn't looking, she gave him a good shake, making him cry louder. Since he had arrived, no one payed any attention to her anymore and she hungered to be the center of importance. Ahead of her, her slightly older brother raced up and down on his pony, trying to look the part of the warrior, although he had not yet counted his first coup. Her toothless old uncle rode just ahead of them on his tired old pony.

"I wish we had brought Father," Gray Dove grumbled again and she shook the baby as if trying to soothe him now that he wailed.

"There was no need," her mother said in Arapaho. "There are no enemies that we know of in this area and your father and big brothers were needed on the hunt."

Her old uncle cackled with laughter as he called back over his shoulder. "What my sister-in-law really means is that she didn't want to bring him along; afraid he would trade all the hides for whiskey like he did last time!"

"It is not respectful to speak so of my husband," her mother said loyally, but Gray Dove knew her uncle spoke the truth. Like too many braves before him, her father had developed such a thirst for the white man's firewater that he often took all the hides they could tan, all the bead work they could produce, and traded it for whiskey at the fort. In the meantime, his women who had done the work did without the small things other Indian women had.

Sometimes, there was not even enough to eat, for Father and her two big brothers would be snoring away in a drunken stupor while the other men went off to hunt. If it had not been for the charity of the other Arapahos in sharing their kill, sometimes the little family would have gone hungry.

Oh, the brother who rode ahead of her tried but he was not yet a skillful hunter. Her toothless old uncle tried, too, but his hands shook now when he held a lance and he couldn't pull a bow with much power in his old age.

The Pawnee war party came out of the trees to the left as Gray Dove straggled far behind. Gray Dove saw the roached-haired devils first and she held the cradleboard and looked around for refuge. Only her mother rode a horse fast enough to outrun the raiders and Gray Dove knew instinctively that she wouldn't try. Her mother would never ride off and leave the others to their fate.

250

The Pawnee yelped triumphantly as they saw the little group and galloped toward them.

"Save the baby!" her mother screamed and she jumped off her horse and started trying to undo the travois of Second Wife's horse so she could ride away unencumbered.

Bile boiled up in Gray Dove's mouth. She had never been so terrified as she clasped the cradleboard and started running for the Platte. If she could make it to the cottonwoods along the stream, she might hide there in safety since she had straggled so far behind, she wasn't sure the war party had seen her.

She faltered as she ran, looking back over her shoulder. Her mother still fumbled with the travois, no doubt hoping they could all gallop away but the red-painted Skidi were too close. Her brother charged the enemy, trying to buy time for the women. His death chant rang in her ears as a lance took him from his horse and the horse stumbled and fell, too. She stared in frozen shock as the fierce braves raced to count coup on the dying boy.

Second Wife screamed, "Go on! You still have time to escape! Leave me behind!"

But Gray Dove's mother acted as if she didn't hear her and kept trying to unhook the horse. The smell of blood and sweat permeated the air and the shrieks of the warriors rang in her ears as Gray Dove ran. Gasping with fright, she glanced over her shoulder as she stumbled and saw her old uncle bring down a Lance Knife soldier with a well-placed arrow. Then a thrown lance caught his horse in the side and it screamed and stumbled. The old man was thrown clear and he was on his feet, bravely shooting arrows at the charging horsemen. One of them threw a tomahawk.

She remembered now that the sun reflected off its blade a split second before it caught the old man in the throat.

Dropping his bow, he pulled with dying fingers at the hatchet embedded in his neck as red blood gushed out over his hands. She didn't think he was yet dead when the whooping savages counted coup and scalped him.

251

Her heart pounded as she ran for the river and the baby cried anew. He was slowing her down with his weight and his noise would give away her hiding place in the grass.

Save the baby! She hesitated only a moment with the crying child in her arms. Alone, she might make it to the river and swim away or hide in the tall grass. She could not save both herself and the crying boy. She dropped the cradleboard and ran on. Behind her she could hear the women shrieking as the warriors surrounded them and the screaming of her little brother abandoned on the prairie. She ran for the river. Her mother had been stupid to try to save the others, she gasped as she ran, knowing if the choice had been hers, she would have ridden away on the swift horse.

Until this moment, she hadn't realized how important her own life was to her. It wasn't so far to the water now and she began to think she might make it as her lungs strained for air. And then she heard the hooves thundering up behind her. She didn't make it to the river. A brave with wolfish yellow teeth swooped down and picked her up, throwing her across his pony as he turned to ride back to the group.

Another brave with unusually large ears walked over to pick up the cradleboard and bring it back. The women's clothes were shredded and they clutched them around their breasts as the wolfish one threw Gray Dove unceremoniously down next to her father's wives.

Her mother tried to fight the big-eared one for the baby, but he shoved her down and took the wailing infant from its cradleboard, holding it upside down by its tiny heels at arm's length.

The chief rode up and dismounted. He was incredibly scarred and ugly. His face twisted in a livid forever grin and his left eyelid drooped almost closed. Whatever had grabbed him had done everything but scalp him alive. *He was lucky at that,* Gray Dove thought as she watched him. A man scalped is a dead man to the Pawnee and they would treat him as such even if he lived.

"Now we shall have some sport!" said the leader in Pawnee and he turned hungry eyes toward Gray Dove's pretty mother.

"Shall we kill them all?" the wolfish one asked. "Bear's Eyes, as leader, you decide!"

"Let us enjoy the pretty one a little first," Bear's Eyes answered.

Gray Dove struggled to keep her face impassive so they would not know she spoke a little Pawnee that she had learned from the traders at the fort.

Her baby brother wailed loudly as the big-eared one dangled him by his feet. Her mother fought like a female bear to protect her cub while Bear's Eyes held her and laughed at her struggles.

Now he ordered, "Someone silence that worthless pup, his crying annoys me! You, Hawk Wing, you hold him, you silence him!"

Gray Dove was too numb to think or feel, but she saw Second Wife staring about as if she could not believe what was happening and her own mother screamed and fought to reach the baby.

The big-eared one called Hawk Wing raised the baby by his tiny heels and slammed him against the rocky outcrop at his feet. He slammed him against the ground three times before the child stopped crying. Then he tossed the small body carelessly to one side as her mother sobbed and struggled to break Bear's Eyes' grip.

The leader turned toward homely, pregnant Second Wife. "We have no use for that pig!" he snarled. "Kill her!"

Gray Dove started to scream a warning, for she knew by the woman's face that she didn't understand. But Gray Dove didn't want to give away the fact that she understood Pawnee. The wolfish one slit Second Wife's throat and took her scalp before she died.

They tossed Gray Dove to one side and she watched in terror as 'the men took turns raping her mother, grunting in satisfaction as they used her. Gray Dove listened to their

253

conversation, understanding they were on a raid to hit the Hevataniu band of Cheyenne. By traveling fast and light, they expected to mount a surprise attack to destroy their enemy. By their talk, she knew they were Kitsita, Knife Lance soldiers, one of the cruelest and most fierce of the Skidi Pawnee warrior groups.

The war party spent several hours enjoying her pretty mother's body and when they tired of mounting her, they staked her out helpless and tortured her with knives and coals from the fire they built to cook their food. The one called Hawk Wing laughed in delight each time he touched her with a burning stick and the woman screamed.

Gray Dove was too terrified to think or feel, knowing that unless she thought of something, she was next when they tired of her mother.

The man put a burning stick in Gray Dove's hand and urged her to poke her mother's belly. She hesitated, fighting to get away but he dragged her back. She wanted to live! She would do anything to live! She would never forget the way her mother looked at her when she touched her with the burning stick.

Forgive me, Mother, she prayed silently. *I just want to live! I will anything they tell me if they will just let me live!*

Someday, she knew, the great God, Heammawihio, would punish her for this unspeakable crime of helping torture her own mother to death with fire. But now, she could think only of her own terror and how badly she wanted to live!

Finally, her pretty mother seemed to have no more screams left and she gave Gray Dove one last look and died.

She could not believe her mother was gone; she who had looked after everything and everyone. And Gray Dove had helped kill her. But she had no more time for regrets, for the men were all looking at her. Kiri-kuruks, Bear's Eyes, fingered his knife as he studied her.

They were going to kill her now, she knew it. She tried to smile as she had seen the women at the fort smile at soldiers.

"I am a virgin," she said in Arapaho, "but I am fourteen

years old and ripe for a man! Take me along! I would be a good second wife for your lodge."

He seemed to consider, his twisted face frowning. Then regretfully, he answered in Arapaho. "Now that I look at you more closely, your soft body might tempt me, but we are on a raid and don't need a captive to slow us down."

The others were nodding in agreement and she smiled at them desperately as she spoke again in Arapaho. "I know of your ceremony of sacrificing a maiden to the Morning Star to insure a good crop and a good hunt. Maybe you would want to keep me for that."

She knew very little of this human sacrifice the Pawnee did except that they didn't do it regularly anymore. But once, the Skidi had been known for this savage ceremony of hanging a beautiful, naked maiden over a fire facing Morning Star and piercing her with arrows to let her blood drip into the fire. Gray Dove had no intention of ending up as a sacrifice, she was only trying to think of any way to delay her own death and perhaps, later, she might escape.

Hawk Wing asked the leader in Pawnee, "What do you think of saving the girl for the Morning Star?"

Bear's Eyes seemed to be considering while Gray Dove held her breath. Then he shook his head. "We only do that ceremony in the early spring at the main village on the Loup Fork River. The old chiefs don't do it much anymore for it annoys our friends, the La-chi-kuts, the Big Knife White soldiers. Anyway, we would have to drag the girl with us on this war party and she would slow us down. Then we would have to hold her captive for months until time for the ceremony. It isn't worth the trouble. I say we cut her throat and be on our way."

It took all her courage not to show she understood his words. Desperately, she stripped off her deerskin shift so they could all gaze on her body. "If you do not want me for the ceremony, I could cook for you along the war trail and warm the warriors' blankets at night." She knew her breasts were still not those of

255

a woman. Her monthly menses had only begun a few months ago so she was narrow through the hips but she knew their eyes now looked at her hotly as she walked up and down, parading her charms. She shook her hair loose from her braids and it was black as a raven's wing as it fell below her hips. She paused, smiling up at each in turn, knowing she would do anything to stay alive.

The one called Hawk Wing looked at her with hot eyes and ran his tongue nervously along his lips as he watched her. "I would like to sample her."

Bear's Eyes grunted contemptuously. "She is not a woman but a child without enough width to her hips or big enough teats to give any man pleasure."

"But she is a pretty child," the big-eared one argued in Pawnee, his eyes never leaving her naked body. "If we aren't going to save her for the sacrifice, what does it matter to take a few minutes to turn this little Arapaho bitch into a woman?"

The others laughed and nodded in agreement as they crowded around.

"Well . . ." Bear's Eyes hesitated. "We need to get to our camp on further down the Kizkatuz, that which the La-chi-kuts call the Platte River, but I suppose a few minutes more won't hurt."

She smiled up at him and he seemed to reach a decision after looking around the circle of lusting faces. "We can only travel a few more miles before sundown and aren't going to hit the Cheyenne camp until dawn. So we will take a few minutes to enjoy this pretty and you, Hawk Wing, may be first since you counted the most coup this day."

The other needed no urging. He jerked off his loincloth and grabbed her, throwing her roughly to the dirt. Always, she would remember the feel of the rough, gritty soil under her naked back and the bruising grip of his hands forcing her slim thighs apart. She wanted to please him, hoping he might beg for her life. But when she saw his naked manhood jutting out she was afraid and did not think her small sheath could take his sword's length.

He struggled to force himself into her and the pain was so great she thought she was being torn apart, but she bit her lips and did not scream for she did not want to anger the men.

Still he tried vainly to take her while the others laughed and hooted at his efforts. "Hawk Wing is a poor marksman! Let one of us show you how to pierce the target!"

"She is so small!" he panted as he threw the whole weight of his body behind his manhood. She could not keep from crying out as she felt something tear. Then he plunged his great length into her and she felt she was being impaled against the ground. She could not help but weep as he drew out and plunged into her again. Gray Dove could feel his manhood throbbing deep inside her. She could not keep from whimpering and writhing under him at the pain as his mouth bit her small breasts.

In another moment, she felt him gasp, shudder, and collapse on her body with his great weight. She trembled, hoping she had pleased him enough. He scrambled to his feet, displaying his manhood triumphantly, covered with her virgin blood.

Bear's Eyes used her next and wiped himself off with her long black hair. Then the others took turns until she reeked of their spilled manseed.

"Enough!" Bear's Eyes said finally. "We have played the dog with this small bitch already too long! Hawk Wing," he ordered in Pawnee, "cut the girl's throat and add her scalp to your belt!"

"Could I not take her once more first?" he argued. "It was good to feel a woman's body clasp my manhood so tightly. I would like to use her just once more before I kill her!"

Her body was one ache of agony but she smiled at Hawk Wing, trying to buy more time for herself, pretending she did not understand what was being said.

"Look at her smile!" Bear's Eyes sneered. "She thinks she has saved her life with her body and that her life is to be spared!"

Hawk Wing looked at her and licked his lips. "Just one

257

more time?"

The chief shrugged. "Have it as you will. The rest of us are moving out and you can join us after a while when you finish with the girl and kill her. We will leave your paint horse for you and you know where we will camp tonight."

The big-eared one grinned, nodding. "I will enjoy her again," he said in Pawnee, "and then cut her throat and join you!"

Bear's Eyes mounted his horse. "Because you have shown much bravery today, I grant you this! But do not take long!"

Hawk Wing nodded, his eyes on Gray Dove's face. She smiled at him, promising him many things with her eyes. Against the whole war party she had no chance. Against one man, she might figure out a way to survive. The other Pawnee hooted and made ribald comments as they mounted and rode out. She and the big-eared Pawnee stood looking after them as they rode away. She smiled at him again as if she did not know he was supposed to kill her when he finished.

Gray Dove was instinctively a survivor and she had just learned two things about men that would serve her in good stead the rest of her life. One was that men often let lust interfere with their judgment and the other, that a man at the height of his passion is as helpless as a newborn colt. This second thing she counted on heavily now as she looked toward the Pawnee with his sharp knife in a scabbard at his waist.

Very slowly, she moved toward him, forcing herself to smile as she watched the war party disappearing over the horizon. She reached out to touch his manhood and made a complimentary remark about his size in Arapaho. He grinned back at her and she stood on tiptoe to kiss him as she had seen the easy squaws who hung around the fort do the soldiers.

He kissed her eagerly, his wet mouth all over her face as she rubbed her small, naked breasts against his chest. He gasped in pleasure and surprise and grabbed for her, but she stepped out of his reach, flaunting herself, stalling for time. She wanted the war party to be as far away as possible before she made her move. She teased him as long as possible before he lost patience and grabbed her, throwing her down on her back to mount her. She arched herself against him as if swept by passion. It was agony to take his length but she knew she must please and distract him.

Wrapping her slim legs around him, she urged him in even deeper, offering her small breasts up to his slobbering kiss as she made sure she would be able to reach his knife.

She dug her nails into his back and whimpered as if enjoying this act. He breathed deeper, gasping into her mouth as she kissed him. As his passion mounted, she shifted her narrow hips to give him deeper penetration.

Abruptly, he moaned aloud and stiffened. And in that brief moment of climax, when he was temporarily unconscious and helpless in her arms, she reached down for his knife. Savagely, she rammed it up to the hilt between his shoulder blades and muffled his scream with her kiss.

She saw his eyes widen in his sudden horror and he struggled to break free of her deadly embrace. But she kept him locked within her legs and smothered his cries with her mouth so that he could not call out after his friends.

After a moment, she pushed his still jerking body to one side and slid out from under him. Coldly, she looked down at him. "You are a stupid food!" she declared to the jerking body. "With no more brains than a rutting buffalo!"

Then she spat on him and turned to catch the paint horse that had been left for the warrior. *He had taken her virginity*, she thought in bitter satisfaction. *She had taken his life. It was a fair exchange,*

Her small body was one raw nerve of agony but she must manage to mount up and get away from here before the dead man's friends came back looking for him. Weakly, she pulled the deerskin shift over her head and mounted the pinto. Flies swarmed over the dead bodies of her family as she surveyed them and held back the tears that would do no good. There was nothing she could do for them now and she must save herself.

Her mother had died because she had stopped to help the others, Gray Dove thought. *Her mother was a weak person. She herself would survive because she would always put herself and her own welfare first.*

She gave only a brief thought to the Cheyenne the Pawnee were riding to attack. She might ride to warn them but she knew none of them and they were nothing to her. Let the Cheyenne look to themselves as she was learning to do. For only a moment, she considered riding back to the Arapaho encampment but she was not sure she could ride that far and, besides, with the death of her mother, the link had been broken. She hated her drunken father and did not want to go back to him. The white fort was not very far away so she rode there.

She was almost fainting when she finally reached it and a red-haired sentry came out as she slid from the paint pony to the ground and collapsed.

The sentry ran off and soon he returned with a sour-faced white woman. As she opened her eyes, Gray Dove knew she did not like the gray-haired woman with thin, unsmiling lips, but she recognized her and knew the woman's husband was the Big Chief of the fort so she tried to smile appealingly up at her.

"Pawnee war party!" she gasped. "Family all killed!" That was not quite true, of course, but this seemed an opportune time to improve her lot and she decided to do so.

"Poor thing!" the woman said. "Bring her to my quarters and get someone to go for the post doctor!"

When she awakened, she was in a clean, white bed at the colonel's quarters and it was very comfortable and warm. It occurred to her that it might be nice to stay with the whites permanently.

The doctor had a white mustache, yellowing around the edges, she noted as he examined her torn body. "How many of them were there?"

"Fifteen or twenty." She sighed and the doctor looked sympathetic.

The colonel's wife entered the room then and her lips pursed in disapproval. "Men! That's all they ever think about!"

"Well now, Mrs. Willard." The doctor scratched his mustache. "You really can't expect savages on a war party to behave differently."

"I wasn't thinking just of Indians," Mrs. Willard snapped. "Now, what on earth shall I do with her?"

He shook his head doubtfully. "I honestly don't know, dear lady. She said her family is dead and no Arapaho brave would want her now for a wife. Perhaps you had better discuss this with the colonel."

"You know how the colonel hates Indians!" she declared in a soft drawl. "Although I keep telling him it's our duty to try to do a little missionary work among these poor savages; to teach them about God."

Gray Dove did not like the white woman. She sensed that in her own way, the colonel's wife was as hard and cold as she herself. But she also saw where her advantage lay.

"Let me stay with you, kind lady!" she begged pitifully. "I can cook and clean for you and you can teach me about your God."

The woman reached over and picked up a big, black book off the washstand and seemed to be considering.

"You can teach me from your book," Gray Dove said and managed to squeeze tears from her eyes. "And someday, I will go out and help you spread the word of your God!"

"Well," said Mrs. Willard self-righteously, "I don't see how I can pass up a chance like this to help spread the Gospel. Besides, I certainly could use some help around here. I never did housework before we came to this awful Nebraska Territory but we had to sell all three negras when we left Virginia. Got a nice price for them, too, but it was too bad we had to split up their family to sell them."

The doctor looked as if he were about to say something and

261

then changed his mind. "Maybe you'd better talk this over with the colonel."

"But here is a lost soul!" the woman exclaimed, clutching the black book. "Don't you see? I'll be doing missionary work and I could certainly use a little household help for just the cost of her room and board."

Gray Dove relaxed against her pillows. She had a feeling that no matter what the colonel himself thought, a decision had already been reached. Even the White Chief had a superior commanding officer, she thought as she looked at the stern woman.

She didn't much like the colonel, either, when she met him. She had a feeling that he was one of those men who never quite did well at anything he tried and had been sent to this out-of-the-way post because the Big White Chiefs in that place called Washington didn't know what else to do with him.

Colonel Willard was as cold and tight-lipped as his wife and seemed to have only two topics of conversation: how much he liked killing Indians and how wonderful it would be next year when he retired and returned to this place called Virginia where he could grow cotton and tobacco and watch the slaves do all the work. It began to dawn on Gray Dove gradually as she fitted herself into the household that there was money and land but it belonged to Mrs. Willard's family.

Gray Dove quickly became so useful around the house that Mrs. Willard was overheard to say time and again, "I declare! I just don't know what I did before she came. Why, she's just as handy as a third arm. And she doesn't eat as much as a negra would, either."

Mrs. Willard was a lazy person, Gray Dove decided as she slaved away day after day, keeping all the washing, ironing, and cleaning done up. The colonel's wife had a particular thing about stoves and stove grates and Gray Dove seemed to spend hours with the messy black polish, going over the wood parlor stove. Gray Dove made sure she was so useful that Mrs.

Willard couldn't possibly manage without her. It freed the lady for time to write long letters home to her friends and which she read to Gray Dove about how she was saving the savage souls and all her trials and tribulations among the heathen.

Gritting her teeth, Gray Dove learned to smile ingratiatingly and parrot verses the lady taught her from the Black Book. Sometimes, Mrs. Willard took her along when she went to Ladies' Bible Class every Tuesday morning for the officers' wives. She liked to have Gray Dove recite verses so she could show off her missionary zeal.

But she didn't take her often, for as she told the girl, "There's so much housework to be done!"

Gray Dove was glad to have the lady's castoff dresses, but as the weeks wore on, it dawned on her one day that the clothes were increasingly tight across the chest and waist. She paused in her endless stove polishing to face the realization that she must be pregnant by one of the Pawnee braves.

This fact threw her almost into a panic and she was not quite sure what to do. She felt Mrs. Willard would send her away and she didn't want to go back to her drunken father's tepee. In spite of all the housework, this was a much easier life she led and she fully intended to stay in the white world. She had already begun to work out in her mind how she would manipulate Mrs. Willard into taking her with them when the Willards returned to this place called Virginia next year.

She knew the colonel already hated her because she was Indian. He seemed to hold all brown people responsible for his being in what he referred to as this "Godforsaken spot." She knew that if he hadn't been helplessly emasculated by his wife's money and family power, he would never have allowed Gray Dove to stay. She decided she must do something about this unwanted pregnancy before her swelling belly was noticed. And if she wanted to go to Virginia, she'd better figure out a way to work herself into the colonel's good graces, too.

So one night soon thereafter she waited until everyone on

the post seemed to be asleep before she sneaked out into the cold, frosty night and stole a rusty scrap of wire from the blacksmith shop. Then she went out to a field where the horses grazed and lay down flat on her back.

What she was about to do was forbidden in most Plains tribes. In fact, the soldier societies of the Cheyennes had been known to whip women with their quirts if they aborted a child. But the Indians would never know, for she never expected to go back among them again. To the child itself she gave no thought, for it was a product of rape by the hated Pawnee and it stood in the way of her own future. She did not intend that anything or anyone ever come before her own welfare. With the old, faded dress pushed up past her hips to avoid bloodying it, she spread her legs and poked and probed with the wire at her womb.

She shivered with the cold as the pain started and she wadded up the dress hem and stuffed it between her teeth to stifle her cries of anguish so she would not be heard by anyone at the fort. She knew she must get rid of this parasite in her womb and be back in the colonel's quarters by dawn to avoid detection. Never had she known such agony, not even when the Pawnee had raped her and she began to think the spasms of pain would never end. But finally there came a rush of hot fluid and it was over. She lay in the grass in her own blood for a long time before she could get the strength to stand and stagger to a nearby horse trough to wash herself. Then she stuffed dried grass inside herself and her underwear to stem the telltale flow.

In revulsion, she kicked a little dirt over the bloody evidence and staggered back to the fort. It was almost dawn when she managed to avoid the sentry and crawled back to her bed.

Mrs. Willard grumbled a little the next day when Gray Dove said she was too sick to work. The lady put one cold hand on the girl's forehead and said it must be something that was going around. She hoped Gray Dove wasn't going to lie abed for more than one day, she sniffed, for no one could expect a lady of gentle birth like herself to scrub floors and polish stoves.

Gray Dove managed to get to her feet the second day and go back to work on the stoves, for she dared not anger the colonel's lady. The officer himself made a very pointed remark as Gray Dove served the dinner about how ridiculous it was to have savages in the house when he had been sent by Washington to kill them.

She thought about it later as she ate her own supper of cold leftovers in the kitchen. Her body was still weak and she was in no condition to be thrown out into the cold weather or try to travel all the way back to the Arapaho, even if she could find them. There was always a chance they had again joined up with their old friends, the Cheyenne, and might have made one of their nomadic moves.

Again, the colonel was pressuring his wife to let Gray Dove go and she began to worry that the lady might do just that. It occurred to her that the colonel was just a man after all, probably with a man's appetites. Now that she thought of it, she never heard him go down the hall past her room to his wife's at night. She decided that she could use her ripening body to insure her place in the household and she put her plan into action a few days later.

Mrs. Willard had sent the colonel down to the root cellar to bring up some apples and when he did not come back right away, Gray Dove suggested that he might be having a hard time finding them and she would go down and help him search.

She went down the stairs, knowing perfectly well that he was down there drinking whiskey. She had found the bottle one time hidden behind the potatoes. The colonel looked up in annoyance as she came down the stairs and attempted to hide something behind his back.

"I know about the bottle, sir," she said softly and winked at him in a conspiratorial manner. "But don't worry, I won't tell!" She took a deep breath, knowing it made her growing breasts strain against the old calico dress.

He brought the bottle from behind his back almost timidly. "What are you doing down here?"

265

"I told your wife I would come down and help you look for the apples," she answered. "Mrs. Willard was about ready to come down herself and I didn't think you would like that." She smiled as if they were partners in a plot. It came to her that she was taking a chance. He might fire her on the spot, but somehow she didn't think so.

He gave her a long, searching look as she reached past him in the crowded dimness of the cellar. As she reached for the apples, she very deliberately brushed her breasts against his blue uniform. He jerked back as if touched by a hot flame but she appeared not to notice.

Looking into the pale, watery eyes, she rubbed against him. Then she stepped back and almost laughed, for he was looking at her with a searching look as if seeing her for the first time.

"I think Mrs. Willard wanted some jam, too," she said, "but it's on the top shelf and I can't reach it. I might if you would help me up—"

Wordlessly, he put hot, trembling hands on her narrow waist and lifted her to reach the shelf. When he put her down, she rubbed innocently against his leg as she turned back toward the stairs.

"I won't tell a soul about the bottle, sir," she whispered. "I'm sure your wife doesn't really understand you."

The next morning was Tuesday and the colonel breakfasted alone as he had an early inspection on the parade ground. As Gray Dove served his coffee, she managed to spill a little cream on his thigh. "Oh, I'm so sorry, sir. That was so clumsy of me. Here, let me clean it up!" She took a napkin and rubbed the spot on the inside of his leg over and over and pretended not to see the sudden bulge of his manhood near where her fingers stroked.

Again, he simply stared at her, but she noticed his hands trembled as he held his knife and fork. Her plan was working as she had anticipated. She intended to seduce the man and then she would have something to blackmail him with.

Later that morning, when the lady had gone to her Bible

study, Gray Dove was changing the sheets on the colonel's bed when she heard the side door open. She smiled a little to herself and went on slipping the clean case over the pillow.

He came into the room.

"Oh, sir!" she feigned surprise. "You're early and I don't have your lunch ready yet."

"Quite all right." He coughed, running a nervous hand through his gray hair. "Is my wife gone to her religious study?"

Gray Dove nodded. "Yes, sir. She won't be back for hours."

He nodded lamely and she looked in disgust at his pot belly. "I—I came back for something I forgot," he stuttered.

She shrugged as if she believed him and managed to brush against him as she moved around the bed, smoothing the blankets.

She stopped in front of him and looked into his eyes with her lips parted in a way that was appealing. "Can I help look for it, sir? What was it, your gloves?"

"Yes," he mumbled, "my gloves, yes!" He seemed to be torn by indecision and she knew that at any moment he might lose his nerve and stride out of the room and her chance would be lost forever. Gray Dove would have to make the first move.

Very slowly she put her hands on his thin chest and looked into his weak, watery eyes. "Did you really come back for me?" she purred.

For a moment, she thought he would turn and run but finally his damp hands went to her shoulders. "God help me! You're only a child!"

"I'm almost fifteen," she whispered, "and many Indian girls my age are already married. And it's not as if I were a virgin. Remember, I was raped by all those Pawnee!"

"Yes, I know," he stammered, his soft hands moist and damp on her shoulders. "It's not as if I were despoiling you. After all, you're just a savage little animal who doesn't understand civilized behavior—"

His voice trailed off and he hesitated again. She was going to have to do it all, she thought disgustedly. Her full, warm lips reached up to kiss his thin, cold ones and she rubbed herself against him from breast to thigh as she did so.

With a strangled cry, he threw aside all inhibitions and jerked her against him, kissing her in a wet, sloppy manner that almost made her retch. She pressed herself against his belly so hard she could feel his thin legs shaking.

She reached up and unbuttoned her faded dress, sending it cascading to the floor at her feet. She wore nothing under it for she had been so sure he would return this morning.

She pulled him down with her on the bed and he was like a crazy man, smothering her lush body with wet, slobbering kisses as the metal buttons of his uniform cut into her tender flesh. "You Jezebel, you!" he gasped as he fumbled with the buttons of his pants. "You little brown Jezebel!"

She feigned passion as she helped him with the buttons. "No, Colonel, it's just that I have hungered for you, the Big Chief of the soldiers, ever since I came here! The other soldiers of this fort have wanted me but I wanted only you!"

She had to help him with his pants since his thin hands shook so much he could hardly unbutton his trousers. He didn't bother to remove his jacket as he kicked the pants aside and fell across her on the bed, pulling her legs apart.

He was no doubt ashamed of his body, she thought, and wondered with revulsion if he had gray hair all over his chest as he did on his head. Indian men had hardly any hair at all on their smooth, muscular bodies.

His thin legs were covered with hair and his man's thing so small she almost laughed aloud but instead she said, "You are built like the big stud bull of the buffalo and I am eager to have you fill me."

But as he fumbled inexpertly to enter, his seed came in a rush on her thigh and he turned crimson with humiliation. "I—I'm sorry! It is always this way. I can't seem to help it!"

She reached up to stroke his sweating face. "It is all right," she comforted him. "I will teach you how to stop this and we

268

have much time ahead of us to love each other. Your wife is gone every Tuesday morning and I will leave my door open at night. . . ."

The next morning at the breakfast table, the colonel said to his wife as Gray Dove served the coffee, "You know, Mabel, I've been thinking and you're right as usual about this Indian girl. It really is our duty to try to educate the savages and she has no place to go. Anyway, my dear, your health is much too delicate to do all that cleaning and scrubbing. We might even take her with us to Virginia when we go this spring since she doesn't eat much and you would be the only lady in Richmond with a real Indian maid."

"Why, John!" She beamed. "I've been telling you that all along. And we don't have to pay her. She's satisfied to work for just room and board. And won't my Missionary Society ladies be just green with envy when they see the savage whose soul I've saved?"

Now through the early spring, the colonel's lady worked Gray Dove a little harder since her husband had acquiesced about keeping the girl. It seemed to Gray Dove that all she did was polish stoves but she put up with the hard work patiently. When she got to the white's city of Richmond, she would figure out another way to make money, for she was very clever.

Every Tuesday morning, she entertained the old colonel, sometimes even in the root cellar. He never got much better sexually and sometimes she had to grit her teeth to keep from scolding him in her sexual frustration. But she was smart enough to feign satisfaction and he always smiled shamefacedly and sometimes slipped her a little money. This she carefully saved toward the time she would start a new future in the place called Virginia.

She never left the fort with the Willards. It was that month the Cheyenne call *Matsiomishi* and the whites know as April that her father came riding into the fort to trade, having long assumed his whole family was dead. She had no interest in returning with him, of course, but there rode with him the most exciting, virile Cheyenne Dog Soldier of about sixteen years or so that she had ever seen.

He hardly noticed her, but when she saw him she fell deeply in love for the first time and dreamed of becoming his woman. He was of the Hevataniu band and it had been them the Pawnee Knife Lance soldiers under Bear's Eyes were riding to attack that fateful day in the autumn when her family's path had crossed the Pawnee's. His father, War Bonnet, had been killed in that attack, she learned, but his half-grown son had fought bravely and the Cheyenne had succeeded in repulsing the Skidi and driven them in retreat back to their own country up on the Platte.

Even now, she remembered how the sun had gleamed on his fine, rippling muscles, his handsome high cheekbones. His back and face were scarred and she wondered about that, never knowing how it had come about. She only knew it was something terrible that was buried in his past among the whites.

She was so charmed by him, although he gave her no encouragement, that she thought of nothing else but returning to the Indian camp in hopes that the young Cheyenne Dog Soldier might take her as his woman. She didn't even mind that her father beat her up and took her small cache of coins she had saved and bought whiskey with it.

The Willards were leaving for Richmond the next day. The colonel's lady had gone off to tell her friends good-bye and left ironing and, of course, the endless stove polishing for Gray Dove to do.

The Indians were ready to ride out when Gray Dove made her final decision. She decided Virginia mattered not at all to her if she had a chance to become the Cheyenne's woman and she ran back to the quarters to gather her few belongings.

The colonel came in as she gathered her things. "Where are you going?" he asked. "The stage doesn't leave until to-morrow."

"I'm going back with the Indians," she answered coldly. "I've changed my mind."

He grabbed her by the shoulders. "You can't!" he stammered. "I—I don't know what I would do without you. I love you, Gray Dove! You can't leave me. I thought you loved me, too."

"Love!" she laughed bitterly. "What you call love is like being mounted by a steer! A gelding! Do you hear! I am sick to my stomach every time you touch me! I can hardly wait to get away from you!" She brushed his bewildered hands away. "You stupid old fool! Do you think I could ever really care for you!"

He collapsed in sobs on the settee and Gray Dove smiled coldly, enjoying the fact that she had wounded him deeply. She gathered her things and looking around, decided to leave a message for Mrs. Willard, a message she could not mistake.

Running back in her room, she took the Black Book from the washstand and tore the pages out, scattering them in a frenzy. Next, she took the black stove polish and carefully poured it all over Mrs. Willard's white blouses that were waiting to be ironed and then all over everything in the house until she used it up.

The colonel still sobbed, a broken man on the settee, as she gathered her things and left, not even bothering to say good-bye.

She ran to join the departing Indians.

That had been ten long years ago. . . .

The thought of Iron Knife brought her back to the present and she realized she had been sitting here motionless for nearly an hour by the pegged-down buffalo hide, the scraper idle in her hand as she remembered the past. For ten years now, she

271

had schemed to become the woman of Iron Knife although she occasionally crawled into the blankets with another warrior if he offered gifts. But her heart belonged to the big Dog Soldier. She had given up a chance at an easy life in the white civilization to stay near Iron Knife, never giving up hope that someday he would realize that she was the right woman for him.

The white bitch called Summer Sky came out of Pony Woman's tepee just then and Gray Dove glared at her in fury. As long as that pale one was in this camp, Iron Knife could see no other.

She would have to get rid of the yellow-haired one, she vowed. *There was no other answer*. Savagely, she scraped at the hide and smiled to herself. She had just decided how to rid the camp of Summer Sky forever!

Chapter Sixteen

Gray Dove laid her plans carefully and waited several days to take action. She figured it would take her maybe two days to ride into Fort Smith and maybe two days back. The war party might be gone a week or more which gave her plenty of time to do something about Summer before the men returned. Then she would feign ignorance when anyone wondered about the girl's disappearance.

In the meantime, the Jesuit priest came to the camp as he made his rounds among the plains tribes in the name of his god. The Indians trusted the frail, saintly man who came and went on his mule and he had free access to all the camps.

She watched from afar as Summer called the old priest into her tepee. Gray Dove hoped she might be asking for help in escaping, but in her heart she was sure the white girl planned a wedding ceremony. The thought made Gray Dove grind her teeth in jealous fury.

So she made her plans, and late one chilly afternoon when no one was around she mounted her dun-colored pony and rode toward Fort Smith.

It was night as she reached the fort at the junction of the Arkansas and Poteau rivers on that rocky bluff the French

273

traders called La Belle Point. The harvest moon shone on the small jumble of brick and stone buildings as she rode into the settlement.

Gray Dove wondered if there really was a big reward out for the missing girl. No matter, reward or no, she determined to hand the girl over to the soldiers and get her out of Iron Knife's arms forever. She wanted this badly enough to risk the anger of the old Cheyenne chiefs. Besides, if she handled this right, no one would ever know where Summer went or who was responsible for her disappearance.

Light shone from the saloons as she rode down the main street. Raucous noise and piano music drifted to her ears. She realized it must be that weekly ceremony the whites called "Saturday night."

Uncertainly, she paused in front of a saloon and dismounted, listening to the crash of chairs and glass from inside. A woman screamed and men roared challenges so Gray Dove realized a fight was in progress. She knew a soldier chief called a "colonel" was probably in charge of the fort, but she wasn't sure where she would find this chief on a Saturday night.

As she stood there, trying to decide what to do next, a big man strode out the swinging doors of the saloon, rubbing his knuckles in satisfaction. "Shoulda finished killin' the sona-bitch!" he drawled as he came down to the hitching post for his horse and seemed to see Gray Dove for the first time.

In the light streaming from the saloon doors, she saw a big man in his middle forties. She could smell him even though she couldn't see him clearly and she thought immediately of the old "Mountain Men."

"A squaw!" he exclaimed, looking her over as he swayed on his feet. "A sure 'nuff dogeatin' squaw. This must be my lucky night!"

She watched as he pulled out a Lucifer match from a small match tin and lit a cigar with unsteady hands. In the sudden glare of the flame she saw he had small, mean eyes and streaks of gray in his beard. He wore a western-type hat with two feathers in the brim and a rough, fur vest.

"Come here, missy, let me look you over." His ignorant drawl was more a threat than an invitation. She thought from his accent that he was from someplace in the South like the Willards.

Touching the small knife hidden in her clothes for reassurance, she moved closer. "I need to see the colonel of this fort. Is he in the saloon?"

He looked at her a long moment as he smoked his cigar. "You speak pretty good English for an Injun," he said. "Whata you want with the colonel?"

"Is he in there?" she persisted, annoyed now.

"Hell, no, he ain't!" The man shook his shaggy head, leaned against the hitching post. "The colonel and some of the officers is off at some big meeting and left that snot-nosed Captain Baker in charge. That kid don't know enuff to pour piss outa boot with directions writ on the heel!"

She moved closer. "You will take me to Captain Baker?"

"Tonight? Gawd Almighty, woman, I ain't gonna risk botherin' an officer this late at night! He'd skin me for sure. They don't pay us scouts much but it ain't worth losin' for wakin' up the captain!"

"You're an army scout?" She put her hand on his beefy arm and deliberately brushed her big breasts against his rough shirt. "Maybe you could point out the captain to me in the morning?"

The man shrugged. "Why would I? I never do nothin' extra 'les there's somethin' in it for me."

She wondered if the scout had any money on him as she brushed against him again. "We could go somewhere and talk."

He took a deep draw on the smelly little cigar and she remembered that at the Nebraska fort she had heard the cigars called "stogies" because the drovers of the big, Connestoga-covered wagons of the settlers favored them.

"Hell, honey." He grinned at her. "I think I could find

275

something better to do with you than talk."

She winked and smiled agreeably. "I'd like some of the white man's whiskey."

He guffawed as he took her arm. "If you ain't the uppitiest little bitch I've seen in a long time! You know they ain't gonna serve an Injun gal whiskey."

"For you, I think they would." She smiled archly at him, knowing she appealed now to his pride.

He laughed as he gathered up the two horses' reins and led her rather unsteadily around the corner to a smaller, grimier saloon.

It was dismal, she thought as they entered. Two men drank at the bar and over in a corner a private lay passed out across a table, his glass overturned before him. A card game was in progress among a tableful of cowboys under the dirty glow of an oil light. At another table, two men sat with white whores on their laps, kissing and fondling them. The women might once have been pretty and young but were neither anymore.

The rough man led her to a table and they sat down. One or two men looked at her with interest and then studied her big escort and looked away.

The bartender came over. "Now, you know I can't serve no Injuns liquor," he whined.

"Two whiskies!" the big man said as if he hadn't heard him.

She watched the bartender man fumble with his apron a moment, looking at the big man. Then he went over and came back with two dirty glasses of cheap whiskey.

She sipped the raw liquor that burned her throat and watched the scout gulp his. Curiously, she watched the two white women and the way the men ran their hands over them as they kissed them.

Her escort laughed as he followed her gaze. "They're playin' something called 'mouth fishin',"' he drawled. "Cowboys usually do it with squaws for fun but those two old bags ain't choosy anymore."

"I never heard of 'mouth fishin.'" Gray Dove shrugged in

annoyance, thinking he made fun of her. "It looks like kissing to me!"

Just then, one of the women laughed triumphantly and extracted a coin from her mouth. The money immediately got Gray Dove's attention.

"See?" the man drawled as he leaned back in his chair. "The gal has to fish the coin outa the man's mouth, *comprende?* He gets a little fun and she gets to keep the money."

Gray Dove looked at him. "You speak Spanish. Are you from the Mexican country?"

"Hell, honey," he boasted. "I been just about everywhere. You gotta speak the lingo if you go anywheres south or west of here." He tipped his hat back and scratched his head absently.

She tried not to stare but she couldn't keep from gaping at the pink, bald spot in his wiry, long hair just back of his forehead.

He glared at her and pulled the hat back down on his forehead self-consciously. "What's the matter? Ain't you ever seen what the Comanche can do to a man? They wasn't even waitin' 'til I was dead yet! I was lucky to come outa that alive! You ain't Pawnee, are you?"

"No, Arapaho." She tore her gaze away from his disfigurement, knowing he asked because the Pawnee considered a man scalped as a man to be treated as already dead. "Show me about 'mouth fishin.'" She got up and settled herself on his lap, rubbing her big breasts against his chest.

He guffawed and pulled a strange little black leather money pouch from his fur vest and popped a coin in his mouth.

Wiggling on his lap, she put her arms around his neck. "I intend to leave here a rich woman!" She laughed.

His hands pawed her breasts. "Missy, you may not leave here at all tonight unless you go home with me."

The two men at the bar ambled over to watch in idle curiosity. The card players paused and looked toward the couple.

Very slowly and deliberately, she put her tongue between

his lips and probed deeply into his mouth. She felt him tense under her and one of his big hands went to her bare knee and stroked along her thigh. She teased him with her tongue, running it along his teeth. She found the coin and took it from his mouth, holding it up triumphantly for all to see.

"Gawd Almighty!" he exclaimed to the other men. "I never had so much fun losin' money. Here, honey, let's do that again!"

"Let's see if you got enough money to keep this up!" she challenged. This time as she took the coin from his mouth, she could feel his fingers probing further up her thigh as she did with her tongue. She started to protest, then decided not to anger him. She wanted the money and she needed him to point out the captain for her the next day.

"Let's go to my quarters, honey." he muttered. "I got something better in mind."

One of the cowboys who had been watching said, "Is this a private game or can anybody play?"

She felt the big scout tense threateningly and she whispered in his ear. "What does it hurt? Let me take the cowboy for his money. I'll buy you some drinks."

He looked at her a long moment and then grinned in agreement. "Missy, you're a gal after my own heart! I never say 'no' to another drink or makin' a little money."

He stood up suddenly, dumping her unceremoniously on the floor. "Sure, Cowboy, you can have a chance at my little Injun gal. So can any of you. But let's see some gold. None of them little silver coins now!"

Immediately, the card game broke up and the men came to the table to watch. Even the two who had been holding the white women on their laps dumped them off in the floor and came over.

Gray Dove took a lot of money from the men in the next hour or so. The scout took over handling the coins, inspecting them carefully to make sure no one slipped her anything to small. *This was easy*, she thought happily. All she had to do was

278

take the coins from the men's mouths while she rubbed her big breasts against their chests and they ran their hands up and down her thighs.

Finally, the scout complained. "I'm tired of watchin' you guys put yore hands all over where I wanta put somethin' else. Come on, honey, let's go to my place!"

She pouted and pulled away when he tried to jerk her off a cowboy's lap. "I want to make money."

"Money mean that much to you?" He smiled cruelly. "I'll show you how to really make money!" He turned to the crowd of men. "You guys want more'n just a sample, come over to my place in a few minutes, you can all have at her. Bring cash!"

Then he took her wrist and pulled her outside to the hitching rail.

Angrily, she shook his hand off. "What gives you the right to offer me to all those men?"

"Listen, you little dog-eatin' squaw." He jerked her around roughly to face him. His eyes were cold and mean. "You probably be givin' it away out in the grass for years. I'm gonna show you how the white whores do it and take a little cut for helpin' you. I'd like to live a little better'n I do now on an army scout's pay."

She sulked as she looked up at him. "I haven't got my share of what I just took in the saloon yet."

He threw back his head and laughed, turned loose of her arm, and reached into his vest for the money pouch. "If you don't beat all! I never saw anyone so money hungry, except me, of course. I think we're two of a kind, missy!" He counted out half the coins and put them in her hand.

They mounted up and rode over to his quarters. The room was small, dirty, and smelled bad.

"I don't think I like this idea after all," she complained, disliking the place. "Soldiers don't have much money."

"They do right now 'cause they just got paid." He peeled his vest off and unbuttoned his shirt. "And what they got, we'll git!"

She scowled. "Why should I cut you in when I do all the work?"

"Because I know how to get you more money! They'd try to cheat a squaw but they'd be afraid to cheat me." He sat down on the edge of the rumpled bed and pulled off his boots. "Listen, honey, I got bigger ideas! I always wanted to own a saloon with fancy women upstairs. You could be one of my main girls. I could dress you up pretty and pass you off as a Spanish duchess or some such."

Gray Dove snorted. "No man would believe that!"

"Sure they would. I'll do something to your hair, put jewels on you like that Lola Montez out in Californy! Them dudes that's startin' to pour in here don't know an Injun when they see one."

She watched him stand, unbutton his pants, and pull them off. "Why should white men be coming here?"

"The gold strike west of here over in the Rockies! Ain't you heard the rumors?"

She pulled her shift over her head. "White men can't go there! That's Cheyenne-Arapaho hunting grounds! They've got a treaty. Do you want to dig for gold?"

He sat down on the edge of the bed again, looking up at her. "Gawd Almighty, no! It's too damned much work. I jest want to take it from the suckers who do find it. And as for the Injun huntin' grounds, since when does that mean anything to whites? If there's gold in that Colorado country, the army'll just move the Injuns outa there! And they'll need saloons and fancy women in those boom towns!"

She stood in front of him nude, and the light from the moon shining through the window silhouetted her lush body as she felt his eyes on her. "Am I a 'fancy' woman?"

"The fanciest!" he assured her as he reached for her.

She evaded his hands. "You are going to pay me for loving me tonight?"

"Hell, no, I don't pay!" He jerked her to him roughly.

"You're hurting me!" she complained, looking regretfully at

his body. He was built like a big, powerful grizzly bear and there were gray hairs in the mat on his chest. She thought of Iron Knife's hairless, rippling muscles.

"I'm gonna hurt you a lot more before I'm through," he promised fiercely as he threw her down on the bed. "I like to hurt women when I love 'em. It makes it better somehow. I like it even better when they hurt me!"

She started to argue, but he was already on top of her. Jerking her legs apart, he pushed her knees up to her shoulders and rammed into her like a big, snorting buffalo bull. He dug his fingers into her shoulders, hurting her but giving him more leverage as he pushed her knees still higher. His tongue was hot in her mouth and she whimpered. That seemed to goad him to dig in even harder. Remembering he had said he liked to be hurt, she clawed his back until she felt the blood come fresh and wet. It seemed to drive him into a frenzy and she hadn't realized how much she liked to hurt men until now.

It excited her to hurt him. But before she could enjoy him to the zenith of her passion, he suddenly exploded within her and lay across her ripe body like a dead man, leaving her angry and unfulfilled.

"For that poor show, I should make you pay money!" she panted in frustration. "I should call the sentry and have him throw you in the guardhouse."

He leaned on one elbow as she squirmed under him and laughed lazily. "Wouldn't do you any good, honey! Who'd listen to a little squaw? Especially if I offered the guard a go at you for keepin' his mouth shut! Don't worry, you little slut, you'll get all the hump you want when the others come in a minute."

"You think they'll come?"

"To have a go at you and them big titties of your'n? Hell, yes, they'll come! Now, let's see if you got any other talents besides just doin' it regular like."

"I don't think I want—" She never got a chance to protest. He rolled over and grabbed up a big whip lying on the

281

bedside table.

"Don't tell me what you don't want," he ordered and his voice held a mean edge. "If you're gonna make big money you got to do special things; know what I mean?"

She wasn't sure she did, but as she hesitated he looped the whip lash around her neck. Gripping both ends, he pulled it tightly around her throat until she gasped for air.

"Ain't this how the dog eaters kill the puppies they're havin' for dinner?" he asked softly. "Just garrote by pullin' both ends of the lash?" He pulled both ends with his big hands and her hands went up in a panic, unsuccessfully trying to get her fingers under the thin leather. He smiled at her fears and she knew he enjoyed frightening almost as much as he enjoyed hurting.

"Missy, it's easy to kill a woman this way, real easy!"

"Please!" she gasped, frightened now. *He was a little crazy,* she thought. "Please! I'll do anything you want!"

"Anything?"

"Anything!" She glanced desperately toward her clothes, where she had hidden her little knife. It was too far away, she couldn't reach it.

"On your knees, bitch!" He jerked her off the bed by the whip lash and she clawed frantically at it. He was not only sadistic and crazy, he was also drunk. For the next few minutes, he did unspeakable things to her, never loosening the lash around her throat. And after that, he wanted her to do unspeakable things to him. She rather enjoyed hurting him. It had not occurred to her that men would pay for such as this. Gray Dove decided she might enjoy working as a white man's whore. She figured it was a soft, easy life and she was basically lazy.

The men from the saloon came about then and as the scout himself dressed, he made her parade naked up and down in front of the men so they would offer more money.

She was not left unfulfilled that night as the soldiers and cowboys paid to mount her. She even began to have a grudging

282

respect for the scout who drove hard bargains for her favors, taking nearly all the money the soldiers had left from their pay.

The men brought the little private along who had been passed out across the table. The scout charged the other men money to watch when the private said it was his first time.

The boy had drunk too much whiskey, Gray Dove thought contemptuously as he sweated and pumped over her for a few minutes with no results. After awhile, the other men started to jeer him.

"Hey, Billy, you done rode far enough to get from here to St. Louie!"

"Hey, honey, you shoulda charged that one by the mile!"

She was tired of this. Shoving him off, she ignored his humiliated face. "Next time, soldier boy, I charge you by the hour!"

The men hooted and laughed. The boy shamefacedly gathered his clothes and they all left.

It was almost dawn now as she turned to the big scout and held out her hand. "Okay, give me my share."

He ran his fingers through the pile of gold coins greedily before dividing them and pushing her pile toward her. "Honey, you just made me as much as I usually make in a month! Give some thought to us goin' in business together."

She smiled and said nothing as she took her share and quickly dressed. *Why should she cut him in when she did all the work?* It occurred to her that if she didn't end up as Iron Knife's woman, she had stumbled on a way to get rich off the whites in the gold mine country. She heard some of the tribes had gotten so bad on whiskey, they were working their women as whores around the white trading posts to buy liquor. She'd gladly whore for Iron Knife if he wanted her to; even give him all the money. But she had a feeling that warrior would not be willing to share his woman with other men.

"It's morning," she said as she finished dressing. "Will you take me to the captain now?"

He yawned and scratched his scalped spot. "I forgot about

that. Why'd you say you needed to see him?"

"I didn't, White Man." She wasn't going to let anyone else carry the story, beat her out of the reward if there was one. Gray Dove had tried to get rid of Summer by killing her and that hadn't worked. This would be easier because someone else would do the work and she wouldn't have to worry about hiding the body.

"Hell, missy, let's go get some breakfast. I'll take you to the captain after that. I'm so hungry, my belly thinks my throat's been cut!"

The sergeant at the mess first thought it might be against regulations to feed an Indian, but he looked like he was afraid not to, Gray Dove decided as she watched him look at the scout. Her admiration for the big man grew. She liked power and fear. He seemed to wield both well.

Now as they walked away after eating, he belched loudly and reached for a cigar. They crossed the parade ground and he pounded on a door.

A high, nasal voice asked sleepily, "Who is it?"

"It's me, sir," the scout said. "It's important."

"It better be!" The young man peered around the door as he opened it. "It's unusual to wake an officer on a Sunday morning for no good reason."

The captain had bad skin, Gray Dove noticed as he peered at her. "You woke me over a damned squaw?"

"She says it's important!"

"I hope for your sake it is! Nothing but trouble and boredom ever happens out here on the frontier. If I ever manage to get transferred back to New York—"

He didn't finish the sentence as he flung the door wide and motioned them in. His shirt collar hung open and he sat down behind his desk and Gray Dove sat down across from him. The white scout stood behind her, smoking his cigar.

"It's about the white girl—" she began.

"What white girl?" He paused in the middle of a yawn. She had his undivided attention now.

284

"The one who disappeared off the stagecoach a few weeks ago."

"Gawd Almighty!" The scout moved around to the side and looked at her with wide eyes. "Honest, Cap'n Baker, if I'd knowed it was that important, I'd have brought her last night."

The officer picked absently at a pustule on his thin face. "Are you talking about Miss Van Schuyler?"

Gray Dove leaned back in her chair, enjoying their undivided attention. She studied them both through the haze of smelly smoke. "I don't know her by that name," she answered. "They call her 'Summer.'"

"Summer! Summer Priscilla Van Schuyler, the missing Boston debutante!" The captain leaned toward her excitedly. "Where is she?"

She laced her fingers together, enjoying the moment. The white girl was rich and important, she could tell by the man's excited tone. "First, is there a reward?"

"Why, you damned, greedy little—!"

"Now, Cap'n." The scout gestured with his cigar. "We both know that girl's rich father sent gold down here as a ransom, and that maid of hers is still in town waitin' with the uncle for some word. This little squaw probably don't know nothin' after all. She's just heard a little gossip."

"You're right, of course." The young officer leaned back in his chair and surveyed Gray Dove. "Just after the money and never even saw the girl."

Now it was her turn to smile. "The missing girl is small, has long yellow hair and pale blue eyes. She was taken from a Butterfield stage a few miles into the Indian Territory. Everyone else was killed. She wore a red dance-hall girl's dress."

The captain sat up straight in his chair and his mouth fell open. "That's right," he said. "We talked with the saloon girl when the maid recognized the blue silk dress the slut wore." He reached into his desk drawer and pulled out a gold locket, tossed it across to Gray Dove. "Is this the girl?"

285

Gray Dove studied the miniature a long moment. "No, this is not the girl," she answered positively, "but she looks a lot like this."

"That was a trick!" The captain smiled, obviously pleased with himself. "If you had said it was, I would have known you were lying. This is a miniature of Miss Van Schuyler's mother. We found it under a seat cushion in the wrecked stage. Otherwise, we'd never have known she was even on that Butterfield."

The scout reached over and took the locket from Gray Dove's fingers and studied the dainty miniature. "If I had a woman who looked anything like this, I'd purdee pay money to get her back! She does remind me a little of a gal I loved once but my gal's hair was a little more red-gold."

The captain took the locket from the man's dirty fingers with an impatient gesture and returned it to his desk drawer before turning back to Gray Dove. "Tell us what you know and I will see you get the reward. Where is the girl?"

She hesitated, trying to decide how to handle this without endangering Iron Knife or bringing trouble to the tribes and, ultimately, to herself. "Some Indians have her."

"Aha!" the captain said triumphantly, jumping to his feet. "And they've heard about the reward and want to bring her in, is that it?"

"Not exactly," Gray Dove hedged. "She's a captive, but the one who has her probably wouldn't bring her in for any amount of money." The thought infuriated her all over again.

"I knowed it!" The bearded man slapped his knee and guffawed. "Some Injun buck's taken a shine to her and we're gonna have to kill him to get her back!"

"No, I don't want you to do that!" She grimaced at the idea. Whatever happened, she wanted nothing to happen to Iron Knife. "You won't have to go to the Indian camp at all. You couldn't find it anyhow."

The big scout tipped his hat back and looked at her with new respect. *Greedy, conniving people always appreciate those qualities in others,* she thought.

"Missy, what you got in mind?"

"You won't have to come to the camp at all," she said quickly. "Just give me the reward and I will bring the girl here." *She would, too,* she thought grimly, *if she had to knock her unconscious and throw her across a horse.*

The captain picked at his face. "You must take me for an idiot!" He snorted. "We just hand over the money and let you ride out, never to see you again! We're not even certain you really know where the girl is."

The bearded man moved over to sit on the edge of the desk and exhaled smoke thoughtfully. "But Cap'n Baker, just suppose the little squaw really does know where she is and we pass up our one chance to get Miss Van Schuyler back?"

"We can't just give her the money and let her ride out of here—"

"Hell, that ain't what I had in mind!"

"I won't take you to the Indian camp," Gray Dove said stubbornly. "He who has her is not there right now. But he would know if the soldiers had been there and would come looking for you. I want her gone before he returns but I will not tell you where the camp is."

She didn't much care whether anyone else but herself and Iron Knife got hurt but she didn't want this betrayal traced to her through the soldiers either.

In the silence, the captain waved the smoke away. "Christ! Put that thing out! It smells worse than you do!"

The scout frowned and tossed the cigar butt into the spittoon next to the captain's desk. "I got an idea that might be pleasin' to everybody," he said finally.

"I don't know about all this," the younger man said uncertainly, "Maybe I shouldn't make any decision at all until the colonel gets back."

"And let him take all the credit?" the scout asked contemptuously as he spat into the spittoon. "Ain't you the one who's been hopin' for some kind of medal or promotion so's you can go back to New York?"

The other's face brightened. "This would do it, wouldn't it? Rescuing the daughter of one of the richest men back East?"

"I won't lead you to the camp," Gray Dove repeated.

"No need to!" the big scout said soothingly with a placating gesture. "We'll meet somewheres halfway. You bring the girl and we'll bring the money; make an exchange."

Gray Dove nodded. "This sounds reasonable. But I get to choose the meeting place." She thought a long moment. "I say the old, abandoned fort." Fort Gibson had been abandoned only last year by the army to please the Cherokee tribe.

She had nothing but contempt for the Cherokee and the others of the Five Civilized Tribes. They had let themselves be driven from their fine homes in the southeast United States and herded to the hostile Indian Territory like sheep. They weren't well received by the savage plains tribes when they finally walked there. More than one-third of them had died on that winter death march ordered by President Jackson. No wonder the march would go down in history as "The Trail of Tears."

"Sounds like a good spot to me, Cap'n," the big man said.

Gray Dove stood up, pleased with herself. Fort Gibson lay about halfway between Fort Smith and the Cheyenne camp so there was no danger of the army accidentally stumbling on the Indians. She would knock Summer in the head and take her to the fort, getting rid of her before the war party returned.

She turned to the officer. "We are agreed, then? Old Fort Gibson four days from now, about sundown?"

The captain nodded.

"Don't forget the reward," she called back over her shoulder as the scout took her elbow.

"Yeah, Cap'n," the scout said. "I'll be right back. We need to talk about this."

The scout escorted her out of the building. Walking across the parade ground, he pushed his hat back and absently scratched the scalped spot. "Gawd Almighty!" He smiled at her. "If you ain't the clever one! Looks like we're gonna be rich, missy."

"*I'm* gonna be rich," she said coldly eyeing him. "Why should I cut you in on my reward. Nobody's even told me how much money it is yet."

He seemed to consider a long moment as they walked toward her dun pony tied at the hitching rail in front of his quarters. "You're plumb right," he said finally. "I got no right to none of it so's I'm gonna see you get every bit of that hundred dollars. You can buy a lot of pretties with that much money."

Gray Dove nodded and smiled as she mounted up. She had hoped it might be a little more, of course, since the girl's father was so rich. Still, she'd never had a hundred dollars at one time in her whole life. The only thing that worried her now was how she could enjoy spending it without everyone in the encampment wondering how she came by it.

The big, dirty man stood looking up at her. "Give some thought to us goin' in together up at the Cherry Creek diggin's in Colorado."

"We'll see," she said. The two of them were too much alike to trust each other very far. As she looked down into his bearded face, she wondered if she should trust him at all. *It was no coincidence*, she thought, *that the Cheyenne word for "spider," "veho," and the Arapaho word for "spider," "niatha," both also meant "White Man."*

"I have to get back to the camp before I am missed." She reined her pony around to leave. "See you in four days at sundown at the old fort."

But he called after her as she started to ride west. "Hey, missy, I just thought, I don't even know your name!"

"Gray Dove!" she called back over her shoulder as she moved out. "What's yours?"

"Jake," he yelled as she rode away. "Jake Dallinger!"

Chapter Seventeen

Summer was almost sure that the Arapaho girl had been missing from camp the last several days, but she didn't mention the fact to anyone. Perhaps Gray Dove had just decided to stay out of Summer's way. She thought about speaking to Pony Woman and Pretty Flower Woman, then decided against it. She wasn't really certain the girl was gone and, anyway, the women might wonder what Summer's connection with the Arapaho girl was.

At any rate, Gray Dove reappeared about sundown one day and the war party rode in unexpectedly at dawn the next morning. Summer forgot about her in the excitement of the homecoming. No one had really expected the war party's return for several more days, but they had found the Pawnee earlier than expected and won a great victory.

At dawn the war party whooped through the camp at a full gallop, Pawnee scalps fluttering at the end of poles. Summer ran out and anxiously looked about, realizing with relief that the blackened faces signaled there had been a great victory with no loss of life among the Cheyenne. The warriors drove a great herd of horses before them as they thundered into the camp.

Summer had never known such excitement and her heart pounded as she searched frantically for his face among the shouting, whooping men, the rearing, snorting horses. Dogs barked and women trilled their high, thin songs of approval. Eagerly, she looked from man to man, peering into each blackened face, looking for the Appaloosa among all the milling, restless horses. Then her heart filled with love and pride as she spotted her man, so much bigger and more virile than the others. There was fresh coup paint on his horse to signify the new victories he had won.

It was all she could do to keep from throwing herself into his arms as he dismounted in the milling crowd. But she remembered herself in time as his eyes found hers. Like a dutiful wife, she stepped forward to relieve him of his war shield and weapons while he gave her a curt nod. Old Scalp Taker and Blue Eagle came forward to grasp his arm and glean details of the victory since both the old warriors had stayed behind from this war party. The cool autumn weather made their old bones ache too much to pull a bow or ride a horse fast.

Proudly, she stood holding his war gear, waiting for him to turn his attention back to her.

"You will be happy to know I counted three coups in this battle," he said formally, "and that I killed Bear's Eyes himself!"

She spoke in the halting Cheyenne that she had learned while he was away. "I am pleased that you have brought so much honor to your family and your tribe."

He smiled and she knew she had pleased him. "I am happy you are learning our language and our customs. Right now, I know you still think of yourself as Summer Van Schuyler, a white girl from Boston, because you have not yet fully given me every bit of your heart, holding nothing back."

"I'm not sure I will ever think of myself as anyone else," she protested.

He nodded, almost sadly. "Maybe the day I hope for will never come, the day you say what I want most to hear that will assure me you are mine and mine alone forever."

Summer turned away toward the tepee. "I am not sure I can

291

ever completely turn my back and close the door forever on my own people and remember them no more. Nor do I know what it is you want to hear."

Iron Knife walked with her to the tepee. "I cannot tell you what it is, but you will know the answer in your heart if you ever have to choose between the two civilizations."

Now they were inside the privacy of their own tepee and he swept her off the floor, crushing her to him in speechless, mutual love.

"Oh, I've missed you so much!" she murmured against his neck and he tilted her face up to his and kissed her deeply.

"I thought I would not live to see you again!" he whispered. "I feel like pulling you inside me so that I will know this is reality and that we are together after all!" He embraced her so hard, she gasped and pulled away from him, laughing a little.

"With broken ribs, I won't be much comfort to you," she teased.

He laughed. "There is no time now for what I want from you. The war party will be expected to be guests of honor at a big feast and there will be dancing all night! I am going down to the river to clean up and then we shall put on our finest for all the festivities."

While he was gone, she laid out his best, softest deerskin shirt with the intricate beadwork, his finest moccasins, and hair ornaments.

For herself, she put on a soft deerskin shift that Pony Woman had left over from the days when she was thin and young.

She had taken down her hair and was brushing it as he returned clean and damp from the river. Wordlessly, he held out his hand for the porcupine tail brush and sat down on the floor with her body between his knees and started to brush her hair.

Sighing, she leaned back against his damp chest, thrilling at the feel of his hard muscles. His breath was warm against her ear. "I can't brush your hair, Little One, with you leaning against my chest."

Summer didn't move and he ran his fingers through her hair. "I love for you to do that," she whispered, closing her eyes as he stroked. *There was something sensual and arousing,* she thought, *in having a man comb or run his fingers through her hair.* She wondered as she enjoyed the feel of his hands why white men didn't seem to realize that women liked this.

"I love to do it," he said softly. "Your hair feels like yellow cornsilk to my touch."

She could feel his damp, naked body against her and the light touch of his fingers made her shiver with anticipation. "You keep this up and we will never get to the feasting!" she warned.

"Don't tempt me," he chuckled as he pushed her forward a little so he could comb her long locks in slow, sensual strokes. He lifted her hair, kissed the back of her neck, and nibbled with small, gentle bites at the base of her skull. "I'd rather stay here with you than go out to the festivities, but I can't disappoint the people."

Summer smirked. "You don't seem to mind disappointing me. I'm aching for you!"

He stood, pulled her to her feet, and kissed both eyelids. "Later!" he promised. "Later!"

It was indeed a great celebration, Summer noted as crowds of Cheyennes and Arapaho gathered. Each tepee sent wood for a big, main fire called *hkao* to be constructed in the middle of the circle for the victory celebration. The festivities started early and were in full swing by dark. The people painted themselves red and black and Summer herself proudly wore three red stripes across the top of her light hair to boast of Iron Knife's new coups.

The food was good and plentiful. Summer helped Pony Woman and Pretty Flower Woman prepare the *mohktaen*, the so-called Indian turnips, and the corn, squash, big haunches of venison and quail, fried bread, and even strong coffee from the traders heavily laced with sugar that the Indians called *vikamapi*.

Someone who had just returned from the western part of the Indian Territory brought in part of a buffalo and the best parts, the tongue and heart, were reserved and served with much ceremony to the members of the victorious war party. But those few like Iron Knife who owned a dream shield, followed the old tabu and did not eat the heart or eat out of the kettle where the heart was cooked.

As darkness fell and the dancing started, whiskey was brought in by some and she noticed the men she knew were from Gray Dove's family were staggering about drunkenly.

Iron Knife shook his head in disapproval. "The white man's liquor will destroy the tribes much faster than bullets. If they are smart, they will not shoot at us but only find a way to bring whiskey to all the camps and annihilate the buffalo. Then we are truly doomed!"

"Oh, let's not be so gloomy tonight." Summer smiled at him in the flickering light of the huge fire. "Let's be happy we are together and not worry about anything else."

Glancing over, she caught Gray Dove's glare and had a strange feeling that the girl was plotting as usual. But somehow, the annoyed face told her something had gone wrong with Gray Dove's plans. But then the dancing started and she gave no more thought to the sullen, dark girl.

The *Heemaneh*, the half men–half women, led the scalp dances. These men who dressed like women and did women's work aroused no scorn among the Cheyenne although they did not hunt or go on war parties like other men, Summer knew. They took no wives and lived with others like themselves. But there was only a handful of them among the Tsistsistas. They were great love talkers and played flutes and composed songs for different warriors who were trying to get a girl's attention. The Heemaneh were in charge of most of the dancing and the music.

One of the dances was "the sweetheart dance." The

Heemaneh stood out in the center of the dance square with the drummers in a line to one side. The women stood in a line facing south, the men opposite them. When the drums started, the man came over to his sweetheart opposite him and took her arm and they danced.

Summer had a wonderful time, dancing in the firelight. In the long line with Iron Knife's strong arm about her, she was proud to display her position as his sweetheart. In the shadows, she saw Gray Dove scowling as the night wore on but she was in too good a mood to let that bother her. If the girl gave her any trouble, she'd take her down and pull her hair again, Summer decided with spirit.

Finally, the hour was late and the old storyteller sat down beside the fire and began to weave his magic spell of words beginning with the Sacred Stories of the Cheyenne's early days. The people gathered around and sat down to listen. The Sacred Stories might be told only at night. To tell them in the daytime was tabu and would cause the teller to become hunchbacked.

Summer was enthralled with the spoken history of a people who had no books, no written word, but told long-ago tales of bravery and things that had involved their folk hero, Sweet Medicine. Finally, the old man stopped. "That is my story," he said. "Can anyone tie another to it?"

There was a long pause and another old man stood and started to weave his magic string of words, telling a story that belonged to him specifically. A story was a possession to the Cheyenne like a dog or a lance and no one might tell a story he did not own. The stories were handed down as gifts to the children and grandchildren or sometimes given to a good friend.

As the old man finished telling his tale, he added as always this traditional ending, "That is my story. Can anyone tie another to it?"

Now Two Arrows stood and told the tale of the latest battle with the Pawnee, some of it in sign language as the members of

295

his family involved, Iron Knife and Lance Bearer, ducked their heads modestly.

Thrilled, Summer realized she understood enough sign language and Cheyenne to be able to follow the story of her love's brave adventures. When Two Arrows made a sawing motion across his left fore finger with his right, she knew he meant "striped" or "cut people" and was speaking of the Cheyenne. The tribe was well known by its striped turkey feather arrows and also for sacrificing pieces of skin they cut from their bodies when asking favors from Heammawihio.

When Two Arrows made a "v" sign and extended his hand, she knew he told of the Pawnee braves. She gasped in shock and thrilled with delight as he told how Iron Knife and Lance Bearer had staked themselves down with the Dog Ropes and turned defeat into victory by rallying the fleeing warriors. It was all she could do to keep from cheering as Two Arrows told the final, climactic battle between Iron Knife and Bear's Eyes and made the sudden, sweeping downward motion of the hand that meant "kill."

She glanced at her lover, sitting straight and modest as the tale unfolded as befitted a great warrior. *Years from now,* she thought, *when a storyteller would finish with "Can anyone tie another to it?" a member of Iron Knife's family, perhaps his son or grandson, would tell the legend of how Iron Knife saved the day against the Pawnee.*

It grew very late and no one added any more stories to the chain. Slowly, people drifted back to their own tepees, savoring their memories. As Summer and Iron Knife walked away, he turned to her. "I have a gift for you. It seems I did not have a pony in my herd fine enough but I do now."

"For me?" She touched her chest in excitement. "You have a horse for me?"

"You do ride, don't you?"

"Of course!" She took his hand as they walked along toward the pony herd. "That's one of the very few things ladies are allowed to do in Boston."

He squeezed her hand. "Life in Boston must have been very

dull for you."

"It was," she agreed with a sigh as they walked. "Only I didn't realize how dull and stifling before I met you. I had nothing and no one to compare my life to."

He led her out to where the captured pony herd grazed in the moonlight. "Many of these belong to me by right of capture. But there is a special one I knew was meant for you the moment I saw her tied in front of Bear's Eyes tepee. See if you know which one!"

The other ponies snorted and wheeled away as they walked among them all except for a small, fine-blooded mare. She was chestnut colored with four white stockings and a blaze face. Her soft, intelligent eyes looked toward Summer and she did not run away.

"This one!" Summer gasped, running to put her arms around the mare's neck. "Oh, I hope it's this one!"

He laughed at her pleasure. "Yes, it is!" What would you have done if I had said she was not the one?"

Summer buried her face in the mare's mane. "Somehow, I knew it was this one!"

The little mare nickered at her softly as she patted her. "Look at the blaze reflecting the starlight. I shall call her Starfire!"

He came over and put his arm around Summer. "I didn't just get her for you, of course."

Her face fell as she looked up at him. "I have to share her with someone?"

He nodded toward the Appaloosa stallion that raced up, whinnying loudly. "Spotted Blanket here seems to think I got her just for him."

Summer laughed. "In that case, I'm not at all upset to share her. He deserves a little love, too."

She felt his arm tighten around her. "It would not look good to have the woman of a rich warrior walk all the way to the Big Timber country. You must ride and see after my travois and my belongings."

She leaned her face against his chest, savoring his nearness,

297

the good scent of the little mare's mane. "But you won't ride beside me, will you?"

She felt his body tense at the intended criticism. "You know the Dog Soldiers must ride at the end to protect the retreat if need be just as the Mahohewas, the Red Shields, will ride point up front. Have you not noticed their two special lances stuck in the ground pointing in the direction the camp is to move?"

She looked up at him, puzzled. "I have seen the two ceremonial lances stuck in the dirt, now that you mention it. Someone always takes them up in the morning."

He nodded. "On the morning you go out and see them pointing toward the Shining Mountains country and they are left standing, you will know we move the camp that day. The standing lances are the signal."

"I'm looking forward to the Rockies," she said, thinking of curling up in his arms during the long snows. He moved his arm around her shoulders gently and they turned back toward camp.

"Should we tie these two in front of your lodge?" she asked, looking back at the pair gamboling through the tall bluestem grass.

"Oh, I suppose not," he said uncertainly. "They are having such a good time and we'll have sentries out, let them enjoy the night. In the meantime, I have something else I have not shown you."

They went back to the tepee and he carefully opened a parfleche box, revealing a fine, full war bonnet.

She drew in her breath sharply with admiration, knowing every feather stood for a coup, an act of bravery. "I have never seen anything so fine." She thought a moment, and then she knew. "Was it your father's?"

He stroked the feathers gently as he nodded. "I recaptured it from Bear's Eyes, who killed him ten years ago on a raid in a place the whites call Nebraska. I think War Bonnet's remains, his *siyuhk*, can rest easy now for he has been avenged!"

She watched him with tenderness. He put the headdress back in the box carefully. "Now you will wear it and be a chief in your father's place," she said proudly.

His face grew troubled as he put the box away. "I can never be chief," he said with finality. "I cannot even wear this headdress for to do so after the thing involving Angry Wolf would disgrace my father. Someone needs to hold an Arrow Renewal to insure the tribe's good luck and clear away this killing. But I cannot, for a murderer cannot sponsor an Arrow Renewal. Someone else must do it."

She turned on him, uneasy about Gray Dove. "No one else knows."

"Exactly! And someday this will bring trouble to my people, this murder, if the ceremony is not done! I should tell the old chiefs and accept exile."

Summer put her arms around his neck. "Let us talk no more of this sad thing tonight," she whispered, looking up into his eyes. "It was not our fault."

She said no more, thinking of Gray Dove and the trouble the girl had caused.

His lips brushed her forehead, light as butterfly wings. "I have hungered for you all these nights," he whispered. "When we reach the Big Timbers, I am going to buy you a 'One Thousand Dress' covered with many, many elk teeth and all the women will envy you."

"They all already envy me." She kissed along his strong jaw line and felt his pulse beat in his neck.

He stood her away from him. "Take your hair down," he whispered. They stood looking at each other in the light of the fire pit. "I love to see your hair swinging free so I can wrap my hands in it."

Her insides quivered with anticipation as she unbraided her hair and let it fall. Then she slowly pulled the deerskin dress over her head and stood naked before him in the firelight. "Your captive awaits your pleasure, my warrior and master."

The flames reflected off the eagle bone whistle and the earring as he pulled off his clothes and stood before her in his natural state. She caught her breath as always at the sight of his broad shoulders and rippling, hairless muscles. His manhood stood hard and erect between powerful loins. His eyes grew intense with passion and need.

She did not say anything, only held out her arms to him as she had first done on a creek bank so many lifetimes or was it only weeks ago? Then she had not known what it was she hungered for as she gifted him with her virginity and he had taught her. *Oh, God! How he had taught her!*

Summer felt his big, rough hands span her small waist and lift her until her breasts were level with his face and she reached out and clutched his face against them. His lips played with her nipples, making her whimper in pleasure.

"Don't stop! Don't ever stop!" she gasped, digging her nails into his wide shoulders and reveling in the heat of his mouth on one breast, then the other. She could feel the warm rush of wetness between her thighs, wanting him; wanting him.

He slid her downward until she was impaled on his hard manhood as he stood there and clasped her to him.

For a long moment, as she trembled impaled thus, she thought he would take her standing. But then he withdrew with a sigh and carried her over to the buffalo robes. He lay down next to her and she pushed him back on his elbows and she nibbled the hard rosettes of his nipples.

"Keep this up, woman," he murmured, "and I may never trade you off for a good horse or even push you to the back of the tepee to take a younger wife."

She leaned over him, her long hair trailing across his chest. "You could not satisfy both me and another wife."

"I think you speak true," he gasped, pulling her down on him. His strong arms locked around her shoulders as with his warm tongue he explored the depths of her mouth. Then he pulled her upward so that her full breasts hung over his face and clasped his hands about her waist as he nuzzled them.

She moaned aloud as she arched backward, feeling the warmth of his lips on her nipples. "I don't think I will ever get enough of that!"

"Tell me that you like it!" he commanded. "Tell me what it is you want me to do to you!"

"I—I can't!" She felt herself blush in the semidarkness. "Women don't talk like that."

"But you are my captive," he whispered. "I command you to tell me what to do and how much you like it!"

"I—I want you to take my breasts in your mouth and lick them."

"Tell me more."

"I want you to drive me wild wanting you!" She gasped as he nuzzled her. "I want you to put your throbbing manhood deep inside me so I can really feel it as you take me. I want to feel you exploding yourself in my depths, filling me with your seed."

Passionately, she kissed him and she pulled at him, trying to turn him, pull him down on top of her. "Take me!" she said feverishly. "Please take me!"

But he pulled her back on top of him. "No, Summer." He separated her thighs so she was astraddle him. "You take me!"

She hesitated. "I don't know— I never—!"

But his hands were insistent. "No, Summer, stay on top! Ride your stallion!"

She could do nothing else but what he demanded. His big hands spanned her waist and as she rose astraddle his loins on her knees, he forced her downward and slid up into her.

Summer gasped at the feeling as she took him deeper that way than she had ever thought possible. "I can't!" she whimpered. "I can't take all of you!"

"Yes, you can! Your body was made for mine! Relax, Summer, relax and let me fill you as you want to be filled. Tonight, I'm going to touch your womb and give you my son."

Trembling, she reared back and came down on him, spreading her thighs so that she took him to her maximum depth and he held her there with the steel grip of his hands.

"I don't think—"

"Yes, you can!" he whispered fiercely, not releasing his grip on her waist as he ground her down onto him. "I'm not going to hurt you, Little One! I'm going to give you pleasure like you've never had!"

She relaxed, believing him, and a warm glow seemed to spread through her body. She felt as if she were impaled on a hot, fiery sword. As she felt him throb deep within her, she moved up and down on him, letting her eager body clasp his. She put her hands behind her on his strong thighs and arched herself, feeling him tremble as he held back his passion while hers built up. In a frenzy, she tried to speed up her movements but his hands held her back.

"Don't hurry, Summer," he whispered. "I want to wait as long as you possibly can, for when you finish I am only going to do it again and again to you. I want to make up for all the long, lonely nights we've missed!"

"I can't wait!" she declared, rising up so that only the tip of his sheath remained in her and she took him again to the hilt of his sword.

Then neither of them could wait and she could not stop herself from almost losing consciousness. Both their bodies shuddered with passion as he gave her what she wanted. As he had promised, she had never felt such pleasure before. She wept in his arms. He wrapped them around her tightly and whispered in her ear as he brushed his lips over her cheek. "I love you, Summer Sky!"

She lay on him, locked in his arms for a long moment until the world stopped whirling. "And I love you, too," she whispered. "I want to marry you."

"I'll marry you," he kissed the tip of her nose, "when we get to the Big Timber country. But I don't know where to deliver the ponies."

She raised on her elbows and looked down into his smiling face. "I mean, really marry me in a legal ceremony."

He seemed lost in a memory. "I almost wish we could go through our first lovemaking again," he murmured. "You were so innocent and eager there on the creek bank."

Frowning, she looked down at him, still held by his manhood. "You don't understand what I'm saying," she said shortly. "I want to be married in the white man's way."

"You don't think the Cheyenne way is good enough?" He

frowned up at her. "Do you need a white preacher man to feel it is okay to mate with a brown savage?" His voice held an angry edge.

"When Father Jacques was here I talked to him and—"

"The white priest has been here and you have seen him?" With an angry gesture, he pushed her off him and stood, grabbing for his clothes in short, annoyed jerks.

She clasped the fur robe to her naked breasts and looked up at him. "I didn't realize it would anger you," she said defensively. "I thought your people trusted the wandering Jesuits—"

"This is different!" he snapped, pulling the buckskin shirt down over his head. "Suppose the priest searches his conscience and decides he has a stronger duty to the whites than to the Indian? Suppose he decides his God would want him to go to Fort Smith and tell the white soldiers where you are?"

Summer shook her head, rising up on her elbows. "I don't think he would do that since I told him I wanted to marry you and stay with your people forever. And he rode west when he left here."

"Did he say he would do a marriage for us next time his path crossed that of our band?"

"Well," she answered slowly, watching him dress with angry gestures, "he asked if I had given it careful thought and if I might regret it later."

"Aha!" His eyes blazed as he whirled on her. "No doubt the good Father will pray over it a little and then go to the fort! I never intended for any whites to see you for just this reason!"

"I don't think he would do that—"

"But you don't really know, do you? Do you realize what dangers you may have exposed my people to if he brings back the white soldiers?"

She sat up, wrapping her arms around her knees as she studied him in the firelight, realizing he really was worried that the tribe might now be in danger. *Would the priest do something like that?* "I wouldn't expose Pony Woman and the others to danger, for now they are my people, too."

He paced the floor in great agitation. "I have known from the first you would turn my life upside down, and yet I was willing to fight anything and anybody who tried to take you from me! Better, I should have let the old chiefs trade you off to the Nimousin, the Comanche."

She stood up naked, put one small hand on his arm. "But you didn't. Why didn't you?"

He paused, his face stormy with inner conflict. "You know why, you pale-haired dream witch! I have too much white blood not to hunger for you! Because from the first moment I saw you I vowed no other man but me would ever touch you!"

Roughly, he jerked her against him and kissed her so savagely he cut her lip and she tasted blood.

She put her arms around his neck and clung to him passionately. "You must believe I never meant to endanger your people."

"I believe you!" he sighed. "But that does not lessen the fact that my people may be in peril! Tomorrow, at dawn, I will go to the old chiefs and tell them not to take the Mahohewas' lances down. We can start the people moving camp quickly just in case the old priest sends soldiers."

She felt the tension in his hard body and knew he battled inner turmoil. Her lips brushed his cheek and she suspected she tasted the salt of a tear. "Would not the soldiers follow us across the Territory if they come here looking?"

"Maybe. Maybe not. Our people have a lot of experience in eluding the soldiers and the desolate plains between here and the Colorado country hold many gulches, rock piles, and other hiding places."

"If the soldiers come," she promised against his lips, "I will tell them I am here of my own free will and do not want to leave. Then they will turn and ride out."

"That's what my mother told them," he said bitterly, "and they took her away anyhow."

"I won't go with them," she said firmly, wondering in her own mind if the priest would do such a thing. Now she was uneasy for the safety of the Cheyenne. "It is still a long time till dawn. Let us rest now, for there is nothing that can be done in the middle of the night."

They returned to their bed and she lay sleepless, staring into the darkness and felt him stirring restlessly. The purple night was faded and the fire had turned to silver ashes before she drifted off to sleep, wrapped in his big arms.

It was approaching dawn when Summer awakened and stretched as she got up and dressed quietly. Her lover lay asleep and she smiled down at him, wondering if he had made good his pledge to get her with child last night. She hoped so. A strong, fat baby was all she needed to round out their love, make their lives complete.

He looked exhausted as he slept and she moved carefully as she picked up her water skins to go down to the river. She knew the war party and the hard ride had been tiring to all the warriors and what they needed was several days' rest without having to move the camp today.

She really thought there was no need to worry about the priest bringing the soldiers but perhaps it had been stupid of her to take the chance.

Wrapping her shawl about her, she took the water skins and started for the river. It was still dark and frosty out; she could feel the frozen grass crunch under her feet. In another hour, the sun would be fully up, burning away the early chill from the scarlet sumac and green loblolly pine of the area.

At any rate, food must be prepared whether the camp was moved or not and the Cheyenne would not use water that had been left standing overnight. They called that "dead water." It was customary to go early to the river for the new day's supply. In a few more minutes, she would be joined by other women coming down to the river.

But for now, as she walked in the semidarkness, she was happy to be alone with her thoughts. She passed the horse herd and the little mare and the big Appaloosa nickered at her as she passed by. *Strange*, she thought, *where are the sentries?* There should be several on the perimeters of the camp, guarding against the approach of enemies that might sneak up on the People. She shrugged it off. No doubt, they were scattered out behind the brush so they could not be seen.

She smiled, thinking of the prospect of a colt from the pair of horses and pleased that the pony might make a good mount for her own son when she had one.

Absently humming to herself, she walked through the wild sand plum bushes near the river's edge and bent down to fill her water skins. *She was more than happy*, she thought, *except for this crazy fear of Iron Knife's that seemed to haunt him from his childhood that soldiers would take her away.* What had happened to his mother simply would not happen to her.

Summer was a stubborn, strong-willed person. She would not leave with the soldiers if they came to the camp. She would explain to the commanding officer that she wanted to stay and he would be satisfied with her explanation and ride off.

She bent over to fill her water skins. Abruptly a hand reached out of the plum bushes and grabbed her, clasping itself over her mouth as she struggled to scream a warning.

Terrified, she battled, thinking of Pawnee and knowing now that someone had killed the sentries. But as she fought, the hands that held her whirled her around. In the faint light of beginning dawn, she looked up into a bearded face, a white face.

The man smiled down at her and did not take his hand off her mouth. He wore a cowboy hat with two feathers in it and a smelly fur vest. The stink of him assailed her nostrils and she tried to bite his dirty hand.

"Take it easy, missy," he whispered. "Don't you understand? We're friends! Old Jake's come to rescue you and brought the whole damned cavalry from Fort Smith!"

Chapter Eighteen

Jake Dallinger looked down at the girl struggling in his arms. Gawd Almighty! She was a real beaut! Even in the dim light he saw the cascade of golden hair, the eyes blue as the waterfall known as Toccoa Falls back in his home state of Georgia. As he felt her satin skin against his rough hands, he understood why some Injun buck had taken a shine to her and wouldn't turn her in for the reward.

"I ain't agonna hurt you, missy," he reassured her in a hoarse voice as she struggled. "We're here to save you from the Injuns!"

But she didn't seem to understand because she kept fighting him. He was glad he had his hand over her mouth so she couldn't cry out and awaken the whole camp. *Probably*, he thought, *the gal had been so raped and brutalized, her brain was addled and she couldn't tell the difference between friend or foe anymore.*

The pimply-faced captain broke through the underbrush at his elbow. "For Christ's sake, Dallinger, what's going on?" He glanced back nervously toward the sleeping camp. "I've got the troopers hid out in that grove of trees like you said but we can't keep the horses quiet forever! What have you got there? Is that a white girl?"

Jake grinned at him but didn't relax his grip on the struggling blonde. "We're in luck, Cap'n. This is bound to be the one we came after! That Injun girl, Gray Dove, was right about what she came and tole us! And it's a lucky break for us, too; we don't have to worry about riskin' her gettin' shot when we attack the camp!"

"Why is she fighting?" the officer asked in his high, Yankee voice. "Doesn't she know we've come to help her?" He peered through the growing light at the girl struggling in Jake's arms.

"She's just plumb crazy with fear right now, sir, and probably don't know friend from foe! But she'll be all right onct we get her back to civilization! I'll just tie her up and leave her here outa the way so she'll be safe until we get through attackin' the camp!"

"Christ! There's no reason to attack the camp now! I'm not going to risk my men when there's no need! We got the girl, let's get the hell out of here!"

Frowning, Jake looked at him over the girl's head as she struggled. "You mean we're just gonna ride outa here without stoppin' to kill all those Injuns? You're sayin' the only ones I get to kill are the two sentries whose throats I cut?"

The young officer looked back at him uncertainly. "Why should we bother? After all, we got the girl and that's what we came for!"

Jake spat to one side. "Maybe that's the only reason you came but I never get tired of killin' Injuns! I hate 'em! Every one of 'em! I'd think you'd be happy to hit this camp hard, seein's as how you're eager to get transferred back to New York! Just think how'd it look on your record that you personally led the charge that wiped out the savages that slaughtered them people on the stage! Why, the Butterfield folks'll probably give you a reward, too! And just imagine how them back East newspapers would make over the handsome young captain that saved the purty white captive!"

The captain tipped back the plumed black cavalry hat, thinking, and as he thought he smiled a little.

He's a purdee danger, Jake thought as he held the girl. There's nothing quite so dangerous as an ambitious man who has neither talent nor brains to assist his ambitions. *God help the country if this one kept getting promoted!*

"You're right, Jake!" The officer nodded. "I'll alert the troops!"

"We got to hit them now, hard and fast before they start comin' awake," Jake cautioned, looking toward the reflected glow behind the eastern hills. "In a few minutes, they'll all be up and someone will find those two dead sentries and give the alarm!"

The captain looked at the struggling girl. "You'll take care of Miss Van Schuyler?"

"I'll tie her up till this is over!" he reassured the officer, enjoying the feel of the warm, struggling girl in his hands. "Jest see to it that you signal them soldiers with hand motions! Don't let no bugles blow!"

Captain Baker nodded agreement and disappeared into the woods.

Jake looked down into the long-lashed blue eyes. "I'm afixin' to do you a favor, miss," he drawled respectfully. "You're gonna wake up when this is all over and be so beholden to me!"

It was awkward to keep his hand over her mouth while he reached for the big whip at his belt. Very lightly, he tapped her across the skull with the heavy silver butt and caught her as she fell unconscious.

"Sorry I had to do that, honey," he said familiarly as he swung her limp body up in his big arms. "I couldn't take a chance on you workin' yore way outa the ropes and screamin' to alert yore big buck! I can just guess why you don't wanta leave this camp!"

Her head swung over his arm, the yellow hair hanging almost to the ground. The stress pulled the deerskin tight across her full breasts. He felt his manhood rise hard and eager for her now that she had aroused him by fighting and resisting. The thought that she was helpless and at his mercy excited him even more. He wished he had the time to throw her down in the

309

grass and take her quickly before he left. After all, she'd never know the difference and he'd never get another crack at an uppity, high-class gal like this one again.

There was a little something about her that reminded him of another woman, another time. Maybe it was that both of the women had courage or "grit," as they called it where he was from down in southern Georgia. She didn't look that much like Texanna, but, still, there was something about this girl . . .

He remembered now that night he had gone to see Texanna a few months after her baby girl was born in Fandango. Jake had been gone from Texas, scouting for the army. But the next time he was in the hill country, he got himself all slicked up and rode out to the small shack on the edge of town.

The place was almost as bad as the one he'd been raised in, Jake decided as he dismounted at the front gate and started across the dark yard. *The gal must be havin' a terrible time of it,* he thought. He paused and reached up to slick down his oiled hair. Not only had he been to the barber, he'd spent a short bit for a bath in the tin tub in the back of the shop. *Yep, he was goin' all out to woo her.* He'd even bought ill-fitting shoes and a store coat.

The moonlight lit up a small, pathetic flower garden as he crossed the yard. Jake surveyed the bright color, sniffed the perfume of the blossoms. Texanna was the kind of woman who would plant flowers in front of a shack, trying to make it homey. A saddled horse tied around at the side of the house so as not to be easily seen mystified Jake. Ladies wanting sewing done usually drove a buggy and Texanna surely couldn't afford a fine-blooded horse like that one.

Jake felt as skittish and nervous as a new colt. He paused on the front porch, wiping the sweat from his face. But as he started to knock, he heard angry voices through the open parlor window, and he peered in to see Texanna confronting her brother-in-law, that uppity Ransford Longworth.

310

"Get out of my house, Ransford." Texanna gestured angrily. "You aren't welcome after this!"

"Now, Texanna," the pompous shopkeeper whined, "I didn't mean to offend. Land O' Goshen, you know how much I think of you!"

She had her hands on her hips as she faced the plump man. "I know you're married to my younger sister. Obviously, you've forgotten that!"

"Well, no." He waved his fat, soft hands placatingly. "Your sister Carolina is a fine woman, but she isn't very warm and loving like I think you must be—"

"So you thought I'd jump at the chance to carry on an affair with you?" Even from the window, Jake could see the sparks in her bright blue eyes.

"Don't put it so crudely." Longworth stuck his thumbs in his loud, expensive vest. "I merely thought some nights when Carolina thinks I'm working or at a civic meeting, I might drop by. After all, since hardly anyone in town will speak to you, you must be as lonely."

"I'm not that lonely, to entertain my sister's husband!" she flung at him, looking him squarely in the eye. Texanna was tall for a woman, almost as tall as her arrogant brother-in-law, Jake thought as he watched.

Longworth sucked his teeth loudly. "Let's just say we both have needs. I need, er . . . companionship . . . and you certainly need a little money and some of the nice things from my dry goods store. We could work out a fair trade—"

She slapped him then, a hard blow across his pasty face that echoed like a pistol shot. "I am not nor have I ever been a whore, Ransford, in spite of what this town thinks! My love is saved for my husband, War Bonnet."

Longworth rubbed his red-marked face. "Husband!" he snorted. "Let's quit pussy-footing and get down to it, Texanna! Your sister and father are so embarrassed because you been sleepin' with an Injun buck, they won't even speak to you. Any tart who'd let some dirty savage between her legs can't be more than a tramp for all your high and mighty talk. You ought to be glad a white man would offer to sleep with you, comin' in behind an Injun!"

"Get out of here!" Her voice rose high-pitched and furious as she pointed to the front door. "Get out of here or I'll tell Carolina you were at my house tonight when she thinks you're at a meeting of the town beautification society!"

But Longworth didn't move. "She won't believe you," he said, "not when I can get a couple of the other important men in town to swear to her I was at the meeting tonight."

"Those same 'pillars of the community' who have come by to offer to 'help' me and my children if I'll just be 'nice' to them?" Her velvet voice dripped sarcasm. "Get out of here, Ransford!"

The man hesitated as if he might argue the point further. Jake had seen enough. He left the window, stalked over, banged on the door, and walked in.

"Maybe Carolina wouldn't believe her sister," Jake drawled as he glared at the man, "but she might listen to me." He strode over and glared down at the shopkeeper. "You get the hell out of here, you pale, soft maggot! And if I ever hear of you comin' near Texanna again, I'll take my whip to you!" His hand went automatically to his belt before he remembered he was dressed up tonight. But the threat was obviously enough as the other stumbled backward toward the door.

"Land O' Goshen, Dallinger," he pulled out a fine linen handkerchief to mop his pasty face, "I didn't realize you had already laid a claim here— I mean, I didn't know—"

"Well, you know now." Jake moved toward him threateningly, his fists doubled. "And you pass the word around town to every man jack that if I hear any more about Texanna bein' bothered, you'll all answer to me for it!"

"Sure, Jake, sure." Longworth stumbled backward out the front door. "I didn't know—! I mean, I—I'll tell the others!" And with that, he turned and fled.

Texanna put her hand on his arm, gratitude apparent on her

lovely face. "Oh, Jake, thank you. All the men in this town have made my life miserable. I guess I could have shot him, but after all, he is my sister's husband—"

"The town fathers probably would have hung you if you shot the uppity bastard." Jake's head reeled with the warmth of her hand on his arm, the clean scent of her red-gold hair. He'd never really courted a woman before. If he saw one he wanted, he took her by force if she wasn't willing. In the awkward silence, Texanna moved over to fuss with the blanket on the baby sleeping in the nearby cradle.

Jake listened to Longworth's horse clopping away toward the fashionable end of town and looked around the small room. The furnishings were so old and ragged that even Jake was appalled but it was clean and shining. The odor of homemade cookies drifted from the tiny kitchen and there was a bluebonnet in a cracked vase on the table.

"Where's the boy?" he asked, running his finger around the too-tight collar of the new shirt.

"Asleep," she sighed. "Tomorrow's a school day." She stroked the baby's head.

"Other kids at school treatin' him bad?" Jake shifted from one foot to the other, uneasy and unsure what to do next.

"Yes." She nodded sadly as she came over to him. "They treat us all bad; you must know that. He's whipped every boy in school so they don't taunt him anymore, they just ignore him. Since the town doesn't want us, you'd think they'd let us go back to the Indians."

"Civilized people couldn't hand a woman back to the Injuns!" he exclaimed without thinking.

She shrugged. "This town feels betrayed. They thought they had a virginal saint who'd given her life to save their wagon train. Then I have the colossal nerve to turn up alive with two half-breed kids."

Jake cleared his throat awkwardly. "You did what you had to do to stay alive, Texanna. I can't fault you for that. I reckon I was purty mean and shocked myself the day the Rangers

313

brought you back—"

"Let's not talk about that day, Jake. It was painful to find out my brothers were both dead. Otherwise, they'd deal with these men now for me." She interrupted with a gentle shake of her head. The light from the coal oil lamp reflected off her red-gold hair, making it glimmer as if touched by fire.

He shifted his huge weight from one tight, hurting shoe to the other and thought how weary and strained she looked as she went over to the big pile of unfinished sewing and picked up a half-done dress.

"What did you want, Jake?" she sighed and her shoulders slumped with apparent weariness. "Were you wanting some shirts made?"

Jake paused, quaking. He had faced down Indians, renegades, outlaws, but he'd never faced a woman and asked her to marry him. If he'd seen a woman he wanted, he just took her whether she liked it or not. He'd killed a couple of men who'd objected to his taking their women.

"No, I don't need no shirts." He felt foolish standing there in his store-bought clothes and slicked-down hair.

She smiled. "You look nice tonight, Jake, must be all dressed up to go calling on a lady friend when you leave here."

"I—I come callin' on you!" Once started, the words stumbled over each other and came out in an awkward rush like a schoolboy's. "Texanna, you need a man to protect you and I always had a hankerin' for you. So what do you say we get ourselves hitched!"

Her face was both shocked and startled as she looked up from her sewing, and for a split second he wondered if she was going to laugh. *By Gawd, he'd kill her if she laughed at him!*

She didn't laugh. Her expression, though startled, was kind and gentle. "Thank you for the offer, Jake, it's very sweet of you—"

"Nobody would dare bother you again, Texanna, they'd have to answer to me for it! We'll leave Texas, make a new start somewheres—"

314

"You didn't let me finish." Her expression now was troubled, strained as she looked down. She fumbled with a button on the dress in her hands for a long moment. "I can't marry you, Jake. I have a man already."

"You mean, that damned Injun buck?" he snorted, his heart starting to sink. *She was going to turn him down after all. That's what he got for trying to be gentle-like instead of just overpowering her like he usually did if the gal weren't willin'.*

His disappointment made his words harsh. "You can ferget that savage. You won't never see him again. And you're mighty uppity with old Jake! You should be purdee grateful I'd be willin' to take an Injun's leavin's. Most white men wouldn't!"

She jerked as though he'd struck her across the face and little blotches of color came to her cheeks. "I might have known you were just like the rest of them." Her voice was cold, hurt. "You all figure if I'd sleep with an Indian, I'm a tramp and should be grateful for your offers."

"That's about the size of it, missy." He's tried the polite approach and it didn't work. He'd treat her like he'd always treated women. His groin was aching with need as he confronted her, put his hand on her shoulder. "Look, Texanna, give my offer some thought. I want you. You know that. I wanted you when we was on that wagon train and I want you now. Never mind that Injun got you first. We'll leave this town, dump those half-breed kids someplace, and go—"

"My children?" Her eyes widened with disbelief as she backed away from him, slowly shaking her head. "You think I'd give up my children?"

Now it was his turn to stare back at her in astonishment. "You didn't think the offer included the kids, did you?" He moved toward her. "I know a good mission orphanage that'll take half-breeds. I couldn't have them kids around, every time I looked at either of them, I'd think about that damned savage forcin' hisself between yore legs—"

"He didn't force me!" Her voice rose in strident anger as she confronted him. "Do you hear? He didn't force me! I took him

315

willingly and, God willing, someday I'll take his children and go back to him!"

Jake felt his small eyes widen in surprise. "You're loco!" he whispered. "They been sayin' it all over town, but I didn't believe them! You do deserve the insane asylum! You're plumb loco!"

Her eyes flashed like deep blue fire. He had forgotten how spirited and feisty she was when she was angry. "Loco, why? Because I'm faithful to the man I love? Because I'm just waiting for the chance to escape and go back to his arms? If that's loco, mister, I plead guilty!"

She was more desirable and beautiful than he had remembered as she glared at him. All the jealousy, frustration, and hunger of wanting her made something inside him go out of control when he realized she was rejecting him. She would never be his, never sleep with him, despite his new clothes and clumsy gentleness.

"By God, woman!" he swore. "I will have you, missy, at least onct!" His big hand reached out, dragged her to him. His mouth covered hers as she tried to cry out and he lifted her off her feet, crushing her in his bearlike embrace. He could feel her full, milk-swollen breasts through the cloth of his coat as he held her and the taste of her mouth was sweeter than he had even imagined in his daydreams.

Yes, he would have her at least once, and then she'd change her mind once he'd put a baby in her belly and take him as her protector. That was how his pa had gotten his mama. Next year, that could be Jake's baby in that cradle, his son sharing those full, swollen breasts with his daddy.

"I'm gonna have you, Texanna, if I have to knock you out to do it," he muttered feverishly against her lips as she writhed in protest. "I know you're used to havin' a man and I'm eager to prove I'm ever bit the stud War Bonnet was! I'll make you forget him when I love you!"

"You rotten bastard, let me go!" Her frantic shriek woke up the baby and it started crying as Jake struggled with Texanna.

The half-breed boy came through the bedroom door then, sleepily rubbing his eyes. "What's the matter?"

"Nothing, son," Texanna answered coolly, pulling from Jake to rearrange her rumpled dress. "Now you go back to bed like a good boy. I'll see to the baby."

Jake smiled benignly at the uncertain child. "Your ma and I is just havin' a friendly visit, that's all. Now you go on back to bed like she says."

He wondered if the boy had caught the tension in Texanna's voice. *She was afraid for the kid's safety. Yeah, she'd let him love her right there on the sofa if he threatened her damned kids.*

Jake and War Bonnet's son eyed each other a long moment while Texanna went over to lift the baby from the cradle and soothe it. Jake wasn't too worried about the boy. Texanna was a good shot, Jake remembered that from the wagon train. But everyone in town said the kid still hunted with a lance or bow and arrow. No, he was no threat.

Texanna put the baby back in its cradle and looked from one male to the other. "Go back to bed, son," she said again.

Almost reluctantly, the boy disappeared into the bedroom and Texanna strode over, closed the door. Before Jake could anticipate her next move, she ran to grab up a shotgun leaning against a wall in a shadowy corner. The slender blonde leveled down on him. "You get out of here, Jake, or I'll blow you to Kingdom Come and you know I shoot well enough to do it."

Would she? Jake knew she was a good shot and brave as they come, but he wasn't sure she'd actually kill a man.

But as he started to advance on her, she hefted the gun and took dead aim at his belly. "I know what you're thinking, Jake, and yes, I would!" Her voice shook a little from fright but her eyes were determined, her hands steady. "Unlike Ransford Longworth," she said, "you aren't a pillar of the community and a lot of folks don't like you. Why, the town might make me a heroine all over again if I killed you!"

"Now, Texanna." He gestured placatingly, but all he could think of was the ache in his groin, how he was going to throw her across the sofa and take her when he managed to get that gun out of her hands. "Let's talk about this—"

"You come one step closer, and you'll think talk," she declared. "Get out of here, Jake, and don't you ever come back!"

Suddenly, the half-breed kid stood in the bedroom door with an arrow fitted to his bow. The arrow was pointed at Jake's belly. "Get away from my mama," the kid said, and his eyes were as brave and savage as any grown Dog Soldier Jake had ever fought.

Jake's lust faded fast as he faced two weapons and knew by the expressions that the woman and boy thought they had little to lose by killing him.

"All right, all right! I'm going!" he muttered, swearing under his breath as the two backed him out the front door. They didn't lower their weapons as he turned and stalked furiously out to his horse. *Damn! If word ever got out he'd backed down to a woman and a kid, he'd be laughed not only out of Fandango, but every saloon and gambling hall in Texas!*

Mounting, he rode toward town, sawing cruelly on his gelding's mouth. He'd wasted all that time and money getting cleaned up and buying new clothes and had nothing to show for it. There was no use wasting all this trouble when there were women at the saloon. Tonight, and the rest of his life, he'd mistreat and brutalize women, trying to get even with a tall, slim girl with red-gold hair who had rejected his clumsy offer of love.

Jake seldom came to Texas after that, but when he did he avoided Texanna's house and hung around the saloon with a woman named Kate. More than four years passed. He didn't see Texanna or her half-breed son again until late one afternoon when he'd caught that devil's spawn of War Bonnet's topping Kate. That started the whole chain of events that climaxed with the town mob wanting to hang the boy after

Jake almost whipped him to death. But gritty Texanna had confronted them all with her shotgun, just as War Bonnet and his raiding party finally rode in to carry her off.

Texanna, he thought. *Texanna. Where was she now after all these years?* He came back to the present with a start and remembered the cavalry was about to attack the Cheyenne village. He looked down at the unconscious girl in his arms.

Almost tenderly, he shifted the Van Schuyler girl so her face rested on his shoulder and he kissed her still lips. Then very carefully, he lay her in a thicket of wild sand plum bushes. Jake checked his Sharps rifle and felt for the hilt of his Bowie knife, still bloody from the sentries' throats. He rolled up his whip and hung it again from his belt. With that, he mounted his scruffy bay pony, swearing a little because he didn't make enough as a scout to support drinking, gambling, and buying a better horse, too. Well, he'd get a fine-blooded horse now, either out of that Cheyenne herd or with the reward money he was going to get for returning the Boston girl.

From where he sat his horse on the little rise, he could see the blue of the troopers' uniforms as they spread like shadows around the camp. Gripping the reins tightly, he held his breath and waited for the first gunshot. His mouth felt dry and he wished he had a shot of strong, sour mash whiskey or, at the very least, a cup of black coffee laced with chicory the way they made it in the Cajun country he had spent a little time in.

Jake licked his lips. The other thing he wanted was a cigar but there wasn't time now that the raid was about to begin. Somewhere in the camp, a dog barked a warning and it drifted on the frosty, clean air as he inhaled.

Almost detached from the scene below him, he watched the Yankee captain bring his arm down in a charging motion and for a split second, he wondered if that sweet little brown bitch, Gray Dove, was in the camp.

He shrugged and spat to one side. It couldn't be helped now if she was and he'd had no way to warn her and get her out. Anyway, she'd be madder than hell at him when she realized she'd been double-crossed and followed back to camp instead of meeting at old Fort Gibson like they'd agreed. He never intended to split that five-hundred-dollar reward with her anyway. He needed it all to open that fancy saloon up on Cherry Creek in the gold diggings they were already referring to as "Denver."

Rifles cracked suddenly in the still air and now all he thought of was charging into the camp, killing as many Indians as possible. He dug his mean Spanish spurs into the scruffy bay nag, raking its flanks cruelly with the sharp steel as he raced into the camp.

The next ten minutes were a blur of noise, blood, and confusion. Half-naked Indians ran out of tepees only to be cut down by gunfire. Women screamed, running about, and children cried out in terror. Dogs raced around the camp barking. The big pony herd, stampeded by the noise, galloped through the camp in a cloud of dust. Here and there, a brave tried to grab a running horse and mount up, but mostly the man attempting it was trampled by the milling, churning herd. Jake grinned as he aimed down his rifle sights at a very old brave wearing a scalp shirt. He had always hankered to own a scalp shirt. If he aimed low and gut shot the old man there wouldn't be any blood all over the front of that fancy shirt. He didn't give it much thought that a gut shot man takes a long, long time to die in agony. *Hell! They was just animals anyways,* he thought as he took aim.

But as he squeezed the trigger, the pony under him jerked nervously, spoiling his aim, and the shot went high. The front of the shirt seemed to explode in a splatter of blood and he swore angrily. Damn! The shirt was ruined now. He couldn't wear it with a big hole and blood all over it! The smell of gunpowder and fresh blood made his horse shy again and he jerked furiously on the reins, sawing the pony's mouth cruelly as he fired a second time. He brought down a running squaw with a baby in her arms. Jake decided not to waste a bullet on the baby. He could hear it wailing over the noise in its dead

320

mother's arms. All around him echoed shooting and screaming. Horses reared and whinnied in agony as bullets struck them. The smell of death and smoke hung over the scene like a shroud as troopers torched the tepees.

The Injuns was making a game effort to defend themselves, Jake noted as he saw a soldier clutch at a lance in his leg and fall from a snorting, stumbling horse.

That lance was thrown by one of the biggest bucks Jake had ever seen. He stood in the middle of the chaos, evidently trying to rally the warriors. *The Injun wore a strange earring*, Jake thought. It looked almost like a button off a cavalry jacket, and from the bone whistle visible in the neck of the deerskin shirt, he knew the Indian was a Dog Soldier, bravest of the brave. For a moment, he thought the man looked familiar, that he had seen him somewhere before. But he dismissed the idea. *Hell! All Injuns looked alike!*

The bigger they are, the harder they fall! Jake thought with satisfaction as he swung the Sharps around toward the big Indian and pulled the trigger. But Jake's horse jerked at the same time the Dog Soldier moved. Though the man went down soaked with blood, Jake figured the shot might have gone a little high. He'd aimed for the heart. *But the Injun shore looked dead from here*, he noted with satisfaction as he reined his pony around, looking for another target. He thought he saw Gray Dove running through hazy smoke toward the woods and he grinned to himself and didn't pull the trigger. There was no need killing her; she was too good in the sack. Sooner or later, she'd turn up at the fort again and he could enjoy her some more. Then, too, if he did get to open that saloon, she could make him a lot of money as a whore. Jake spat to one side. Yes, she'd come to the fort again because she was too lazy and greedy to stay with the Indians. But if the Cheyenne ever found out she was the one who betrayed them, she might not have enough hide left to hold her meat and bones together. Angry squaws would beat her to death if they got the chance for revenge.

321

The Indian men stood their ground valiantly now, making a last ditch effort to buy time for the women and children running to the thick underbrush and woods to escape.

"Don't let them get away!" Jake shouted, whirling his horse around. He'd like nothing better than a chance to ride some of them into the dirt. He grinned with satisfaction. "There's plenty more to kill!"

But the young captain on his gray gelding was already signaling the bugler to sound recall.

"We ain't killed 'em all yet!" Jake protested.

"This slaughter makes me want to puke!" The officer gestured toward the burning tepees, the wounded horses struggling to stand and neighing in pain, the crumpled human bodies. "I'm sorry I let you talk me into this, Dallinger!"

He signaled the bugler who blew again. "I always thought fighting Indians would be glorious, but, Christ! I feel rotten! Let's regroup and get the hell out of here!"

"I'll go back to the river and get the girl then." Jake ducked his head humbly, hating the uppity Yankee but knowing enough to hold his tongue. "You might want to have them soldiers gather up that horse herd, sir, to keep the Injuns from comin' after us! An Injun afoot is purty helpless!"

The captain nodded curtly and rode off to assemble his troops.

Jake jerked his pony's mouth savagely as he turned back toward the wild plum thicket. Disgusted and annoyed, he thought about the missed chance to take a few scalps, do a little looting. It was probably just as well that the colonel would be back tomorrow and that sissy little captain wouldn't be in charge anymore. He had had a bellyful of that snot-nosed kid. There was a rumor that some of them, including the scouts, might be transferred up farther north soon. *Everybody said there was gonna be a hell of a good fight in "Bloody Kansas" between pro and anti-slavery settlers,* Jake recalled. The gold-seekers flooding across Kansas toward Colorado were adding to the confusion. Anyplace there might be a fight and some killing, Jake wanted to be there. He smiled with satisfaction as he rode to the river.

The blond girl still lay unconscious in the grass where he had left her. *Gawd Almighty! She was one purty gal!* He swung off his horse and stood looking down at her, waiting to see if she stirred. When she didn't move, he knelt beside her and touched her with an eager hand. Encouraged by her lack of response, he pushed her deerskin shift up and found she wore nothing beneath it. His dirty hand trembled as he reached out to touch one rosebud nipple. He could remember only one other girl so beautiful.

Unbidden, his thoughts went again to the only woman he had ever really loved. *He'd near about driven himself crazy thinkin' about shovin' it to that Texas gal.* She was the only woman besides his own ma that he had ever felt tender toward, offered to marry. And she'd turned him down for a damned, dog-eating savage! Thinking about her made his manhood grow hard and his anger and frustration over Texanna came back to haunt him now. He looked down at the unconscious blond girl in the grass.

He licked his lips. *Another damned Injun had gotten to this one first, too, but it didn't matter none; nothin' really mattered to him since he'd lost Texanna.* This time, Jake was going to make up for it. He could have a quick one at her expense and the unconscious girl would never know the difference. The fact she was helpless excited him and she looked enough like Texanna that he could pretend. Texanna's hair had been redder, of course, almost strawberry blond and her eyes had been the bright blue of the Texas wildflower.

He'd never gotten to lay Texanna but he could have this one and get even with these two damned women who fought him off while they opened their legs to a rutting savage. Unbuttoning his pants, he positioned himself between the blonde's satin thighs and ran his hands over her. *It wasn't like she was a virgin,* he rationalized as he pulled his manhood from his pants. Besides, if some buck had already been enjoying her, it wasn't gonna hurt her to give her rescuer a quick sample.

Five minutes was all he needed, he thought, looking down at her as he ran his hands over her full breasts. Five minutes would ease the ache in his groin that had been hurting ever since he'd seen her, started thinking about Texanna. Jake laughed to himself, thinking what a big joke it would be on her high-class pa if nine months from now, she came up with a white baby and nobody, including herself, could figure out how she'd come by it.

Jake would know, he thought, looking down at the small, port wine stain between his fourth and little finger on his right hand. The Mark of Cain his pa called it, and every Dallinger had it. Yes, if he put a child in her belly, it would have that telltale birthmark. All the Dallingers had marked their children that way for several hundred years now.

He made ready to enter the girl. *Yep, that would be a joke on the rich folks if they had to raise a poor white trash baby.* There was only one thing Jake hated more than Indians and women and that was high-class, snotty men who treated him like dirt. That's the way Ransford Longworth, Texanna's brother-in-law had treated him.

He heard a movement in the trees behind him and jerked away just as he was about to rape the girl.

"Dallinger?" the captain called. "Dallinger, where are you? If you've got the girl, let's get out of here!"

Swearing silently, Jake scrambled to his feet, forced his erection back in his pants, buttoning them quickly. Then he jerked the girl's dress down to cover her ripe body. *He'd have an ache in his groin all the way back to the fort now,* he thought savagely, thinking how good it would have been if he'd just had another five minutes! Hell, he could have done it in three!

"I'm over here, sir!" he called out. "And I got the girl safe and sound! Be right there!"

Regretfully, he swung her up in his arms and kissed her lips. For a long moment, he pretended she was Texanna and frustration and anger overcame him as he looked down at the limp girl. "Missy," he whispered. "You just barely missed gettin' ole Jake's big rod rammed right down your little musket barrel. I kin only hope someday I may get another chance at you, willin' or unwillin'. If you damned women will let some Injun have you, you deserve to be raped or put to work in a whorehouse!"

With that, he turned, caught the reins, and mounted up, easily swinging the small, limp body up on the saddle before him. Now he rode out to join the troops who were already rounding up most of the big pony herd to take with them.

Smoke rose in a thin column. Tepees burned and the dying moans of men and horses drifted on the suddenly silent air. The high, trilling wail of grieving women started and he smiled in satisfaction. *There'd be a lot of cut legs and shorn hair among the Cheyenne tonight,* he thought, and he wondered suddenly about the big Dog Soldier he had killed.

Damn! That savage had had a knife in his belt that Jake would like to have for a souvenir. *No,* he decided, *what he really wanted was the buck's hair to make hisself a warrior's scalp shirt.* He hesitated, thinking about riding back in and taking the warrior's scalp. And maybe he'd take his heart, too. Some of the plains tribes believed if you ate a brave man's heart, it made big medicine. He wasn't sure he believed it, but still . . .

Yep, he'd leave the girl with one of the soldiers and go back for the big Dog Soldier's scalp and heart. He imagined lifting it in his bare hands, still warm and bloody from the man's chest. The idea was almost as exciting as raping the unconscious girl. He'd pretend it was War Bonnet's. *Damn you, Texanna, what'd you see in that savage anyway?* He gritted his teeth, relishing the thought of eating the bloody Indian heart as he reined his scraggly pony around.

Chapter Nineteen

But as he reined around, that snotty pup, Baker, yelled at him. "Hey, where do you think you're going?"

Jake hesitated. "I forgot something back there—"

"For Christ's sake, whatever it is, we aren't going back! We got the girl and that's what we came for."

"Yes, sir." Jake scowled, hating his superior but afraid to dispute him. He could forget about the Indian's knife and scalp. Although he'd been looking forward to seeing the captain puke in front of all the troopers when Jake came riding back with that bloody heart in his hand.

Yeah, he had enjoyed the morning's work, he thought as he glanced back at the burning camp before regretfully rejoining Captain Baker. The Cheyenne were clever all right, he had to hand it to them. If it hadn't been for Gray Dove, nobody would have known which tribe hit that stagecoach. The raiders had done such a good job leaving Pawnee and Crow lances and arrows around, even Jake had been fooled. That was hard to do when it came to Indians.

Behind him, he could hear the keening trill of the grieving women over their dead. He looked down at the unconscious girl in his arms and smiled with satisfaction and fell in beside the captain in the line of march. The cavalry rode toward the east, driving the big pony herd ahead of them. He hadn't enjoyed anything so much as he enjoyed this morning since a few days ago when he'd heard about the mistaken raid against Bull Hump's Comanche down at the springs near Rush Creek. The Second Cavalry from Camp Radzimski led by Captain Van Dorn had attacked the Comanche in a bloody slaughter. An officer from another fort had arranged for them to come in for a peace parlay at the Wichita village but someone forgot to notify Van Dorn and old Sul Ross at the other fort.

Wasn't that typical of the government, Jake thought with glee as he rode into the rising melon-colored sun, *never let your left hand know what the right one's doing*.

Wal, Jake thought as he rode alongside the captain, *the sooner the stupid government quit tryin' to parlay with Injuns and just went ahead and wiped them out or herded them onto reservations, the better off white folks would be. And Injuns were no better than animals anyway*. His hand went unconsciously to tip his hat back, finger the bald spot in his hair. *Damned Comanche!*

The captain looked over at the limp girl in Jake's arms as they rode along. "Christ! What's happened? She isn't dead, is she?"

"Naw, she ain't dead!" He reassured the officer as they kept their horses in an easy lope toward the east and the new day. "I think she musta fell and hit her head on a rock back at the river. After while, she'll come to and be grateful as hell to you, Cap'n! Probably gonna give you a big kiss!"

He heard some of the troopers riding behind the pair snicker and had to agree silently. No girl in her right mind would want to kiss the little pimply-faced captain from New York.

"I'm having second thoughts about that raid," the captain grumbled. "We slaughtered those people like flies! And I didn't even have permission from the colonel to leave the fort!"

Jake yawned. Discussions about moral issues always bored him. "Gawd Almighty! You only had two men wounded and none killed. I reckon you can always 'lose' the report and tell the boys not to talk about it none. That way, nobody will ever really know about it if you was worried about the history books." He guffawed.

Baker said nothing for a long moment as they rode back toward Fort Smith. "Christ! I may just do that," he said finally.

It sure didn't matter to him. Jake spat lazily as he adjusted the girl's limp form on the saddle before him. Once when no one was looking, he patted her thigh and then rubbed his hand under one of her full breasts. If she didn't revive soon, he would get worried he'd hit her too hard. Automatically, one hand went to touch the silver butt of the big whip that was as much a part of his personality as his right arm. When anyone heard that twelve-foot lash snap, they didn't have to ask why the ox and mule skinners from his home state were called "Georgia Crackers." Yep, the boys from Georgia could really handle the oxen teams. He was an expert with the deadly lash, able to make it sing harmlessly out over a team of the giant Connestoga covered wagons or cut the eyes out of a man in a fight. He'd done both.

It seemed like an eternity ago now that he'd had to flee Georgia when he was just a young kid. He went to work as a lowly oxen drover on wagon trains moving down the trail known as the Texas Road. He was green and inexperienced, riding point too far out in advance of the train when he'd been ambushed by the Comanche war party. Unconsciously, he reached up to touch the bald, pink scar under his hat. The savages had been in the process of scalping him alive and laughing at his screams when men from the wagon train rode up unexpectedly and rescued him. After that, he never let Indians make the first move. He'd shoot them down like rabid coyotes and then ask questions. Jake had an underlying fear that sometimes gave him nightmares. In them, he was being tortured by Indians, tortured and killed while the warriors laughed.

A couple of years passed. It was the spring of 1832 and he was working as a scout for the wagon trains. But now, he was hard and experienced, one of the best scouts on the trail, everyone said. The Mexicans didn't want any more Gringos. They were worried too many white immigrants would finally want to govern themselves and break away from Mexico. So the wagon trains had to take a chance on getting caught as they sneaked across Indian Territory into the Mexican holdings. He remembered now it was four years before the Gringos rose up and declared their independence at the Alamo. *Yep*, he sighed, *1832 was the year he met Texanna, the year the Cheyenne had carried her off. . . .*

He was scouting for a train headed to a Texas hill country town called Fandango. The girl with the glimmering red-gold hair, Texanna Heinrich, had been with that train along with her old father and spoiled younger sister. The Heinrich brothers were already in Texas.

The limp girl in his arms moaned and moved a little. Jake studied her face and thought again that there was a slight resemblance between this one and his beloved Texanna.

His emotions were a mix of anger and anguish as he looked down at the girl and remembered another girl, another time and what happened that fateful morning. . . .

The wagon train had already had more than its share of bad luck when, just south of the Red River, their luck ran out completely. It was dawn on the north Texas prairie and the wagons were still circled up. The little group had just finished burying the wagon master, leaving the train without a leader. Jake appointed himself that spot, knowing the immigrants were too afraid of him to argue the point. The people started gathering up to move out.

Jake frowned, remembering. A big Cheyenne war party had

crossed their path and surrounded them.

He gritted his teeth even now, remembering the virile, dark warrior on his black and white stallion. The chief looked resplendent in a long feathered bonnet and garish war paint. The braves outnumbered the settlers so they had sent the preacher out to parlay, see what they wanted. The preacher came back pale and shaken and repeated the message: "Send out the girl with the red-gold hair and I will let the rest go on their way unharmed."

That had started one hell of a fuss, Jake thought, listening to the scissortail flycatchers in the trees around him as he rode alongside the captain with the unconscious girl cradled in his arms. . . .

Texanna's mild little father had gasped and exclaimed, "Ach, are you sure, Herr Schmidt? Perhaps you misunderstood what he said! Maybe if we give the savages some food and trinkets—"

"*Nein.*" The preacher readjusted his wire-framed spectacles. "Their leader spoke English and he said he wanted the girl for his woman. He mentioned red-gold hair several times."

"Wal." Jake pushed his hat back and glared at the magnificent chief waiting just out of rifle shot with his men. "He ain't gonna get Texanna."

The preacher nodded, "*Ja,* I told him that; I told him we would fight to the last man."

One of the other men asked, "Then what'd he say?"

The minister sighed and looked around at the silent women and children of the party. "He said they outnumbered us and if we didn't give her up, they'd take *all* the women when they'd killed *all* the men."

Mrs. Johnson started sobbing then. "We're all going to be killed! We're all going to be killed!"

Hands on her hips, Texanna looked out toward the Indians with a defiant shake of her head. "The colossal nerve of the man! You'd think he was bartering for a bracelet or some such bauble."

Her father, the frail little tailor, looked around the circle of silent faces desperately. "You can't expect me to hand over one of my daughters to satisfy barbaric lust!"

Jake stepped in, took charge. "That savage bastard ain't gonna get her." He glanced over at Texanna's lovely, troubled face. When the train got to Fandango, he intended to marry her himself although she'd told him she wouldn't have him.

There was a chorus of frightened voices. "What are we going to do? Shall we fight? Can we give them horses or something to make them go away?"

"Shut up, everyone!" Jake shouted, gesturing. "Looks like we only got two choices: we can fight and we're outnumbered, or we can give them a woman—"

Old man Heinrich protested again. "Not my Texanna!"

"I tole you it wasn't gonna be Texanna!" He scratched his beard thoughtfully. "This is sort of like being in an overcrowded lifeboat. We got to sacrifice somebody so the rest can live."

The immigrants nodded slowly. They understood this talk of ships. Most of them were fresh off the boat.

But the minister took off his glasses and stared at Jake. "This whole thing is immoral. I don't think—"

"Gawd Almighty!" Jake swore and the man hesitated, backed away. "You can talk about right or wrong all you want, preacher, but the fact is, it's either one sacrificed or they kill all the men and take every one of you women!"

The women shivered and looked uncertainly at each other.

Jake leaned over, began to pull dry grass stems. "That ruttin' Injun don't know one white woman from another. All he can think of is creamy pale titties! We're gonna have us a little drawin' here, and every woman but Texanna will draw! Whoever gets the short straw gives herself up to that chief—"

"But the chief was adamant," the minister protested. "He said over and over, 'the one with the red-gold hair'!"

Mrs. Johnson ceased sobbing and wiped her eyes. "If the Injun wants Texanna, she's the one we should send—"

Jake glared at the woman. "It ain't gonna be Texanna."

Texanna drew herself up proudly. "It isn't going to be anyone. We're not animals here. We'll fight rather than hand over a hostage."

"Of course you'd say that." Mrs. Olsen sniffed disdainfully. "Since he wants us to send you out!"

"We ain't givin' him Texanna," Jake said, and his tone was cold and ugly. He put his hand on his pistol and glared into each face. "If we got to send one with light hair, we'll send Mrs. Olsen or Carolina Heinrich."

Both those women broke into hysterical sobbing and Joe Olsen pushed to the front of the crowd. "You can't send my Hilda, we got two small children."

Herr Heinrich faced up to the man. "Your wife's got no more right than my Carolina."

Jake pulled out his pistol. "What I say goes. Anybody don't agree with me is gonna get a taste of this gun rammed down his throat or my whip on his back. I say all the women draw straws except Texanna—"

"That's not fair, Jake." Texanna's bright blue eyes flashed. "I'll draw along with the rest of the ladies, but don't put my little sister Carolina in the hat, she's only fourteen—"

"But my wife has two kids," Joe Olsen protested. "How am I supposed to raise two little kids without a mama to cook and wash for all of us?"

"My wife shouldn't be included, either," someone else shouted. "She's in the family way and it ain't fair!"

Mrs. Schmidt, the pastor's wife, stepped forward, her lips trembling. "I—I'll go myself rather than send one of these others."

"No!" the preacher exclaimed. "Not you—"

"Well," exploded Mr. Olsen. "If not her? Who?"

The whole group acted like a pack of fighting hounds. Jake remembered now as he rode along toward Fort Smith. Everyone wanted some other woman to go. While they were arguing and exchanging blows over who they'd force to be the sacrifice, brave Texanna slipped away from the train and started walking across the prairie toward the war party. She'd decided to give herself to save the others.

As long as he lived, he would never forget that scene; how courageous and alone she had looked walking through the bluebonnets from the wagon train to the Indian war party. He screamed at her, tried to get her to come back, told her he'd force someone else to go. But she only gave him that serene, brave look and walked on. She was too far from the wagons by then to risk running out to grab her. He saw the chief look down at her, offer his hand. She took it and he lifted her up on the saddle of the big black and white paint stallion ahead of him. The sunlight glinted on her hair as the war party turned and galloped away toward the north. . . .

Jake swallowed hard, remembering. The settlers thought her dead after that, of course, and they talked about what a heroine she was. When they got to the new town site, the people built and named a school in her honor. Then, years later, Texanna returned. The Texas Rangers had brought her back by mistake, thinking they'd found the missing Cynthia Ann Parker who'd been carried off by the Comanche.

Even now, he could remember riding like hell to get there when he'd heard she was being brought back. And he also remembered his disgust and the town's horror that their saintly dead heroine was not only alive, but had a half-breed kid and a swollen belly. That gave evidence that she'd let herself be taken by a savage instead of killing herself like she was expected to do.

War Bonnet. The name came back in a rush after all these years and he gritted his teeth, hating the man who took Texanna's body and her love when Jake had hungered for both and got neither.

Of course, living with the Indians had made her a little crazy. Everyone in town agreed that was the only reason she wanted to run off and go back to that Cheyenne chief. But when they threatened to lock her up in the asylum and put the two kids in an orphanage, she quit trying to run away. Jake kept thinking she'd finally see his point; give those damned half-breed kids to anyone who'd take them and marry him. Instead, one Friday evening in the spring after she'd been in Fandango five years, that boy decided to mount Jake's fancy woman at the saloon and that was the last straw. He was in such a blind fury, he got the town rowdies all fired up to lynch the kid. . . .

"You got a cigar, Jake?" The captain broke abruptly into Jake's memories.

Jake felt around in the fur vest. "Just my regulars, Cap'n." He stuck one between his lips and offered one to the officer across the girl's unconscious form.

"Forget it, then," Baker growled as he shifted in his saddle and waved his hand away. "Those stogies stink almost as much as you do! Christ! Don't you ever take a bath?"

Jake didn't answer. He knew his smell annoyed the more civilized, which delighted him. He never noticed it himself. As he lit up with a match from his little silver match safe, he remembered suddenly why he didn't like Captain Baker. The kid from New York, except for the accent, reminded him of that uppity St. Clair boy who owned the plantation near the Dallinger's tumble-down cabin on the edge of the Okefenokee swamp. . . .

Jake glanced at the port wine stain between his fingers as he held the cigar. *Yep*, he thought. *It seemed like every Dallinger had killed somebody in his lifetime.* Pa said Great-Great Grandpappy had started it all by killing his brother and the mark had been passed down through the bloodline ever since.

In fact, that's how the family ended up in Georgia in the first place. Great-Great Grandpappy was in that first shipload of convicts that were among the first settlers of the state. They were all supposed to be debtors, of course, but some thieves and murderers had gotten into the bunch, figuring life in the new wilderness was better than the gallows. The English used to settle a lot of new colonies with convicts, Jake recalled.

Great-Great Grandpappy had got himself a woman on that ship, a serving wench who had stolen a duke's purse. The Crown thought most of those convicts would die, but they didn't. The outlaws and scum had retreated back into the remote hills and swamps and there they lived, generation after generation, inbreeding with their own relatives. They scraped a bare living out of the earth, hunted and trapped a little, robbed and stole, and sometimes made and sold whiskey.

Jake's ma had been a pretty little thing, he remembered, hardly more than a barefoot child when Pa had raped her and then abducted her because she carried his son. Maybe she was a trifle dim-witted from so much intermarriage in her family, but Jake had loved her like he'd loved no other but Texanna. *If Ma had been real smart, she never would have gotten mixed up with young St. Clair while she was cleaning at the big plantation house to make a little extra money. . . .*

Them damned uppity St. Clairs! If he'd said it once, he'd said it a thousand times! Jake ground his teeth together as he rode along with the girl in his arms. The St. Clairs always called Pa's family "poor white trash." But the night they'd needed someone with a reputation for handling a whip, they'd sent for young Jake. Old Mister St. Clair himself requested Jake to come bring his whip to the thousand-acre cotton plantation and make an example of a runaway slave.

Even now, he could remember it all vividly, the crowd of white men gathered by torchlight under the big live oaks with the Spanish moss trailing like ghostly fingers. The St. Clairs herded the slaves out to watch so they would pass the word to all the other plantations about what happened when an uppity black tried to stir up insurrection.

Gawd Almighty! he thought. That big slave was bloody already and had been chewed pretty bad by the tracking hounds. But he was still defiant and fought the men as they dragged him out and hung him up by his hands in front of the barn with his feet barely touching the ground.

"This the only one?" Jake drawled, uncoiling his big whip. He was right proud to be asked to do a man's job in front of all the white plantation owners and overseers in the area. All the money he'd make this past year from hunting and trapping had gone into paying for that silver-handled whip and he was pleased for a chance to show it off.

Old Mister St. Clair ran his hand through his white hair. "This is the only one left," he drawled, his voice as slow as the rhythmic cicada insects in the trees. "Dogs killed one of the others and two of them was lost in the Okefenokee as we chased them. You know how the quicksand in that swamp is!"

Young Mister St. Clair, not much older than Jake himself and just back from school in New Orleans, leaned against a wagon wheel and watched. Jake relished the idea of showing off in front of the young dandy. *Junior was such a snotty sonovobitch*, Jake thought, *mostly never botherin' to speak to the poor whites whose cabins clustered on the edges of his vast holdings.*

Drawing back his lash, Jake reveled in being the center of attention. The only time he got noticed at home was when Pa got drunk on homemade moonshine and beat him up. He could remember even now how good it felt to be the center of the drama with the men gathered around, urging him on in the ghostly torchlight. He could almost smell the sweet, decaying scent of the nearby swamp and feel the bite of small mosquitoes humming on the humid air.

The big black screamed as Jake's lash cut a scarlet ribbon across his gleaming ebony back.

"Hit 'em harder, Jake!"

"Lookit the muscles in that white boy's arm!"

"Wouldn't y'all hate to have him use that whip on you?"

Young Jake gloried in the approval of the men as he went to work on the black with a flourish. The men shouted approval as he swung his whip and someone brought out a jug and passed it around the circle. The punishment took on a festival atmosphere. Probably most of them were pretty drunk within a few minutes, he remembered now as he rode toward Fort Smith with the unconscious girl in his arms. Leastways, that's all he could figure for letting him whip that slave to death. He'd expected to be stopped after a few minutes because big, strong bucks like that one were worth a thousand dollars or more down in the cane fields of Louisiana. Down there in the swamps, they'd soon take the fight out of that black.

But no one stopped him from whipping the huge slave. After the first few blows, the runaway hung unconscious from his wrists and Jake stepped back while someone threw a bucket of water on the man to bring him around.

Old Mister St. Clair nodded approvingly as the slave stirred and moaned, water dripping from him. "Ain't no use in punishin' a nigger if he can't feel it and know he's bein' whipped!"

The whiskey jug went around again and Jake himself took a few swigs with the encouragement of old Mister St. Clair who was stumbling drunk by now. Jake felt like a real man tonight and he knew his whole future lay in the way he was handling the whip. By tomorrow, half the county would know what had happened here tonight. In another month, the story would have spread over a wide section of Georgia. He might be offered jobs as overseer on several plantations with a nice cabin of his own and maybe a pretty little mulatto housemaid to warm his bed any time he ordered her to.

But tonight, it was already enough to be the center of attention with men he admired complimenting and encouraging him. He'd never used his whip on a human being before, not that anyone really considered blacks human. Otherwise, the good Lord wouldn't put them in circumstances to be driven and worked like animals. That damned government up in Washington had passed a law a few years before against importing new slaves from Africa. Of course, there was still a market for them so it was worth the risk to get the extra money for running the blockades. Since the most experienced seamen came from New England, quite a few Yankee fortunes were built on "Black-birding" profits. Why, Jake had heard there was some family with a Dutch name that had made almost a million dollars running the blockades before they became respectable.

Young Jake whipped the slave for two solid hours until his arm was almost too tired to lift the whip. Even throwing water on the black didn't bring him around anymore. The man's back was such a bloody map of lash marks that Jake couldn't see each new one he added to the pattern. Old Mister St. Clair finally stepped forward and jerked the slave's head up off his chest by his woolly hair. "You can quit whippin', Jake." He laughed. "Ain't no use punishin' a dead man! I believe you already taught him all the lessons he's ever gonna learn!"

Jake remembered now how the white men guffawed and slapped their knees at the good joke and how the slaves had rolled their eyes in terror as the body was taken down.

He hadn't realized how exciting and arousing it was to hurt someone and make blood run. No wonder his pa always knocked his ma around when he made love to her. *Like a pair of cats fightin' and lovin' at the same time,* he thought.

"Here, Jake, these is for you." Old Mister St. Clair leaned over the dead body with his penknife and cut something off, handed it to the other. "You deserve this little trophy and, after all, this nigger don't need his balls no more!"

The crowd roared with laughter as Jake examined the prize along with the gold coins the man handed him. It was the black man's scrotum. Jake had had the skin tanned as a souvenir and still carried it. Absently, as he rode toward Fort Smith, he reached up to touch the little black coin pouch. Sometimes, he was uneasy about it, for a preacher had told him once each man carried the seeds of his own destruction, whatever that meant. But he never felt uneasy enough about it to throw the coin pouch away. Jake had the slave's woman the same night he accepted the black's manhood.

Old Mister St. Clair grinned at him as young Jake wiped the blood off his whip and coiled it up.

"Jake, you ever had a woman?"

"Jest a couple of the little nigger gals I caught out in the cotton patch," he said, smiling shamefacedly.

"Hell, boy!" the old man cackled. "After what you done tonight, you deserve a real grown woman! I'm gonna give you this dead buck's gal for the night! She's locked up down there in his cabin, one of the men will show you the way." Mister St. Clair winked at him. "Just don't put too many marks on her, we're sellin' her down the river tomorrow. She's too wild for me or my boy, either!"

She was wild, all right, Jake remembered even now with relish. Not that anyone could hear her fighting and screaming because there was such a drunken brawl for the slave catchers going on up at the big plantation house. His ma had been called in to serve and clean up during the party. But he liked his own little party at the slave cabin better so Jake didn't go up to the big house. He would never forget that girl, black as a voodoo night and wild as a swamp panther. He'd never had a full-grown woman before and she was beautiful and big-titted, carried herself like an ebony princess. He'd have bought her himself if he'd had that much money.

She'd fought him, but he was bigger and stronger than most full-grown men and somehow the fighting and blood made it twice as good. He'd taken her five times before dawn when the men came to take her away. She'd bit and clawed him and he'd hurt her back. Both of them had been smeared with blood and his manseed.

In the morning, the crowd was still drunk but they all gathered up to accompany old Mister St. Clair down to the river. They took along the slave's body, too, in a wagon, so they could show it at all the plantations they passed and teach the blacks a lesson. Jake didn't go, he was too tired, and he noticed young St. Clair wasn't in the rowdy crowd, either, as they mounted up and accompanied the buckboard down the road.

His pa rode up about then, coming to fetch Ma who was still up cleaning at the big house. Pa hadn't been here last night, he had a batch of sour mash cooking that he'd had to stay home and watch. He looked like Jake, right down to the port wine stain mark.

He and Jake both walked up to the deserted big, white house and went around back like blacks and poor whites always did. But nobody answered their knock and the door stood wide open. When no one responded to their calls, they started looking through the big rooms for Jake's ma, figuring she was cleaning somewhere in the house. They blundered into an upstairs bedroom and found her naked in bed with young St. Clair.

Even now, Jake remembered the fury and jealousy on Pa's face as he faced the pair. "Junior St. Clair, I call you out!"

Young St. Clair threw back his head and laughed easily as he got out of bed and reached for his pants on a chair by the fireplace. "Why, you piece of poor white trash! You ought to know better than that! Only a real gentleman can call another gentleman out for a duel! Riffraff like you don't duel! Anyway," he gestured toward the pretty, confused woman in the bed, "she ain't hurt none! Everybody in the county but you two know I been diddling her pretty regular when she comes up to clean. I'm tired of her anyways and I think she's expecting so I'm already looking for a new gal! Just think, Dallinger, I may have added a little blue blood to upgrade your no-account, poor white trash family!"

Pa hit him then. He grabbed up a poker from beside the fireplace and hit the snooty, smirking face over and over until it was unrecognizable. Jake stood frozen in shock, knowing what would happen for killing an important planter like the St. Clair heir. Then he tried to grab Pa's arm and stop him but it was already too late.

About that time, his pretty little dim-witted ma saw all the blood and began to scream.

"Shut up!" Pa shouted. "Shut up! You'll bring all those men

back here with that noise!"

But she didn't stop screaming. Pa hit her to shut her up and her head snapped back. Her skull must have hit the sharp edge of the heavy wood bedstead. Jake lifted her, looked back at the blood on the bed, and then felt it on his hands. "Gawd Almighty, Pa, you've killed her! You've killed Ma!"

His father sagged a little, all the color draining from his face. "I never meant to hurt either of them," he said tonelessly. "I only came to fetch her home. But Junior St. Clair said everyone knew, and he laughed! He laughed! If only she hadn't screamed—"

"We can't worry about what's past, Pa!" Jake laid the nude, limp body back across the bed with a sigh. "We'll have to get out of here before they come back from sellin' that slave girl."

"You? You don't have to run, you didn't do nothin'!"

Jake shook his head. "You think them men will believe that? They'll be lookin' for both of us, Pa! We got to get out of here!"

But the other still stood and looked in shock at the pretty, nude body. "I was crazy about her," he whispered. "If only Junior St. Clair hadn't laughed—"

Jake grabbed the man and shook him roughly. "Snap out of it, Pa! We can't worry about none of that now! The St. Clairs is the richest, most powerful family in Georgia! Our lives ain't worth spit if we don't clear outa this whole state!"

"You're right, son. We'd better each go a different direction so's they will have a hard time trackin' us! I'm gonna take my own chances in the swamp! I know it purty well and it's hard for dogs to track a man through there!"

Jake remembered his own terror even now. "Gawd Almighty, Pa! You ain't gonna try to make it across the Okefenokee! Iffen the quicksand don't get you, the alligators and the water moccasin snakes will!"

"I don't got much choice with the reward old St. Clair will be offerin' for my hide! You head out west, boy, and if I make it, our paths will cross again sometime!"

Jake nodded, sensing he was seeing his father for the very

341

last time.

Pa turned toward the bed and there were tears in his eyes. "Always remember, boy, a woman caused this! They're all like that, lettin' any man hump 'em that has a little gold or pretties to give 'em. Remember, all women is whores at heart so just use 'em when you feel the urge and toss 'em aside! And treat every man like he's gonna cheat you or try to kill you 'cause most of 'em will. If you'll remember all that, Jake, you'll survive in this dog-eat-dog world!"

They'd separated then and Jake blinked back tears as he left the house, thinking of his ma. But he had no time for sadness as he fled for his life. With only his whip and the gold St. Clair had given him, he'd made a run for the wilderness and found himself a job as a drover with a bunch leading wagon trains to Texas.

Pa never made it across the swamp. Jake wasn't out of the state yet when he heard folks talking about that poor white trash fellow who'd been lost in the trackless Okefenokee. It seemed St. Clair's hounds lost track of him on the edge of a deep, slimy pool of quicksand that seemed almost bottomless.

How many years ago had that happened? Twenty-eight? Thirty? He tried to figure as the girl in his arms moaned a little and brought him back to the present. He'd taken Pa's advice and lived as ruthless and cunning as any predatory animal. He asked no quarter and gave none. And he treated all women like whores because in his heart he was sure they were. Only Texanna had made him think of marriage and in the end she was no better than the others. She'd turned him, a white man, down, while willingly spreading her legs for that savage chief.

The blond girl in his arms stirred a little and her long lashes flickered uncertainly. "Hey, Cap'n Baker," Jake said. "The lady's finally beginnin' to come to!"

"About time! I was beginning to worry!" The captain rode over and peered down anxiously at the semi-conscious girl.

"By the way, Dallinger, what about the reward money? What happened to the Indian girl?"

Jake took one last drag on the cigar and tossed it away. "Gray Dove?" He shrugged. "Who knows? Like I tole you before, it was smarter to trail her back to that camp than to trust her to bring the girl to us like she promised. Them Injuns might have decided to move the camp too fast or Gray Dove might have decided to double-cross us. Anyway, I figure I'm entitled to the reward money now."

"You mean, *we're* entitled to the reward money," the captain said. "I figure I should get half."

"Anything you say, sir." Jake gritted his teeth, knowing better than to argue the point. *They was all the same,* he thought, *all them high-class, uppity folks like the St. Clairs who wanted to make it miserable and stomp all over poor folks.* "I would like to have one special horse outa that Injun pony herd." He smiled humbly at the officer. "Iffen you don't mind, sir, I'd be mighty obliged iffen you was to give me that strange-colored stallion."

The boy picked at his face absently. "You mean that bay with the funny white blanket rump with the red spots?"

"That's the one! I never seen a horse colored like that before and I'm hankerin' to own it."

The captain laughed good-naturedly. "Christ! Why not? Nobody but an expert tracker like you could have followed Gray Dove back to that camp."

The girl in Jake's arms moaned and her eyelids fluttered. "She's comin' around, sir. Maybe we should stop and rest the horses anyways. That was shore some big buck I killed."

"The one with the earring? Strange, it looked almost like a cavalry uniform button."

"Yeah, that's the one, the big Dog Soldier! Did you ever see so much blood when he went down?"

The girl jerked suddenly in his arms and said something unintelligible.

Jake reined in his horse and spoke respectfully as he had

learned to do to survive among his betters. "You're okay now, miss, you done been rescued!"

She looked up at him with those great blue eyes and he saw both hate and fear there. *I shoulda humbled you, you sassy little bitch*, he thought, *if I'd just had two more minutes there by the river . . .*

Gawd Almighty! It was a long way back to Fort Smith, he thought as the troop pulled up for a rest. He'd like some sour mash whiskey, but right now just a cup of coffee would taste mighty good with a cigar!

Chapter Twenty

Summer came back to consciousness gradually, her head aching. Her mind was alert several minutes before she stirred and she listened to the conversation, dimly aware she was being held by someone on horseback. The words were English, not Cheyenne, and her ears picked up two accents, one ignorant Southern, the other a high-pitched Northern voice.

The smell of the man who held her assailed her nostrils as her face pressed into his dirty fur vest and she couldn't imagine how she got here. The last thing she remembered was walking down to the river to fill her water skins. Then someone had grabbed her and clasped a hand over her mouth to stop her from screaming out a warning. Somehow, it seemed a long time had passed since then.

Warily, she opened one eye and looked up at the man who held her and the blue sky past his shoulder. *Yes*, she decided, *this was the man she'd fought with on the riverbank*. She thought she recognized the other voice, too. There had been an officer at the river. She remembered that they had talked about Gray Dove as she struggled to break free. *Gray Dove.* She tried to make her mind stop whirling. *Gray Dove had betrayed her and brought the army down on the Cheyenne camp.*

Stubbornly, she tried to open her eyes again and make them focus. She stared at the man's hand, a large, dirty hand with a small birthmark between the fingers. Her head ached and her mouth tasted very dry. What was it the men were saying?

That was shore some fight today . . . did you see that one big buck I shot . . . the one with the earring. Strange, it almost looked like a cavalry uniform button. . . .

They couldn't be speaking of Iron Knife! Her dazed mind couldn't unscramble the jumble of words that made no sense to her. The man who held her spoke to her and she tried to protest the logic and the reality of his words that echoed through her brain: *Did you see that one big buck I shot . . . the one with the earring . . .*

It was all some horrible dream, Summer thought. Any minute now she would awaken safe in her lover's arms by the fire pit of their tepee. But first, she would have to erase all those terrible words and images before she could awaken snug by his side. She who was so strong-willed, willed herself to faint back into unconsciousness again so she could wipe out the nightmare.

Summer knew a long time had passed as the horses reined up and the big man who held her dismounted and lifted her off his horse. As he seemed to realize she was fully conscious, he stood her on her feet and held her up as she swayed.

Abruptly, all her senses came alive, her head cleared. She realized she stood on the parade ground of a fort, surrounded by dismounting cavalry soldiers. Now she knew that this was reality and she couldn't creep back into the blackness and pretend it was all a bad dream. Looking around, she saw her plump Irish maid and her stooped, gaunt Uncle Harlow rushing across the parade grounds toward her.

Anger swept her and she turned on the big man in a fury of small fists and sharp nails, screaming curses at him she didn't even know she knew.

His small, mean eyes widened in astonishment as he threw up his powerful arms to protect his bearded face. "Gawd Almighty, mah'm! I don't understand what's ailin' you—"

"You've killed him!" She screamed, attacking him with her fists. "You've killed him!" But her words all ran together in a high, unintelligible wail.

The young captain's eyes widened with shock as he grabbed her flailing arms. In a frenzy, she attacked him, too, leaving bloody scratches down his pitted face.

"Christ! What on earth is happening?"

The big man tried to help the captain hold her as she struggled and fought. "You better send for the post doctor, sir! The lady's been under a terrible strain!"

She would always remember the astonished faces of the troopers around her and Mrs. O'Malley wringing her plump hands helplessly.

"May the saints preserve us!" The Irish brogue stood out among the other voices. "What on earth—?"

Summer tried to tell the maid what was wrong but realized that it all ran together in hysterical screaming. She looked into the dour, disapproving face of her uncle and saw him tap his head as a signal to the red-faced doctor who ran puffing with his little bag.

The memory came back with crystal clarity of what Iron Knife had told her of his mother's ordeal when she tried to return to the Indians. *An asylum*, she thought with a chill. *If I'm not careful, they might lock me away in an insane asylum.* With that thought, she quit fighting and collapsed.

She was only dimly aware of anything that happened the next several days except that the fat doctor came and went. Someone returned her locket to her with the chain repaired. Around her, everyone seemed to be making preparations for her return to Boston and no one asked her what she wanted to do, which, of course, was go back to Iron Knife.

No, she couldn't do that. The thought came back to her troubled mind. He was dead as were many of the others among the Cheyenne she had known and loved. So when no one watched her, she hid her face and wept in deepest grief.

Now there seemed to be immediate plans to leave and the gray-haired Irish maid attempted to dress her in strange, uncomfortable clothes.

"But these aren't mine!" Summer protested as the woman laced her into a tight corset that narrowed her waist and made her gasp for breath. "My dress is deerskin with lazy stitch work of pony beads."

The short woman looked at her with kind, watery eyes. "Don't you remember, Lamb? You left these clothes behind when you fled the hotel."

Yes, that was right, wasn't it? For a moment, she had been confused as to her identity. She had almost begun to think of herself as someone else. But who?

The maid's double chins waggled as she slipped the long, full dress over Summer's head and put tiny, handmade shoes on her that pinched her feet. *These couldn't be hers.* Hers were soft, comfortable moccasins. *But no,* she reasoned, *the moccasins belonged to that other girl and she didn't exist anymore. Maybe she had never existed except as a forlorn hope in Iron Knife's mind.*

Uncle Jack Harlow came to escort her and Mrs. O'Malley to the stage that would connect with the eastbound train at St. Joe. She sat in the stage unmoving as her uncle leaned over to give her a dry peck on the cheek. Summer thought that his black suit smelled like a musty closet that was seldom opened.

"Remember me to your father," Uncle Jack said stiffly, "and pray that you will conquer this terrible sin of being so stubborn and headstrong that caused God to bring all this trouble and woe upon you."

She looked into his dour face, too saddened and burdened with grief to retort with her usual fire and spirit, but she did her best just as the stage pulled away.

"Uncle Jack?"

"Yes, my dear?"

"Go to hell!"

The memory of his shocked face and his mouth hanging

348

open made her laugh for the first time in days as the stage pulled out and she heard the Irish maid muffle a delighted giggle.

On the train headed east, she brought the image to her mind again and again to hearten her, for the only other thing to do was watch Mrs. O'Malley's short fingers knit endlessly. Summer stared at her own tired reflection in the window glass for hours while the wheels clicked out a rhythm that said over and over: *Who are you . . . ? Who are you . . . ? Who are you? Are you? You? You?*

She was Summer Priscilla Van Schuyler, of course. The thought came to her as she and the Irish maid stood forlornly at the Boston station in a pouring rain waiting for someone to meet them. Her dark blue print dress made her feel morose.

"Sis! Hey, Sis!"

Summer looked around the station to see her blond twin brother fighting his way through the crowds to reach her.

"Oh, David! I'm so glad to see you again!" They fell into each other's arms, both talking excitedly at once while the maid tried to get a word in.

"Are you well, Sis?"

"Of course! And you? How is Harvard and are you still painting?"

David hugged her to him, his sensitive face alive with feeling. "One question at a time!" He laughed. "Harvard and I are not getting on too well, I'm afraid. And yes, I'm still painting but on the sly! You know what Father thinks of such useless frivolity. Mrs. O'Malley!" He embraced the chunky woman. "Good to see you, too! Mother has been worried sick about you! Did you have a good trip?"

"Aye! And 'tis glad I am to be back to civilization." She adjusted her bonnet which David had knocked slightly askew with his enthusiastic embrace.

Flannigan, the bulbous-nosed family coachman, arrived on

the scene, nodded politely to the ladies, and attended to the luggage.

In the carriage, Summer tried her best to be cheerful for David's sake, but the cold, rainy gloom of the crowded city depressed her as the horses clopped along.

"Well!" she exclaimed a little too brightly. "How is everyone? Why didn't anyone else come to the station to meet us?"

David looked embarrassed as he glanced over at the Irish maid who had pulled out her knitting. "Frankly." He hesitated. "Father seemed afraid to come, afraid the reporters would hear of it and do a big story about your return. I think he hopes no one in town will even remember you were gone. You know how important appearances are to him. Besides, he was busy with his many business appointments, as usual."

"Of course." Summer tried not to sound bitter but there had never been much love lost between her and her father. He wanted everyone to do exactly as they were told without question and Summer couldn't or wouldn't do that. This was one more small way of punishing her for daring to cross him in the first place. "And Angela?"

"Our spoiled baby sister is now in Miss Priddy's Academy. She's in class today as they struggle to turn the brat into a well-mannered young lady." David shrugged as the carriage rolled through the narrow, twisted streets. "It does amaze me how Father dotes on her and thinks she can do no wrong while neither you nor I ever seem to do anything right!"

"I don't know why it should amaze you," Summer replied shortly. "Everything about Angela is a mirror image of Father and you know how much he thinks of himself."

"Now, now, you two." Mrs. O'Malley's double chins waggled disapprovingly. "You're both behavin' like two jealous cats. Young Miss Angela may not ever be the popular belle you was, Miss Summer, but she will be a great beauty someday and make her father proud."

"You're probably right," Summer said grudgingly. "I'm not

350

usually so mean-minded. Speaking of cats, David, does she still have that monster?"

"Coaldust?" The slim, blond boy nodded. "I'm sorry to say that black tomcat is more a companion to her than either of our parents. I'm away at Harvard, of course, and Father has his business, and Mother . . . Well, you know about Mother."

Summer sighed audibly. "I had hoped she might be better and would come to the station to meet me." She stared out the carriage window at the old North Church tower of Paul Revere fame as the carriage drove toward the family estate.

"Saints preserve us!" The Irish maid looked at David over her knitting. "I had hoped your dear mother might have improved some while we were stranded in that wild, heathen place."

David didn't answer and Summer felt the crushing sadness of reality like a weight on her heart. She herself was a strong person and would finally come to grips with the reality of her lover's death. But whatever it was in Priscilla Van Schuyler's past that grieved her only seemed to make her flee deeper into the haunted maze of sherry and that new opium derivative called laudanum. All the society doctors were prescribing it for that nebulous condition called "nerves."

Mother had not yet lost complete contact with reality but she seemed to be attempting such. How often Summer remembered now had she seen Mother sitting in her rose garden, staring into space at ghosts only she seemed to see or seated before the fire looking into the flames for hours as she drank.

The carriage rolled through the big estate gates and Summer became even more depressed as they stopped out front. Father had built the house as a display of wealth when Summer was a small child and it was a grandiose mansion in the style known as Gothic Revival. But as Flannigan helped her out and she looked up at the cupolas and turrets, she knew she would always think of the fashion as Ugly Victorian. The chill, early November gloom encased the large home like a wet shroud.

Evans, the British butler, took David and Summer's wraps and welcomed them with stiff formality. The entry hall was as cold and cheerless as it had been in memory.

"Well!" David said too brightly, rubbing his hands together. "Does it look like you remember it?"

"Yes, it's exactly as I remember." She sighed, breathing in the musty, decayed smell. Could she ever have forgotten the dark, ornate furnishings, the heavy drapes, and murky oil paintings? Bric-a-brac seemed to be everywhere and large, Oriental rugs lay faded on dark walnut floors.

Her thoughts went unbidden to a simple, cheery tepee with a warm fire pit and only a few buffalo robes and willow backrests for furniture.

Tears came to her eyes at the thought and she blinked them back. "I—I'm tired, David. It's been a long trip. If you don't mind, I'll go to my room and see everyone at dinner."

"Of course!" Her twin sounded puzzled but he had always been so understanding and sensitive to others. "I'll help Flannigan see to your luggage."

Quickly, Summer turned to the maid who had just shaken the rain from her bonnet and cloak. "Mrs. O'Malley, I know you're eager to see Mother and your friends. I can manage just fine for a while."

"Well, I don't know, Lamb. It's me duty to shake the wrinkles out of your clothes and all—"

"No." She wanted desperately to be alone for a while. "No, you go along," Summer insisted as she started up the ornate curved stairway. "I think I'll nap a while."

The maid needed no further urging to seek out Priscilla who would be, of course, up in her room. Summer knew Maureen O'Malley had come over in the Great Famine of 1845 when the Irish potato crop failed. A million people starved to death during that time. Anyone who could scrape up the money left for America. Mr. O'Malley had died on the trip over of typhus and Priscilla Van Schuyler had found the hungry widow roaming the docks aimlessly, trying desperately to find work when no one would hire the Irish.

Summer trudged up the stairway behind the puffing maid and went down the hall. Thinking about going in to see her mother, she hesitated, then went on to her own room. She needed time to prepare herself to face all this again. Summer was glad David had been perceptive enough not to put her through the ordeal of having all the servants lined up to greet her.

After Flannigan carried her trunks into the bedroom, she quickly closed the door against the world and thought how much she was becoming like her mother.

Summer looked about the room, and realized nothing had been changed or moved. *A million years ago, I was a silly, immature happy girl in this room* she thought, *and now I am a very mature and sad woman.*

Her room faced south and was the only cheery bedroom in the house since it got the winter sun when it shone through the turret windows onto the cushioned window seats. Absently, she walked over and looked out at the steady downpour, remembering how many, many hours she had curled up and read books on that window seat since there wasn't much else to do in this sad, lonely house.

The room colors were her favorites, pale yellow and cornflower blue. Even the faint, sweet scent of her perfume, lily of the valley, still hung on the still air. Absently, she ran her hand over the delicate satinwood French bed. On the wall was a large print of Jenny Lind and Summer smiled now in pleasure as she remembered the concert she had attended. Tickets had been all sold out, of course, but Silas Van Schuyler had gotten tickets anyway.

A fire blazed in the ornate fireplace and she pulled off the damp dress and spread it over a chair to dry. Then she drew up a wingback chair and sat down, enjoying the warmth after the cold carriage ride. The latest copy of *Godey's Lady's Book* lay on the table nearby and she thumbed through it listlessly. Hoops were going to get wider and skirts more full. She didn't care about such silliness or fashion. Boston was always behind in styles and she'd only just purchased her first hoop a few months before she left. The thing probably still hung in the closet.

She stared into the flames and remembered another fire, another time. And in the flickering blaze, she saw a man's bronzed, gentle face. *Yes, a million years ago, a vain, silly schoolgirl had run away on a stagecoach and a fierce, passionate man had awakened her to womanhood. She could never go back to what she had been, never be the same again.* Tears blurred her eyes and the image of the man in the flames and she leaned back and closed them. When she opened them, Mrs. O'Malley knocked stubbornly on the door.

"Are ye all right, Lamb? It's straight up six o'clock and you know how your father is about dinner."

"I'll be right down." She jumped to her feet, jerked a green cotton dress from the closet, and was still buttoning it as she rushed toward the stairs. Six o'clock meant dinner in the formal dining room day in and day out, month after month, year after year. No one ever questioned it because it was one of Father's inflexible rules. It was one small thing he used to rule with an iron fist. Several times, when she was small, she had come to the table late and been sent back up the stairs without dinner as punishment. She had forgotten how unhappy she had been in this dismal house, had always been. The big grandfather clock in the hall struck six times and the deep chimes echoed through the house.

They were all already seated as she rushed into the large, burgundy dining room.

Her mother stood up at her end of the table a little unsteadily. "Summer, my dear! I'm so glad you're home!" She put her arms around Summer's neck and kissed her with warmth and Summer hugged her. She had forgotten how thin and vulnerable Priscilla always looked as her gaze swept over the expensive rose-colored dress. Although in many ways she was a carbon copy of her daughter, Priscilla had a little gray

354

among the blond strands now and the dark shadows under her eyes seemed to have deepened in the months Summer had been gone.

David smiled encouragement at Summer as she walked to the opposite end of the ornate mahogany table. Had she never noticed before how her parents faced each other like adversaries the length of the long table?

"Hello, Father." She gave the lean, hawklike man a quick peck on the cheek without any real warmth as he half stood, frowning at her with ice blue eyes. His sharp, prominent nose and the way his thin hands grasped the arms of his chair reminded her of a bird of prey.

"Hello, my dear," he said. "I'm surprised you are late to dinner. You remember the rule: six o'clock straight up, you know."

"Sorry." Summer gritted her teeth. She had been lost for weeks and he could only scold her for being late for dinner. Nothing had really changed while she was gone.

She smiled down at Angela and tried to hug the child who stared back at her with no give to her stiff little shoulders at all. Summer noticed a black furry tail sticking out from under Angela's chair but said nothing but "My! How you've grown! You're becoming such a beauty, Angela." *She was becoming a beauty*, Summer thought, *but there was something missing in her that other little girls seemed to have. Warmth? A capacity for love?*

The child fixed a baleful, icy gaze on her. "Tell me about the Indians."

"Angela!" David and Mother said in unison, looking both pained and annoyed.

"Now, now!" Father boomed, smiling at his favorite as Summer stumbled to her chair in confusion. "It's just natural curiosity. No need to scold the child!"

Summer sat down in her chair, looking at the reflection the large oil chandelier cast on the sparkling, crystal wine goblets that, in turn, created little pinpoints of light on the deep burgundy walls.

"Well, now." Mother put her glass down with an unsteady hand and Evans sighed disapprovingly as he refilled it with red wine. "Isn't it wonderful that we're all here together with the holidays so close and all?"

"It's delightful," David agreed too heartily as the butler brought the heavy silver server of roast lamb to the head of the table and Father served himself.

"Oh, it's going to be a great holiday!" Summer put in desperately as she picked up the fine silver fork, placed the imported damask napkin in her lap. She caught David's eyes and they confirmed what she had already guessed. Mother was drinking more than usual these days.

Priscilla had already drained her glass and held it up. The stuffy British butler paused with the decanter and looked toward Father who shook his head and scowled. "You've already had enough, my dear," he said. "Let's not play the fool tonight, shall we not?"

Priscilla reddened and Angela laughed. Summer looked at the tall, lean man at the end of the table and recalled how seldom he smiled. Did he love any of them except Angela? Had he ever loved Mother or had he always treated her so coldly? She looked into the smug, smiling face of her younger sister and had an almost terrible urge to reach across the table and give her a good shaking.

Summer took a bite of the lamb and mint jelly. It was tasty, of course, but her memory went to deer meat roasted simply over a small fire pit. It suddenly dawned on her that Father was addressing her.

She looked into his ice blue eyes. "I'm sorry, sir, I didn't hear you."

"You're getting as bad as your mother." He frowned as he peered at her. "I merely asked after the health of your uncle Jack."

"Oh, he's fine. He sends his regards." It was an effort to keep from smiling at the memory of the dour man standing open-mouthed, staring after the departing stagecoach. She wouldn't tell Father about that, of course. "Do tell me about Harvard, David," she stammered, ducking her head so she could avoid the glare of the cold eyes.

"David's doing fine at school," Silas Van Schuyler said crisply as if he dared anyone to doubt it.

"Well, as a matter of fact, sir," David began hesitantly. He paused with his fork halfway to his lips and Summer felt dreadfully sorry for him.

"Yes?" It wasn't a question, it was a dare.

"As a matter of fact," David rushed on manfully, "I've been thinking of another field rather than business."

"Nonsense!" Father paused in gulping his meat and Summer thought again how much like a hawk he looked. "You'll need all those commerce classes to take over your rightful place in my businesses."

David looked a little desperate now and Summer saw Mother give him just the slightest shake of her head but her brother plunged in despite the warning. "I don't think I'm cut out for business!"

Angela smirked. The brat was really enjoying this, Summer thought miserably.

"Ridiculous!" Silas dismissed the idea. "Now if you're wanting to ship out on one of our vessels for a while, get to know the business from the ground up, I couldn't approve more! Did it myself as a youngster. Different business then, of course." He leaned back in his chair. "My grandfather built his fleet of ships on slavery and my father enlarged it on the illegal profits of 'blackbirding.'"

"What's 'blackbirding'?" Angela's pale eyes gleamed with interest as she slipped another bite off her plate to the cat under her chair.

"Please, Silas!" Priscilla protested weakly. "I'm not sure this is suitable conversation for the child!"

Father grinned almost maliciously at Mother before he turned back to the curious child. "A 'blackbirder' was someone who ran slaves past the blockade after the idiot government decided no more blacks could be imported into this country. My great-grandfather started out working someone else's ship up in New York harbor where my family landed after they came from Holland. I miss the fun I had as a youngster of helping my father outwit those ships that lurked out there, trying to catch us bringing the slaves in."

The child smiled at the idea. "Are we like pirates?"

"Not exactly." Father fairly beamed at her as he pushed his plate back. "Although a few of the jealous have been known to call me a 'robber baron.'"

"What did you do with the slaves when you got them here, Papa?"

"Sold them, of course, Sweetie, and made good profits doing it. Only one time we had to take a loss. A U.S. frigate moved in on us sudden-like and we couldn't be caught with the evidence, so we threw them all overboard!"

Angela laughed with delight. "Didn't they swim away?"

"No, of course not!" He leaned back and smiled faintly at the memory. "Those leg chains made them sink like rocks!"

Summer saw Mother's face pale and she herself tried to blot out the image the story brought to mind.

"Silas," Priscilla said again, rather weakly. "I do wish you wouldn't tell those stories! She might repeat them to the girls at school."

"I am damned tired of you and your blue-blooded, snobby ways!" Father roared, throwing his napkin down across his plate. "I'm not ashamed of how my family made its money! Look at that prissy cousin of yours, Elizabeth Shaw! They may be the cream of Boston society and own half the textile mills in the state, but I happen to know Robert Shaw's grandfather was a rag picker in the slums of London!"

"Sir," David said manfully. "I wish you wouldn't speak that way to Mother."

Summer's hands trembled as she watched Father turn his angry attention to her twin. "And I wish your blue-blooded mother would quit sticking her mouth in where it doesn't

358

concern her. She married me for my money, now how dare she get squeamish about how it was made!" His face was dark as thunder as he looked to the delicate blond woman at the other end of the table. "I'll run the business, my dear, you look to your drinking! You seem to do that well enough!"

Priscilla staggered to her feet, overturning her chair in doing so. With a whimper, she ran from the room.

Angela laughed. "Papa's right! She drinks too much!" she said to Summer.

Gritting her teeth, Summer fought the urge to reach across and grab the child. "Angela, you are a monster, and, Father, you are a rotten bastard!"

Then she, too, raced up to her room and slammed the door protectively behind her. Rain beat against the windows as she flopped down in front of the fire and saw the image in the flames.

"Oh, my darling!" she whispered. "I can't live in this unhappy house! I'm not even sure I can go on at all! What am I to do?" But no answer came to her and finally weariness overcame her and she dropped off to sleep.

The rain had turned to snow at dawn. Summer awakened with a start as Bridget, the cook, knocked timidly, then entered with a breakfast tray.

"Good to have you home, Miss Summer." Bridget's nose wiggled when she talked and Summer thought of a small mouse.

"I'm glad to be home, Bridget," she lied as she accepted the tray and took a gulp of the dark, rich cocoa. Hungrily, she reached for the salted kippers and hot, buttered muffins complete with port wine jelly.

With a sigh, she watched the cook scurry away. Summer was not sure how she could live in this miserable household. Only the fact that she might possibly be carrying the Cheyenne warrior's child cheered her and gave her some hope to cling to.

The consequences would be terrible, of course, but worth it.

Mrs. O'Malley peeked into the room as she finished her cocoa. "Feeling better, Lamb? Did you sleep in that dress?" She didn't wait for Summer's nod before continuing. "Your father says he understands how tired and out-of-sorts you were last night and says he forgives you."

Summer didn't answer, having played this charade before. Somehow, she wasn't sure she had done anything to be forgiven for but she never seemed to do anything right.

"Now, Love." The Irish maid rubbed her hands together in satisfaction. "Your friends will all be wantin' to call on you this morning, so I must get you ready. How shall I do your hair?"

Summer closed her eyes, remembering his big hands stroking and brushing her hair, tangling his fingers in it as he braided. Tears came to her eyes. "What ever you think," she answered quietly.

"Ah, now here's something nice!" She could hear the maid's voice echoing from the depths of the closet. "I don't believe you've ever had this on."

Summer didn't argue with the maid as she brought the clothes out, helped her out of the rumpled green dress, and laced her into the tight corset and hoop. The skirt Mrs. O'Malley selected was a full, bright blue wool with the matching "polka" or "monkey" jacket that had been in style several years. The new dance was all the rage but the jacket also looked like something an organ grinder's monkey would wear. Actually, Summer knew the military look with its braid and brass buttons had come into style because of the Crimean War the British had just finished fighting.

"I've got the curling iron heating, Love." Mrs. O'Malley bustled about, helping her with the tiny, handmade shoes.

Summer was submitting to the hot iron and wrinkling her nose at the smell of burned hair when a knock sounded at the door. "Mum?"

"Yes, Evans?"

"I'm asked to announce your friends from school. Miss Peabody and the two Misses Osgoodes are awaiting you in the music room."

"Very good, Evans. Tell Bridget to serve tea there in a few minutes."

As she heard the butler's footsteps fading, she wished she could send down a message that she was ill and unable to come down. But that was what Priscilla would do and she was definitely not her mother. Resolutely, she stuck out her chin, gathered up her skirts, and descended the stairway.

Before she could open the music-room door, the voices inside drifted to her. "What do you suppose those Indians did to her. You know what I mean." Susan Osgoode said.

"Why, Sister, what a terrible thought!"

Maude Peabody's deep voice floated to her. "I'm sure the Indians wouldn't have dared do anything at all! Remember the money and influence of the Blackledges and the Van Schuylers."

Summer smiled. She could almost imagine Maude's plump form, her large, deep-set eyes. Only Maude could have chained herself to the State House doors and lost the key. It would never occur to the Boston girl that Indians would not be impressed by money and social position.

"But what about those terrible stories we read in the papers about the horrid, unspeakable things savages do to white women?"

"That proves my point!" Maude answered glibly, "Everyone knows when a real lady is touched by a black or a savage, she is supposed to kill herself to erase the shame!"

Summer leaned against the door a long moment, her mind going back to powerful arms sweeping her up, big hands pulling away her clothing. Her skin tingled with the remembrance of his touch. *If it were shame, she wished she could be shamed forever!*

But she swallowed hard and pulled herself together before she flung open the door. "Good morning, girls!"

361

"Summer! We're so glad to see you! You look wonderful. You honestly do!"

She watched them exchange worried glances, afraid she might have overheard them as they rushed forward to hug her and exclaim how well she looked.

Evans entered with the large silver tea service. "Shall I pour, Miss Summer?"

"No." She dismissed him with a wave of her hand. "I can manage." And she poured as he retreated from the room.

The conversation was too hearty and too bright, Summer thought wearily as she sipped her tea and looked around the music room past the prim Osgoode sisters. It was on the south side of the first floor and done in pastels with pale Chinese rugs on the light wood floors. A very fine grand piano stood in the corner and a harp was positioned near the fireplace.

Summer found it very hard to make small talk with her former classmates but she tried. She had lost both her innocence and her heart in the past weeks. There was such a chasm of emotion and experience between her and the silly schoolgirls because it was not likely they would ever experience such passion and devotion. She lost track of the conversation and merely smiled and nodded now and then as the girls prattled on while she enjoyed the strong, hot tea.

She suddenly realized Maude was asking a question of her for the second time. "Sorry, my mind wandered. What did you say?"

Maude's sallow skin reddened. "I asked, casually, of course, whether David was in town for your homecoming?"

"Yes, certainly. He met my train. But he's going back probably tomorrow, I think."

Maude did have the most unfortunate habit of choosing unbecoming colors, she thought sympathetically. Bright purple was not her shade at all.

Maude looked disappointed at her news of David and promptly announced that she really must be going.

The Osgoode girls suddenly gave the same excuse. Summer

protested that they had really just arrived but she was rather relieved as she saw them to the door and climbed the stairs.

She ran into David in the upstairs hall. "Why, David, you should've come down. You just missed seeing Maude Peabody."

"Good!" He smiled grimly. "I've been lurking up here for an hour, afraid to walk past the music-room door for fear her ears would perk up at my step."

Summer smiled in spite of herself. "Now, David, that's not fair! Maude adores you!"

"So does Grandmother Blackledge's King Charles spaniel who bears an uncanny resemblance to your friend and has about the same amount of brains."

"Well, her eyes may be a little large and her nose a little pug—"

"You've just described Grandmother's dog!" He laughed in delight. "But the dog is at least quiet most of the time while Maude makes inane chatter. Just because she is an only child with a rich, widowed father and Silas would love an alliance with the Peabody banking interests—"

"Maude wouldn't make a bad wife for you."

"She wouldn't make a good one!"

Summer bestowed a warm look of devotion on him and decided to abandon that conversation. "What were you trying to tell Father last night?"

"I'm trying to tell him I'm going to drop out of Harvard and do whatever it is that I want to do which is not slaughter whales for oil! I may try to make a living with my painting or go into medicine or the ministry."

Summer was aghast. "Father will be furious! I can't remember when anyone didn't do exactly as he wanted—"

"Except you, of course, Sister." His fine, sensitive face looked into hers. "In the meantime, what are your plans? Surely you don't intend to stay in this unhappy house the rest of your life?"

She shrugged and turned away. "I—I don't know what

to do."

He put a sympathetic hand on her shoulder. "I took the liberty of contacting Austin the minute I heard you were on the way home. He's frantically trying to get leave to come from Washington for the holidays."

She turned a troubled face toward him. "I wish you hadn't done that, David."

Evans came up the stairs.

"Yes, what is it?" David asked testily. She knew he had no liking for the snooty butler.

"It's Mr. Austin Shaw," the butler announced grandly. "He says to tell Miss Summer he's awaiting her in the library."

Chapter Twenty-One

Summer almost panicked for a long moment. David gave her a puzzled, troubled look as he dismissed the butler, "Thank you, Evans, tell him Miss Summer will join him shortly."

Twisting her hands with indecision as the butler went downstairs, she turned to her brother. "I—I really don't want to see him, you know."

David frowned. "Sis, you'll have to see him sooner or later. He's gotten leave from his post in Washington just to see you and he'll be in town all through the holidays."

"I don't know what to say to him."

"For heaven's sake, Sis!" His tone was warm and reassuring as he took both her hands in his. "You're acting like the man is a complete stranger! It's good old Austin, remember? He's my best friend and we've been a constant threesome all these years, not to mention we're distantly related through our relative who was hanged as a witch in Salem."

She paused, thinking. *Would Austin be able to look at her and know she was no longer a virgin? Could he possibly stare into her eyes and see all the passion another man had taught her?* Sometimes she had an eerie feeling that Austin had an uncanny perception, almost able to read others' minds. She thought again of Angela Blackledge, the skeleton in the distant closet, the so-called witch.

"Has it to do with your ordeal?" David asked sympathetically. "Austin will not ask, you know that. Would you like me to come down with you?"

"No." She pulled away from him. "You're right. Sooner or later, I must face everyone's curiosity and Austin will be the warm, wonderful person he has always been."

Resolutely she lifted her skirts and descended the curved stairway, remembering that the Cheyenne would disapprove any talk of marriage between two people even distantly related. The old people of the tribe checked into these things and if the couple were as much as sixteenth cousins, the marriage was called off.

Opening the library door quietly, she studied Austin standing before the fire. He was five years older than she and every inch the polished, aristocratic gentleman he looked in the blue uniform with the second lieutenant's insignia.

He seemed to sense her presence and turned, striding toward her slim and tall. "Summer, I've been so frantic about you!" He crossed to her, acted for a moment as if he might take her in his arms, then characteristically hesitated and took her hands in his instead.

"Hello, Austin," she said, feeling his soft, fine hands on hers and trying not to remember the touch of large, callused hands. She had forgotten how handsome Austin really was with his wavy brown hair and deep hazel eyes.

"I've just been worried to death!" His voice was cultured and educated. He squeezed her hands again.

"I'm fine, Austin, really I am. There was no need to worry." Disengaging her hands, she tried not to look into his eyes as she glanced around the dark library with its endless shelves of books and dark Oriental rugs.

Austin's eyes worshipped her and it was truly disconcerting.

"You do look so handsome in your uniform!" she exclaimed, thinking that only his weak jawline and thin, compressed lips detracted from his good looks. "I thought you couldn't appear any more handsome than you did in your West Point uniform when you graduated last spring but I was wrong! You're positively dashing!"

"Do you truly think so?" He exuded so little self-confidence that she wondered if he could ever function as an officer. "I don't like the army as well as I had hoped I might, but Mother says a military background is absolutely imperative if I'm ever to run for public office; image and all that, you know."

"I remember your mother was wanting one of her sons to go into politics and Todd is rather hardheaded about letting your mother make his decisions. Senator Sumner has not improved in health while I've been away?"

"No, not much." He clasped his hands behind his back and cleared his throat. "The poor man has hardly made an appearance in the last three years so our state has only one vote most of the time. Imagine the effrontery of that Representative Brooks from North Carolina nearly beating a United States senator to death with his walking stick!"

"I remember the uproar and the indignation," Summer said. "I suppose feelings are running high on this slavery thing if one man will nearly kill another over a Senate speech."

"Of course the speech was about Kansas and that's a terrible controversy," Austin said. He hesitated again. "Would you mind terribly if I smoke?"

Automatically, she shook her head and watched him fill his pipe and light it, enjoying the scent of tobacco.

"I can't imagine such a fuss over a little prairie territory." She shrugged, trying to keep him talking so they would not get to more important, more intimate words.

"The reason they call it 'Bloody Kansas' has nothing to do with that Territory at all, it has to do with power and whether the pro- or the antislavery forces will control Congress. Both sides are evenly matched right now and how Kansas representatives and senators would vote may swing the balance."

"Then there's going to be war?"

"Probably. In fact, a lot of young officers like myself are

367

counting on it." He puffed his pipe.

She gave him a long look. "That doesn't sound like the gentle Austin I know."

He cleared his throat, obviously stung by her implied criticism. "A war brings rapid advancement. Mother says if I reach major or colonel, in a few years, with the Shaw money and influence, I could easily become a senator."

If he quoted his mother one more time, she would break a tooth from gritting them, Summer thought grimly. She went over and sat on the cold leather sofa. *If there were a more formidable dragon in Boston's high society than the tiny, birdlike Elizabeth Shaw, she didn't know who it was.*

"How is your brother?" she asked to change the subject.

"Todd? Well, I suppose. I've been off in Washington as you know so I haven't seen much of him, but I don't think either he or David want to stay at Harvard. He wrote that he has no intention of taking over Father's mills and is considering the newspaper business or going off with the antislavery faction to Kansas."

"That Todd!" Summer laughed, thinking how different the two brothers were. Todd was even more handsome, more dashing and reckless. "But he always seems to go his own way, no matter what! Is your mother having one of her famous fainting spells over it?"

He cleared his throat and fiddled with his pipe. "I'm sure you're not implying that Mother's illness is not real!" he said defensively. "And I don't think Todd has told her of his plans. You know he is the apple of Mother's eye."

She felt sympathy for Austin. "Well, it's your mother who has been leading the Boston social set against slavery. She should be pleased if Todd goes off to Kansas to fight slavery."

He smiled, chagrined. "It's very fashionable in the best circles to come out against slavery right now. Mother's been helping raise money to get all those settlers who are opposed moved to Kansas so they'll be a majority vote when the time comes. And of course the Union will need all that gold that's rumored to be in the western Kansas area of the Rockies if there's war!"

Her heart sank. "That's Cheyenne-Arapaho hunting grounds. We can't just start invading that area by the thousands, digging for gold."

"You think not?" He fiddled with his pipe. "The army will just push those savages out of the Rockies. You don't really think the government would let a few Indians stand in the way of our Manifest Destiny policy? It is our duty to expand our country's borders from ocean to ocean and from Canada to Mexico. No one cares what happens in the process to a bunch of ignorant savages!"

Summer felt small blotches of color come to her cheeks. Austin saw her expression and evidently misread it. "Forgive me, my dear!" He put his pipe down on a nearby table and came over to sit next to her, taking her hands. "I had forgotten your ordeal among them. It was unkind and thoughtless of me to mention them and bring back what surely must be terrible memories."

Memories. Yes, there were memories.

"It's perfectly all right, Austin," she murmured tonelessly, pulling her hands from his. "Are you going to be home throughout the holidays?"

"Yes, Mother and Father arranged it so I could stay until after our New Year's Eve ball."

She stood up suddenly and went to the window to watch the snow fall. "Would it surprise you very much, Austin, if I tell you I get a little sick of your mother sometimes?"

He came over and put his hands on her shoulders very hesitantly and his lips were close to her hair. "I don't understand why you're upset!" he stammered. "Please don't let's quarrel, Summer, that's not why I came all this way at all! I keep thinking that whatever has happened to you is my fault. I should have overridden my mother last summer when I finally was graduated from West Point and married you. If you had been my wife, you never would have gotten mixed up in

369

that silly protest and your father wouldn't have sent you away."

She didn't answer as she watched the big flakes fall and wondered if it were snowing now up at the winter camp in the Big Timbers? Tears came to her eyes and trickled down her face.

His fine hands trembled on her shoulders. "I never meant to upset you and make you cry."

She knew he was trying to get up the nerve to take her in his arms with reckless passion, but she knew, too, he could never do it. He was too timid and inhibited. *If only, just once in all these years, he had swept her up into his arms with heated daring and said, "You're mine! I'll not take no for an answer!"*

Her mind went to the other man, the one she would never have met if Austin had stood up to his mother last summer. She would have married Austin then, probably. Now her heart belonged to a dead man.

"Summer," he began hesitantly and his hands tightened on her shoulders. "I wondered if . . ."

He was going to ask and she had no idea what to say to him. "I think I hear David out in the entry," she said quickly as she fled across the room. "David! Do come in and speak to Austin!"

She flung open the door. "Come in, David!"

Her brother had been going out the front door but he returned with her to the library. "Austin, old friend! Glad to see you!" They shook hands warmly. "How's Washington?"

"Buzzing with talk of Kansas and war. What do you think of Harvard?"

David smiled and clapped him on the back while Summer gave her brother a look of appreciation.

"I find Harvard dull, frankly," David said. "The only real pleasure I get is sneaking off to set up my easel and paint. Like Todd, I'm thinking of dropping out."

"You'd better give that a lot of thought," Austin admonished as he went over, picked up his pipe, knocked the

370

ashes into the fireplace, and pocketed it. "I never do anything without giving it a great deal of thought. Haste makes waste, as Mother says."

Summer rolled her eyes in desperation at David and he took her cue and came to the rescue. "I was just thinking of getting the sleigh out. Why don't you two come with me?"

"What a wonderful idea!" Summer feigned enthusiasm. "It'll be just like old times! Isn't it a wonderful idea, Austin?"

He looked unhappy at the interruption but he nodded reluctantly as she ran to get her heavy blue cloak with the white fur around the hood and the matching muff.

In minutes, they were climbing into the small sleigh, with Summer in the middle. Austin pulled the fur robe over their laps as she shivered in the cold air.

Stunned, she reached out a trembling hand to stroke it. "What—what kind of fur is this?" But she already knew.

"Buffalo," David answered as he flicked the little whip. They skimmed across the glittering white crust. The brass bells on the red harness of the black gelding jingled. "Buffalo lap robes are coming into fashion. I'm told they'll be shipping more and more of the hides back east as they find ways to use the leather."

"Well, there seems to be an endless supply of the beasts." Austin nodded. "And no one has any use for them so far but the savages."

Her hand shook with remembered passion. She stroked the fur ever so gently and saw a fleeting image of flickering firelight and strong, rippling muscles, *Summer, my little love . . . my dearest, take me now . . . Please take me . . .*

The men did not seem to notice her silence. They fell into easy camaraderie, talked and joked about past times.

"Hey, I know!" suggested David. "Let's sing!"

"What shall we sing?" Summer tried to sound enthused and keep tears from gathering in her eyes.

"That new song that came out last year about sleighing."

"Very appropriate!" Austin judged. "I'll start: 'Jingle bells,

371

jingle bells, jingle all the way!'"

"'Oh, what fun it is to ride',"David joined in lustily, "Sing, Sis! Sing!"

She did her best to oblige as she breathed in the icy air. No one would ever know of her secret sorrow. *She would survive,* she thought grimly as they skimmed along with the men singing happily. *She would survive because she was too strong to give up. Her beloved was gone. Still, she might be carrying his child and the thought strengthened her.*

As the days passed, she thought of nothing else as she made excuses to avoid Austin. *But what of Austin? If she were pregnant with a savage's child, would he still want her? Would he gather the nerve to stand up to his domineering mother? Could she make up her mind to marry him when her heart belonged to a dead man?* She would think of all that later; right now, she could only hope for a child.

But her hopes were dashed in a few days as her monthly period began and she had to face the fact that there was no child, would never be a child. She had nothing to remember Iron Knife by.

No, that wasn't true, she thought as she curled up in her bedroom wing chair before the fire. *She had wonderful memories and she could live on those. She would hold onto each precious remembrance like old love letters and bring them out when she was low in spirits. He wasn't dead at all; he lived on in her heart.*

She noticed in her mirror that she was getting shadows under her eyes and thought she looked more every day like her mother. The thought frightened her and she promised herself she wouldn't retreat from life like Priscilla had done. Sometimes as she went up the stairs, she paused before her mother's closed door and listened to the tinkle of the old music box from within and wondered what maze of time Priscilla inhabited.

No, she was much stronger than her mother, she thought grimly

372

as Christmas approached. Mechanically, she went through the motions of living. She would face life and give as good as she got. But what was she to do? There were no jobs open to a respectable young woman of her social class and she had no funds of her own if her father should cut her off.

Her thoughts went to friends and relatives but she saw no permanent solutions there. The only aunt she really cared for was an impoverished governess in New York so she saw no help there. Her mother's parents, the Blackledges, were reclusive, crabby people who only seemed to care for spaniels. *Could she work as a governess herself?* She winced, imagining her references being checked and the would-be employer finding the Boston arrest and the scandalous sojourn among the Indians.

She began to see herself, years in the future, trapped as a powerless, graying spinster in this horrible house. Unmarried, childless, she imagined herself playing with David and Angela's children when they came to call. She had little of any value to sell and she thought because of the cavalry raid, she would not be welcomed back by the Cheyenne if she should go back West. As the holiday approached and she stared into the fire, only one answer came to her though she thought about every angle: *Austin.*

She had been careful never to be alone with him the last several weeks so that he would not have a chance to ask the question she was not sure how to answer. *Austin adored her and always had.* Before that fierce Cheyenne warrior came into her life, she had thought she loved Austin, too. *Austin would take her out of this house, love her enough to soften her sorrow.* She would have everything: power, money, social position. He might even become a senator and she would be part of the Washington scene. *Would it be fair to him? Would he care that she did not love him as he loved her? Would he know that she had once made love to another man if she didn't tell him?*

Night after night, she stared into the flames and puzzled over the problem of her future. The *Harper's Magazine, Godey's*

373

Lady's Book, and old copies of the discontinued *Lily* all lay unopened on the chair-side table. She had never had much interest in fashion and the suffragette movement seemed to fade in the reality of her own problem. Anyway, perhaps the answer for women was not to be so militant, but to exert gradual, constant pressure. Even water can finally wear down stone if it drips long enough.

At last it was Christmas and the gloomy mansion gleamed with unaccustomed lights and gaiety. The Shaw family, Maude Peabody, and her elderly father joined the Van Schuylers for the festivities of Christmas Eve. The Blackledges were invited but declined, preferring the company of their spaniels.

Summer helped Mrs. O'Malley dress Mother in soft pink before selecting a blue velvet gown for herself. Much laughing and joking prevailed as the party gathered in around the tree. A Christmas tree was still a novelty to most Americans except for the German immigrants who had brought the custom with them. But when Albert, Queen Victoria's German husband, took the custom to England, it quickly spread throughout the richer class and crossed the ocean.

The huge fir dominated the center of the music room with its scent and greenery. Summer played carols on the harp while they all sang. The portly, florid Mr. Shaw read *The Night Before Christmas* with gusto. Everyone else strung cranberries and hung the delicate German decorations. Finally the tree was finished and lit with dozens of small candles that cast a yellow glow out the windows and flickered on the snow drifts.

It was so beautiful that everyone exclaimed in wonder and even Angela seemed in a friendly mood.

Evans came in just then. "Dinner is served!" he announced rather grandly.

Lights glimmered from the chandelier over the long dining table. The snowy damask cloth shone white under Mother's best china, that with the pink and burgundy roses around the rim.

Each gentleman seated a lady and Summer muttered under her breath, struggling with the hoop under the full skirt.

Austin's paunchy, red-faced father, Robert, sat to Mother's right, across from Summer who sat to her left. Austin sat next to Summer. Tiny, birdlike Mrs. Shaw sat to Father's right with Todd across from her. The others were scattered alternately up and down the table.

David gave Summer a quick wink and she winked back, both noting that Father had carefully arranged the seating so that Maude Peabody sat next to David.

"Isn't this a great party?" Mother asked a little too loudly and almost knocked her wineglass over with an unsteady hand.

Summer caught it before it spilled and ignored the murderous look Father flashed from his end of the table. She could only hope Priscilla hadn't seen it.

Priscilla reminded Summer of a gentle, lovely, slightly befuddled dove. In contrast, her distant cousin, Elizabeth Shaw, moved in quick motions like the vicious little shrike bird, the one that impales its victims on a thorn bush.

The big grandfather clock in the entry started its deep chiming. Father pulled out his pocket watch and frowned. "Half a minute out of time," he snapped to no one in particular. "We always sit down at exactly six o'clock." Then he picked up his goblet of white wine and stood. "I propose a toast!" he announced.

Everyone raised his glass and looked toward the hawklike man expectantly.

"Here's to Christmas of 1858 and to the New Year ahead! Here's to our children! May they prosper and add many generations to our table and more wealth to our families!"

"Hear! Hear!" Everyone lifted their glasses and drank.

The pointed hints were not lost on Summer as she rolled the dry, tart wine on her tongue and watched Evans enter with the silver tureen of rich turtle soup.

Robert Shaw smiled expansively across the table as he

375

attacked the soup. "We're all so glad you're home, Summer."

"I'm happy to be home," she lied as she watched Maude gobble the soup. Her friend was a kind, generous person but she would never be able to buy the class she craved with all her father's money.

"I'm so glad you invited Father and me to join you," Maude gushed as she slurped the last drop.

Father smiled expansively at the girl. "The pleasure is ours, Miss Peabody. I'm sure we'd like your company more often, wouldn't we, David?"

"What? Oh, yes, of course!" David blurted and Summer tried hard to keep a straight face as David said lamely, "Why, Miss Peabody, what an—interesting gown you're wearing tonight."

Summer glanced at it, thinking the poor girl did have the most unfortunate habit of choosing clothes that made her sallow complexion look worse. The scarlet taffeta gave her the overall appearance of a barn on fire.

"Thank you." Maude smiled modestly.

Mr. Shaw looked down the table toward Maude. "It's those new aniline dyes we have in the textile industry now. Ladies don't have to wear pale colors anymore, they can all wear bright hues and look just like Miss Peabody!"

Maude reddened at the compliment as David began to cough into his napkin.

"Were you about to say something, son?" Father demanded as he glared.

"Well, no." David coughed and Summer suppressed a grin. "I was about to say, sir, that it is a wonder what is being invented these days."

"You can say that again, young man." Mr. Peabody's hand shook as he dipped the rich soup. "Why, who would have ever believed they would lay that transatlantic cable so the Queen of England could send a message to our President!"

"Humph!" Mr. Shaw snorted. "Dang thing broke down after three weeks! I don't know if I can see any sense to this telegraph thing."

"Now, Father," Todd argued, "you've got to move with the times! They say in a few more years, they'll have that wire all the way to California!"

"Exactly!" His father crowed. "Why would anybody in their right mind want to contact California? Except for the gold strike, the whole place is worthless! Know what they're doing now? Importing camels to haul freight!"

"Now, Robert," Mrs. Shaw said firmly with a quick, birdlike gesture, "if Todd thinks it's a good idea, I want you to buy stock tomorrow."

Summer saw Austin scowl slightly and felt sorry for him. No matter how hard he tried, he could never replace his younger brother as his mother's favorite. It seemed sad since Austin so obviously craved her favor.

She glanced at Todd as he ate. He was everything his brother was not: popular, dashing, more handsome, gregarious. Women were always drawn to him and, in truth, at one time he had made Summer's heart flutter a little. But he never hung around with the other three because they were perhaps too dull and serious for him. Besides, she had soon realized that he lacked Austin's sincerity and depth.

Her attention came back to Father as he peered down the table. "Well, I think you're right, Robert. Everything west of the Mississippi is just a desolate wasteland."

"Oh, but it's not!" Summer protested before she thought. "There's lots of hills, sparkling water, and green trees. It's so big, you can't imagine how uncluttered and beautiful it is!" She realized suddenly that all eyes were turned toward her and her wistful description. Until now, she hadn't fully realized how much she loved the wild wilderness that she would never see again.

Evans entered at that moment with a large, roast goose and a great tenderloin of beef and started to serve, diverting everyone's attention.

"Well," said Todd, "I'm glad to hear a firsthand opinion

377

that the West isn't such a terrible place! I've made a decision to join up with the Massachusetts Immigration Society's next group headed for Kansas right after Christmas!"

For a moment, in the shocked silence, Summer thought Elizabeth Shaw might really faint. She gasped and fanned herself with her napkin. Immediately Austin was up out of his chair, rushing to her side.

"Really, Todd!" he scolded as he pulled her smelling salts from her chatelaine that was pinned to her dress and waved them under her nose. "You should be ashamed to upset Mother so!"

"I'm not upset!" the woman declared grimly, taking another whiff of the smelling salts. "After all, I have been a leader in the fight to get antislavery people to move there so we can outvote the other side! The Shaws have donated a great deal of money to help the Reverend Beecher send both bibles and rifles to Kansas. Sending a son is an even bigger commitment to this holy cause!"

Maude sighed and rolled her eyes. "I think it's an utterly romantic and idealistic thing to do! Perhaps I should consider being a pioneer. But do I have to miss the New Year's ball to do it?"

David was right, Summer thought as she took a mouthful of the savory roast beef. *The girl really did have the brains of Grandmother's spaniel.*

"I've had the idea for a long time, actually," Todd explained as he helped himself to the roast goose and vegetables. "Ever since last year when that wool buyer from Ohio was here in Boston for the big, antislavery rally."

Angela had been sitting quietly all this time slipping bits of food off her plate to the cat under her chair. "You mean the man with the eyes like coals and the beard like Moses?"

"Oh, I remember him now that you describe him." Maude paused in shoveling in food. "He had a common name like Smith." She thought a moment. "Brown, that was it. John Brown."

"Yes, that's him!" Todd's hazel eyes sparkled. "He really set everyone on fire with his zeal, didn't he? I think if the South doesn't yield on this, we'll have war!"

"The furor over that Kansas-Nebraska Bill combined with the Fugitive Slave Act is certainly pushing our side that direction." Mrs. Shaw waved Austin away and he returned to his chair.

"Well, just in case," Robert Shaw said, his florid jaws chomping like a bulldog, "I've already started stockpiling cotton for my mills from the big plantations. The St. Clairs and some of their cousins down in Georgia and Tennessee are working closely with me on this. If we do go to war, I won't be able to get cotton up the river and my mills will be in trouble."

"I've been thinking about expanding my own investments." Father pushed back his empty plate. "The whales can't last forever and I understand some fellow named Drake has been over in Pennsylvania looking for something called petroleum. I may contact him."

Mr. Peabody cackled as he finished his beef. "The market's been a little slow because of the panic last year, but it looks to me gunpowder and munitions factories might be a wise thing to put money in right now."

"With the shape this country's in," Mr. Shaw wiped his expansive jaws, "what we need is another Whig president."

"There is no more Whig party, Robert." Elizabeth Shaw used a tone one would take to a rather stupid child.

"I know that! That's why the country's in the shape it's in! I don't think that new party, the Republicans, will ever make a go of it."

David leaned back in his chair and looked at the rich nut cake and coffee the butler placed before him. "You didn't think much of that fellow who just lost the Senate race in Illinois last month?"

"Hah!" Father snorted as he dug into the cake. "That gawky, ugly nobody! That's his second loss running for the same office! You'd think Lincoln would realize he has no talent for politics and go back to his piddling law practice!"

Summer sighed and sipped her coffee, barely tasting the rich, brandied cake. *Had conversations at this table always been so much wrangling? Of course they had.*

"Well," said Maude, looking up and down the table as if to make sure she was the center of attention, "if I can't be a pioneer, I may decide to do what my friend Louisa May Alcott says she is going to do in case of war."

She had everyone's attention now.

"Which is?" Summer prompted, holding her breath.

"Well, we're talking of going to the front and helping our brave boys in uniform by being nurses!"

Summer thought for a moment Mr. Peabody might drop his coffee cup. "No daughter of mine is going to do something as scandalous as that!"

"Miss Alcott is not getting any younger," Father said icily. "It might behoove that strong-minded spinster to spend her energy looking for a husband which she certainly won't find after getting involved in such a dubious field as nursing."

"Louisa May intends to support herself by writing books!" Maude retorted with such spirit that Summer suddenly admired her.

"Books!" Father wiped his mouth and threw down his napkin. "Who'd buy a book by a woman?"

"That's exactly what you said when Mrs. Stowe came out with *Uncle Tom's Cabin*," Summer snapped, throwing down the gauntlet to him verbally.

Father glowered at her and she held her breath. But before the battle could go any further, Mother came out of her fog and stood up. Naturally, all the gentlemen scrambled to their feet.

"I think the ladies will retire to the music room," she announced loftily with the slightest glance of congratulations at Summer. "I'm sure the gentlemen are ready for their cigars and brandy anyway."

"In the music room, each lady accepted a glass of sherry as Summer poured and they sat in the glow of the Christmas candles and opened gifts.

Coaldust prowled about like a small, menacing panther, climbing the tree, tearing ribbons from packages. Maude tried to pick him up to pet him and he snarled and scratched her, running under a desk to hide.

Angela snickered and Mother said, "I'm sorry, Maude, at times, animals do reflect their owner's personalities."

The child glared back at Priscilla and her look made Summer shiver. *She was not really a child at all, had never been. Angela was a spiteful, cruel adult trapped in a child's body.*

"Here's gifts for everyone!" Summer put in quickly, passing the rare oranges around while everyone exclaimed in delight and reached for the gifts Summer handed out. There was a magnificent blue sapphire necklace for Summer from her parents. She expressed delight although she knew someone in Father's office had no doubt chosen it for her. Mother seldom went out and Father couldn't ever be bothered with such small details. There was also expensive jewelry for Mother, no doubt purchased the same way.

Angela tore into her packages in a greedy frenzy and held up a wooden mallet with puzzlement. "What is this? A joke?"

Her pouty little face clouded and Summer held her breath, wondering if they were about to be treated to one of the child's kicking, screaming tantrums.

"My goodness!" Maude gushed, visibly impressed. "A croquet set! What a lucky girl you are! That's the new game that's so popular in England. They say it will soon be all the rage here!"

Mother nodded vaguely. "I do remember Silas saying he was having a great deal of trouble getting one of his employees in London to track the game down and get it on a clipper so it would arrive in time for Christmas."

The child looked a little less sullen, obviously pleased that she had put someone to a great deal of trouble. "What do I do with it?"

She swung the mallet wildly and Summer grabbed the

crystal wine decanter to keep the mallet from smashing it.

"Well," said Maude with enthusiasm, "I've never played it, of course, but I think you are supposed to put those little wire things out on the lawn and knock those wooden balls through them. Just thing how much fun we will have out on the lawn next spring with it."

Summer yawned in spite of herself. "Sounds a little dull to me." She picked up the decanter and poured another glass for Mrs. Shaw.

"I suppose it's at least a game women can play," Mother said, holding out her goblet unsteadily for a refill. "There's so few sports that are ladylike enough that men would approve or that women could actually do in a tight corset and hoop skirts."

With a sigh, Summer gently took the goblet from Mother's shaking hand and set it on the desk. One more and there would be a terrible fuss later. By not refilling Priscilla's goblet, perhaps she could protect her from Father's wrath.

Mrs. Shaw regarded Summer with satisfaction. "Now, Summer, I've been thinking about Austin's and your wedding."

"You're a trifle premature," Summer said shortly as she reached for a piece of candy. "Austin has not asked me to marry him."

"Oh, I've spoiled the surprise!" Her hand went to her mouth with a quick gesture of feigned dismay. "But of course he's going to ask you! I'll admit I was a little uneasy about it last summer when he mentioned it since I thought you might be a little—shall we say, too spirited for him. But I've reconsidered."

Summer regarded her coldly. "Even my father would be the first to admit a little spirit in either a woman or a saddle horse is not all bad!"

"Touché!" said Mother.

In the sudden silence, Summer and Mrs. Shaw studied each other like two opponents and Summer saw respect in the other's eyes. The woman knew a worthy adversary when she saw one. Summer could best her on all fronts and she seemed to know it.

Mrs. Shaw seemed to decide to ignore the remark. "Anyway, Austin and I have discussed the honeymoon and I told him Nahant at the seashore was the fashionable place to go right now since it will be a June wedding. A grand tour of Europe was more what I had in mind, but the war department might take a dim view of Austin leaving for six months with all this war talk."

Summer smiled a little too sweetly. "I'm sure you know someone in high office who could pull the right strings and aren't you kind to plan both my wedding and honeymoon and save me all that bother!"

Mother looked both amused and troubled. It occurred to Summer that Mother didn't really like her cousin at all.

"Why don't we sing some more carols?" Maude said a little desperately, rushing to the piano. She played very badly but it broke the tension for the rest of the evening.

Todd Shaw left for Kansas right after Christmas, not even waiting for the Shaw's annual ball. The weather was none too good but he said the group wanted to get out there and get themselves organized so as to be ready for early spring planting. The settlers would be dependent on their crops to survive the next year. Summer wondered if he were all that interested in Kansas or just trying to get away from his mother.

Then it was New Year's Eve. Summer had chosen her dress with great care, knowing there would be dozens of people there she hadn't seen since her return who would inspect her curiously. The dressmaker created a gown of yellow satin that complemented her light hair. The skirt was so full over the hoop that she thought she might have trouble getting through doorways. The neckline was cut low to show off her smooth shoulders and the soft swell of her creamy breasts. The pale blue satin sash accented her small waist and was just the color of the sapphire necklace which reflected her blue eyes.

Mrs. O'Malley outdid herself on Summer's hair, piling it up on her head in a great mass of curls entwined with more sapphires and small wisps of ringlets about her heart-shaped face. Summer put a few drops of the sweet lily of the valley scent on her wrists and in the shadow between her breasts.

She thought Mother looked almost happy and a little more steady on her feet as Summer and the Irish maid helped Priscilla into a magnificent pink and burgundy gown with diamond jewelry.

Since the hoops were so full, both women could not squeeze into the carriage at the same time so Flannigan first drove the parents over to the neighboring estate and then came back for Summer and David.

They were both silent for a moment as the horses started away and Summer said, "Have you still said nothing to Father about your plans?"

"No, but my mind is made up," he replied stubbornly. "I'm going to remove myself from that miserable household sometime soon."

Summer sighed. The occasional visits from David when he came from school were the only bright spots in her life. How could she stand to live there without her twin?

David cleared his throat. "I've never pried, Sis, but I've always had a feeling you left a man behind you out west."

She ran her tongue over her lower lip. "Yes, I did," she admitted quietly.

"Then for God's sake, why don't you go back to him? I realize that if you did, Mother and I would probably never see you again. But we could stand it, knowing someone in this unhappy house had finally found a little comfort."

She wondered if she should tell him, decided she trusted him enough. "He's dead, David."

"Oh." He paused. "I'm so sorry, I didn't realize—" A long moment passed while she listened to the horses' hooves clatter

384

on the street.

"Summer," he said. "I know Austin is going to ask you to marry him tonight. What are you going to tell him?"

She studied him in the dark carriage. "It would make you very happy for me to marry your best friend, wouldn't it, Brother?"

"Yes," he said grudgingly, "but I wouldn't want you to do it for that reason. If you don't love Austin—"

"I love him," she answered, pulling the expensive cloak more closely about her against the biting chill. "Not like I loved the other one, but I suppose I have always loved Austin. But I don't know if it's enough. He's a fine person. I wouldn't want to hurt him or give him less than he deserves."

"Then what are you going to tell him?"

"I—I don't know! I just don't know!"

The carriage pulled up in front of the big Georgian mansion. Ornate coaches were parked about the grounds. Drivers and footmen gathered in groups, visiting. Elegant ladies and gentlemen arrived in fine carriages for this annual and most important of Boston's social events. The faint sounds of the orchestra drifted on the frosty air and light streamed through all the windows, reflected by the drifts of shimmering snow.

Torn by indecision, Summer let Flannigan assist her and her brother out and they went inside to the ball.

Chapter Twenty-Two

The large entry and the ballroom beyond were ablaze with lights. Summer and David entered and gave their coats to the butler.

Austin had obviously been watching for them. He rushed up and took both Summer's hands in his. "My dear, you are easily the most beautiful woman at the ball!"

"And you are so handsome in your uniform." She meant it as she smiled at him.

A large crowd of Boston's most prominent families filled the ballroom and many spoke to her. Austin took her arm and guided her across the floor while David stopped to visit with friends. She saw bold curiosity on some faces but she stuck her chin out and didn't flinch as she returned each look boldly.

Let them talk, she thought defiantly. The gossips would gradually lose interest in speculating on her adventures out west and finally stop whispering.

The orchestra struck up a tune. Austin grabbed her hand and pulled her out toward the dancers. "Oh, it's a polka, Summer! We must dance this one!"

The new dance was so popular that a woman's jacket had been named for it, she remembered. Then she had no time for thought as he whirled her out onto the floor. They danced briskly among the other couples out under the giant chandeliers. She found herself laughing and really enjoying herself for the first time since she had returned to Boston.

The music ended. She laughed almost breathlessly and patted the slight dew of moisture from her cheeks as they left the floor. "That was such fun, Austin! I don't remember when I've had such a good time!"

He smiled at her as he took her arm. "This is only the beginning, I assure you! I intend your life should always be full of fun and happiness! Would you like some punch?"

She nodded and they made their way through the crowd toward the refreshment table, stopping to speak to different ones. Austin was well liked and respected among the older crowd. They joined David and Maude at the punch bowl.

"My!" Maude simpered. "Isn't it a wonderful party? What a pretty dress, Summer! So chic!"

"Thank you, Maude dear," she answered politely, thinking "chic" must be the latest word from the fashion magazines. Maude didn't read anything else. When "elegant" and "stunning" had come into being several years ago, Maude had worked them both into every sentence she uttered.

Austin smiled kindly at the rotund girl. "That is certainly an—interesting gown you're wearing, Miss Peabody."

"Thank you!" Maude reddened with pleasure.

"Such a bright green!" Summer stammered, trying to say something nice. Maude looked a bit like a large Christmas tree.

The new dyes had brightened all the ladies' dresses, Summer noticed, looking around at the garish colors.

The musicians started a slow waltz and Maude looked longingly toward the floor. Summer knew that the beefy girl was a poor dancer. A sedate waltz was one of the few steps she could manage. Summer decided to do something about her friend's plight.

"Isn't that a lovely waltz?" she noted innocently. "And I know you waltz divinely, Maude. I'm sure David is trying to get up the nerve to ask you, aren't you, Brother?"

"What?" David gulped. "Oh, of course! Would you do me

the honor, Miss Peabody?"

"Delighted, I'm sure!" Maude simpered and they moved out onto the floor. David went at it with the dogged determination of a captain steering an unwieldy vessel.

Austin watched them. "That was a kind thing for you to do, Summer, although I'm sure David won't think so."

She shrugged and sipped her champagne punch. "It won't kill David! It occurred to me how terrible it would be to stand all evening and never be asked to dance!"

"You've never had that problem, have you?" He winked at her. "You've always been the belle of these balls. But I've already warned all the gentlemen not to cut in on me tonight. I don't intend to share you for even a single dance. However, I will ask Maude for a dance myself and see that some of the others ask her so she will have a wonderful time."

Summer looked up at him a long moment. "Sometimes I forget what a kind, caring person you are, Austin."

"You bring out the best in me; you always have." He gave her such a tender look that her heart was touched. *There were many things worse*, she thought, *than to spend the rest of her life with a kind, caring man who offered deathless devotion.*

Across the floor, one of the Osgoode girls danced by and waved to her. She could see Mother and Father in conversation with the older Shaws.

David and her friend returned to them as the waltz ended. Maude puffed like a beached whale and gulped her punch. Summer wondered if there were any kind way to change her friend's manners and decided it wouldn't be worth it to hurt her feelings.

David wiped his face and said, "I do hope you give me a chance, Austin, to dance with my own sister at least once if we can keep the usual rogues from monopolizing her."

Austin laughed. "I've passed the word weeks ago they should all stay away from her permanently. But speaking of rogues, I want to introduce you to one of my younger classmates from the Point."

A handsome, almost pretty blond cadet in jaunty short gray jacket and white pants joined them. He offered his hand. "Good to see you, Austin, you were kind to invite me to the ball."

"Fannie! So glad you could come!" The other shook hands with the young man vigorously.

"Fannie?" Summer questioned.

Austin laughed. "It's a joke, of course! Fannie is what the others at West Point call him. They say he's as good-looking as any girl. Miss Van Schuyler, Miss Peabody, David, may I present George Armstrong Custer."

The handsome boy bowed charmingly and shook David's hand. "I'm enjoying my short trip to your fine city."

Summer sized him up. He was probably not much older than she and every bit as blond and blue-eyed. "Where are you from, Mr. Custer?"

"Ohio, originally, but I really think of Michigan as my home. I've lived with my sister there much of the time and my sweetheart's there."

"And how do you like West Point?" David inquired politely. "Austin used to tell us the Point was tough and the discipline hard."

Custer laughed easily. "Well, I don't make the grades Austin did and I must admit to often being in trouble over the discipline."

Austin blushed modestly. "What Fannie isn't telling you is how popular he is with the other men and a born leader! I think as an officer, his men would follow him anywhere without a backward glance! And when he does get into trouble, things always seem to work out for him. The others are beginning to call it 'Custer's luck.'"

Now it was the young cadet's turn to flush. "I don't know about that but I do hope my luck holds out and the war doesn't start until I graduate. There's going to be a shortage of officers and that will mean a golden opportunity for ambitious young men."

Summer sighed. "All I hear is talk of war. I'm sure another

389

way can be found to settle the differences."

"Well, if war does come," Maude waved her hand in a melodramatic flourish, "I intend to be on the front lines as a nurse! If Florence Nightingale can do it, so can I!"

"How interesting!" Custer had a winning smile. "If I'm wounded in the fray, I do hope I'm lucky enough to be attended by such a charming nurse as yourself! Perhaps we'll all meet someday on the battlefield."

"You can count me out," David said stiffly. "I don't care to go even if congress passes a draft!"

The others eyed him with such obvious disapproval that Summer felt compelled to rush to his defense. "What my brother means is he's going to be so badly needed in our business, we won't be able to spare him. He'll reluctantly have to pay someone to go in his place as will a lot of other young men."

"What I mean is," David said, a bit testy, "I don't have any intention of getting mixed up in this glorious game. It's not going to be a lot of fancy parades and uniforms, it's going to be terrible bloodshed, brother against brother, father against son!"

Custer stared at him. "You'd just let the South pull out of the Union?"

"I would!"

There was a long, awkward silence. The orchestra struck up "Jeannie with the Light Brown Hair."

"I do wish they wouldn't play Stephen Foster's songs," Maude prattled inanely. "You know he writes for those blackface Christy Minstrels and his songs are so common!"

The young cadet offered his arm gallantly. "Even if it is a common song, Miss Peabody, I'd be charmed to have this dance."

Maude simpered as she took it and they pushed through the crowd to the dance floor.

"Really, David," Austin scolded gently, "if I were you, I'd keep my thoughts to myself. Most of us are eager to give those

Rebels a good whipping! Why, it'll all be over in a month, once it starts!"

"I'm sorry if I made it awkward for you just now with your military friend." David shrugged. "But I think you are all taking this too lightly. The idea of all that suffering and bloodshed breaks my heart."

Austin put his hand on David's shoulder. "If war does come, I hope there are going to be a few medics or chaplains out there who care as much as you do. Now I need to talk to your sister."

David nodded as Austin took Summer's arm and they moved away toward the conservatory with its jungle of plants.

"David is very concerned about anything involving suffering," she said as they entered the dim greenhouse.

"I know that, Summer," he said gently. "He's my best friend, remember? David is one of two people I care most about in this world." He hesitated. "You surely know who the other is."

She didn't answer as she sat down on a bench among the steamy atmosphere of the potted palms. There were times that away from the competition of his more dashing brother and his scolding mother, Austin changed in personality, becoming, almost, a man she could love.

He sat down on the bench beside her. "Do you remember the first time you were ever in this conservatory?"

"I'm afraid not," she confessed.

"I suppose you don't because it doesn't mean as much to you as it does to me. The first time I ever saw you that I recall was right here. You had come with your mother when she came over to check on the new house your parents were building next door."

"I must have been very young," she said, laughing. "I'm afraid I don't remember at all!"

"I remember. I remember every small detail. I was only eight years old and I remember the small child with the beautiful pale hair and a dainty blue frock. I fell in love with you that day and waited all these years for you to grow up so I

391

could marry you."

Such adoration made her uneasy. "So many things have changed since then, Austin! I'm not that innocent child you idolized all these years. There are things that if you knew—"

"I don't want to know!" he said almost savagely, taking her face between his fine hands and looking into her eyes. "I—I don't care what has happened and I don't want you to ever tell me! My life stopped the day you disappeared off that stagecoach and only resumed the day I heard you'd been found. Whatever has happened, let's forget and never speak of it. I love you too much to think of it!"

She felt her eyes widen in surprise as she looked up and saw the jealous pain and suffering in his eyes. *He knows!* she thought in puzzlement. *He knows somehow about the Cheyenne warrior and is willing to forget it if I can and make an attempt at a future.* She tried to hold back the tears as she thought of the dead brave but one rolled down her flawless skin.

Austin reached for a handkerchief and wiped her eyes gently. "Whatever you have endured, I'm going to make you forget," he promised. "I know you've never cared for me as much as I did for you, but I'm willing to take the gamble that you might learn to."

Summer turned her face away. "Your mother—"

"Forget about Mother!" he said so sternly that it surprised her. "If it comes to a choice between you, there's no contest! I have plenty of money of my own, Summer. Where would you like to live? Washington? England? France? Whatever it takes to make you love me, I'll do! Whatever you want, I'll buy! I intend to devote the rest of my life to making you happy."

She looked up at him, touched by his ardent fervor, thinking how few alternatives she had. *Could she ever learn to love him as he loved her?*

He took both her hands in his. "Summer, please say you'll marry me."

She hesitated a long moment and considered. And in that moment, she closed the past as one does a book that is finished.

Her beloved was dead but somehow she must try to pick up the pieces of her life and go on. *The best place to bury a dead love is deep in the depths of memory where it can be cherished forever. No one could ever take those few short, wonderful weeks away from her. She would have them always. But life is for the living . . .*

Summer swallowed hard and she knew her voice was a whisper. "Yes, Austin," she answered. "I—I'll marry you."

He gave a small sound of relief and gladness as he kissed her. It was a proper, prim kiss. As his lips touched hers lightly, she could not keep her mind from thinking of powerful arms lifting her, a hot, passionate mouth forcing hers open.

But she must not think of that anymore, she reminded herself as she returned the prim kiss. She must be fair with Austin and try to give him as much love as he gave her and maybe, somehow, it would all work out.

He pulled away and reached into his pocket for a small box. "I didn't dare hope, but I brought this along tonight anyway." His eyes shone with moisture as he brought out a magnificent sapphire ring encrusted with flawless diamonds.

"Oh, Austin! It's beautiful!" she gasped as he slipped it on her finger.

"I'm glad you like it," he answered happily. "It's a family heirloom. I've had our lawyer holding it for many years until you grew up. The first time I saw it, I knew it was meant for you because the stone is a perfect match for your sky blue eyes."

She winced at the memory. *Sky blue eyes. Summer Sky . . .*

"Is something the matter?" he asked anxiously. "Have I said something wrong?"

"No," she said. "I—I'm very pleased with the ring. Sapphire has always been my favorite."

"I can't wait for everyone in Boston to know how lucky I am!" He jumped to his feet eagerly. "Let's go ask Father to make the announcement to the crowd!"

Had she made a mistake? Was there any alternative for her?

"Yes, let's go announce it," she agreed.

There were many toasts to the couple although she thought

Mrs. Shaw looked a little annoyed. Mother whispered to her, "Come to my room afterward. I want to talk to you."

Summer nodded in surprise. Mother seemed almost sober tonight.

Finally the clock struck twelve and the new year of 1859 was ushered in with a cheer.

It was the wee hours of the morning before the party broke up and Flannigan took her parents home and came back for her and David. She looked doubtfully at the ring glittering on her finger as the carriage moved away from the Shaw estate.

"I'm so glad you accepted!" David said cheerfully. "I was afraid you wouldn't and I know he is the man for you! It'll be a wonderful life; you'll see!"

She thought about Mother a long moment, wondering what she wanted. "You know, Brother, I came back from the West with a changed outlook, a more mature outlook. I see things I never saw before." She paused a long moment. "David, do you think Father really loves Mother?"

"What a question to ask when you should be thinking about your own marriage." He sounded evasive.

"I am thinking about marriage," she answered. "It's funny I never noticed the unhappiness, the tension between our parents before. And you are evading my question."

For a moment, she did not think he would answer and when he finally did, his voice was almost a whisper. "Somehow, I think he must have adored her a long time ago," he said. "He's older than she, you know, and Mother was a reigning beauty in her day. There's something between them that's turned his love into almost an impotent rage and I sense she never loved him."

"Then why on earth do you suppose she married him?" Summer looked out at the snowdrifts as the carriage rolled along.

"You've heard enough to know it has to do with money. From bits of gossip over the years, I've decided her father had made some bad investments. The family was almost penniless when along came the brash, rich New Yorker who yearned to be accepted in blue-blooded society. I suppose her father pressured her into it. Maybe she just couldn't see any alternatives."

The words made Summer shiver. "Have you not wondered why they don't share the same bedroom?"

"Sis," David hesitated and the horse's hooves seemed very loud on the pavement. "I'm going to tell you something I've never told anyone before, something that happened one winter night when we were nine years old."

She looked at him uneasily. Even in the pale moonlight, she could see the conflict on his face. "Yes?"

"My room is across from Mother's and yours is down the hall," he said, "so the noise didn't wake you, I suppose, but the noise and screaming woke *me* up one night."

"They were having an argument?"

"An argument?" he snorted. "Father was tearing her door down to get in! I heard the door splinter and he screamed something like, 'If I can't have your heart, I'll take your body! By God! I've paid enough for it!' I jumped out of bed and ran in there when she started screaming."

He didn't say anything for a long moment and closed his eyes as if he couldn't bear the memory.

"And?" she prompted.

"The room was a wreck and Father was naked. He and Mother were struggling as he held her in a tight embrace and her nightdress had been ripped to shreds."

"Oh, my lord!" Summer gasped.

"When he looked up and saw me standing in the doorway, he shouted at me, 'Get out of here! This doesn't concern you! This is between her and me and that Goddamned ghost! Go back to your room!' His face was absolutely distorted with livid rage. When I returned and ran out, he slammed what was left of the door behind me and I could hear Mother crying, 'No, Silas, No!'"

"What did you do then?"

He shrugged almost guiltily. "I was only a small child; what could I do? I heard Father screaming something about 'I'll

395

have what I paid for one last time, by God!' and Mother's weeping. I went back and hid under my pillows so I couldn't hear the fighting. I don't suppose anyone else in the house heard the struggle but me."

"Not the servants?"

"The servants' quarters are on the third floor," he reminded her.

Summer collapsed limply against the cushions as the carriage pulled up before the Van Schuyler home. Mentally, she did a quick calculation of Angela's age and the facts crashed down on her. That strange, sinister child had been conceived in rape and violence. No wonder Mother couldn't love the girl. Angela was a constant reminder of a terrible ordeal.

"I never meant to tell anyone, Summer," he said. "I meant to carry that to my grave."

She didn't answer as Flannigan came around to assist them out of the coach and Evans opened the door, took their wraps.

But at the top of the stairs, she stopped and looked at him. "No, I'm glad you told me, David," she said. "I can almost understand now and feel sorry for them both. There are only a few pieces of the puzzle missing and I don't think either of us wants to know what they are. At any rate, I'm now sure I'm making the right decision to get out of this house." *Was she— or was she doing exactly what her mother had done?*

David put his hand on her shoulder gently. "I'm sorry that, as a woman, you don't seem to have as many choices as I do."

"And what choice are you going to make?"

His sensitive face mirrored his indecision. "I don't know yet, but I promise not to cause any disruption until after the wedding. I love you both too much to create trouble for you."

She had never loved him so much. "Good night, David." She hugged him briefly and they parted.

Mrs. O'Malley yawned grumpily as she assisted Summer off with her ball gown and into a fine, silk dressing robe before plodding heavily back up to her third-floor room.

The light shone from under Mother's door. Summer took a deep breath before rapping softly as she looked to the very end of the hall. There was no light under Father's door.

"Come in," Priscilla said.

It was like stepping into another time period. Summer frowned. The decor hadn't been changed since the house was built. Mother's large room was done in pale pinks and burgundies with large cabbage roses on the walls and fabrics. *It looked like the sanctuary of a woman who does not care about the present, has no hope for the future, and prefers to live in the past.*

"You really ought to redecorate," Summer said without thinking. "The wallpaper is yellowing."

"I like it just the way it is," Priscilla said from where she stood before the fire. She wore a dressing gown of pale pink velvet and Summer looked at her and knew she was seeing almost the ghost of a great beauty.

There was an open, crystal box of potpourri on the table and Summer took a deep breath of the scent of faded rose petals saved from her mother's garden. It hadn't occurred to her before but the whole house seemed to have that faint scent, that ghost of dead roses about it.

"You wanted to see me?"

"I thought, just once," Mother said uncertainly, moving to stare out the window, "I thought we might try to carry on a conversation."

Summer bit her lip, deciding not to make a bitter comment about how impossible it was to communicate with someone who is in an eternal narcotic haze. Incredibly, Mother seemed sober at the moment.

She waited, not knowing what to say next to this pathetic stranger who was her mother. She wondered if Priscilla had forgotten Summer was in the room. Mother stood staring out at the rose garden that lay below her window.

"I hate winter," she whispered so low that Summer strained to hear her. "I hate winter," she said again. "It's very dreary and lonely and my roses die. Summer is my favorite season;

397

that time that roses bloom and warmth and love flourish."

She wasn't sure if Priscilla expected a reply. Mother seemed to have forgotten anyone else was in the room and was talking to herself.

The music box sat on the table where it had always been since Summer could remember. She ran a finger over it, really looking at it for the first time. It was a cheap, small music box and Summer wondered idly about it as she opened the lid. Father's pride would never have allowed him to give such an inexpensive gift.

As she opened the lid, the music tinkled out: *'Tis the last rose of summer left blooming alone . . . all her lovely companions are faded and gone . . .*

"Don't touch that!" Mother said so sharply as she whirled around that Summer snapped the lid down with a startled motion. Priscilla's face reflected a storm of emotions and she acted as if she were about to speak and then turned back to the fire.

Why have we always been such strangers? Summer thought sadly. *Is it that we are too much alike? Is reality so hard for you to bear that you must escape to your sherry or your rose garden? Like me, did you think you had no alternatives?*

"You're really going to marry Austin Shaw?" Priscilla didn't turn away from the fire.

"Yes, in late June."

Priscilla laughed mirthlessly. "That should make Silas very happy! The only thing that would make him happier than getting his hands on some of the Shaw interests is marrying your brother off to the Peabody banking money so Silas can own that, too, when her father dies."

"I'm afraid he's going to be disappointed there," Summer answered, wondering what this was about. "I think David has decided to go his own way no matter how furious it makes Father."

"Good for David!" she said with such a flash of spirit that Summer was astonished. "Silas has bought everything he ever wanted with his damned money, including me! There ought to

398

be one person in the world who can't be bought! Although those who make a bargain with the devil shouldn't be bitter when their note is called! It really isn't sporting!"

Summer stared at her, startled at the rare show of energy and courage from a woman she had come to regard as a rather pathetic, helpless dove. *Once*, she thought, *her mother had had all the passion and spirit of Summer. Was she seeing herself as she would be twenty years from now?*

The thought was disconcerting and troublesome. "You're behaving very strangely tonight, Mother. Are you telling me you do not approve of my marrying Austin?"

Priscilla looked her directly in the eyes. "Do you love him?"

Uneasily, Summer avoided the direct look and question. "After all these years, it's interesting that you are suddenly terribly worried about my future."

"New Year's Eve has a way of making people reflect on their past and futures, making old ghosts come back to haunt them. I know I haven't done right by any of my children and I'm attempting now to rectify my mistakes by stopping you from going down the path I took."

Summer stared at the faded roses on the walls. "Surely you must have expected that after all these years I would probably marry Austin Shaw."

"I have nothing against the Shaw boy although I detest his bitchy mother heartily! I think you can best her easily. But ever since you returned, I keep seeing something in your eyes that tells me you are in love with another man, probably someone your father wouldn't approve of or you would already have told Silas about him."

The scarred, bronzed face came to her mind. "You're right, of course! I haven't given you enough credit, Mother, for perception. Yes, on all counts! Father would disapprove of the man heartily!"

"Then that's probably the one you belong with!" She came over to Summer. "I want you to go back to that man. I have a little money hidden away, not much, but certainly enough for a train ticket one way! Go back to your soldier, or rancher, or whatever he is with my blessings!"

Tears came to Summer's eyes. "How could you know about the other man? And why, tonight, are you deciding to go up against Father?"

She paused, almost wistfully. "Because, tonight, as you announced your engagement to a rich man, I saw myself as I was twenty years ago and I don't want you to make the same mistake I did. Not every woman gets a chance at a once-in-a-lifetime love and if you're lucky enough to find it, run after him, damn the consequences, and don't look back! Do you hear me? Don't look back!"

The realization dawned slowly on Summer. "Who was he, Mother?"

A very soft, gentle look came over her mother's face as she remembered. "His name was Shawn O'Bannion and he was very poor and Irish Catholic. He had very black wavy hair and eyes as green as shamrocks. Shawn was strong and sensitive and had a way with the soil. You should have seen the roses he grew. That's my only link to him now; my roses."

She tried to imagine her mother wrapped passionately in a man's arms as Priscilla stared regretfully into the past. It occurred to Summer that she had never seen her parents in a loving embrace; not even once.

"Did Shawn not want to marry you, Mother?"

"He did. But I was already engaged to Silas Van Schuyler and my parents were pressuring me to marry Silas. Shawn and I had only that one summer and then, with winter, I had to make a decision, a choice."

"And you chose Silas Van Schuyler instead?"

Priscilla tried to laugh and her voice became a ragged sob. "I know you can't understand that, can you? Now that I look back, neither can I! But you have to understand Shawn was so poor and all I could think of was how terrible it would be to have no money and how Boston society would laugh when they heard about it. I couldn't see any other way out since my parents had lost their fortune."

"Was Shawn so terribly unsuitable?"

The deep silence was broken only by the crackling of the fireplace logs. Summer heard the big grandfather clock downstairs chiming as she waited.

"Shawn was my father's gardener," Priscilla said finally. She went back to the window and stared out at the falling snow as Summer regarded her in stunned silence.

"It was snowing that night, too," Priscilla said as if speaking to herself. "I was supposed to meet Shawn under the street lamp across from my parents' home and we would run away together. I remember standing at the upstairs window with my luggage, looking down on him as he waited patiently for me."

Summer stared unbelievingly at her. "And you didn't go down to meet him?"

Priscilla shook her head as she stared unseeing into the night and her shoulders trembled slightly. "No, I let the man I loved turn and walk out of my life because I was afraid and weak. Other people's opinions and luxury meant too much to me. I have to live now with that choice I made and isn't it ironic that I've got all the money and social position I want? I'd give every bit of it away to have a chance to go back and make that decision again."

Tears came to Summer's eyes. "Do you not know where this Shawn O'Bannion is? Have you never heard from him?"

"No. He's never tried to contact me again. Does that surprise you? Can't you imagine how he must have felt as he walked away that night through the snow?" Priscilla's voice was tinged with regret and bitterness.

"And is that man my father?"

Priscilla bit her lip. "I wish to God he were! No, you're Silas Van Schuyler's children, all right; all of you. I let him purchase me like a fine-blooded brood mare, and so I've cheated him, too, you see. I wanted luxury and money: He wanted a beautiful, blue-blooded wife, whether she loved him or not. We both got what we thought we wanted, and in the end, we have nothing to share but bitterness and regrets. But just once, I would like to see someone in this miserable house make a wise choice and be happy."

She went over to her desk and fumbled in the top drawer. "I do have a little cash of my own, Summer. Let me buy you a ticket, send you back to your lover."

Summer choked back her tears. "I—I don't get the luxury of a choice like you did, Mother. You see, the man I loved is dead."

Priscilla paused and looked up at Summer. For just an instant, their eyes met. They understood each other, not as mother and daughter, but as two women who have loved and lost and know the pain it brings.

"I'm so sorry," Mother said, pouring herself a glass of sherry from the decanter on the desk. "I didn't understand. I—I didn't realize . . ."

"So you see now why I'm going to marry Austin Shaw next June."

"I don't blame you, then." Mother gulped the liquor. "I don't blame anyone for trying to escape from this house, from the wreckage your father and I have made of our lives."

She lifted the lid of the music box. As the sad little tune tinkled out, she took her drink and went back over to stare out the window at the falling snow. "I hate winter," she said in a whisper. "Summer is the time for roses, and love, and the cold brings only sad memories and regrets . . ."

Summer watched her mother drain her goblet and stare out the window at the snow, knowing Priscilla had forgotten her daughter was even in the room.

Very quietly, Summer walked out and her mother never turned around. Even with the door closed behind her, she could hear the faint music. She went back to her own room and wept for herself and for Priscilla locked in a prison she had made herself. She could not erase the image of the young, handsome Irish face staring hopefully up at the window of the fine Beacon Hill home of her grandparents. She could almost feel the heartbreak and the indecision of her mother as she let the man leave without her. But Priscilla Blackledge could have had the man she wanted; Summer lacked the luxury of the choice.

She lay sleepless on her bed the rest of the night, listening to the chimes of the grandfather clock echoing through the big, gloomy house as the hours passed. Grimly she pushed the scene from her mind and began to make wedding plans.

Her brother David was the one in the family most excited about the marriage although Silas was in as good a mood as Summer had seen in a long time. Even pouty little Angela smiled at the prospect of all the festivities and the part she would play in the wedding as the flower girl.

Only Mother retreated back into her narcotic haze as if saddened by the coming wedding and hardly spoke to anyone at all. It was almost as if she and Summer had never talked that night. The mental door that had seemed to open slightly now slammed shut forever.

Austin returned to the city of Washington after the holidays but wrote daily letters full of adoration. Summer tried to write words of love to him but the best she could do were short, gossipy notes about how the wedding plans were shaping up and what was happening among Boston society during the following weeks.

Mrs. Harrison Gray Otis, the well-known Boston social leader, gave a ball in March to raise money to build a tomb for Washington at Mt. Vernon and it was a great success. Summer attended with David during one of those weekends he was home from Harvard.

Now that she had committed herself to the marriage, Summer didn't allow herself second thoughts or regrets. There was much to be done to put on a wedding that would be the biggest event of the summer social season among the wealthy. A message was dispatched to Todd to get himself home from Kansas in time for the June wedding but weeks passed with no answer from him.

Crocus pushed up through the melting March snow and

Austin was home on leave, joining Summer and the ladies in the music room as they worked on decisions concerning the wedding. Only Mother drank her sherry and stared out the window with a remoteness that showed her lack of interest. Summer, Mrs. Shaw, Maude, and the Osgoode sisters showed Austin the fabrics that had been chosen and tried to keep Coaldust, with Angela chasing him, from becoming tangled in their ribbon samples.

Curious, Summer looked up as she heard a loud, impatient rapping with the brass knocker on the front door and Evans hurried to answer it. Robert Shaw burst into the room, his florid complexion even redder than usual. He stalked in waving a crumpled piece of paper.

"Why, Father Shaw." She rose hurriedly to meet him. "Is something wrong?"

"It's Todd!" he blurted, waving the paper. "A message finally got through! Todd is missing!"

Before anyone else could move, Elizabeth Shaw shrieked, half-rose, then collapsed back in her chair.

"Quick! Her smelling salts!" Austin rushed to her side.

"Mrs. O'Malley," Summer said as the maid poked her head through the door, "please bring a glass of water." She had to grit her teeth to keep from adding, *to pour on Elizabeth Shaw who insists on being the center of attention even in the middle of a real tragedy.*

The other women broke into chatter like a gaggle of excited geese. Summer moved hurriedly to Mrs. Shaw's side. Priscilla turned around to watch, almost as if she were a disinterested spectator at someone else's home.

Robert Shaw knelt on one side of his wife's chair, rubbing her limp hand frantically while Austin waved the smelling salts under her nose. "Are you all right, Elizabeth?" the man asked several times before her eyelids fluttered weakly.

Mother's eye caught Summer's and seemed to confirm what Summer was already thinking: *What a mother-in-law Elizabeth Shaw was going to make with her continual fainting spells even though she was as tough as her pilgrim ancestors and would probably outlive everyone in the room.*

"What—what has happened to my dear son?" Her hands fluttered as she clutched at her heart and her eyes seemed to glance around to make sure everyone was hovering anxiously.

"Now now, dear." Her husband tried to get his considerable girth up off his knees by her chair. "It may not be all that bad! All I know is that he soon tired of the dullness of Kansas farms and went off to Cherry Creek to seek adventure in the gold strike."

"Cherry Creek," Summer thought aloud. "That's Cheyenne hunting grounds somewhere around the Arkansas River and Bent's Fort."

Austin looked up from his vigil at his mother's side. "You've been there?"

"No." Summer shook her head. "I just know the area from hearing the Indians talk. There's a new town at the gold strike called Denver."

Maude rolled her spaniel eyes. "Do you suppose the Indians got Todd?"

This comment evoked fresh wails from the tiny, bridlike woman and Summer glared at the banker's daughter.

"Now, Mother, don't worry!" Austin cleared his throat and hesitated a moment. "Knowing how much this will worry you till we hear from him, I'll go out there myself, find Todd and bring him back."

Mrs. Shaw stopped moaning immediately and looked around in triumph. "What a wonderful idea! Why, I never would have thought of that! Will the army let you do that?"

"Of course they will!" Robert Shaw stopped pacing the Chinese rug. "Of course he can do it! If that will make you happy, Elizabeth, I'll use my influence in Washington to get Austin assigned to Fort Leavenworth on a temporary basis. It won't be any problem from there to take an army patrol and go search western Kansas and the gold digs."

"But what about the wedding?" Maude whimpered. She had obviously been looking forward to her role as maid of honor.

Summer had already been annoyed with Mrs. Shaw over

today's discussions. Austin had wanted to use David as his best man but Elizabeth Shaw was insisting on Todd in that capacity. Austin's mother had just won that round before Mr. Shaw walked in. Summer had begun to have doubts about whether she really wanted to go through with this at all. She felt a mixture of both guilt and relief as she heard Maude's question. She had only felt a little relief that this new calamity might delay the whole thing; now guilt brought a dark cloud to her face.

"Don't worry, Summer," Austin said, evidently misreading her expression. "This won't affect our wedding plans at all. Tomorrow is the first of April and the wedding isn't until the end of June. That's plenty of time to go find Todd and get him back here for the wedding."

The Irish maid puffed back into the room with a glass of water and handed it to Mrs. Shaw. "Here 'tis, missus!"

Elizabeth Shaw didn't even thank her as she took the glass and sipped it. "But the Indians! Suppose, like Maude says, the Indians have gotten Todd?"

Angela looked around at all the people, the big cat in her arms. "Summer knows the Indians well enough to bargain with them and she speaks the language, too."

All faces turned toward Summer. "Well," she began uncertainly, "I do speak a little Cheyenne, not much. I do know enough sign talk to carry on the barest conversation with many of the plains tribes."

Mr. Shaw turned and eyed her thoughtfully, his hands clasped behind his back. "Didn't you say that area was Cheyenne country?"

"Yes, but—"

"That's it!" Mrs. Shaw leaped to her feet. "That's the answer! You can accompany Austin and the patrol to look for Todd!"

"Now, Mother." Austin cleared his throat and pulled out his

pipe nervously. He acted as if he might put it in his mouth, looked at all the ladies, returned it to his pocket. "Now, Mother," he said again, "I don't think taking Summer out there is a good idea at all! After all, she's had a terrible ordeal in the West and it would almost be like reliving it to return to that area—"

"I really wouldn't mind," Summer said quickly, remembering how much she had loved the wild country. She would like to see it one more time, inquire after the safety of the others of the tribe before she closed the door forever on that part of her past. "If it will be of any assistance in helping find Todd, I'll be happy to go along and do what I can."

"But you just can't go off out there unchaperoned!" Maude declared dramatically. "Think of your reputation!"

"I don't like your insinuation!" Austin flushed. "I would never do anything ungentlemanly or even think such!"

No, he wouldn't, Summer sighed, thinking wistfully of the uncontrolled passion of another man.

"I've got an idea that should solve everyone's problem." Mother suddenly entered into the conversation with a gleam in her eyes. "I'm sure Silas will agree to let her go if we send Mrs. O'Malley along to look after her and chaperone."

"May the saints preserve us!" The Irish maid's eyes rolled heavenward and she crossed herself.

"Well, it's settled then." Mr. Shaw rubbed his hands together with obvious satisfaction. "Just as soon as I can make arrangements, the three of you will be leaving for Fort Leavenworth!"

Summer shivered in spite of herself, feeling excitement tempered with a sense of danger. She wanted to return one more time but she wasn't at all sure the Cheyenne would be glad to see her if their paths crossed.

"Start packing, Mrs. O'Malley," she said, trying not to look too excited though her heart pounded. But in her mind, there was a trace of sadness as it went back to that terrible October day the cavalry had attacked the camp.

Chapter Twenty-Three

Ohahyaa! Ohahyaa! The wailing cries of grief rang out all around Gray Dove. She looked about at the destruction and the soldiers riding out that October morn. Death and destruction reigned as tepees blazed and wounded horses tried to rise, and, failing, lay there kicking and neighing pitifully.

But there were too many human dead to think of wounded horses. Sadly, the survivors dug through the wreckage. A new, trilling cry went up each time they found another body or one seriously wounded among their friends and relatives.

Gray Dove stood numbly, watching her own tepee burn, knowing her own father and two brothers must still be in there. When the fire went out, she found them with the empty whiskey bottles beneath them. Probably they had been in such a drunken state they never knew what was happening as the cavalry charged into the camp. But they had been dead to her long before today. *The white man's liquor had taken them a long, long time before*, she thought bitterly. Gray Dove stood and looked at the charred bodies without tears. A small child wandered past her, shrieking for its mother but she did not bother to comfort or help it.

All she could think of now was Iron Knife. Turning, she ran toward his tepee, the wail of women and the terrible smell of burning flesh stinging her nostrils.

She could almost taste the rage of her betrayal. Jake

Dallinger had been responsible for this, trailing her back to camp instead of meeting her at the old fort as she had planned. She hadn't been so smart after all. *He was even more cunning and evil than she was herself,* she thought grimly as she ran through the smoldering camp.

His tepee still stood undamaged but he lay crumpled his back before it.

"Iron Knife!" she screamed. "Iron Knife! Are you alive?"

He did not answer and desperately she knelt at his side. He seemed to be breathing shallowly and there was a large, bloody wound gaping in his shoulder. *Someone had probably been aiming for the heart and missed.* Frantically, she tried to drag him inside the tepee, out of the cool air, but he was too big for her to move alone. She found Lance Bearer and another warrior helping Two Arrows, who was slightly wounded. They helped her drag Iron Knife into his lodge. Pony Woman and Pretty Flower Woman stayed to help the other, while Clouds Above went in search of the medicine man.

Quickly, Gray Dove washed the wound and covered him with warm buffalo robes. The old man entered with his bag of medicines and charms.

"Many have been wounded or killed!" the old man sighed as he opened the bundle. "The smell of death is everywhere!"

"Can you save this warrior?" She hovered anxiously. "I will give you any ponies I have left of my father's herd if you will help!"

"I will do all I can because I am a friend of this Dog Soldier and knew his father well. But think not of ponies since the army has run off all but a few stragglers."

He got out his rattles and medicines, spread white sage on the tepee floor.

Iron Knife opened his eyes as the old man stopped the bleeding and began his singsong chants, shaking the rattle over the wound. "What happened?" he asked weakly, and, seeming to remember, tried to get to his feet. "My lance! Give me my knife!"

Gray Dove restrained him gently, relieved that he was strong enough to resist. "Rest easy, big warrior, the soldiers are gone now."

But he struggled to get up. "We'll want to ride after them and attack—"

"There are no horses left to ride," Gray Dove said, taking his big hand in hers. "And most of the warriors are too hurt to fight—"

"My family!" He struggled to get up.

"They're alive," she reassured him. "Lie still!"

"Summer!" he gasped, struggled up on one elbow. "Summer Sky! Where is she?"

Gray Dove gritted her teeth so hard she hurt with the jealousy that consumed her. *Would she never heard the end of the white bitch?* "That one has gone with the soldiers!" she informed him. "She is no longer in this camp!"

"Summer . . ." Tears came to his eyes and he swore white man's curses. "I thought she loved me! I never thought she would leave!"

Gray Dove pushed him down and ran her hand gently across his scarred face. "Remember this! It is I who have loved you without limits all these years! I would never ride away with the soldiers and desert you!"

"The white priest!" he gasped. "I told her he might betray the Cheyenne and go to the fort! I was going to warn the old chiefs to move the camp this morning!"

She hardly dared hope as she stroked his face and watched the old medicine man work his charms. "You knew the girl talked to the priest?"

He closed his eyes almost as if he could not believe what had happened. "She said she had asked him to do the white marriage vows for us. It must be him who brought the soldiers. Who else could it be?"

She almost smiled to herself at her luck and moved in to take advantage of his confused thinking. "She probably didn't ask him about marriage, she probably lied to you! No doubt what she did was ask him to send the soldiers for her. Remember this, you can trust my love as you could never trust a white girl's. She has not only betrayed you to the soldiers, but in doing so brought death and destruction down on your people!"

He drifted into unconsciousness, still protesting weakly. "I thought she loved me . . . She said she would never bring trouble to my people. . . ."

"Sleep, my love," she whispered. "There is no reason for the soldiers to return. They got what they came for."

"The horses," he whispered. "Did they get my stallion and the little mare called Starfire?"

The mare he had brought as a gift to the other girl, she thought savagely, but she only said, "Yes, they are both gone as is most of the herd. Maybe sometime when all the men are recovered, they can raid the fort and get back some of the horses."

"Summer . . ." he whispered faintly over the medicine man's chants. "Summer, where are you? I need you. . . ."

Gray Dove stayed by his side as he drifted off to sleep. She felt no guilt or shame in letting him think the white girl and the kindly priest had betrayed the Indians. She felt only a sense of relief that she was covering her own tracks, knowing how vengeful the Cheyenne could be to a traitor. She had meant to get rid of her rival and it was only Jake Dallinger who had complicated things. She grimaced angrily, thinking of his trickery, of the reward he had done her out of. If she ever got a chance, she would deal with the cunning scout.

She never left Iron Knife's side all night sitting there cramped and cold. Without sleep, she watched his face, willing him to live, holding water to his fevered lips when he moaned.

Outside, the trilling for the dead continued through the night as dogs howled and searched through the wreckage for a scrap to eat. But the people were too cold and hungry to think of dogs. Most of the dried meat for the winter, the buffalo robes, and tepees had been burned by the soldiers.

In desperation, to keep the big warrior alive, she took a haunch off a dead pony and cooked it, spooning it between his lips. But she dare not tell him what it was. Horses were like brothers to the Cheyenne and they would not eat such meat unless they were starving. They were not like the Kiowa, the

411

Dotaine, who relished the taste of horse meat and thought it a delicacy.

Within a day, the camp took on some semblance of order and those who were not hurt gathered up a few horses and went hunting. The tepees and clothing that were not burned were shared generously by all. The dead could not be wrapped ceremoniously for lack of robes. They were taken out to high burial scaffolds with few possessions.

Old Scalp Taker was among the dead, shot in the chest. His body, in the bloody scalp shirt, and a few prized possessions were placed on the scaffold on a windswept hill. Had he been killed far away on a war party, his body would have been left where it fell as was the custom. But now he was carried up to the hilltop followed by the shaman and grieving friends and relatives to be left forever between earth and sky.

The shaman sang, *"Ma Ka mai yo tsim an stom ai,"* over and over, meaning "Great Spirit-making Maker!" as the people following along entreated Heammawihio in behalf of the fierce old chief who had served his people long and well.

One of the fine remaining horses was led beneath the death scaffold and killed so he might go with the dead man. "Go, Little Brother!" The shaman gave instructions to the pony as he stabbed it. "Go carry the warrior up the Hanging Road to the sky where buffalo run plentiful and free so the brave chief may chase them through the clouds forever! *Ohahyaa! Ohahyaa!"*

Old Scalp Taker's second wife and daughters slashed their legs and cut their hair short to show their grief. His old first wife did all that and sacrificed two of her fingers with a sharp knife to display her sorrow.

The trilling sounds of grief went on for days as the dead were gathered and placed on scaffolds. It seemed to Gray Dove as she listened that the wailing went on forever. Even as she kept constant vigil by Iron Knife's bed, she could hear it through the night and it awakened her. She was uneasy that the people might learn who was responsible. Many among the Arapaho had lost loved ones, too, and they would thirst for revenge

412

almost as much as the Cheyenne.

One of Pretty Flower Woman's brothers had been shot through the hand by a soldier and the bones shattered. When Gray Dove saw it, she knew he could die since the Cheyenne did not practice amputation. What good was a badly crippled man to either himself or his tribe in this hard struggle for survival?

The hand was treated with the medicines available and chants sung over it. Then they could only wait and watch his brave, stoic face grow gaunt with suffering. Soon red streaks ran from the wound up the arm and it began to fester and smell.

Seeing his face as he sat quietly, Gray Dove knew he suffered great agony. But he did not cry out for such was not the way of the tribe. Word went through the camp that he had called in his older brother and asked him to take the grieving young wife and children as his own so they would not starve.

Finally, the young warrior's jaws seemed frozen in place and he could not open them in that mystery Gray Dove knew the whites called "lockjaw." His grieving little wife tried to spoon broth between his teeth. But at last, he wrapped himself in his blanket, turned his face to the back of the tepee, and died. After his body was taken to a burial scaffold, the tepee was torched because he had died there. His belongings were given away and his sad little family moved to become part of the older brother's brood.

Days passed and the weather grew colder. It was long past time for the camp to be moved but the lances of the Mahohewas, the Red Shields, were still taken down each morning. There were too many badly injured to be moved even though they might be in danger of a second attack if the soldiers decided to return. But who knew what the whites were thinking?

Two Arrows recovered and all three of the men of that family toiled hard at the hunting to keep the camp supplied with meat since there were many hurt. Pony Woman and Pretty Flower Woman tried to check on the big Dog Soldier, but Gray Dove kept her vigil jealously and wouldn't let them do anything. No task was beneath her in caring for him and she worked possessively, washing his muscular body and cleansing the wound. *No woman would touch him again but herself*, she vowed, *and someday he would recognize and appreciate her devotion.*

Sometimes as she washed his fevered body with cool water, she wondered at the scars on his back. The sun dance marks and old wounds from his many battles were common. What mystified her were the scars on his back and face like those made with a lash. Gray Dove had loved him from the first moment she had seen him as a young warrior riding into that fort in Nebraska so many years ago. But of his past among the whites, she knew nothing except what everyone knew of the stolen girl, Texanna. Something terrible had happened to him to drive him back to the Cheyenne but that had happened before she first saw him.

Day after day, she sponged his fevered face and spooned food into his mouth. At night, often, he moaned and muttered, but she crawled under the robe and held him close to quiet him and whispered, "It will be all right, my love. I am here and I will never leave you."

He would mutter and pull her to him and cry out, "I thought you had left me! Don't go! Don't leave me!"

Gray Dove knew he thought of the white girl, but as she pulled him against her and warmed him with her body, she was satisfied. He could not love a ghost forever when he thought the yellow-haired one had betrayed him. Only once in all these ten years had she managed to tempt him into making love to her and that had been a long time ago. As a young warrior, he had tried the firewater once and he was almost senseless in the grass when she followed him there in the darkness and offered her body. He had taken her like any male animal might take a female; not knowing or caring, she thought. And the caring made all the difference in the world between lust and love. She'd had the one from him, now she hungered as always for the other.

Gradually, his mind and his strength seemed to return to

him and with it a great sadness so that he sat and stared into the fire without speaking.

Gray Dove did not mourn her dead father and brothers since they mistreated her when they drank and worked her hard to get more money for whiskey. As far as she was concerned, all the family she had had died when the Pawnee had attacked the little party up on the Platte.

Finally, one morning Iron Knife seemed strong enough to walk about the camp and watch the preparations that were being made to move the band. When he returned to the tepee, he breathed heavily as he came in and sat down.

"Rest!" she commanded him. "You are not strong enough yet to move too much and it will be awhile before you are fully recovered. Here," she thrust a bowl of warm stew in his hands, "I have made food for you."

He took the bowl and looked at her a long moment. "You have been very kind," he said finally. "Everyone says I owe my life to your care."

She shrugged. "Have you ever doubted how much I think of you? I have waited a long time to show you my devotion and love."

He sighed. "It is good for a warrior to have a woman for his tepee. I thought Summer Sky loved me as I loved and trusted her, but I suppose I was wrong."

"Of course you were wrong!" She almost snapped at him for mentioning the other's name. "I would never betray you and go off with the whites. That is what you get for trusting those of the pale skin when they have demonstrated time and again they are unworthy of trust. You are Cheyenne, Iron Knife, and you should remember that and not put your faith in any white at all!"

He looked at her a long moment. "No doubt you are right, although my heart does not want to believe it. I do not know what to do to demonstrate how grateful I am to you." He finished his stew and set the bowl aside.

"Do you not?" She set her own bowl down and reached out to touch his cheek. "I have no relatives left, no place to go. I am at the mercy of any man who will offer me shelter and food."

He reached out and caught her hand, looking into her eyes. "I suppose I owe you that much, although I cannot promise my whole heart."

She moved close to him and saw the sudden need in his eyes. "I am willing to gamble that I can change all that, make you really care for me."

He was close enough that she could feel his breath on her cheek. "I have been all these weeks without a woman."

In answer, she took his hand and placed it on her full breast. "And I have not had a man all this time I have cared for you," she whispered. "Let me pleasure you so that you will think of no other. I can take you in my arms and wipe the memory of anyone else from your mind."

She ran her hand lightly across his hardening manhood. He gasped softly and reached up to tangle his hand in her ebony braids, pulling her hard against him.

Eagerly, she opened her lips to his, taking his tongue in her mouth as she had always wanted to take his manhood. His mouth searched hers in a passion so savage, she tasted blood. Savagery always excited her and she responded by stroking his throbbing manparts. She felt a growing wetness between her thighs, signaling her own body's hunger and need.

His hand went down to stroke her there, and she opened her thighs to his touch, willing him to touch her yet deeper in her innermost being. But she was too hungry for him and she could not stop herself from arching against his hand as her body surrendered to the touch of his fingers. She tried to hold back but she couldn't stop herself as she gasped and shuddered in a frenzy of passion.

Her reaching the pinnacle of desire seemed to drive him wild. "Why didn't you wait for me?" Savagely, he ripped the front of her deerskin shift and her breasts spilled out like ripe fruit to his hungry mouth.

Eagerly, she clasped her arms around his dark head, clasping his face against her breasts as she arched against him. His lips were hot and wet on the dark circles of her nipples and there was nothing gentle about him at all.

"I want you!" he gasped. "My body is eager for yours!"

"You will have me, my darling! Now and as often as you need me!"

He had said nothing about love, but she knew that his desire for her might sometime turn to love. Now she was satisfied to be able to drive the small white bitch from his mind. Gray Dove knew there was no one as skilled at dealing with a man's passions as she was.

His hungry mouth nursed her breasts until she was shaking at the touch of his tongue, wanting his body to invade hers.

Roughly he pushed her down on her back, shoving her thighs apart with brusque, violent moves. Somehow, she had expected he would be a gentle lover, but he took her now with almost a vengeance. But it was enough to her that she lay in his arms. He rode her with a savage intensity that told her there was nothing but lust in his mind. Still, she knew that as skilled as she was at mating, he could be thinking of nothing but her as she tilted herself up so she could take his full length. No man had ever been so virile and powerful and she did not mind too much when he bit her lips instead of kissing them.

Feverishly, she ran her hands over his scarred back as she spread her thighs even farther, wanting to take his seed deep in her womb so she might give him a son. Surely, a man could not keep from loving a woman who gave him that.

Never had she known such ecstasy as he filled her and drove home hard again and again. She arched herself against his sinewy body and reached up to brush his nipples with her warm lips. Then she could not stop herself and she was soaring in her passion like riding a dream stallion in a rush across the clouds with the wind blowing wild and free against her naked body.

She never wanted to come down from that surging peak, but as she returned to consciousness she felt him begin his rise to passion and he drove into her hard. She dug her nails into his rippling back and knew with satisfaction that she had driven thoughts of any other from his mind as she took his virile seed.

But as he came, he whispered, "Summer! Summer! I love

417

you so much! Don't ever leave me again!"

Heya! She had never been so furious! No man had ever made love to her and called out another's name. Trembling with uncontrolled rage, she rolled out from under him and stood, pulling the torn remnants of her dress together.

"I save your life, care for you without ceasing, and you return my love by calling out the white bitch's name as you make love to me!"

He half raised from the pallet and held up a placating hand to her. "I am sorry to hurt you. I never meant to. But surely you must have realized that only she held control of my heart!"

"How could you?" she wept with jealous rage. "I thought I could at least push her from your mind during lovemaking!"

He stood slowly, adjusted his breechcloth. "I never lied to you, Gray Dove. You took advantage of my need for a woman when otherwise I would not have touched you. Summer Sky will never be completely gone from my heart."

Iron Knife tried to reach out to her, but she slapped at his hands furiously and backed away. She was past caring about anything, only wanting to hurt him as he had hurt her.

"Can you understand now why I was so desperate to get her out of this camp? Why I tricked her into leaving and sent Angry Wolf after her to kill her?"

He looked at her almost as if he didn't comprehend what she was saying. "You were responsible for Summer's first escape? You sent Angry Wolf after her?"

"Men are so stupid!" She threw back her head and laughed viciously. "Yes, it was me! I hated the white girl so much, I plotted to get her out of the camp when you were gone hunting! All I could think of was how much I hated the thought of her in your arms and would do anything: You hear me? *Anything* to get her out of this camp!"

She saw the sudden, stunned look of realization cross his face as he stared at her. "Then you, Gray Dove, you are the one who betrayed this camp and brought the soldiers, aren't you?"

"Yes! Yes!" she raged, not caring any more that he knew. "I told her I would help her leave and she told me that she loved

418

you and intended to stay with the Cheyenne forever and be your woman! You look so shocked!" She sneered. "Did you not realize how much she loved you? That she would never have left your side?"

He advanced on her and she saw the anger in his face. She was past caring about anything but her revenge in hurting him with her slashing words. "Yes, it was me who went to the fort and told the soldiers! But I was tricked and followed back to camp by the scout, Jake Dallinger!"

He swayed on his feet with the impact of her words and she saw rage in his eyes such as she had never seen before on a man's face. "You have turned the woman I love over to a man called Jake Dallinger?" His hands grabbed her throat. "For this one thing alone, I will kill you!"

For a long moment, as his fingers tightened in furious passion on her neck, she did not even care if she died. Without his love, life was nothing to her. But she was a survivor and her primeval instincts took over. She fought for her life as she stumbled backward out of the tepee, not seeing the curious faces of the others outside.

"Kill me!" she gasped as she fought to break the steel grip of his fingers on her neck. "Kill me! If I could do it again, I would still bring the soldiers to take the white bitch away!"

She started blacking out as he choked her. She struggled, trying to break his grip as he gradually cut off the life-giving air. Never had she seen such a murderous rage on a man's face and she knew he would not stop until he killed her.

Dimly, she could feel people pulling him away from her, breaking his grip. Gasping for air, she fell on her knees and realized that in her jealous fury she had told all.

She looked up into a growing crowd of hostile Cheyenne and Arapaho faces.

Old Blue Eagle stared down at her. "Is this true what you say? Was it you who betrayed us to the soldiers?"

She tried to deny it but as the faces around her grew more hostile, she knew her guilt must be written in her eyes and many had heard her incriminating words.

"Turn her over to the grieving women," Blue Eagle ordered. "They will know how to deal with her!"

Helplessly, she looked around for a friendly face, but saw only angry ones. Voices called out for revenge for the death and destruction she had brought. Almost, then, she told of what she suspected of the death of Angry Wolf. But she loved Iron Knife still and because of this, she did not tell as she faced the hostile crowd defiantly.

The women attacked her with sticks and quirts and she struggled to fight them off as they ran her through the camp like a cur dog gone mad. She threw up her arms to protect her face but the hard blows rained down. As she stumbled and fell, she began to lose consciousness and could feel the deep bruises and the blood running sticky down her body. But still she fought, for she would not die easily.

Then she heard Iron Knife's voice. "Enough!" he ordered. "This is a dirty business! It turns my stomach to watch even one such as this being beaten to death. She has saved my life and now I ask you to spare hers so we will be even and I will feel obligated to her no more!"

The young widow of Pretty Flower Woman's brother cried out, "You are right. It is too easy to kill her! Let us send her into exile instead so she can know all the anguish and the loneliness she has visited on this camp!"

There was a chorus of agreement. "Yes! Exiling is more hurtful than death! Send her out of this camp!" A straggly, thin pony was brought forward and someone picked her up roughly, threw her upon it.

"Leave this camp!" Old Blue Eagle ordered. "And never show your face among the Cheyenne-Arapaho again! You are banished from our camps forever!"

"But how shall I live?" she gasped, holding to the horse's mane to keep from falling off. "I have no people save these!"

"Then you have no people at all," the old chief said with finality. "You are now a dead person to us."

The young widow pushed forward. "Yes, go to the whites! Maybe you can be one of them, for you are no longer one of us!

420

If you ever try to come back, the women will not be stopped again from torturing you to death!"

So saying, she struck the horse hard with her quirt. It bolted and galloped wildly from the camp with Gray Dove hanging on for her life. The pony ran a long way before it tired and slowed to a walk.

She tried to decide what to do. Word would go out to all ten bands and their comrades, the Arapaho, too. She would not be welcome in any camp. Exile was usually a death sentence since no one could survive against cold, hunger, and their many enemies alone.

She would go to the whites. They had accepted her long ago and she had nowhere else to go. And if she got a chance at the fort, she intended to kill her rival, Summer Sky, and the white man who had betrayed her and brought her trouble. Now she remembered the reward money that Jake Dallinger owed her. She thought she might survive if she could insist he give her that money.

It took more than two days to ride to Fort Smith. She did not think she would make it as she shivered through the cold and her body ached with green and purple bruises. All that kept her going was her strong sense of survival and her thirst for revenge. If she got a chance, she would kill the white girl and Jake Dallinger.

When she finally arrived it was almost dusk. She sent the sentry looking for Jake, telling him she would be at the scout's quarters.

Limping into the tiny room, she looked around. The room was a mess, clothes and gear piled everywhere. Obviously, the scout was going somewhere.

He entered just then, acting happy to see her. "Wal, if it ain't the purty little squaw!" Peering at her more closely, he swore under his breath. "What happened to you, gal? Looks like someone tried to beat you to death!"

She reached into her clothes for the small knife she always carried. "Because of you! Because of your raiding the camp, I have been thrown away by my own people!" She tried to attack

421

him but she didn't move fast enough. He grabbed her arm and they struggled for a moment over possession of the knife.

But it was no contest. He twisted her arm cruelly as he took the knife from her and, opening the door, tossed it outside. Then he slapped her, throwing her backward on the bed. She held her throbbing arm and whimpered as he grinned down at her. "Don't ever pull a knife unless yore sure you can use it and don't give no warning first! If you hadn't given me such a good tumble in the hay last time you was here, I'd have made you eat that blade!"

She lay on the bed, helpless in her pain and rage. "You are rotten! You tricked me by following me back to the camp and needlessly attacked and killed my people! You are as ruthless and cunning as the lean lobo wolf that runs down the baby deer and tears its heart out before it is even dead!"

He leered at her. "That makes us two of a kind, don't it, honey? Neither of us ever lets scruples get in the way of what we want! Why did you come here, anyways?"

"The white girl!" she snarled. "I came to kill her!"

The big man laughed and slapped his leg. "If you ain't something! She's already gone, missy, gone on the train, the Iron Horse, understand? Has been since a couple of days after the raid! Matter of fact, I'm leavin' at dawn tomorrow myself. You almost missed me."

"You are leaving?" She sat up on the bed. "I have no place to go now, take me with you."

He sat down on a corner of the chest by the bed and lit a cigar. "Why should I?" he asked coldly. "I'm bein' sent up to Fort Leavenworth because of all the trouble in Kansas. The army's tryin' to keep peace until Congress decides whether it's gonna be a slave state or free."

"But I have no place to go! No money!" She held up her hand to him appealingly. "You promised me a hundred-dollar reward and then you tricked me!"

"Don't ever trust nobody who's as rotten as you are yourself." He blew smoke toward her. "I got the reward okay; got it right here." He pulled a strange little leather pouch from his vest, then put it back.

"Why didn't you wait?" she raged. "I would have brought the girl to the fort!"

He laughed easily and scratched his dirty beard. "Maybe you would, maybe you wouldn't! But the army couldn't take the chance that something might go wrong and we'd miss a chance to rescue the little bitch! She was a beauty, all right! I can see why the brave didn't want to give her up. She musta thought plenty of him, too! I had to fight her to get her out of there!"

She glowered at him. "What is it all men seem to see in that white girl?"

He took a deep, thoughtful puff on the cigar. "Wal, she's a purty thing, but that ain't it. There's lots of good-lookin' women out there." He blew smoke toward the ceiling. "No, that weren't it! She had a strange combination of softness and steel to her, a conflictin' mix of innocence and passion that would make a man give up a front seat in hell just to have her love him once!"

She pouted. "I thought you liked my body!"

"I do, honey, I do!" he said soothingly. "But you ain't been innocent since you was a baby! There's no mystery, no interesting contradiction to you at all! Hell, if you had as many pricks stickin' out of you as have been stuck in you, you'd look like a west Texas cactus!"

She decided to bargain. "You talked of going to the gold fields once, I want to go there with you."

"Gawd Almighty! Not in the wintertime!" He shook his shaggy head and snuffed out the cigar with his boot. "It's cold up there! What I got in mind is lay around Fort Leavenworth and take off next spring when the weather warms up. Then's a good time to fleece them miners."

She looked at him and took a deep breath so her big breasts swelled against the ragged buckskin. "Take me with you to Fort Leavenworth, then."

She could see him looking at her breasts as he licked his lips ever so slowly. "You'd be a lot of trouble to take along, although I could probably make a little money off you among

423

the soldiers up there. Reckon you're so bruised up right now, men might not hanker much for you."

She reached out, took one of his big hands, putting it inside the torn dress where it could cup the soft swell. "Can you look at me now, hurt as I am and not hunger for me? Have you forgotten what it was like with me?"

She felt his hand close and squeeze cruelly. "You're a hot little piece, okay," he admitted grudgingly. "I reckon in time you'd heal up and lonely soldiers would pay me good to hump you."

Without removing his hand, he moved to sit on the edge of the bed. "You'd be a real drawin' card all dressed up in my saloon if they thought you was a Spanish duchess or something like that Lola Montez who created such a ruckus in Californy." He ran his hand from her breast down her belly and she smiled at him invitingly.

Gray Dove eased onto her back and pulled at him. "Let me show you how grateful I could be for your taking me to Kansas with you."

"Let's see how grateful you are!" he challenged and she pulled open the front of her torn dress, revealing her full, big breasts. With a muttered gasp, he buried his shaggy face in her bosom while she glanced over to the cast iron bootjack laying on the bedside chest. It was what white men called a "naughty lady," shaped so that the boot heel went between her cast iron legs. *That would do nicely,* she thought coldly, regretting the fact that Jake had thrown her knife outside.

Letting him nuzzle her like a greedy baby, she looked about the room and saw his coiled big whip lying by his things. One misstep and he would probably beat her to death. She could make no mistake.

"Take me with you," she whispered in his ear while he pawed her body and she unbuttoned his shirt. "Think how I can warm your bed all winter and keep your clothes washed and cook for you!"

"Missy, I'm not sure I can turn down your offer. It's beginnin' to make sense."

Slowly she unbuttoned his shirt, running her fingertips over the matted fur of his bearlike chest. The hair repelled her, for she thought of a big, dirty animal. Indian men's bodies were almost hairless, as were their faces.

His slick, wet mouth made slimy trails across her bruised skin as he mouthed her nipples. "Honey, you shore do make a convincin' argument. I believe I will load you up and take you along!"

"I would be very grateful!" she breathed into his ear. Running her tongue deep inside, she felt him gasp and shiver.

He threw her across the bed and his face was flushed with passion. He jerked open his pants and took her, not even bothering to take his pants off, and the big metal belt buckle cut cruelly into her torn flesh. She whimpered in protest but that only seemed to excite him more, made him more brutal.

"I love it when I hurt you!" he gasped. "And I like it even more when you hurt me! Hurt me some more!"

She needed no encouragement as she raked his back and sides with her nails until she could feel the fresh blood wet on his skin.

He drove into her hard, cutting and bruising her lush body with the hard belt buckle. The more she whimpered in pain, the more excited he became. She enjoyed clawing him and biting his lips until they bled since there was an anger that only hurting him could fulfill.

She let him ride her with savage abandon although she cringed at the pain he caused her injuries. He gasped as she dug her nails hard into his hips. As he shuddered and went into climax, she reached for the bootjack. The lesson the Pawnee had taught her she would never forget. In that split second when Jake Dallinger was rigid and helpless in her arms, she grabbed the Naughty Lady. He never knew what hit him as she brought it down with a crash.

He collapsed on her body with a grunt and she slid out from under him. Repairing her clothing, she looked at the unconscious man with satisfaction. "Don't ever trust nobody who's as ruthless as you are yourself." She echoed Jake's words with a mirthless grin as she looked down at him.

It would be hours before he came to life again. Gray Dove had a terrible urge to go get her knife and stab him to death, then she reconsidered. If she killed the scout, the army would come looking for her because the sentry had seen her. If, on the other hand, she only knocked him out and robbed him, he wouldn't tell anyone because he would look the fool. Other men would laugh at him since it happened often enough on Saturday night in the saloons.

"Filthy dog!" She spat on the limp form as she used all her strength to turn him on his side so she could reach the vest. There was more money in the pouch than expected and it dawned on her the reward had been bigger than he had told her. There was $250 in the leather pouch. She took the gold and hid it in her clothing, throwing the pouch down.

Now that she had the money, she didn't need Jake Dallinger. He had told her everything she needed to know to start her own pleasure palace up in the Colorado gold country. It wouldn't be much at first, but with the love-starved men up there, she could quickly add to her money and hire more girls to work for her. With fine clothes and paint like the white saloon girls wore, the Arapaho girl, Gray Dove, was about to disappear forever to be replaced by a high-class Spanish madam. Stopping to pick up her small knife, she rode out of the fort unnoticed.

Darkness spread like velvet across the hilly forest and it was a very long way to the Rockies for an injured woman alone. But she was a survivor and she had not come through all this to die along the trail. Shivering in the damp cold, she rode northeast, listening to the small screech owls in the shadowy woods and thinking of the *mistai*, the ghosts who walked about.

Her mind went again and again to Iron Knife. She would always love him and she knew she would probably never see him again. The memory of his angry face came to her. She remembered now how he had kept them from killing her and stared after her in rage as she was driven from the camp.

Chapter Twenty-Four

Iron Knife had stood watching in fury as the vindictive women quirted Gray Dove's horse and drove her from the Cheyenne camp. He felt no compassion for her. The horse galloped into the trees and was lost to view.

"Are there enough horses left in camp at all to make up a small war party?" he asked.

Lance Bearer gave him a troubled look. "There are a few horses, but I am not sure the old chiefs will approve of a war party. We are trying to leave for the Big Timber country right away before the soldiers return. The revenge is not worth what it will cost us in lives. Forget about the white girl. If she loved you, she would have returned or never left. Take a girl to wife from one of our own or from the Arapaho."

Iron Knife shook his head. "I want only her light skin and hair like pale gold."

His cousin frowned. "Then we will hit a ranch somewhere. We'll raid one of those wagon trains that goes near our hunting grounds on the paths the whites call the Santa Fe or the Oregon Trail. I'll help you steal another white girl or maybe two if you want them."

"No, I want none but Summer Sky," he sighed. "And I ride to the fort, not only to bring her back to me where she belongs, but to take revenge that scout owes me from long ago."

427

Two Arrows joined in the conversation. "There is only one good reason to ride to the fort," he said logically, "at least, only one the old chiefs would approve. The bluecoats drove away nearly all our horses and we must have more to pull the travois and carry the people when we leave for the Big Timbers. Let us go talk to the old chiefs and see if they will consent to a raid to get back the stolen horses!"

The old chiefs did consent for that reason. It was the next day before the war party could be readied and it was not a very large group that rode toward Fort Smith. Many were dead or still too injured to ride. Near the fort, they located the stolen pony herd and saw no guards around it.

"The soldiers do not expect us after they have raided us so savagely." Iron Knife sat his borrowed black gelding easily. "But I do not see my spotted Appaloosa stallion in that herd."

From their position on a small rise, his eyes searched in vain but he did see the little chestnut mare, Starfire.

"Summer is here!" he trilled with excitement.

But the small boy they sent in to beg at the fort so he might spy for them reported back differently when he returned through the early November frost.

"The white girl has been gone a long time from what the soldiers say," the boy informed him. "They have put her on the Iron Horse and sent her back to her people."

Iron Knife's spirits fell. He would never see her again. "And the scout? I will kill him for his part in this as well as what I already owe him." He patted the big knife in his belt.

The child shook his head. "He is also gone. The Great White Father had him sent farther north and he took your stallion with him. Gray Dove has been here, too, but she left. But she did not leave with the white man."

Iron Knife swore bitterly in the white man's tongue. Anguish twisted his insides until he almost cried out at the knowledge he had lost Summer Sky. It was salt in the wound that Jake Dallinger had had a hand in this and added insult to injury by stealing his beloved stallion.

428

"We will attack the fort anyway!" he cried. "And then we will ride after this scout and try to find him so I may kill him!"

His cousins exchanged glances and Lance Bearer said, "No, we will not do this thing. The girl and the man are both gone from here. There is no reason for our small group to attack the fort since we can easily steal the ponies back without fighting bad odds."

He touched Iron Knife's arm gently. "Someday, you may cross this man's path and take revenge. But now we must put the People first. That means we take the horses and ride out of the Indian Territory and on toward our mountain hunting grounds as fast as we can!"

"You are right, of course," Iron Knife agreed grimly. "The survival of the Cheyenne means more than either love or revenge! We will wait until dark to raid the ponies and by the time the soldiers realize what has happened, we will be on our way back to our camp."

And that was the way it was. The Cheyenne moved like a swift whirlwind in the darkness. There was great confusion and shooting, but the Cheyenne lost not a man. Now they drove the thundering pony herd ahead of them in the night and the victory was sweet in the mouth.

When they reached the encampment, the band was waiting for them with tepees already down and travois loaded. On that morning the lances of the Red Shields did not come down and they pointed the way northwest as the tribe moved out. As always, the Dog Soldiers brought up the rear, expecting that any time they would have to fight a delaying action and give up their lives to the avenging soldiers.

But the soldiers did not come. *Perhaps they weren't sure which Indians were to blame,* Iron Knife thought. Maybe they thought the ponies were not worth the trouble. But the People were afraid to linger, to camp along the trail. Who knew when the soldiers would decide to follow? The only thing that gave him pleasure as he left the memories behind and started northwest was the little mare. She nickered and raised her pretty ears. Because they were short on mounts, he put four children on her back.

Makhikomini, the month of the big, freezing moon the whites knew as December, would be here before they could ride all the way to the Rockies. The winds turned cold as the tribe set its march across that desolate waste of the panhandle the whites called No Man's Land.

It was already too late into the winter season to move the camp. But they were afraid to stay where the soldiers had attacked them, afraid the soldiers might attack again. They hoped to be fortunate enough to make it to the Colorado area of the Shining Mountains before the first blizzard caught them.

They almost made it all the way before Hoimaha, the Old Man All White who brings the cold from the north, blew in on his churning snow clouds with his frosty breath.

They were so close to safety, and yet so far as they fought their way through the drifts and abandoned most of their gear and anyone who could not keep up. All that mattered was moving forward. Several old people fell in exhaustion and were left to die because there were not enough travois and the northern movement could not be stopped. To the northwest lay shelter with the other clans among the foothills of the Rockies and, at all costs, the tribe must survive.

A baby was born in the howling snow and died in the cold. Its father had been one of those killed by the soldiers. The baby's widowed mother placed it among the rocks and gently covered it with her shawl. But Pony Woman took the shawl from the small body and shook her head. "We cannot afford even this small luxury," she said with a sob, and she took the shawl and wrapped it about a still living baby who shivered with cold.

Iron Knife helped the woman cover the tiny body with stones so that the hungry coyotes would not get it. Then he gave the woman his horse and buffalo robe and pretended not to see the tears freezing on her face. As he staggered through

430

the snow, leading the horse, he thought of another time, another dead baby. . . .

He did not want to remember Texanna's death, but the howling wind became a baby's plaintive cry in his mind and he could not stop his mind from reliving the tragic drama. . . .

She had less than a year to live that night she had stood off the irate whites with her shotgun to save her son. At the last moment, War Bonnet had galloped in, jerked the two up on his paint stallion, and rode out just ahead of the mob.

War Bonnet had still not taken another wife although his woman had been gone for five years.

Iron Knife smiled a little as he bent against the blizzard, remembering now the joy of their homecoming. The clan had turned out to greet the two, Texanna, and the boy who had been called Falling Star. His laconic, stern father had not given way to emotion until he had them both inside the tepee.

"I have waited and never given up hope," the great chief exclaimed, hugging them to him. "Several times, I have led a war party down to Texas to find my family. But it is such a big country and we never knew where to look. A trapper passing through our camp said he had seen a woman with red-gold hair in the Texas hill country and gave me directions."

Falling Star saw the tears start down Texanna's face and he marveled because she seldom cried.

"It doesn't matter, my love," she whispered as she went into his father's embrace. "All that matters is that we have finally made it back to where we belong and we will never leave you again in this lifetime."

But War Bonnet pulled away, looked down at her with a puzzled frown. "Golden One," he exclaimed. "In the excitement of the rescue, I forgot the new child—"

"A beautiful little girl," Texanna answered sadly, "with a loud wail and a fiery temperament like your own. I called her Cimarron."

War Bonnet nodded, satisfaction on his stern, dark face. "'Wild One'. It is a very good name. But what has happened—?"

"The baby was sick," Texanna answered with regret. "And the angry mob was between me and the child who had been left with the minister and his wife."

The boy apologized to his father. "We did not mean to leave her behind. When we rode out ahead of the mob, there was no time to tell you of her."

"It will be all right," Texanna assured the chief. "The preacher will be kind to her and soon we will sneak back into the town some night and reclaim her. But for now, let us not think of anything but the present and our happiness at having the three of us reunited."

But they had so little time left to them, so little happiness before them. Iron Knife sighed now as he clutched his thin blanket around his shoulders and waded the snow drifts, still leading the horse.

In less than a year from that joyous reunion, Texanna would be dead. In another, War Bonnet would be bleeding his life away in his half-grown son's arms. No one ever got back to Texas to reclaim the small sister. Falling Star had thought of it many times, but when he mentioned it to his uncle, Clouds Above had shaken his head.

"The girl has been with the whites too long to reclaim her now. Her feet are set in the white path and she would never adjust to the Tsistsistas way. Besides, with the Texas Rangers and our Comanche brothers continually fighting each other, and the White Chief in Washington often warring on the Mexicans, it would be hard to slip through and reclaim the girl."

The boy nodded sadly. "What you say is true, my uncle. But someday I must see my small sister again. I have sworn this on the body of my dead mother."

My dead mother. Iron Knife thought of Texanna as he faced into the cold north wind and icy needles stung his face. His feet

432

seemed numb and without feeling, but he knew the band must keep moving. They would all be safe if they could make it to the winter camp near Bent's Fort.

The grieving woman on the horse he led sobbed quietly and he thought of her dead infant, the one who never had a chance against the harsh elements. A small pile of stones back on the trail was the only monument that the tiny being had ever existed except for the pain in its mother's heart.

He sighed as he walked, remembering. They had placed Texanna's dead new baby in her arms when his grieving father placed the Golden One on the burial scaffold. Then they left her on the desolate plains.

Such a little time for love War Bonnet and his mother had had together after the return from the whites, Iron Knife remembered bitterly.

No, he must not be bitter, he reminded himself with a determined shake of his head. Most couples never shared as much love and devotion in a lifetime as his mother and father had shared in those few months between the time she returned and the day she died in childbirth.

Only she needn't have died. Iron Knife gritted his teeth, hating the Pawnee and glad he had brought Bear's Eyes to justice. He had owed it to both his parents.

The weather had been cold the day of the Pawnee attack, too, he recalled now, but Texanna hadn't died of the cold. Most of the men were gone hunting. It was the month of *Mahkohktsiutsi*, the Big Wheel moon the Whites called February, and it was often a hungry time if the hunt was not good. There was no meat in the camp. War Bonnet had led most of the men on a hunt, looking for deer, rabbits, anything to fill many hungry bellies. If no meat were found, they would be forced to eat the horses and this was distasteful to the People. Horses were like brothers.

He remembered now how eager he had been to go on the hunt. But his father had insisted someone must stay behind to look after Texanna who was in her seventh moon of the new baby growing within her.

"But Father," he argued, "I am almost a man. Next season, I shall join the Dog Soldier society. I want to go on the hunt, not stay behind with the women and small children."

War Bonnet smiled from the back of his black and white paint stallion. "No, my son. Someone must stay behind to guard the camp and I leave you the responsibility of my most precious possession."

His eyes went to Texanna who stood looking up at him.

Falling Star frowned. "There is no reason to be on guard. No one, not even the Pawnee, would attack in terrible weather such as this."

"That is the reason to be on guard," his father admonished as he patted the stallion's neck. "The Pawnee sometimes strike when it is least expected. I leave you to guard your mother."

He would never forget the way his father had looked down at Texanna, the way she had looked back up at him. Iron Knife remembered now that she smiled like Mother Earth, glowing with good health and love as she regarded the man.

Iron Knife winced at the memory as he trudged on through the snow.

If only . . . No, it wasn't good to have regrets, to think what might have been differently. His grieving father had said it was not the boy's fault, there was nothing he and the other few guards could have done when the Pawnee rode unexpectedly through the camp in a surprise raid. War Bonnet said over and over that he held his son blameless. But it didn't ease Falling Star's burden of guilt and pain as the two sat beside Texanna's buffalo robe bed and watched her die.

If only . . . he thought again. If only more warriors had been left behind to protect the village, if only those who were there had had more notice that a Pawnee raiding party was on its way . . . If only the hunting party had returned an hour sooner . . .

But by then it was too late for blame, too late for regrets, too late for anything except to sit by Texanna's bed, each of them holding one of her pale hands as she slowly bled to death. The medicine man shook his head and indicated he had done all he knew how to do. Then he left the tepee and went out in the howling storm, leaving the two males to hold vigil over their dying woman.

Her son clasped her hand and watched her shallow breathing that couldn't be heard over the blizzard outside. "It is my fault, Father," he muttered. "You gave me the responsibility. I should have watched after her better—"

"No, my son," War Bonnet said heavily. "It is my fault."

The boy looked at his father's grief-stricken face and thought he had never seen him look so old although the man had only a gray hair or two in his ebony braids.

War Bonnet clasped her other hand and looked down at her pale face. "I should have sent someone else to lead the hunt so I would have been here when the Pawnee dogs rode through . . ."

His voice trailed off and there was no sound save the crackle of the small fire and the wind crying outside. It cried like a small, lost child and Falling Star thought of the new baby brother, the one who would never grow up to love or fight or be a great chief. It had been born too soon and the small one had given only one small cry like the whimpering wind before it gasped feebly and died.

His father shifted positions, running a finger tenderly across Texanna's cheek.

"Was it Bear's Eyes who led the Pawnee carrion?"

"I think so," the boy answered. "They came in so fast. We had no warning before they were attacking and everyone was running—"

War Bonnet gritted his teeth. "Promise me that neither of us will rest until we hunt this cunning coyote down and kill him. First he steals the Sacred Arrows and we have had little but bad luck since. Now he has cost me the life of my new son, and more than that, I am going to lose my whole world . . ."

His voice was a ragged sob as he stroked Texanna's pale cheek and Falling Star was suddenly very much afraid. Never

435

had he seen tears in the great chief's eyes before. He had not known War Bonnet could cry. To see the great man crumble like an ordinary mortal was to feel the earth give way beneath his feet.

The boy felt compelled to tell the story again as if to relive his own guilt, as if retelling it would change the outcome.

"She ran, Father." He nodded toward the slim form between them. "The Pawnee rode through the camp, killing and setting fire to tepees. She grabbed up a lost small child and ran with it toward the woods. The Pawnee Lance Knife brave never touched her, but his horse trampled her and she fell. The fall brought on the babe too soon . . ."

They both looked toward the tiny form wrapped in soft deerskin, awaiting the end of the blizzard, awaiting the end of his mother's life so they might bury them together.

Such a few, brief months his parents had had together. Even now, he could remember that glorious summer and fall, the two of them running across the prairie together. He could close his eyes and see his stern, laconic father laughing like a child as he swung Texanna up in his big arms and carried her off to a secluded nook. He only watched from afar when his father took his mother in his arms thus, knowing that they were sharing something secret and wonderful that he could not be a part of.

But the summer and the fall were gone and they were left with the cold, tragic events of February. Now the boy looked over at War Bonnet and saw crooked trails down the dark, stoic face. Then his own vision blurred and he realized his own eyes were not dry.

His father's finger caressed her pale face. "Texanna," he whispered. "Texanna, Golden One . . ."

At the sound of her name, the bright blue eyes flickered open and she looked first to Falling Star.

"Son?" Her eyes were puzzled. "I—I don't remember what happened—?"

"The baby," he blurted without thinking and his father looked across her small form and gave him a warning shake of

436

the head.

"Oh, yes, the baby." Texanna smiled faintly. "In the spring, we must go down to Texas and get her. Promise me, my love?"

The boy watched the man struggle with his emotions as they both realized she was lost in another time, another place.

"I—I promise, Golden One," War Bonnet managed to say— and maybe only the son saw the hard mouth tremble. "As soon as the weather warms and you are well, we'll all ride down to Texas."

His voice choked off and Falling Star squeezed his mother's hand once and stood up, moved away. Whatever few minutes she had left belonged to War Bonnet, the great chief who had loved her from the first moment he saw her.

Texanna's lovely face was so very pale, her eyes such a bright blue. Her long hair spread around her like a red-gold halo, reflecting the firelight.

The boy thought of the fine mare War Bonnet had given her years before. It was a strawberry sorrel just the color of Texanna's hair. She still rode it, he thought, but she never would again. He moved to sit in the shadows at the back of the tepee, listening to the wind whimper and whine outside, listening to his mother's shallow breathing.

For a long moment, the only sound was the crackle of the small fire and the scent of pine needles as the yellow flames devoured the wood. He tasted salt in his mouth as he watched his parents and knew he would never forget the bitter taste of grief.

Texanna stirred faintly and the man took both her hands in his, gripping them like he could keep her from slipping away from life, and his face was a mask of agony.

Texanna stirred again. "Texas . . ." she whispered. "Do you remember Texas?"

"How could I ever forget?" War Bonnet murmured so softly Falling Star hardly heard him. He knew suddenly his parents were retreating into a very private world of memories where he might not intrude. *The world of memory is full of love*

437

and one need not deal with pain, or death, or regret.

A tear ran down the man's stoic face and he wiped his face against his shoulder quickly rather than turn loose of the woman's hands.

"Yes, I remember Texas," he whispered. "I was leading a war party to steal horses from the Comanche before we made peace with them. We rode across north Texas, returning with many ponies. Then just at dawn I reined up on a small rise and looked down to see a wagon train circled below."

Texanna nodded ever so slightly. "The wagon master had died," she remembered. "We had just buried him and were getting ready to move on. . . ."

War Bonnet nodded as he seemed to join her in her world of memory. "At first, I intended to kill all the whites as they had done my family. But then from the rise I saw a young girl walking across the circle of wagons and the rising sun reflected off the red-gold of the girl's hair. . . ."

Texanna laughed faintly. "You told me later you had never seen hair that color before and you thought I was the reincarnation of Ehyophstah, the Golden-Haired Woman of the Cheyenne holy legends, the one who brought the buffalo to the Tsistsistas."

"When I saw you from that hill, my heart turned over and I knew you would be my woman, no matter what the cost."

"The war party outnumbered the settlers," she remembered faintly, "and could have overrun them and killed them all. . . ."

War Bonnet squeezed her hand and nodded. "I sent them a message: 'Send out the Golden One and I will let the rest of you live.'"

"Your message caused a big fuss," she whispered. "Some wanted to fight, some wanted to draw straws to see which blonde they sent. Jake Dallinger even wanted to send out my younger sister, Carolina."

The man reached out to stroke her hair. "They could not have fooled me. I had already vowed not to leave that place till I claimed you as my own."

Her eyes flickered open and she smiled up at him, a special smile as though the man who looked down at her was all the world she ever had or wanted.

"I decided to take matters into my own hands," she whispered. "And while the wagon train argued over what to do, I started walking across the prairie, giving myself up to you to save the others. . . ."

"Oh, my beautiful, brave Texanna!" War Bonnet's voice was ragged as he bent to kiss her lips. "Always," he said, "always I will remember how you looked walking across the prairie toward the war party."

"I was so frightened." Her voice grew faint. "I remember it seemed such a long way to where you sat your paint stallion, how forbidding and grim you looked to me. . . ."

"The bluebonnets were in bloom." He smiled down at her. "I always think of you when the bluebonnets bloom because of Texas, because of the color of your eyes. . . ."

His voice trailed off as if the image were more than he could bear. Texanna, lost in her memories, didn't seem to notice as her breathing grew more shallow.

"Yes, I remember the bluebonnets. . . ." She barely nodded. "The flat prairie was covered with them and as the breeze blew, the flowers moved like an endless blue sea."

"And there were dragonflies," he reminded her. "And I thought it a lucky sign that dragonflies rose up around you as you walked through the bluebonnets since the dragonfly is my spirit animal."

"Dragonflies—" she gasped. "Their gauzy wings were green and gold and reflected sunlight so they seemed magic. . . ."

"Oh, Texanna!" he said and his voice broke, "my girl of the bluebonnet eyes! If I had only let you go with the wagon train that day, you might have lived to an old age among the whites—"

"I have no regrets, my love; none at all . . ." Her voice was only the faintest whisper. "I would do it all over again because our brief time together was worth the price . . . Look after our

439

son . . . Ne-mehotatse . . . I love you. . . ."

The man bent over her, weeping openly now. "Texanna,
don't leave me, Texanna . . ."

But she was already gone. It was almost as if the great god
Heammawihio leaned over from the heavens and blew out a
weak, flickering flame.

Texanna, the Golden One, the girl with the bluebonnet eyes,
had left this life behind. For a long moment, Falling Star stared
in horror, unable to believe it. Always, her calm serene
presence had been the sun of his existence and now the sun was
eclipsed, leaving the two men in a blackness of grief.

In a daze, the son watched the great chief gather the slim
body into his arms as if he might breathe life back into her. And
the wind howling outside the tepee drowned out their cries of
sorrow.

The two gashed themselves and cut their hair in grief.
Texanna's body was dressed in finest deerskin with the baby in
her arms and placed out on the lonely prairie up on a burial
platform. And the last thing they did before they rode away
was kill her strawberry mare beneath the scaffold.

"*Ohohyaa,* hear me, Great Spirit," War Bonnet intoned to
the sky, "Let my Golden One ride her favorite pony up the
Hanging Road to the Sky until that day soon when I join her
and we ride together through fields of bluebonnets that bloom
forever. . . ."

Iron Knife swallowed hard, retreating from the memory as
he led the struggling horse through the snow. He looked back
at the grieving woman on the horse he led. She had just buried
a child and would live through it, somehow. He had buried
both father and mother and now he had lost Summer Sky. But
he would survive, the tribe needed him. All he had left of his
love was Summer's delicate little mare that staggered under
her load of children. She was all that was left of his memories
and if she fell and could not get up, he was not sure he could go

440

on and leave her for the hungry coyotes.

Finally they were at the winter camp and it was warm and safe in the tepees of their friends. Those already there welcomed the newcomers and fed the starved horses and took them into little groves out of the wind.

Iron Knife went to see his friend at Bent's Fort, Kit Carson, to ask anxiously about how to get to Boston. Carson was visiting from his job as Indian agent to the Utes and Apache in New Mexico.

But his friend shook his head in sympathy and told him the distance could never be ridden on a horse. Besides, if the woman had loved him, why had she gone away?

Reluctantly Iron Knife accepted the logic of this and spent a long, lonely winter staring into the fire, remembering laughing pale eyes and hair the color of the sun.

The hunting was good in that country and all waxed full and happy as they visited with their friends and the Bents who had married into the Cheyenne. A number of girls tried to get his attention, hoping in vain he might offer ponies to their fathers. He did not even seem to see them.

So the long winter passed slowly for him, and now wildflowers pushed through the melting snow. As the area became less frozen, greedy whites looking for the yellow metal swarmed through the area and the soldiers looked the other way at these trespassers.

But Iron Knife hardly noticed what went on around him. He only wondered if a white man now made love to Summer Sky and wherever he looked, he seemed to see her lovely face.

Chapter Twenty-Five

There were two things about himself that he had always kept from everyone, Austin Shaw thought as he sat across from Summer and Mrs. O'Malley on the train headed toward St. Joe.

Number one was that he hated his mother. Number two was that he was psychic and occasionally saw things in his mind that were happening elsewhere or would happen sometime in the future. He never told even his closest friend, David Van Schuyler, about this phenomenon. It always made him think with trepidation of the family's ancestor who had been hanged as a witch.

As the train headed west, he had a lot of time to think about these two things since Summer seemed withdrawn. The Irish maid rambled on and on as she knitted, never giving him time to comment.

He'd never dared tell anyone how he really felt about his mother despite his solicitous behavior toward her. Austin sometimes wished she would die and leave him in peace but he felt guilty about having such thoughts. Austin was certain well-brought-up, respectable men from Boston should not dare to think such terrible thoughts. Besides, he'd once had a sudden vision of his mother as a very old lady placing flowers on his grave. He was determined to outlive her and have the last laugh after all.

Summer said almost nothing the whole trip, staring out the

442

train window while she fiddled with the gold locket she always wore. Her silence seemed to deepen as they transferred to the stagecoach that carried them on to Fort Leavenworth.

Finally, the two of them sat across from the fort commander, Colonel Burton, who reminded Austin of a nervous little terrier dog.

The colonel looked at the papers in his hand. "Yes, Lieutenant Shaw, I've been sent orders concerning your mission." He rattled the papers and frowned. "I would say by these that your family wields considerable influence in Washington."

Austin felt the flush creep up his neck above the blue uniform. He cleared his throat, a defense mechanism he had acquired as a child to give himself a few seconds to pull his thoughts together. "I guess one would have to say my father does have a few friends at the nation's capital."

"I'm instructed to give you a sergeant, a scout, and a patrol so you may search the western borders of this territory, Arapaho County, for your missing brother."

Why did he feel the implied criticism? He was hypersensitive to criticism since that's all he ever seemed to get from his mother.

Nervously, Austin felt for his pipe. "Do you mind if I smoke?"

Both the officer and Summer shook their heads.

"My brother came out here with the Massachusetts Emigrant Aid Society," Austin said as he filled the pipe with Lone Jack tobacco. "I was afraid he wouldn't stay put very long before farming got too dull and he went looking for excitement."

"I understand that particular group has spent five million dollars bringing antislavery settlers in here." The colonel pursed his lips. "And well-meaning preachers like that Henry Ward Beecher are taking up collections to send

443

in 'Beecher's Bibles.' "

Summer raised her eyebrows in curiosity and the colonel explained. "That's what we call those high-powered Sharps rifles the Northerners are sending in to help the antislavery faction. However, some of those would-be settlers are finding the gold rush more exciting and heading toward the Rockies."

Austin puffed his pipe, giving his nervous hands something to do. "Frankly, I've always thought Todd was perfectly capable of looking out for himself. It was my mother who was about to have a heart attack over his safety." *He wondered if the tables were turned, would Mother prevail on Todd to come looking for him? Probably not.*

Summer frowned. "But aren't those thousands of people digging in that area creating trouble with the Indians?"

The colonel snorted. "Miss Van Schuyler, any time now we can expect a major Indian war to break out because of this wholesale trespassing into the hunting grounds! Of course, Representative Curtis from Iowa is already suggesting to Territorial Governor Denver that what we need to do is take that area away from the tribes and create a whole new Territory out of what is now western Kansas's Arapaho County. He wants to call it 'Jefferson Territory', but some of us like the name 'Colorado' better." He sighed and shifted in his chair. "Curtis has a son at the Cherry Creek diggings."

"But what about the Indians?"

"What about them?" The officer looked tired and defeated. "We'll do the poor devils like we always do; make them sign a new treaty and push them a little farther west."

Austin smoked and watched her troubled face. She seemed unusually sympathetic to the savages after what they had done. The memory came back of that day late in the afternoon last autumn. Austin had been seated at his desk in Washington when he had had a sudden, crystal clear vision of Summer naked on a riverbank, arching herself with abandon against a muscular, bronzed man. The flash was so strong, he could feel the heat and passion between the two. Sickened at the vision, he'd had to go back to his quarters for the rest of the day.

Now she played with the chain of the little gold locket. "We have reason to believe my fiancée's brother is somewhere around the Cherry Creek area."

"If I may be so impertinent to say so," the senior officer tapped his fingertips together, "what with the Indians, the miners, and the Jayhawkers, western Kansas and the Rockies are no place for a white woman!"

"My mother thought Miss Van Schuyler might be of some assistance." Austin cleared his throat. "She does speak some Cheyenne and sign language."

He saw the sudden curiosity on the other man's lined face, and knew also he would not be impolite enough to ask about it.

Austin himself had asked no probing questions about Summer's sojourn among the Indians. Other than the one vision, he had no clue as to why she seemed to have changed so much and he wasn't sure he really wanted to know. As always, he felt guilty because he had bowed to his mother's wishes instead of marrying the girl last summer. It was not only ridiculous but embarrassing to him that the girl had gotten herself mixed up in that silly suffragette protest. Certainly, as his wife, she would conduct herself with proper decorum although he had to admit her spunky, spirited behavior was what had always attracted him to her.

"Really, Colonel." Summer interrupted Austin's thoughts. "Isn't all this newspaper publicity about 'Bloody Kansas' a trifle overdone?"

"No, my dear young lady, it isn't!" The man looked impatient as he drummed his fingers on the desktop. "I'm sitting on a powder keg that the army's been trying to keep from blowing up for several years now. You obviously don't understand how high feelings can run over the slavery issue!"

"But I thought the Missouri Compromise forbade slavery this far north."

"It did." The colonel nodded. "But the Kansas-Nebraska bill in Congress opened up the possibility of this Territory coming into the Union as a slave state. The resulting senators and representatives from Kansas would be able to swing many important votes in Congress one way or the other since power is fairly evenly divided now."

Puzzled, Austin puffed his pipe and enjoyed the aroma of the tobacco. "But surely there aren't many slaves in Kansas. Why don't they just let the settlers vote on a Constitution and decide for themselves whether Kansas will come in as a slave or free state?"

The officer smiled faintly and shook his head. "We've already voted; several times. Both sides stuff the ballot boxes and a United States senator from Missouri, Atchison, makes no bones about bringing men across the line to vote in our elections. Add to those two factions the outlaws, Jayhawkers, and a few thousand hostile Indians, and you see what I'm dealing with!"

"Has there been much bloodshed?" Summer asked.

Colonel Burton snorted. "Bloodshed! First, the proslavery bunch sacked the town of Lawrence. Then that crazy John Brown led the other side to murder some proslavery settlers over on Pottawatomie Creek! He's dropped out of sight right now although we're looking for him! No telling where he'll turn up or what he'll do next!"

"The unstable situation out here is what prompted my family to send me looking for my brother Todd, and also," he smiled faintly at Summer, "he's to be best man at our wedding!"

"Congratulations," the colonel said shortly and Summer looked away, not meeting Austin's glance. "Anyway, Lieutenant, I'm already short on men so I'm afraid the men of the patrol and its sergeant, Meridith, are a little green, but I'll give you the best scout on the whole frontier. He was just transferred to Leavenworth before Christmas and—"

There was a sharp rap at the door. "Come in," the colonel ordered.

A man entered—one of the biggest, ugliest men Austin had

ever seen. His beard was gray-streaked. A bald, pink scar above his tangled, shaggy hair could barely be seen under the western hat with two feathers in the brim. Austin wrinkled his nose at the rancid smell of the man's rough clothes and fur vest.

He heard Summer's quick, shocked intake of breath and glanced over at her, puzzled as he stood to be introduced to the newcomer.

"Miss Van Schuyler, Lieutenant Shaw," the senior officer gestured. "This is your scout, Jake Dallinger."

"Lieutenant." The other held out one big paw and Austin hesitated only a split second before shaking it. He wouldn't want to offend the man, but the hand looked dirty.

"I believe the young lady and I have already met." Dallinger doffed his hat humbly.

Austin's sensitive psychic antenna picked up unbelievable waves of hostility and anger as he glanced with curiosity toward Summer. But her face was a closed white mask, betraying nothing.

"Yes, I believe Mr. Dallinger was part of the cavalry that took me out of the Cheyenne camp," she said crisply with a slight nod in the man's direction.

Austin hesitated, wondering why she should feel anger toward the man who had rescued her. He had a sudden premonition that he should grab Summer's hand and hurry back to Boston as fast as he could. Great waves of sadness and feelings of danger washed over him. He dismissed the mental warnings with a shrug. His forewarnings were not always accurate and, besides, he cowered at the idea of facing his irate mother without his younger brother in tow.

"You've been told about our mission?" Austin asked.

The scout nodded, fumbling with the brim of his hat. "Beggin' yore pardon, sir, but we ain't got a snowflake's chance in hell— Excuse my language, miss. But they do say there's almost a hundred thousand men out there diggin' for gold, hopin', to strike a bonanza!"

Austin cleared his throat and sucked his pipe. The fire had

gone out. "Mother suggested we could get word around the gold camps quickly if we posted notices everywhere that there's a sizable reward. I've brought almost a thousand in gold with me!"

The scout whistled. "If any white man's seen him, that'll loosen their tongues for shore! But if Injuns got him, you can forget it! Them savages would take gold pieces and use them for necklaces and hair decorations!"

"Just because you haven't heard from your brother in a while," the senior officer glared at the scout, "doesn't mean the Indians got him! Communications out of that wilderness are poor and he may just be too busy to try to get a message out."

"Beggin' yore pardon, sir," the scout said, "iffen we're leavin' early in the mornin', I better go see about the gear and supplies."

"Dismissed," the colonel said, standing up himself as the scout nodded to Summer and Austin, then withdrew.

"Now, Lieutenant," Colonel Burton said. "Allow me to show you and your young lady a tour of the local sights around the fort . . ."

Summer remained tight-lipped and remote all evening although she was obviously attempting to be polite. Several times Austin had a feeling she was going to mention something, something she wanted to talk about. Somehow, his sixth sense warned him it had to do with the Indian experience and the big scout, Dallinger.

Whatever it was, Austin knew it was something he didn't want to hear, didn't want to admit even to himself. So all the rest of the day he was careful not to be alone with Summer. Even at supper that evening, he kept up a constant, nervous prattle to discourage her attempts to tell him whatever it was she wanted to share and he didn't want to know. Finally, she retreated into a moody silence and he felt guilty relief as he watched her at supper. If he never let her put it into words,

448

maybe it had never happened, didn't exist. *It was cowardly of him*, he thought as he watched her toy with her food, but he didn't want to know why she obviously objected to and didn't want the company of the big scout.

The officers at supper were noticeably smitten with her delicate beauty and vied with each other for her attention. It never failed to make Austin nervous to see how men were affected by her. He still couldn't believe he was going to be lucky enough to marry her. For years, he'd lived in nervous apprehension that some more charming, more handsome man such as his brother Todd, might steal her away from him.

At dawn the next morning, he went out to where the patrol was saddling up. A tall, lanky sergeant approached and saluted. "Meridith, sir, assigned to you."

Austin saluted. "Oh, yes, Meridith, I think the colonel told me at supper that you're from Vermont. What do you think of this new Territory?"

"Hate it!" the New Englander spat between his gapped teeth. "Like to see houses and trees myself. Nary a thing to see out here but miles and miles of emptiness!"

"Interesting that you feel that way," Austin chuckled. "I'm sort of acquiring a taste for the endless horizon; gives me a giddy sense of freedom I've never known before."

"They do say sometimes settlers out here go crazy from not enough contact with other folks and lookin' at all that nothin'. I'm hopin' to get sent back to civilization next time around."

Austin watched the patrol load the supply wagon and saddle up a sorrel horse for himself and a gray for Summer. The two ladies had not yet appeared from breakfast. The scout joined the group and he looked no different from yesterday except that he now wore a Bowie knife and a big whip hanging from his belt. The scout rode the most strangely marked horse Austin had ever seen, a big bay stallion with a white rump. Brown spots splashed the white blanket of the horse.

He turned and saw Summer and Mrs. O'Malley coming out of their quarters and his heart sang at the sight of her lovely face. She had pulled her hair back under her bonnet and she wore a soft chocolate brown and blue riding habit. She smiled at him as she approached, and then she seemed to see the scout's horse for the first time and her face blanched and looked stricken.

"Where—where did you get that horse?" she asked in a stunned whisper.

"Ain't he a beaut?" The scout nodded proudly. "The cap'n in charge of that Injun raid where we rescued you, mah'm, let me cut him outa the herd! 'Course I have to quirt him purty hard to get him to mind me and I got to remember to mount him from the right side like an Injun would!"

Austin frowned and stepped forward to take Summer's elbow. She looked like she might be feeling faint. Again, he got vibrations of warning that he decided to ignore. All night the prairie wind had seemed to blow and whine around the corners and through the loose shingles of his quarters. It almost seemed to whimper, "Go back! Go back!" at him.

He wouldn't mention it of course. He'd already heard enough comments about his witch ancestor. But there was some terrible conflict between Summer and this scout that Austin sensed but was afraid to ask about. He was certain it concerned his vision of the love scene on the riverbank. *Those two knew something Austin didn't know.* He considered cornering Summer later and asking. Mentally, he quailed and decided against it. Whatever it was, he didn't think he wanted to know.

The color gradually came back to Summer's face and she shook his hand away. Austin reached idly for his pipe while he studied the stallion. "I don't think I've ever seen such a strangely marked horse."

"And you ain't likely to see another, beggin' yore pardon, sir." The scout pulled out a cigar. "Someone told me they call 'em Appaloosas. Don't know what it means or where this horse

450

come from originally, but I'll bet there ain't another one like it for a thousand miles."

Austin puffed his pipe and tipped his hat politely to the heavy Irish maid. "Did you have a good night, Mrs. O'Malley?"

"I said Hail Marys all night," she informed him, "just thinkin' about what me and me darlin' lamb are facing in this wild country. You, there!" She waved at a soldier and gave a sharp order. "Be careful with me trunk as you put it on that wagon!" Her double chin shook as she allowed a trooper to assist her up on the wagon seat next to the driver. Austin was reminded of a plump hen fluffing her feathers as she settled down and got out her knitting.

"Are we ready to mount, sir?" the sergeant asked.

Austin nodded as he helped Summer to sit sidesaddle on her gray and then swung up on the sorrel he was offered.

It was interesting to him to watch Summer's face come alive as they rode out through the bustle of soldiers, prospectors, and immigrants crowding the muddy streets of the surrounding settlement. Everywhere were covered wagons with banners proclaiming Pike's Peak Or Bust! The saloons were in full swing with their raucous pianos though the hour was early. Swaggering prospectors and ragged immigrants passed each other in front of the bustling stores. An endless sea of prairie that yesterday saw only savages and buffalo now hosted civilization.

Summer's face shone with excitement and her love for the wild country. It occurred to him he might make her very happy after marriage by accepting an assignment with the cavalry out here. Then he shook his head. Mother wouldn't like it if he got stuck off out here hundreds of miles from civilization as Boston knew it. Besides, the advancement opportunities were in Washington where a well-placed, ambitious young lieutenant could make a mark for himself with the country's leaders.

* * *

451

The journey went smoothly. After a couple of days riding west, the little party saw less and less of the droves of gold seekers who seemed to be moving across the plains. Austin was awed by the vast emptiness of Kansas. Three days west of the fort, they ran across a great herd of buffalo. It seemed to be one great brown sea, undulating like muddy waves as the animals shifted, grunting and rolling in the dust. When the herd moved forward, it echoed like thunder.

The sea of beasts made Austin uneasy. "There must be thousands of them!"

"Millions!" The scout spat to one side. "They say, maybe a hundred million roam the plains and them big wallows where they roll will be there years after them buffalo are gone. 'Course the hunters is startin' to kill off a lot."

The lanky sergeant rode up and stared uneasily. "Scares me to think about gettin' caught in a stampede of those things! Wouldn't find enough of you left to cover a buffalo chip, much less bury!"

Austin felt both danger and excitement as he stared at the great, moving herd. There was nothing like this in the narrow, crowded streets of Boston or Washington, either. The smell of their hot bodies and droppings made him wrinkle his nose in fastidious distaste.

Summer rode up and sat looking at the great herd. "The buffalo is the Indians' pantry," she said quietly. "Without them, the tribes would starve!"

"Now, there's a worthwhile thought!" Dallinger drawled as he reached for one of those small, stinking cigars he always smoked. "The only way we'll ever be able to corral them savages is to kill off all the buffalo."

Austin shook his head as he watched two great bulls fighting. The air floated with red dust as they pawed the earth and snorted. "Since there's millions of them, it doesn't seem likely they'll ever make much of a dent in the herds."

"Reckon not," the scout agreed, smoking his cigar. "Although the hide hunters is killin' a few. That panic in '57 has got a lot of men lookin' for a way to make an extra dollar. The farmers shoot 'em, too, to keep them from eatin' and tramplin' their crops."

Austin tasted gritty dust on his lips churned up by the great herd. There seemed to be no beginning and no end to the moving brown sea. Even rising up in his stirrups, he could not see anything but brown fur in every direction.

The sun reflected off the sapphire and diamond ring on Summer's hand as she clasped her saddle horn. *The thought came to Austin that wearing a priceless gem like that out into this lawless country was probably as foolhardy as carrying a thousand dollars in gold in his saddlebags.* Then he shrugged it off. What better protection could one have than an armed cavalry patrol?

He could feel such hostility between Summer and the scout that it made him uneasy. Though she was friendly and pleasant to the rest of the group, she treated the scout with such remote disregard that he was almost embarrassed by her lack of manners. He wondered if many years from now he would ever have the nerve to ask her why she hated the scout and decided he would regret her answer.

Mrs. O'Malley never seemed either to cease talking or knitting. Austin felt sorry for the wagon driver when he rode close enough to hear the thick, Irish accent.

"We do need to move on, sir." The sergeant broke into Austin's thoughts. "If anything spooked that herd and it began to run, there's nothin' taller or stronger than a sunflower in any direction for us to climb."

Dallinger nodded. "The sergeant's right. Besides, there's usually Injun huntin' parties around these big herds in the spring and I'd jest as soon not run onto Injuns!"

It took the small party two full days to move past the big herd and Austin grew more puzzled the farther they got into the wilderness. The more they moved west, the more remote from all of them Summer became. It was almost as if she were reliving some adventure she either couldn't or wouldn't share with anyone, not even him. He tried to talk to her as they rode along, discuss their future, but she seemed almost lost in the past. Her expression chilled him when it finally dawned on him where else he had seen that lost, dreamy expression. *Summer's mother, Priscilla, often looked just that way.* He could feel Summer slipping away from him like gold dust through his fingers and he seemed powerless to pull her back to him. He watched her dreamy gaze as he rode next to her across the prairie and had the most terrible urge to turn the patrol around and ride back to the fort, leaving Todd to look out for himself. *But what would Mother say?*

"What are you thinking about?" Summer glanced over at him as they rode along the flat landscape.

He laughed. "I was just remembering the story of Joseph in the Bible. Remember? He was his father's favorite who could do no wrong and his father bought him a many colored coat?"

"Yes, I remember." She nodded. "The older brothers finally got so fed up, they sold him into slavery in Egypt."

Austin smiled in spite of himself. "When I think of Todd, I can't help but remember how guilty I used to feel in Sunday school because I cheered for the older brothers!"

Summer threw back her head and laughed and he relished the sound. She had a soft laugh, like tiny, silver bells.

"I wish you wouldn't look at me like that," she said, suddenly serious.

He cleared his throat awkwardly. "I can't help it. I adore you, Summer. I always have. You know that."

She patted her horse's neck. "It makes me uneasy to be worshiped like a marble statue on a pedestal. I want to be loved like a flesh and blood woman."

He didn't answer as he pursed his thin lips and tried to imagine making carnal love to Summer. It made him feel both filthy and guilty to think about her that way, and yet . . .

The image came back to him of his beloved arching her virginal body against a bronzed Indian stallion and he was so torn by jealousy and pain that his hand trembled on the reins. It had been his fate to be second in his mother's affections.

Now it appeared he would be the second man in Summer's affections, too. But he would be grateful if he got that much from her.

Two days later, following a dry little creek, they ran across the little pioneer family in their sod hut. The farmer plowed, using a thin milk cow to break the hard dirt.

"Mama, we got company!" he cried out, running awkwardly to meet the group. "You all get down and set a spell! We ain't had anybody ride through since last fall!"

A woman came out of the sod hut accompanied by two small boys. Her face had the appearance of tanned leather and they were all barefoot. "All you folks get down! We're mighty glad to see you, Lieutenant."

"We'd appreciate a little water if you have it," Austin said, dismounting. "We're almost out and the creek's dry."

The man came forward eagerly, holding out his hand which felt callused and horny to Austin's own.

"Name's Landry, sir. Been tryin' to farm this for a year now but don't get enough rain and the grasshoppers get a lot of it. We got a hand-dug well, kinda muddy, but drinkable if you're thirsty enough."

Austin looked over and saw Summer and the kindly Irish maid exchanging sympathetic glances. The little family did look bone-thin and their clothes were almost in rags. The home was built of the only building material available on the prairie, blocks of sod cut and stacked against a little rise. The floor was dirt and it couldn't be very warm in winter, Austin noted.

The woman ran one big, bare foot over the other in embarrassment. "We'd be pleased if you'd join us for supper, iffen you'll eat potatoes and flour gravy."

Her husband nodded. "It was a tough winter, all right, but it ain't gonna run us out! We're here to stay! The ox died last fall and we got so desperate we ate the only horse we had last winter. We didn't dare kill the cow 'cause we needed the milk

455

for the young'uns. Old Bessie don't plow none too good, but I got to get my crops in or we won't have nothin' to eat later."

Austin wiped sweat from his face. "We're grateful to get the water, Mr. Landry, so the United States Army will provide food tonight. We'll have a little party! Sergeant Meridith, have the men make camp."

One of the men helped Mrs. O'Malley down from the wagon and she clucked like a fat, fluffy hen. "Saints preserve us! You folks living out here all alone?"

The woman's eyes followed Summer's hands as she shook the dust from her fine skirt. "Oh, we ain't alone, missus," she said. "There's another family five miles down the creek. We seen them just last Christmas."

Austin took off his hat and slapped it against his leg and the dust billowed. He saw another soddy a few hundred feet from the house with a rope tied between.

"What's that for?"

The man sighed and scratched his weather-beaten face. "That's the barn. You got to have a rope to follow in a blizzard or you get lost." He looked sad and pensive. "We lost Bobby that way last January. I guess he went out to feed the cow and let go of the rope. Didn't find him till the thaw in early March." His eyes went to a mound on a nearby rise with two small sticks tied in a handmade cross.

As the men went about their jobs of setting up the camp, the scout lit a cigar. Austin noted the way Landry's eyes watched it hungrily, then looked away. The scout didn't offer the settler a smoke.

"Mr. Landry," Austin said, "I hate to smoke alone. If you've got a pipe, I brought along a lot of extra tobacco that I'd like to give you in exchange for your hospitality."

The scrawny man frowned. "Don't take no charity."

"Got plenty!" Austin lied. "I'd be offended if you didn't join me for a smoke. I believe the sergeant probably even has a little whiskey in that wagon somewhere."

"Wal," the man said, licking his lips eagerly, "just so's you

456

won't be offended and to be sociable like!"

It became a party and Austin enjoyed himself immensely. The sergeant saw to it that there was plenty of food and the patrol pretended not to see the way the starved family gobbled everything in their mess kits. One of the little boys stared at the big sack of sugar and Austin pretended not to notice when he saw Summer slipping it out of the wagon and into the soddy. So what if the patrol ran out of sugar before they found a town again?

He watched Summer digging out a dress for the woman, explaining it would not fit her anymore and she'd only throw it away anyhow because it was so old. Austin smiled gently at her kindness. The expensive dress was almost new. Summer had bought it a few weeks ago while he trailed along behind her on a shopping trip.

After supper, Sergeant Meridith got out his harmonica and played "Listen to the Mockingbird." Before the evening was finished, he taught the oldest child to play it, too. The rest of them sat around and talked beside a fire that was fueled by cow and buffalo chips. There wasn't a tree within eyesight except for three cottonwoods on the dry creek. That night as they sat around the fire, they saw a big, lonely lobo silhouetted on a small rise howling at a bright spring moon that hung like a twenty-dollar gold piece over the flat prairie.

The next morning before they rode out, Austin had the sergeant cut the biggest, sturdiest horse out of the small remuda the patrol had brought along.

"Just say the army appreciates your hospitality," Austin said when the farmer protested. "No use ruining a good milk cow."

They mounted up and the lanky sergeant reached down and gave his harmonica to the small boy.

"Are you sure you people will be all right out here, Mr. Landry?" Summer asked anxiously. "Wouldn't you like to go on to the next settlement with us?"

"And give up our farm?" His weather-beaten face questioned her incredulously.

"I know it don't look like much now." The thin woman stood proudly in her new dress and rubbed one big, bare foot against the other. "But we'll make a go of it. That's what built this country, folks like us.

"Yes sirree!" The man put an arm around his wife proudly. "We're partners, me and the wife! Share and share alike! Someday, there'll be folks all over Kansas and someone might be proud to know their kinfolks helped build this state!"

Austin was impressed by their bravado. He touched his hat in salute and led the patrol out. The four people looked very small standing together on the vast plain as the group rode away. For at least a mile, they could hear the faint, off-key sound of the harmonica.

It seemed forever they rode toward the Rockies, looming up ahead of them, before they finally started moving from flat plains to high elevations. They ran across a new mining camp every few miles. They always stopped to ask if anyone had seen or heard of Todd Shaw, left a description, and told of the reward. No one had heard or knew anything about Austin's brother. Too many men roamed the Rockies and many of them did not want their names known.

Finally, on a fast flowing, icy creek a few miles south of the new town of Denver, they found yet another mining camp.

"Hallo the camp!" the scout shouted and immediately a dozen or more grizzled faces appeared from everywhere.

"Look, it's an army patrol!"

"Hey, they got women with them! White women!"

"White women? I ain't seen nothing but squaws for months!"

Five of them scrambled from the cold stream and dropped their gold pans, running to meet the visitors. Austin smiled as he dismounted among the tall spruce trees. The miners surrounded him eagerly, asking for news of the outside world. He helped Summer from her horse and kept her protectively by his side. Still, the miners ganged around her just to stare at her beauty. Another group ran to help Mrs. O'Malley from the wagon and the woman reddened with pleasure, obviously never having had that sort of rapt attention before. *A woman was a rare and valuable item on the frontier, which made the Western men appreciate and treat their ladies much better than their Eastern counterparts,* Austin decided.

The arrival took on a festive atmosphere and no one did any more work that day. The miners roasted a deer and made something called Sonvagun stew that Summer pronounced delicious although Austin ate it hesitantly, not sure he wanted to know what it contained. He was just too civilized to relish the raw, frontier world although he had to admit the freedom of the wild appealed to him.

That night they sat around the fire and discussed events in the outside world and the fact that this area would fight on the side of the North should a war begin.

Now a miner brought out an old fiddle and someone passed a jug around. As the fiddler struck up a chorus of "Oh! Susannah," the lanky sergeant bowed before Summer.

"With the lieutenant's permission, I'd like the honor of dancing with his lady."

"Oh, I really don't feel like dancing," she protested.

But Austin urged her on. "Go ahead, dear! All these men will want to dance with you. They don't see a white woman very often and you might hurt their feelings."

So Summer stood and went out in the dirt circle by the fire and immediately the men lined up for a chance to dance with her.

A group also formed around Mrs. O'Malley and the expression on her face was pleased as the men fought over who got the next dance. She puffed her way through a few songs until she was breathless.

459

As in most mining camps where there weren't enough women to go around, some of the men tied handkerchiefs around their arms to designate them as "ladies" for the evening so there would be partners for everyone.

Austin watched the light flicker on Summer's golden hair, thinking how he would love to tangle his fingers in it and then frowned guiltily. *No, that was a savage thing to think. Mother would not approve at all.*

A bearded old miner with a crippled left hand came over and sat down next to Austin. "Now what did I hear you was doin' up here, Lieutenant?"

"I'm looking for my brother Todd." He sighed. How many times had he told the story?

The old miner scratched his beard. "What is he wanted for? He kill somebody?"

Austin noted the caution in the man's voice. The frontiersmen protected their own.

"No! No!" Austin reached for his pipe. "He really is my brother and he hasn't done anything wrong! My mother's worried something has happened to him, is all, and we want him to come back East temporarily so he can be best man at my wedding."

The thought annoyed Austin. *He really wanted David in that position of honor. Could he never win an argument with his mother?*

The miner grinned. "You marryin' that purty thing?" He motioned with his crippled hand toward Summer.

Austin cleared his throat as he nodded. "The only thing holding us up right now is finding my brother. There's a reward—"

"Hell, mister." The miner laughed. "We all already got more gold than we can spend! Not that there's much to spend it on, although there's a new fancy house in Denver that's really worth the price when we get up there now and then."

"A fancy house?" Austin didn't understand for a moment.

"You know!" The miner gave him a broad wink. "Most

460

popular place in Denver! Run by some Spanish duchess who appeared out of nowhere a few months ago, I understand. Becoming one of the richest, most important women in town, they say!"

"Oh." Austin tried not to redden as the man's meaning became clear. He didn't mean to be a prude, he just couldn't help the way he felt about women. He'd never actually had one yet although the West Point boys had gotten him as far as the front door of a whorehouse before he panicked and left. The image came to him again of Summer in the throes of passion in a savages's arms and he couldn't bear the thought that another man had had her before him. *But he loved her enough that he would try not to hold it against her, never throw it in her face.*

"Is it possible you might have run across my brother anywhere here in the Rockies?" Austin asked, fumbling with his pipe. He didn't want to think about Summer making love to another man.

The old miner ran his tongue over his lips as they both watched the dancers. "Well, I did see a handsome young fellow at the duchess's place that didn't seem to quite belong with the rest of us. He was a little too refined, if you know what I mean. Just a minute, let me ask my partner what he remembers. Hey, Bill. Come here!"

A bent man with a slight limp paused in clapping his hands and came over to them. "What's going on?"

"You remember that young fellow, the good-lookin' one with the funny accent at the duchess's place?"

The other's lean face took on a guarded expression. "Yeah, I remember him. What's he wanted for?"

"Nothin'!" The other laughed. "This here's his brother, tryin' to find him. What do you remember about him?"

"Well." The other wrinkled his face thoughtfully as the music whined on. "He was good-lookin', sort of a dandy, I'd say, but a regular fella. Everybody liked him. He's workin' for Byers at the newspaper, the *Rocky Mountain News*."

Austin couldn't control the excitement in his voice as he

461

gestured with his pipe. "That sounds like him. Can you remember any more?"

The miner spat tobacco juice to one side. "Name's Tom, I think."

"Could it have been Todd?" Austin asked.

The man's eyes lit up. "That's the name! Todd! Do believe he mentioned something about Boston but he said he liked the West and the newspaper business."

Austin stood up, excited. "That's got to be him! How far is it on to Denver, anyway?"

The first miner took a swig from the jug as it passed him. "Oh, a couple of days north of here, more or less."

Austin turned toward the dancers just as the big scout tried to cut in on Summer and the miner she danced with. Summer stopped abruptly, gave Dallinger a look of cold hatred, and stalked out of the circle.

"Summer!" Austin said excitedly, "they've seen Todd! He's up in Denver!"

"Austin, I'm so glad!" She took his arm and they walked away from the dancers. "Is he all right?"

"He sounds like he's having the time of his life," Austin said as they walked through the shadowy spruce, away from the fire. They stopped and he knocked the ashes from his pipe and slipped it in his pocket. "We'll leave for Denver at daybreak, but it sounds like he's not going to want to leave this area."

Summer paused and looked up at him. "I don't blame him," she said almost wistfully. "I love it here, too. I wish I could stay forever!"

She was standing close enough that he could smell the faint lily of the valley perfume she wore and the clean smell of her golden hair over the woodsy spruce scent around them. He took both her hands in his, looked down into her small, heart-shaped face intently. Austin could feel himself trying to hang onto her and it was like grabbing futilely at star dust. "You are coming back to Boston and marrying me, aren't you, Summer?" he asked almost desperately.

462

Was there the slightest hesitation in her voice? "Of course, Austin." But she didn't sound too sure. "I'll need something to do with my time, though. Would you mind terribly if I went back to my women's rights meetings?"

Austin felt horrified but he tried not to let it show in his eyes. "What would that do to a future politician, to have his wife involved in something like that? Why, when you were arrested before, Mother said . . ."

He let his voice trail off without finishing as he saw the fiery spark in Summer's eyes and the stubborn set of her chin.

"It has suddenly occurred to me anyway," she said, "that when votes for women are finally won, it won't be in civilized places like New York and Boston. No, it'll be here on the frontier where men really appreciate women and are willing to share with them as equal partners!"

"Now, Summer, you know I would never mistreat you—"

"No!" she flared, "but mentally, you've got your foot on my neck and I don't like it! Maybe the reason I have so much trouble getting along in Boston is not my fault, maybe it's Boston's! Perhaps like the little pioneer family we saw on the plains, I ought to be in an area where a man would be ashamed to treat me as an inferior simply because I'm a woman!"

He didn't want to fuss with her over something so stupid and controversial as women's rights. Matter of fact, Austin didn't like confrontations at all. He paused a long moment. "Let's not fight, Summer. After all, we're going to be married soon."

She nodded reluctantly and looked away but she didn't pull her hands from his. "You're right, of course. Maybe I shouldn't get so upset. We'll work all that out later."

Austin stood looking down at her adoringly. He loved her so much, he didn't care what she wanted to do. If she wanted to lead protests and get thrown in jail again, maybe he could learn to deal with it. But he flinched, thinking what Mother would say. Only the right man who would treat her as an equal partner would get Summer's love. Austin had to be that man, no matter that it went against everything he believed in to treat a woman as an equal.

He hesitated and cleared his throat. "May I— May I kiss you?"

In the dim light, he thought she looked a bit annoyed. "It may surprise you to learn this, Austin, but there are men in this world who wouldn't ask! They'd just do it!"

Now he was really puzzled. He didn't understand whether she was giving permission or criticizing him. He decided to take the chance. Letting go of her hands, he took her in his arms and his thin lips brushed hers gently. For a moment, she was stiff and cold in his embrace. Then she started to melt. Her mouth opened greedily to his and she molded herself so hard against his uniform, he could feel her firm breasts pressed against him. For only a moment, they clung thus and he had an overpowering urge to sweep her up in his arms, carry her into the woods, and make love to her with abandon. He imagined their wild rapture on a soft carpet of leaves under a canopy of shadowy trees.

The image and her hot passion shocked him so much that he pulled away from her abruptly. "Summer!" He couldn't keep the shock and the disapproval out of his voice though he tried. *Girls men married weren't capable of such low passion, were they?*

But as he looked down into her startled eyes, he realized sadly that it was not he who thrilled her. Her look told him she had forgotten he even existed. She had been lost in some long-ago embrace as her warm lips responded to his automatically.

"I—I'm sorry, Austin! I don't know what came over me!" She whirled and ran into her tent.

He stood there alone with the moonlight making fragmented patterns through the trees. Taking a deep breath of fresh pine and a faint trace of lily of the valley that lingered, he tasted again the sweetness of her mouth on his. Through the trees, he could hear the faint fiddling and the clapping of the dancers over the roar of the icy creek nearby. He leaned against the rough bark of a tree, thinking as he hesitated. His groin ached with his need and he had the almost overpowering urge to go to her tent and sweep her up in his arms, taking her in passionate abandon, making her his for all time.

Would Summer like that? He had seen a flash of her that he hadn't realized existed and he ground his teeth, knowing where she had learned it. *Would his bedroom be haunted forever by this savage from her past? Did it matter as long as Austin finally possessed her?*

In the end, he didn't follow through. Austin was too civilized to respond that way and he could almost imagine his mother's disapproving face at the idea. Instead, he went to his tent and lay there for hours, cursing himself because he hadn't swept her up in his arms and loved her with mad passion. The sooner they got out of this primitive country and back to civilization, the better off they'd all be.

Early the next morning, the little patrol took the trail north toward Denver. Most of the men seemed to be suffering from hangovers. Mrs. O'Malley appeared to be so sleepy from all the dancing, she kept dozing off on the wagon seat. Austin himself was tired and cranky from his restless night and Summer seemed as remote as she had ever been. He felt such an overpowering sense of disaster that he was loath to ride out of the miners' camp. But of course, they had to get to Denver.

In the middle of the afternoon, it happened. Austin just glanced up as they rode along the trail and saw a small puff of smoke. Apprehension rose in him and he didn't watch the path in front of his horse. He peered at the distant mountains as his eyes scanned the horizon. He saw a puff of smoke, then another. Prickles of hair rose on the back of his neck as if his ancient ancestor were trying to send him a warning.

Indians! he thought. *We're being trailed by Indians!* Abruptly, he felt his horse step in a prairie dog hole in the path. As it stumbled, he grabbed at thin air and felt both himself and the horse falling.

Chapter Twenty-Six

Gawd Almighty. What now? Jake looked back over his shoulder at the sound and saw the lieutenant's sorrel horse stumbling to its knees. The uppity Yankee officer grabbed desperately at empty air and then fell from the saddle as the pony went down.

The lanky sergeant reined around. "You hurt, sir?"

The blonde slid from her gray gelding. "Are you okay, Austin?"

Damn! Jake spat disgustedly. Why had he ever taken this patrol out of the fort anyway? It was a wonder this bunch of greenhorns hadn't gotten lost or killed a dozen times these last few days. If it hadn't been for him, they wouldn't have made it this far. He didn't really care if they made it the rest of the way or not.

He leaned on the Appaloosa's saddlehorn and watched, feigning interest as the sergeant and the girl inspected the officer's ankle. His sorrel mount stumbled to its feet, limping slightly. "Horse is all right." Jake looked it over critically. "Just a little lame, is all. What about you, Lieutenant?"

Shaw grimaced. "Just a sprain, I think." He gestured toward the horizon. "I wasn't paying attention; watching that smoke instead."

Everyone else turned to look but Jake didn't bother. He'd

466

seen the smoke talk and the other Injun signs a few minutes after they'd left the miners' camp this morning. Yes, he'd been aware they were being trailed all day long. The bird calls of a type not found around here had alerted him first. He'd only been amazed this green bunch hadn't noticed the smoke signals before now.

They all turned questioningly toward Jake. "Yep, it's Injuns, all right." He nodded as if he, too, had just discovered them.

That fat Irish woman said something like "Holy Mother of God!" and crossed herself with stubby fingers. The blonde put her hand over her mouth and looked shaken, but she didn't say anything. *She was a brave one*, Jake thought approvingly. *Lots of grit to her, just like Texanna*. He wondered again what had ever happened to her and her half-breed son after they had ridden out ahead of the mob that long ago night.

Jake spat to one side. "There's a clearing about a hundred yards ahead, sir," he suggested respectfully as he tipped his hat back on his head. "I reckon we ought to move ahead up to there where we can take shelter in the rocks. We don't want to get caught on this narrow ledge."

The lieutenant nodded as he tried to stand, supported by the sergeant and the blonde. He hobbled along and the patrol moved up. One of the men caught the limping horse and led it.

"Maybe we should ride ahead to Denver," the officer suggested as the patrol dismounted in the clearing.

"Denver's too far ahead of us," Jake answered as he dismounted. "We'd be easy to pick off one at a time movin' along that narrow trail. If we got to make a stand, I'd rather do it here."

The sergeant ran his tongue around the gap in his teeth and looked wistfully behind them. "What about tryin' to make it back to the miners' camp?"

Jake scratched his beard and belched. "Same problem as tryin' to move forward."

The officer limped over and sat down with his back against a

467

big fir.

"What about firing some shots?" the blonde asked hopefully. "Maybe the miners will hear them and come to our rescue."

Jake coolly lit a cigar. "By the time they git here, it's gonna be too late! Any help we git is just gonna be ourselves! Anyways, I'd save my bullets if I was the leader of this patrol! We're gonna need every single one."

Jake was so pleased with the turn of events, he was having a hard time keeping it from showing in his face. He'd been riding along for days now trying to figure how to work this whole thing to his advantage. All this time, he'd been wondering how he could take that money the Yankee carried and steal that blonde, too. That ring she wore must be worth a tidy fortune, not to mention what he could make off the girl working her as a whore down below the border.

Shaw cleared his throat. "I'm sure Dallinger is right, men. Find any shelter you can around this clearing and we'll make a stand here if we have to!"

Jake checked his old Sharps rifle and reached for the reassuring feel of his Bowie knife and whip as he smoked. He'd never carried a pistol. He'd rather kill a man at a distance and if they got any closer than that, he trusted only his blade and the long lash.

He watched the girl help the officer off with his boot. Even from here, he could see how discolored and swollen the ankle looked.

The blonde ripped off a piece of her white petticoat and ran to the nearby stream. "Maybe some cold water will help," she called back.

She was a real beaut! Jake had hungered for her ever since he'd first seen her in the Cheyenne camp. But he'd never expected to see her again once she got on that eastbound train. He'd just about given up hope on his plan since they were only a few miles out of Denver. He could hardly take the woman and the money right out from under the noses of an armed cavalry patrol. *Now, the Injuns had come along and opened up some interesting possibilities.* Jake hadn't figured out exactly how he was going to pull it off, but there had to be a way.

As for the Injuns, he wasn't afraid. If he had been, he'd have sounded the alarm this morning, when he first noticed them and there was still time to retreat to the safety of the miners' camp. Naw, he could blend into the trees and disappear like magic. He was going to stay around and try to get away with what he wanted in the panic and confusion. If that didn't work out, he'd just mount the Appaloosa and disappear, leaving this stupid bunch of greenhorns to the mercy of the war party.

The lieutenant's face looked strained. *That ankle was hurtin',* Jake thought, *but he was tryin' to take the responsibility and be a good officer.*

"I'm afraid most of my fighting has been book strategy at West Point," he confessed. "I'm going to have to count on your experience to get us out of this, Dallinger."

"I'll do my best, sir," he answered with just the right amount of humbleness. "I jest been sittin' here tryin' to think what move to make next."

And that was God's truth, too, he thought with a slight smile. *Just how was he gonna get that money and that woman outa here? He didn't want to wait for that war party to come riding into the clearing.*

The officer called him over. "Dallinger, maybe we can bargain with the Indians. You know, give them some horses and supplies—"

Jake snickered. "We could if they turn out to be Ree, Crow, Shoshoni, or Pawnee. They're peaceful and a little cowardly. The army uses them tribes for scouts a lot of the time. But if they're Arapaho, Sioux, or, God forbid, Cheyenne, you better say your prayers!"

"Don't talk so loud!" the lieutenant commanded. "No need to scare the women! I've got a thousand dollars in gold in my saddlebags. Maybe we could offer them that and they'd let us leave."

Jake tried not to show his greed at the mention of the money. "Injuns don't know about gold, sir. They'd just punch holes in them coins and use 'em for necklaces."

"What about just riding out and leaving them all our extra horses and the supply wagon?" Shaw gestured toward the spare mounts grazing on the edge of the clearing.

"Why should they settle for our spares when they can kill us and take *all* the horses?" Jake took a final drag off the cigar and tossed it aside.

The officer's thin lips trembled in exasperation. "Then what in the devil do you think they want?"

For answer, Jake turned deliberately to look toward the women who were carrying ammunition to each trooper. "With a beauty like that one travelin' with us, you gotta ask what they want?"

"Good God!" Shaw's face paled as Jake's words seemed to sink in.

Yep, she was a beaut, all right! Jake thought as he watched her. He was going to enjoy her himself for a while until he humbled the snotty little bitch, then he'd either sell her to some Mexican general or make her whore for him. That made him think of Kate. *That damned slut!* Automatically, his hand went to the big whip. *He hadn't really meant to kill Kate, but he'd been in such a rage when he caught her with Texanna's half-breed son that he'd strangled her with the lash before he thought.*

He hadn't believed for a minute the boy had been raping her like she said because he knew Kate and her eye for a man too well. Maybe he wouldn't have cared except that it was War Bonnet's son she took a shine to and he hated that chief because of Texanna. The sheriff and the mob had been all too eager to believe his story about finding Kate dying and how she'd blamed it on the Injun kid.

The sergeant joined them and looked toward the forest around them anxiously. "What do we do now, sir?"

The lieutenant looked toward Jake. "What do you think, Dallinger?"

470

Jake spat to one side. "Can't be a very big war party or they would have already attacked us. Let's wait and see what they got in mind!"

He looked around at the little patrol. *They were all scared, all right, scared enough to do anything he suggested because they were leaderless.*

That uppity young officer may have looked mighty good out on the parade ground at West Point but he didn't have enough faith in hisself to give men confidence enough to follow him to the outhouse, Jake thought. He couldn't figure out why that blonde would be plannin' on marryin' the guy. Must have plenty of money, that had to be it. He was good-lookin' in a sissy sort of a way but he couldn't have much to offer a woman in bed, especially one that was used to bein' humped by some big Cheyenne stud. Jake tried to imagine the little blonde naked in bed and his groin ached, thinking about her.

The last really good lay he'd had was that Arapaho gal, he thought. Matter of fact, she was the reason he was still scouting for the army. After she'd knocked him in the head and got off with his half of the reward money, he had no cash to start that saloon with so he'd stayed on as a scout. He had to admire her even though if he ever saw her again, he'd kill the bitch. She was every bit as ruthless and full of tricks as Jake himself.

He checked his rifle again and looked around at the men, silent and waiting behind the rocks. The lieutenant still sat against his tree. Jake started to suggest he take cover, then thought better of it. *Hell! What did he care if the officer was the first to take a bullet? That'd make it easier for Jake.*

The lieutenant grimaced and tried to prop his swelling ankle into a more comfortable position. "We just going to sit here all day?"

Jake shrugged and tipped his hat back. "You got any better ideas, sir?"

Shaw shook his head. The way he was favoring that swollen ankle, Jake decided, that man wasn't going to chase after any Injuns or Jake, either, for that matter. The lieutenant would have to finish his ride to Denver in the wagon.

Jake ran his tongue over his yellow teeth and sniffed the clean, cool air, considering the possibilities. It would be dark in about three hours. *If he could get some kind of ruse going, he might take the girl and sneak off.* In the trees off to one side, he saw movement but the others didn't seem to notice. *He had been right about one thing*, Jake thought coolly. *It wasn't a big war party or they would have already have attacked.*

A fly buzzed around his face and he brushed it away, pulling his hat down over his eyes to cut the glare. Then on the edge of the clearing, four painted braves rode out, yelping and waving blankets, trying to run off the extra horses.

The sergeant from Vermont leaped to his feet. "If that's all there is of them, sir, let me take the men and go after them!"

Summer looked around wildly. "Weren't those Dog Soldiers? I didn't get a good look, but—"

"Let me go after them, sir!" The lanky sergeant interrupted her.

"I—I don't know." The officer glanced uncertainly toward Jake. "I'm not sure going after them is a good idea—"

"Shore it is, Lieutenant!" Jake said eagerly. "Let the men go after those red devils and teach 'em a lesson! You can't ride so's you and me will stay here to protect the ladies till the patrol gets back."

"That's not a good idea," Summer blurted. "I think—"

"I'm the Injun expert around here." Jake glared at the girl, then looked back to the officer. "Beggin' yore pardon, sir, but take a man's advice. Women don't know nothin'!"

The little blonde tried to protest again, but Shaw evidently agreed with Jake's opinion of women. "Mount up!" the lieutenant ordered Meridith.

Jake had a hard time holding back the laughter as the green officer gave the command that sent the novice patrol to mount and ride out in hot pursuit. Sure them was Cheyenne Dog Soldiers! He'd recognized them at a distance and they were pulling the oldest trick in the books! How many greenhorn

atrols had been ambushed just that way, led away by a handful
f braves only to find there was half a hundred waiting out
here behind a hill to surround them?

He scratched his beard and watched the patrol ride out. *He
wasn't sure what the Cheyenne hoped to gain by this trick, but it
didn't matter none,* he thought. By the time the Dog Soldiers
doubled back and rode into this clearing after losing the patrol
or killin' them, he intended to be long gone. All them Injuns
was gonna find was that fat Irish sow and the officer.

*But he'd have to be real careful now. If a single gunshot
sounded, that would alert the patrol and they'd swing around and
come back.*

Jake looked at the two women. "Either of you ladies got a
gun or know how to use one?"

They both shook their heads. "No," answered Summer.
We aren't carrying guns. Neither of us knows how to shoot
one and we didn't figure we'd need to with an armed patrol
along to protect us."

Jake glanced over at the officer propped against the tree.
What about you, sir?"

"Come to think of it, Dallinger," Shaw said, "all I've got for
my pistol and rifle are the ammunition that's in them. You
might bring me some more shells from my saddlebags."

"Yes, sir," he said humbly, picking up his own Sharps as he
walked to the lieutenant's horse. He lifted the heavy
saddlebags off the pony. Then he walked over and threw them
behind his own saddle on the Appaloosa.

The officer stared at him, uncomprehendingly. "What are
you doing—?"

Jake grinned in evil delight as he swung around and leveled
his rifle at the man. "Okay, you stupid greenhorn! Toss that
pistol and that rifle away from you as far as you can and don't
none of you make a sound!"

The three of them looked at him blankly, almost as if they
didn't understand what he wanted.

"What is this?" the officer asked. "Some kind of joke?"

473

"Yeah, it's a joke," Jake said, waving his rifle. "Only the joke's on you! You should have listened to the little lady. She' a smart one, all right. Now, toss them guns away like I told you to!"

He stalked over and stood pointing the Sharps down at the man's chest. Gathering up Shaw's guns, he took them over and threw them into the creek.

"You uppity bastard!" He came back to look down at the lieutenant. "I'm gonna take your woman and your money and clear out of here!"

The maid gave a choking sound and crossed herself and he thought she might scream. "Don't you yell, you fat sow, or you'll never live to hear it echo through these mountains!"

"You rotten, no good—!" The blonde's eyes flashed. " should have known you'd try something like this!"

Jake grinned. "You're a cool one," he said. "Feistier and braver than I thought! We're gonna make a good team! Now honey, you take some of that damned yarn that maid's alway knitting with and tie her up and gag her with a scrap of you petticoat!"

Jake stood with his rifle almost against the lieutenant's ches as Summer moved to comply. When she was finished, he turned back very slowly and deliberately cracked the office across the skull with his gun butt before Shaw realized wha was happening.

The blonde gave a smothered cry of protest as she ran over and knelt by the limp form. "You've killed him!" She tried to take the bloody head in her arms but Jake grabbed her and dragged her away from the unconscious man.

"No, I ain't, missy, I've just put him to sleep for a few minutes, that's all! Now you and me has got some hard ridin' to do!" He gripped her arm and looked down into her eyes as he leaned his rifle against a tree.

Summer stared back up at him in horror, trying to pull out o his grasp. She looked desperately from Mrs. O'Malley to the limp form of Austin. The maid rolled her eyes at her but her voice was muffled by the gag. No one could help her, Summer realized as she struggled; no one but herself.

She had known back there in Colonel Burton's office that she should have protested, asked the officer to assign them another scout. But she'd been afraid Burton and Austin both would ask why if she made that request.

She couldn't tell the two officers why she didn't want Dallinger, and she'd been afraid the scout might if she raised any kind of objection to his coming along on the patrol. She didn't want Austin to know the truth. The truth was she hated the scout because he had killed her Indian lover and Dallinger might suspect that. Nor did she want him to tell Austin he'd had to fight Summer to take her away from the Indians because she didn't want to leave!

Dallinger dragged her toward the horses.

"You'll never get away with this!" she gasped as she fought him.

"Sure I will, missy, you jes watch me!" he drawled as he jerked her up against his rancid smelling body. "Your boyfriend is gonna sleep through the whole thing and that fat maid ain't gonna help you none. The patrol is either bein' led on a wild goose chase through the hills or bein' ambushed this very minute!"

Almost on cue, gunshots and savage shrieks echoed through the mountains and Jake laughed. "I think the U.S. Cavalry jest met up with the Injuns they was lookin' for! They ought to keep each other busy long enough for us to take the gold and clear out of here!"

Summer clawed his face as she struggled to get away.

"You shouldn'ta done that, honey," he said with evident relish. "Pain excites me!" He pulled her to him and kissed her while she fought him. His breath smelled sour and she tried to spit in his face as his mouth covered hers.

"You little wildcat!" He slapped her hard across the face and

475

she could feel the sting of the blow as one of his dirty paws squeezed her breast roughly. "I'll teach you not to spit at me you uppity bitch! Keep fightin' me, though, honey! I love t take a woman that way!"

She needed no urging as she struggled. She saw the lust ir his eyes as they fought and then she felt his leg behind hers forcing her to the ground. His hot, wet mouth ravaged hers a he fell on her with his great weight.

"You're softer than a featherbed, missy," he snickered "You need humblin' worse than any woman I ever saw! I go no time to play with you right now, we got to get out of here There'll be lots of time later for us to play this game!"

She paid him no mind and kept fighting. The more she fought, the more aroused he seemed to become. She could fee one of his big, rough hands gradually working her skirt uर under his heavy body and him fumbling with the buttons of his pants.

"Maybe just a quick one!" he panted. "Two minutes is all I need!"

In panic, she fought him as she felt the sudden heat of his bare manhood against her naked thigh where he had pushed uर her skirt. He forced himself slowly between her legs as one big hand cupped her breast cruelly. When he tried to kiss her, she bit his lips and he bit her back.

"Gawd Almighty!" he breathed rapidly, "you drive me crazy that way! I'm gonna take you quick and then knock you in the head! When you wake up, you'll be miles from here, headed fo the Mexican border!"

"Never!" she vowed. "Never!"

"Never's a purty final word, honey," he said with a grin holding her down with the weight of his huge body. "You never had a stud like me before and you're gonna love it, so quit tryin' to stop me!"

He came up on his knees, positioning himself to come into her as she fought to get out from under him.

A twig snapped as he readied himself. She looked past his

houlder in terror at the big form silhouetted against the sun so
hat she saw only the outline of a tall man standing behind
ake. She froze in terror, thinking Jake had a partner and now
ll was lost for her. She couldn't fight them both off.

Then the man moved slightly and the sun reflected off the
avalry button earring and the head of the lance he carried.

For a split second, she stared up at him, sure she had created
he image out of her own terror for it couldn't be! It just
ouldn't be!

The scout seemed to realize from her sudden stillness that
omething had changed. He looked into her wide, staring eyes,
nd slowly turned his head to look behind him. Frantically he
ried to scramble to his feet, his naked manhood still visible in
is unbuttoned pants.

But the other man was already reaching, tossing the scout to
ne side with an enraged roar.

Summer looked up at the intruder, almost disbelieving. Her
eart had never been so full and for a moment, as she tried to
et up, the tears came and she couldn't speak. "Iron Knife!"
he finally whispered. "I thought you were dead!" She swayed
o her feet and ran into his arms, sobbing uncontrollably.

Very gently, Iron Knife held her quivering body in his big
rms for a long moment, his face buried in her golden hair. His
eart overflowed with emotion. Reluctantly he stood her away
rom him and turned to the big scout who still stood almost as if
e had seen a *mistai*, a ghost. "And now, Jake Dallinger, we
inally meet again!" he said coldly as he gripped the hilt of his
ig knife.

But the scout only stared at him with his mouth hanging
pen as if he didn't know him. Then a slight recognition crept
nto his mean little eyes. "You're—you're that Dog Soldier I
hot and thought I killed last fall when we raided the Cheyenne
amp! I was shore I killed you!"

"You should have made sure you finished the job!" Iron

477

Knife flung at him to control his rage as he glanced again at th bruised, weeping Summer. "Take a better look, you worthles Coyote whelp! Take a good look and remember a helpless boy i Fandango, Texas!"

The scout's face worked in horror for a long moment as if h couldn't believe the fact that was slowly dawning on him "No— You ain't— You can't be— You can't be Texanna' half-breed son!"

Iron Knife smiled mirthlessly. "I will carry scars all my lif because of you. I have waited long for revenge! Now I find yo in possession of both my horse and my woman!"

The other crouched, uncoiling his big whip. "Texanna?" h asked. "Where is she?"

Iron Knife felt the old sadness. "She's dead. Texanna die where she wanted to be, in War Bonnet's arms—and he's dead too!"

The rage and pain on the other's face was indescribable "You damned Injuns!" he snarled. "You've cost me the only woman I ever really loved! If I had realized who you was las fall, I'd never have ridden out without makin' sure you wa dead!"

"And if I had recognized you at the same time, I would have tried to see you never rode out of that camp alive! I've searchec for you all these many months in vain. But a messenger came from the buffalo hunt to say the big Appaloosa was riding with a Bluecoat patrol. I knew it had to be you since there is no othe stallion like mine on the plains!"

"Then, take a good, last look at him, Injun." Jake spread the lash behind him as he crouched warily. "Take a good look at him 'cause after I kill you, I'm gonna take that stallion and the girl and ride out!"

Iron Knife crouched with his big knife, anger making his voice rise as he faced the scout. "You'll never make it! My men have deliberately drawn the soldiers away so I could ride in here, but they'll swing around and come back before you can leave with my woman!"

478

"*Your* woman, huh?" Jake's head turned toward the sobbing girl as he spat to one side. "I'll enjoy her twice as much then when I rape her and make her whore for me! I'm gonna treat your woman like I've been treatin' your horse! They both need a heavy quirt and sharp spurs to break their spirits and show 'em who's boss!"

Iron Knife felt his face darken with fury at the image the other's words brought to mind. "It's even odds now, Dallinger! You're not dealing with a young, scared boy anymore! You're too yellow to face up to a grown man when you're so much better at brutalizing helpless women and horses!"

Out of the corner of his eye, he saw Summer glancing around vainly for help, but he knew that his blade and lance were the only help she would get. The fat woman was tied up by the big rock and a cavalry officer lay unconscious with a bloody head over near a fir tree. Gunshots echoed through the canyons as Two Arrows and Lance Bearer led the cavalry on a fruitless chase. The plan had been to keep the patrol occupied just long enough for him to ride in and rescue Summer and his horse. He hadn't believed she was along, at first, but the sun glinting off her pale hair from the top of the ridge had been unmistakable.

Dallinger cracked the whip with evident relish. "I don't need any help for what I'm about to do! I'm gonna finish the job I started in the town square years ago! When I finish, there ain't gonna be enough hide or face left for anyone to know you was anything but a raw hunk of meat!"

Iron Knife hefted his big blade easily and gripped the lance in his left hand. He saw the other's gaze go to the rifle leaning against a tree behind Iron Knife's back. The scout couldn't get to the gun without getting past him. Iron Knife had never handled the white man's firearms enough to know if he himself could load or aim one. He felt confidence only in the weapons he held in his hands.

Warily he circled, remembering to stay out of the range of the big whip. He could remember the sting of it on his body as

479

though it were yesterday and he knew its deadly accuracy. Glancing over at Summer, he saw she was untying the plump woman but he thought he would not be able to depend on them for any help. Most white women were not like his mother, they knew nothing of guns or weapons.

The lash cracked abruptly, and Iron Knife stumbled backward, remembering how far it reached and that its tip stung like a thousand angry wasps. The scout drew the lash back and cracked it again.

Iron Knife tried to twist away but he wasn't fast enough. It wrapped around his chest, cutting the deerskin shirt almost off his body. He grabbed at the thin leather squeezing his naked chest like a snake and felt the warm blood run from the wound. Summer screamed in horror. He glanced at her and saw she had managed to untie the woman. The lieutenant moaned as he regained consciousness.

Iron Knife feinted with the lance, trying to find an opening, hoping to impale the other. But Dallinger brought the whip back over his shoulder and even as Iron Knife readied for his throw, the whip reached out and jerked the lance from his hand.

He heard Summer gasp in terror but there was nothing it seemed she could do to help. He had only his knife against the twelve-foot lash and he couldn't close enough to use it. Hopelessly he looked toward the rifle, wishing he knew more about using the white man's firearms. He wasn't even sure it was loaded. If he dropped his guard and tried to pick the gun up, Dallinger could lash him a dozen times while Iron Knife tried to handle the unfamiliar weapon.

Cautiously he circled the white man, feeling the blood from the whip slashes running down his body as the torn buckskin fell away.

"I was jest playin' with you that time," the scout sneered. "Now I'm gonna take your eyes out one at a time like I did a Greaser once at Sonora! You ever seen an hombre stumblin' around with his hands over empty eye sockets? Take a good look

480

at your woman, 'cause it's the last look you're ever gonna get!"

Desperately Iron Knife tried to decide if he dared charge in under the lash or if he should take a chance on throwing his big knife from here and catching the other in the throat. If he missed with his blade, he would be completely defenseless. He knew from past experience that Jake Dallinger would have no qualms at all about whipping him to death in front of Summer.

He looked toward the girl. She stood almost directly behind the scout as he flicked the whip back over his shoulder, spreading the lash to aim so he could make good his promise to blind Iron Knife with his next move. Iron Knife dodged as the lash came down with all the power of the man's arm. He wasn't fast enough. The snakelike leather cut into his arm and Summer screamed.

Futilely he glanced toward his love, thinking what would happen to her if Dallinger killed him. The whip kept him too far out of range to fight effectively. He only had one chance now. He paused, steadying himself, trying not to see Summer trembling with fear in the background behind the scout. Then, he threw the big knife, its hilt red with blood that had run down his arm. Almost, he got Jake, but the fur vest deflected the blade ever so slightly. The scout jerked away and it clattered harmlessly to the ground.

"You brown bastard!" Jake screamed, and then seemed to realize for the first time that Iron Knife was completely defenseless.

He spread the whip lash behind him and advanced menacingly on Iron Knife. "Now, Injun! Now we finish this!"

Slowly Iron Knife backed toward his horse. If he could reach it, there was a bow and arrows and his short Dog Soldier quirt. Dallinger moved toward him, licking his lips, the whip lash trailing along behind him, the other hand on his big Bowie knife. Unless some miracle occurred, Iron Knife was going to be whipped to death before the two women and the semiconscious lieutenant.

But he hadn't counted on Summer. His mother had once

saved his life and Summer had, too. Now she did it again. She ran up behind the scout, wrapped her hand in the trailing end of the lash, and hung on even as the scout brought the whip up for the savage blow. But her tenacious gesture stopped his move.

"Why, you little bitch! Let go of that!" he swore at her, jerking viciously on the lash. But Summer hung on, even though Iron Knife could see the blood on her hands as the whip cut into them.

Dallinger turned around and charged her like a maddened bull, bringing back his arm to strike her with the heavy silver butt. Her action had delayed the scout's an instant. But that instant was all Iron Knife needed.

Deftly he charged in, colliding with the huge man as he tackled him. They both went down, rolling in the bright spring flowers. As they fought and tumbled, the scout let go of the whip and Iron Knife saw Summer grab it up in her bleeding hands and toss it away into a gully where it lay, its silver handle gleaming dully.

Iron Knife hit Dallinger with the pent-up rage and force he had saved for all these years. "This is for the beating you gave me as a boy!" He hit him again. "And this is for the misery you caused Texanna and what you planned for Summer!" He struck him again and again.

But the scout came back, roaring like an enraged animal and swung his fist into Iron Knife's jaw. He tasted the salty taste of his own blood as the fist cut his mouth. Iron Knife grabbed the other by the neck, but Dallinger broke his hold and slammed him back against a boulder.

Iron Knife picked up a broken branch and swung it hard against the other's throat. The man fell, strangling and coughing under the hooves of the rearing, plunging horses as the fight continued beneath their feet.

"I'll kill you for that!" Dallinger choked out, "like I should have done years ago in Texas!"

Iron Knife swung with a hard fist against the huge man's

jaw. "And this is for what you did to Kate! You cowardly woman killer!" He hit him again and they meshed and tumbled across the grass.

Iron Knife could see Summer running back and forth, trying to do something to help, not seeming to know quite what to do. She grabbed up the rifle, tried to fire it, tossed it away as it jammed.

His attention diverted, Dallinger hit him, knocking Iron Knife backward. "When I finish with you, Injun, I aim to enjoy your woman!"

But Iron Knife swung again and made contact with the other's chin. It was a dull sound like a great buffalo bull makes when it goes to its knees. "I promise you this, Dallinger! You have raped your last woman!"

But the big scout staggered to his feet, tackled Iron Knife about the knees, and brought him crashing. Dallinger's mouth dripped blood and he roared like an *ahke*, the Cheyenne legendary monster, as he fumbled for the Bowie knife in his belt. "Now!" he roared. "Now it's time to get serious!" He had Iron Knife flat on his back, trying to bring the big Bowie down for a final thrust.

Iron Knife tried to hold the man's wrist. He could see the sun glinting off the blade, hear the fat woman's screams. Summer attacked the scout from behind with her fists, beating him about the shoulders and head.

Like slapping at a worrisome fly, Dallinger swung at Summer, striking her and knocking her away from him. That second his attention had been diverted by Summer enabled Iron Knife to grab the scout's wrist and twist it as he threw the big man off him by sheer superior strength.

And abruptly Iron Knife had the big Bowie! He swayed to his feet as he glanced toward Summer. She lay like a damaged doll, blood running from the corner of her small mouth as she struggled to get up.

Iron Knife's fury flared out of control as he saw the injured girl. "And this is for Summer!" He came in fighting and slashing like a deadly machine. With one flashing stroke, he gelded the scout with his own knife.

The man went down, screaming in anger and disbelief. Iron Knife moved in for the kill. But Summer had staggered to her feet and gripped his arm, pulling him back. "Don't kill him, Iron Knife! I can't bear to see even that beast killed because of me! What you have just done to him is punishment enough for any man!"

He paused, the bloody Bowie knife dropping from his nerveless fingers. Dallinger clutched himself and went to his knees, moaning and cursing. "You've gelded me!" he choked out in disbelief, "like a rancher does a steer!"

Iron Knife went over to reclaim his own knife and lance, then stopped to inspect Summer's injuries. She had only a cut lip and few bruises. "You're right, Summer," he said, glancing toward the whimpering scout. "To castrate a great bull and turn him into a steer is punishment enough!"

The plump woman knelt by the injured lieutenant who sat up against a tree.

Iron Knife asked the puzzling question as he looked at Summer. "What are you doing here in the Rockies? I thought you went back to Boston?"

He could not be sure of her emotions as she looked up at him since her eyes filled with tears. "We came looking for Austin's brother. We thought he was lost but he isn't after all. I thought you were dead in the raid or I never would have left on the train!"

"And I thought briefly that you were the one who betrayed the Cheyenne, but it was Gray Dove instead."

The officer moaned and Summer turned and ran to him. "Austin! Are you all right?"

Iron Knife watched with a sinking heart as she touched the man's face, looked into his eyes almost tenderly.

"I'm okay, just a little stunned," the bluecoat answered as he took her hand and stumbled to his feet. "What happened?"

"May the saints preserve us!" the fat woman exclaimed.

"That evil rascal!" She pointed toward Dallinger sitting helpless on the ground. "That terrible man was intending to steal your money and kidnap Miss Summer, but that savage showed up in time to save us all!"

Iron Knife glared at the man leaning against the tree. *So this was "Austin," the man she had called for in her delirium, the man from Boston.* "I have sworn to kill any man who tried to take her!" he remembered aloud, fingering the hilt of the big knife.

"No, don't kill him!" Summer flung herself protectively in front of the injured man. "Please don't kill him!"

Iron Knife looked at them both a long moment. *She loved Austin after all. It would tear his heart out to leave her but if Austin was the man she wanted, he would not kill him or force her to go with the Dog Soldiers. He would never do anything to make her cry.*

Resolutely he strode over, caught up the reins of the Appaloosa. His old friend nickered a welcome. Iron Knife took the saddlebags and tossed them to the lieutenant's feet. "I suppose this belongs to you like everything else around here."

With a heavy heart, he mounted up. Iron Knife looked back at Summer one more time, loving her still as he reined the Appaloosa around to ride out. "No, Little One," he said gently. "If you love this man, I won't kill him. I give you his life as a wedding gift."

He took one last look at her and started to ride away.

Summer looked back at him as he started to ride out of the camp. As she watched him leaving, she saw a vision, a vision of a young Irishman walking away through the snow because her mother had made the wrong choice and let love walk out of her life forever.

"Iron Knife, wait!" she called out impulsively.

He reined in his horse, looking back at her questioningly as she stood by Austin's side.

But Austin put a restraining hand on her arm and looked at

her with stricken eyes. "Summer, you couldn't possibly think—? I mean, you wouldn't—"

She hesitated, looking from one man to the other. She could have either one and they both awaited her decision. And it was not only a choice between two men: they offered two different worlds, two different civilizations, two different lives.

Austin gripped her arm frantically as she failed to respond. "No, Summer, you can't be thinking that! You know I can offer you everything! Money! Clothes! Jewels! Social position! We'll go anywhere you want, Europe, maybe! I have money and the power to give you anything you desire!"

Iron Knife stared at her impassively and sighed. "He's right, Little One. Stay with him. I know he will take good care of you. He has everything to give and I have nothing at all except my love. Take care of her," he ordered Austin and turned again to ride out.

Almost on a scale in her mind she weighed the two men's words and knew they both spoke the truth. The white one offered her everything in the world, the brown one nothing but his love. But real love can't be bought and her heart belonged to the Indian. The scales came down in his favor with a final thud.

"Wait!" she called out desperately, looking from one man to the other. As the warrior halted the stallion and looked back, she slipped the big sapphire and diamond ring slowly from her hand and laid it in Austin's palm.

"You can't do this!" Austin gasped in horror. "The tribes are running on borrowed time! It will only be a little while before the army kills them all or sends them to reservations!"

Iron Knife nodded in agreement. "Already the Cheyenne are being hunted down and slaughtered like the fierce timber wolves! Our time is fast running out and my world is full of danger and hardship! There is no place at my side for a rich, Boston girl like Summer Van Schuyler."

But she ran out and caught the stallion's stirrup as the brave started to ride away. She looked up into his eyes and in that instant she made a final decision; the one with her heart. She knew in that instant who she really was. And in that moment, she closed the book on her past forever.

"Summer Van Schuyler? I don't know that spoiled, white girl," she said in soft, halting Cheyenne words. "I am Summer Sky of the Hevataniu band of the Tsistsistas, and I am Iron Knife's woman!"

She saw the sudden glint of moisture in his eyes and his jaw worked as he seemed to remember his long-ago words.

"Are you sure?" he asked slowly, looking at her.

She held up a hand to him. "I am very, very sure!" she answered in Cheyenne.

Only she saw his strong hand hesitate ever so slightly before he reached down and took hers, lifting her to the saddle in front of him.

Austin swayed toward them, staring up at her with disbelieving eyes. "Have you lost your mind, Summer? You can't do this! Think of the consequences!"

"I'm sorry, Austin, I didn't mean to hurt you but I'm not sure we could have made a go of a marriage. You see, you wanted a shy, retiring Boston-type girl and I wanted to be a man's partner, his equal. I belong in this frontier country. I belong with this man!"

Just then the war party rode in and there were only four others: Two Arrows, Lance Bearer, Clouds Above, and one of Pretty Flower Woman's brothers.

"We have lost the patrol and come back for you as you told us," Two Arrows said. "But we must ride fast! They are not far behind us!"

"We are ready to ride out!" Iron Knife answered. "I have everything I came for!"

But Mrs. O'Malley ran forward and looked up at Summer. "Holy Mother of God, Lamb!" There was consternation on her plump face. "What on earth will I tell your family?"

Summer hesitated. For her remote father and her strange, hostile little sister, she had no message at all.

"Tell David I wish him love and luck and maybe our paths will cross again someday," she answered.

"And your mother! What in the name of goodness will I tell her, Miss Summer?"

She thought of Priscilla, lost in the past because of a long-ago love, playing Shawn O'Bannion's little music box over and over.

"Tell Mother the man we spoke of New Year's Eve wasn't dead after all and I decided to take her advice. She'll understand."

The old Irish maid looked up at her, puzzled. "Saints preserve us, what did she say to you?"

Summer saw the image of her mother's tragic face before her. "Tell Priscilla that I got a chance at a once-in-a-lifetime love. Like she told me, I ran after him, damned the consequences, and didn't look back!"

She leaned against Iron Knife's big chest with a sigh. *She was safe and loved,* she thought, closing her eyes. No one would hurt her as long as she had her love's arms encircling her. But as the little war party turned to ride out, the cavalry patrol rode in. In seconds, the five Indian ponies were surrounded by the soldiers, each pointing a rifle at the braves.

The lanky sergeant turned to the lieutenant. "Okay, sir, we got them! What shall we do now?"

All looked toward Austin's face and Summer held her breath and pleaded with her eyes. He could wreak vengeance on his rival now, take them back to the fort. He might think he could regain her love if he hanged the Indians or threw them in prison. Should she barter with him? Offer to desert her love if Austin would only let Iron Knife leave in peace without her?

But as she studied him, she saw a different Austin, a more decisive Austin than the one she had always known. He straightened up and he seemed almost like a self-confident, seasoned officer.

"No, Sergeant," he ordered in a firm voice. "Let these people ride out. They've done nothing wrong. But get a rope and tie up Dallinger!"

He gestured toward the scout sitting moaning on the ground. "I'll tell you the whole story later, but it looks like he may do time in the stockade for everything from attempted robbery to attempted murder! One of you men go look for that big whip! If at all possible, I'm going to see he gets a public lashing back at the fort! But first, we're riding on in to Denver to see about my brother!"

"Yes, sir!" The Sergeant snapped him a salute and Summer saw the new respect in the man's eyes.

Austin turned and looked up at her. She saw the love in his eyes and she was sorry she couldn't love him enough.

"Be happy!" he said gently.

"Thank you, Austin," she whispered. "I'm sorry it had to end this way for you. What will you do now?"

He shrugged. "I may just stay here in the West and serve with the cavalry. I like this country! Maybe I'll end up joining up with my friend Custer somewhere. I'll decide all that later!" He tipped his hat to her and tried to give a brave smile. "I somehow always knew that you wouldn't be mine. And I suppose you are leaving with the one man who loves you as much as I do."

"I love her even more!" Iron Knife declared, and there was respect in his voice as he nodded to the lieutenant. "You have been a fair man, Lieutenant. May the great god Heammawihio smile on you!"

Summer sighed and leaned back against his chest, feeling his big arms gripping her possessively as the war party rode out of the clearing.

She didn't look back as the horses started down the mountain trail. This was her man! She had chosen him, and of all the places she could spend the rest of her life, she wanted to spend it in his arms.

Chapter Twenty-Seven

The war party returned to the camp in the Big Timbers not too far from Bent's Fort. It seemed to Summer the whole band had turned out to welcome them.

"The war party has returned!"

"The men have come back!"

"Look! Iron Knife has reclaimed his woman!"

They were cordial and friendly. Pony Woman and Pretty Flower Woman, who was round with pregnancy, came running to Iron Knife's tepee with clothing for Summer. She visited with them and put on the deerskin shift and the soft moccasins, glad to be rid of the uncomfortable Boston clothing. She gave the clothes to any eager squaw who wanted them, keeping only the small locket with the painting of her mother.

Iron Knife went off to report to the old chiefs in detail about the journey.

When he returned, he led the small chestnut mare. The Appaloosa stallion nickered in recognition, glad to see the dainty mare again.

"Starfire!" Summer exclaimed and ran to throw her arms around the pony's neck. "I never thought I would see you again!"

Iron Knife came to her side. "And I never thought to see you again, but I kept your mare. Having her around made me think of you and I see Spotted Blanket is also glad to see her."

They both laughed as the stallion nuzzled Starfire's face.

"Let's go for a ride!" she cried. "I have dreamed for months of galloping along with you beside me!"

They both mounted and rode out of the camp in the warm spring sunshine. Pausing on a ridge overlooking the purple-shadowed, snow-capped Rockies, they surveyed the green valleys below.

"Has anyone found out about Angry Wolf?" she asked.

"No," he said soberly. "But someday it must come out and then there will be trouble for us both. But until that day, I have everything a man could want! I will pack a lifetime into whatever time is left to me or my tribe because I have your love!"

She smiled at him. "You are right. Let us not borrow trouble by worrying too much about the future. And to think we almost lost each other because of that hateful Gray Dove!"

He frowned. "When the women found out she was the one who betrayed us, they ran her out of the camp. But Gray Dove is a survivor. Wherever she is, she is alive and doing well because she is so ruthless."

Summer studied the towering mountains and sniffed the clean, pine-scented air. *Yes, they were living on borrowed time, she knew that. The army, the settlers, and the gold prospectors were crowding in. Eventually, there would be no room left to roam for the fierce nomads of the plains.*

"I would rather live only a few years with your love than a lifetime without it," she said.

Iron Knife smiled. "Pony Woman is supervising the making of a 'One Thousand' dress decorated with elk teeth. When that is ready, I will marry you in the Cheyenne way. If I ever find a white preacher who will do it, I will marry you in the white man's church, for I have never loved and trusted a woman so much."

She looked at him with love and her happy laughter sounded like tiny silver bells. "Let's race!" she challenged, and she urged the chestnut forward at a lope across the meadow through the bright spring flowers.

She loved the freedom of the gallop and the feel of the wind blowing through her loose hair. He caught up with her at a small creek and they both slid from their horses as he swung her up in his big arms. The horses stared at them curiously and dipped their muzzles in the icy stream to drink.

He laid her very gently on the stream bank. "It was on just such a creek as this that I first made love to you, remember?"

She lay on the soft grass and watched him lean back next to her on his elbows. "Do you think I could ever forget? It was on a warm, wonderful day just like this one! Was it only a few months or maybe a million years ago that two people who were meant to be together finally found each other?" She remembered as she looked at him, her heart almost too full to speak. "You taught me about passion."

"And you taught me about love, real love," he murmured, leaning over to brush his lips across her forehead.

Summer winked up at him. "Many Cheyenne men take more than one wife. Will I someday be pushed aside by a prettier girl?"

"You know better than that!" he declared. "You are the only woman I will ever want! Do you remember, that first time, the gesture you made?"

She knew immediately what he was talking about. Very slowly, she opened her arms to him and he came to her, taking her in his embrace, kissing her fiercely. The taste of his mouth, the feel of his arms around her was even more wonderful than she remembered. Eagerly, she pressed against him and his lips took hers with all the gentle wanting of the long, empty months.

She felt his hard muscles rippling under her hands as he pulled away her clothes. She could feel his manhood against her and he looked deep into her eyes.

"I have felt like the eagle deserted by the wind currents," he whispered. "Like the soul of me fled with you. Now I am whole again."

"Then let the eagle soar," she answered in her halting Cheyenne. "And let my devotion be the song of your *tasoom*. *Ne-mehotatse*, my darling. You are now and forever my once in a lifetime love!"

He kissed the pulsing hollow of her throat and all her senses were alive with desire. Always she would remember this moment, the sweet scent of the grass, the sound of the creek roaring over the rocks, the horses stamping lazily. The colors surrounding her were dazzlingly brilliant. The snow-capped mountains appeared to be sparkling with spun sugar as they reflected the sun.

His warm mouth came down on hers and she arched against him, wanting him as he had taught her to desire him. His strong hands lifted her so his lips brushed her breasts.

"Summer Sky!" he gasped.

"Yes, oh, yes!" she answered, parting her thighs and running her hands in a frenzy down his scarred back. This moment was everything she had ever dreamed of as she sat by her lonely fireplace in Boston.

"*Ne-mehotatse*. I love you, Little One!" he gasped as he plunged into her.

"Take me!" she breathed as she surrendered to her passion. Then she had no time to think as he impaled her with his hardness and she wrapped her legs about him, arched herself against him. It was too good to last forever. She surrendered to her ecstasy and began a dream ride at dizzying speed across the Ekutsihimmiyo, the Milky Way. Nothing could be better than this peak of passion they were approaching together.

So there in the soft, sweet grass of a tiny valley in the Colorado Rockies, they reached ever higher to ride a crest of love and fulfillment and it was as wonderful as the very first time!

To My Readers

As Summer predicted, it was a frontier territory, Wyoming, that first gave its women the right to vote in 1869. But when applying for statehood in 1890, the U.S. Congress suggested the territory rescind this brash action. Gallant Wyoming fired back: "We may stay out of the Union a hundred years, but we will come in with our women!"

In spite of this, Congress regretfully gave them statehood. The constitutional amendment allowing all American women the right to vote would not come about until 1920.

The friendship pact the Cheyenne-Arapaho made with the Kiowa-Apache, Comanche, and the Kiowa tribes in 1840 has never been broken up to this very moment. For those interested in history, Bull Hump's Comanche were attacked by mistake on October 1, 1858, near the present town of Rush Springs as I indicated. Little Buffalo, Aperian Crow, and the unwilling Cheyenne had yet to play out their roles in the terrible Indian uprisings now known as the "Great Outbreak of 1864."

Here in my home state of Oklahoma, the Cheyenne still gather to dance the sun dance at the ancient site of Cantonment (Canton). All over the state in the hot summers, thousands of plains Indians still powwow even as they did more than a hundred years ago when my grandfather was an Indian agent. I attend sometimes with my Irish-Choctaw husband and my Chickasaw brother-in-law and I always leave saddened for a way of life that is as close to extinction as the once-great herds of buffalo.

I do in-depth research for my stories, tracking down such small items as the exact time the stagecoach left Fort Smith and details on Indian rituals. However, Cheyenne Indians do not belong in the hilly forests of eastern Oklahoma. Their territory has always been (and still is) the flat plains country to the west and north. Since the Butterfield stage did not run through western Indian Territory, I was in a dilemma until a friend with a Ph. D. in History pointed out there were several known incidents involving plains Indians riding into eastern Oklahoma to raid the Five Civilized Tribes.

Curious people often ask me about the Cheyenne Sacred Arrows and I will share with you a secret that only a handful of white people know. Yes, the Arrows still exist and are as important and sacred to the Cheyenne as ever. In fact, the tribe pays the Keeper of the Arrows to look after them. At the moment of this writing, the official Keeper of the Arrows is Joe Antelope out in Watonga, Oklahoma. Watonga is deep in the heart of the old buffalo plains near Canton and Roman Nose State Park, named for the famous Cheyenne warrior.

The Sacred Buffalo Hat also still exists and is in the possession of a northern Cheyenne family living in southern Montana. The day did come when the Buffalo Hat was damaged and defiled. That started a whole new series of calamities and adventures for the Cheyenne people.

Meanwhile, down in the Texas hill country, Iron Knife's beautiful half-breed sister, Cimarron, Spanish for "wild one", was growing up. She would meet a dashing Spanish vaquero on a great ranching empire during the Civil War. This was the time called "The Great Outbreak of 1864," when the fierce Plains tribes realized the soldiers had gone east to fight and the western frontier was set ablaze and soaked with blood. Cimarron would be caught in the middle of the fierce

Comanche-Comanchero raids involving El Lobo, Little Buffalo, and Aperian Crow. Spirited Cimarron dared any man to tame her or steal her heart. Then she came up against the handsome, moody cowboy called Trace who expected wild mustangs and women to submit to his will.

But the story of sultry Cimarron is the next tale I will tell in this series. . . .

Although my research encompassed some fifty books, I wish to acknowledge these in particular:

The Cheyenne Indians, Their History and Way of Life, Volumes I & II, by George B. Grinnell.

The Fighting Cheyennes, by George B. Grinnell

The Southern Cheyennes, by Donald J. Berthong

And special thanks to Indian friends who told me things never found in print.

Ne-mehotatse,
Georgina Gentry